W9-BBB-511

FAVORITE SONS

FAVORITE SONS

A NOVEL

ROBIN YOCUM

ARCADE PUBLISHING
NEW YORK

Arcade Publishing books may be purchased in bulk at special discounts for sales promotion, corporate gifts, fund-raising, or educational purposes. Special editions can also be created to specifications. For details, contact the Special Sales Department, Arcade Publishing, 307 West 36th Street, 11th Floor, New York, NY 10018 or info@skyhorsepublishing.com.

Arcade Publishing® is a registered trademark of Skyhorse Publishing, Inc.®, a Delaware corporation.

Visit our website at www.arcadepub.com.

10 9 8 7 6 5 4 3 2 1

Library of Congress Cataloging-in-Publication Data is available on file.
ISBN: 978-1-61145-004-0

Printed in the United States of America

Acknowledgments

This book would not have been possible without the women in my life.

The first is Frances Kennedy, who found the sample chapters of my manuscript on the slush pile at the Doe Coover Agency. Frances, bless her Irish heart, liked what she read and passed them on to Colleen Mohyde.

There are many talented writers out there who are never fortunate enough to find an agent like Colleen. What a gem. She has been a warrior on my behalf and I am extremely appreciative.

Colleen put the manuscript into the very capable hands of Lilly Golden, who wisely snatched it up. Her deft touch in editing my manuscript made it a much better read.

In Columbus, we are fortunate to have a terrific literary center—Thurber House. The executive director is Susanne Jaffe, who has been a friend and constant motivator during my journey to get a novel published.

Prologue

My entire professional career has been spent prying secrets out of the accused. When it comes down to it, it's not a complicated job. The path to learning the truth is simply decoding lies and uncovering layers of secrets.

The lies are easy. Every accused in the history of the criminal justice system has lied. Big lies. Little lies. White lies. Monster lies. It's a given. Fortunately, most criminals are not Harvard graduates. It is relatively easy to sort through their statements and pick out the improbabilities and impossibilities. What remains is a semblance of the truth.

It's the secrets that cause police detectives and prosecutors heartache.

Secrets can be fragile. Their structure can be torn apart by a whisper, a faint betrayal into the ear of another. Secrets also can be powerful, for they can control and haunt lives for many years.

In 1983 a woman showed up in the lobby of the Summit County Prosecutor's Office and said she wanted to report a homicide. These were the types of water runs that the new guys got sent on, and as I had been there less than a year I was summoned to the lobby. Her name was Angela Swan and she claimed to have witnessed the homicide. She was fifty-two years old and had deep creases running away from tired, rheumy eyes. As I walked with her to a nearby conference room, Swan nervously rubbed her hands together and said that even at this late juncture, she was feeling guilty about what she was about to tell me.

The homicide had taken place when she was six years old. She had been out with her father, riding in the passenger seat of his pickup truck. He bought her a bottle of pop and told her that he needed to stop and talk to a man. She remembered that he pulled off the road into a parking lot and gravel crunched under the truck tires; bright orange and red leaves adorned the trees. Her dad patted her on the knee and said, "You wait here, sweetheart," then got out of the truck to talk to the man. When the talk turned loud, she strained to look over the dashboard as her dad pulled a pistol from under his jacket and shot the man, maybe in the chest. The blast scared her and she spilled orange pop down the front of a blue and white dress embroidered with butterflies. The gun exploded a second time and a thin line of blood squirted across the windshield. The man fell and her dad fired the gun three more times. She didn't know what triggered the argument or where the parking lot was located. The truck fishtailed and she slid hard against the door as they sped from the lot, gravel pelting the wheel wells, and the panicked look on her father's face brought her to tears. Somewhere on the way home he pulled to the side of the road and wiped the blood from the windshield with his handkerchief, then stuffed it between the steel grates of a storm sewer. When he jumped back in the truck he cupped her face in his hands and said, "Angie, sweetheart, you can never tell anyone what happened today. Not your friends, your teacher, your grandma and grandpa, not even your mommy. It has to be our secret. Do you understand?" She nodded, and had faithfully kept the secret for forty-six years.

When she was young, Angela said she and her dad occasionally spoke in whispers of that day, and each time she renewed her vow of silence. Her dad told her the man he shot was a very bad guy—just like the desperados in the westerns they watched at the Paramount Theatre. It was a great game.

But as she grew older, she witnessed other disturbing actions of her father, which she didn't want to discuss—more secrets. She began to wonder if the dead man had been, in fact, a very bad man.

She wondered who he was, wondered if he had a little girl who missed her father and was tormented by not knowing why he had been murdered. Angela couldn't get it out of her head. But she could never betray her father. Wouldn't even consider it.

Her father had died a week before she showed up in the lobby. Now that he was gone, she felt obligated to report the homicide. Her father's name was Philip Economos. She doubted that anyone was around who remembered the dead man, and didn't know if anyone even cared, but she had to get it off her chest.

Since she didn't know where the shooting had taken place, I went to the library and searched the newspaper microfilm for the fall of 1937, the year Angela Swan was six and the time of year when the leaves would be changing color. On October 13, a story appeared on the front page of the *Beacon Journal* about a man found dead in a roller-skating rink parking lot—shot once in the chest, once in the shoulder, and three times in the back of the head. His name was Willie Backus and he owned the roller rink. He had no criminal record. Neither his lone surviving brother, his ex-wife, nor his only son could shed any light on what may have precipitated the shooting. The reason Willie Backus died, it seemed, was itself a secret that died with Philip Economos.

Angela was a rarity. She kept her secret, smothering the information for forty-six years. Most people can't keep a secret for forty-six minutes. Those who commit crimes without witnesses quite often cannot keep their own secrets. They precipitate their own undoing because they feel compelled to talk. They tell a friend or a girlfriend, who one day becomes a former girlfriend, and soon it is no longer a secret.

I kept my secret, not as long as Angela kept hers, but for a formidable number of years. I didn't tell my mother, or my now ex-wife, or any of the friends and girlfriends who passed through my life. I could never reveal my secret and relieve myself of its crushing burden. To do so would not only have destroyed my life, but the lives of those who were once most dear to me.

Secrets are central to misdeeds, infidelities, and betrayals. Without wrongdoing, there would be little need for secrets. The consequences, whether you're a six-year-old girl with an orange

Nehi, a teenage boy running with his buddies, or a man sworn to uphold the law, may not be realized for decades. There is no way to project to the future and know what those consequences will be. You wait and wonder, not if, but when the rogue asteroid that is circling your life will make its fiery reentry, and with each passing year, the consequences grow, lives become intertwined, and the pain in the chest refuses to subside.

Hutchinson Van Buren
Akron, Ohio
October 14, 2004

PART I

Chapter One

Petey Sanchez was a troubled human being, a stewpot of mental, emotional, and psychological problems manifested in the body of a wild-eyed seventeen-year-old, who cursed and made screeching bird noises as he rode around town on a lime green spider bike with fluorescent pink streamers flying out from the handlebars. Mothers could never relax when Petey was in the neighborhood. He had been banned from every backyard in town, but that didn't stop him from pedaling through the alleys and around the blocks, watching, staring, circling like a wolf on the lighted fringes of an encampment. Occasionally, an angry mother would shoo him off with the gentleness normally reserved for stray curs. "Get out of here, Petey. Go on, git. Go home." He would scream like a wounded raptor and flee, only to return a short time later, circling from a safer distance—pedaling and watching. Crystalton was a little less than two miles long and only about five blocks wide, squeezed hard between the Appalachian foothills and the Ohio River, so even when Petey wasn't in view, he was never far away, a wispy, ubiquitous apparition looming in shadow and mind.

From an early age, I learned the difference between Petey and the other kids who rode the little yellow bus out of town each morning to the school for the handicapped and mentally retarded in Steubenville. To my mother, most of them were objects of pity. There was a girl who lived down the street from us, Sarah Duncan, a frizzy-haired little kid who was cross-eyed, wore bulky, metallic braces on her legs, and struggled to the bus stop every morning, swinging each stiffened leg in an awkward arc. When she passed our open kitchen window you could hear with each footfall the clack of the steel braces and the squeak of the leather restraints, which would cause my mother to sigh, push an open palm to her breast, and say, "That poor little thing." Then, she would turn and glare at me, the corners of her eyes and lips crinkling in anger at my apparent lack of appreciation for the gifts I had been given, and say, without pause for a breath, "You should count your lucky stars that you were born with ten fingers, ten toes, and a good mind. Don't ever let me hear that you were teasing that little Duncan girl. Do you understand me, mister?"

"Yes, ma'am."

"You better. If I hear a word of it I'll knock you into tomorrow."

And she would have. Miriam Van Buren was a sturdy, humorless single mother who meted out discipline to her three children without impunity. She had strong wrists and heavy hands, which I had felt everywhere from the back of my head to my ass. Never mind that my various infractions had never once been for making fun of any handicapped kid. Mom always felt duty bound to forewarn me against potential indiscretions.

But she had no such sympathy for Petey Sanchez, of whom she said, simply, "Stay away from that boy; he's not right in the head."

I didn't need the warning. From an early age I had both detested and feared Petey Sanchez, and bore a J-shaped scar on my chin that I received in the fifth grade after he shoved a stick into the spokes of my bicycle, locking up the front wheel and sending me hurtling over the handlebars face-first into the asphalt parking lot at the elementary school. On our way back from the emergency room my mother stopped by the Sanchezes' to talk to Petey's mother and show the gash that had taken eight stitches to close. When Mrs. Sanchez saw us standing on her front porch with a gauze bandage taped to my chin, she sighed and shook her head, weary of the steady stream of neighbors and police officers knocking on the door with complaints about their feral son. "I'm awfully sorry, Miriam," said Lila Sanchez, a sickly thin woman with train-track scars along the base of her neck from a bout with thyroid cancer. "I know that boy's out of control, but I can't do a doggone thing with him."

As we climbed back in the car, my mother reiterated her early admonitions. "Stay away from the boy." That seemed to be the solution offered by most parents. Unfortunately, staying clear of Petey had its own challenges. He cruised the streets of Crystalton with more regularity than our police department. Throughout elementary and junior high school, if I saw Petey pedaling down the street, or heard his screeching cry, I would duck between houses or hide behind trees to avoid him. If you made eye contact with Petey he would call you a queer and a faggot, his favorite words, and try to run you over with his bicycle.

Petey was the second youngest of the nine children born to Lila and Earl Sanchez, who worked as a coupler on the Pennsylvania Railroad and had lost four fingers and a thumb to his job. The Sanchezes lived at the far north end of town in a paint-starved Victorian house with chipped slate shingles and sagging gutters that was wedged between the Chesapeake & Ohio Railroad tracks and the water treatment plant, where following each heavy storm, effluvium overflowed into the drainage ditch behind their house. They were all skinny, pinched-faced kids with stringy hair the color of dirty straw and the unwashed smell of urine. Petey had a similar look, except he had bad buckteeth that were fuzzy and yellow, rimmed with decay and foul-smelling. However, the feature that overwhelmed his narrow face was a calcified ridge that ran from the bridge of his nose and disappeared into his hairline, the result of a botched birth during which the doctor grossly misused a pair of forceps. If all this wasn't misfortune enough, his forehead ran back from the calcified ridge, giving his thin face a trout-like quality. This battering of the skull and brain was most likely the genesis of Petey's cocktail of problems. Lila had told my mom that there were times when Petey would roll around on the floor of their living room, sometimes for hours, squeezing his temples between his palms and crying like a fox in a leg trap.

My first introduction to Petey Sanchez was when I was six years old and riding my new bicycle with training wheels down the sidewalk from the house. Behind me, I heard someone making a noise like a police siren and soon Petey flew by me on his bicycle, head tilted upward, mouth agape, howling away. He stopped broadside on the walk, blocking me. I was terrified. He was wearing a dime-store police badge on his T-shirt and carrying a small pad and the stub of a pencil in his hip pocket. Pointing a grimy index finger at my face, Petey slobbered down his chin while admonishing me in a tongue I did not comprehend for a violation I could not fathom. He then pulled the pad and pencil from his pocket, wrote some nonsensical drivel on the paper, ripped it out and handed it to me, then continued down the sidewalk in search of his next traffic violator. When I returned home and showed my mother the "ticket" and told her of my encounter with the strange boy who talked but couldn't say words, she shook her head and for the first time in my life I heard, "That was Petey Sanchez. Stay away from him. He's not right in the head."

Petey's traffic cop antics continued for several years. It seemed harmless enough at first, but after a while Petey started demanding that the young violators pay their fines with whatever change they had in their pockets. Parents complained, but it didn't stop for good until the day Chief Durkin walked out of Williams Drug Store and saw Petey making a traffic stop with a very realistic-looking .38-caliber revolver stuck between his belt and pants.

"Helping me with some speeders, huh, Petey?" Chief Durkin said as he approached Petey and a terrified little girl on the verge of tears.

"Uh-huh," Petey said.

"Did you get the license plate number of her bicycle?" the chief asked, pointing to the rear fender of the girl's bike. When Petey turned his head, Chief Durkin snatched the revolver. Petey screamed, called the chief a queer and a faggot, and lunged for the weapon, which looked realistic because it was, and fully loaded. A highly agitated Chief Durkin put Petey in the back of the cruiser and took him home. "What the hell is wrong with you, Earl, leaving a loaded gun around where a boy like that can get his hands on it?" the chief asked. "Why in hell do you even own a gun? You don't have enough fingers left to pull the damn trigger."

It was one thing after another with Petey. For a while he ran through the streets at night with a black cape, pretending to be a vampire. During another stretch he lurked in bushes and behind fences, pretending to be a tiger, leaping out and scaring young and old, then running off, growling. Twice he got angry with his parents and set his own house on fire, though miraculously the tinderbox was saved both times.

Parents in Crystalton worried that Petey would someday badly hurt or kill another child. Still, most would not reprimand Petey for his misdeeds because they feared he would return in the night and set their houses on fire. Thus, there was a silent but collective sigh of relief among these parents when on the evening of Tuesday, June 15, 1971, a berry picker found the body of Petey Sanchez on Chestnut Ridge.

Chapter Two

At 8:30 a.m. on Monday, June 14, 1971, Deak Coultas tapped twice on the back screen door and walked into our kitchen. His face was freshly scrubbed, pink acne medication applied to his considerable eruptions, hair neatly parted, his khaki shorts cuffed and a pair of tube socks pulled up just below his knees. A Boy Scout knapsack was slung over one shoulder. I was still rubbing sleep out of my eyes and had pulled a ball cap over my uncombed hair. My last fried egg was congealing on the plate; I slid it between two slices of dry wheat toast and we headed down Second Street.

My name is Hutchinson Van Buren and I grew up in the eastern Ohio village of Crystalton, which anchors a slight, southwest bend in the Ohio River. Crystalton was named for the glass and crystal business that thrived there from the mid-1800s until the Brilliant Glass Works closed in 1932, its doors slammed shut by the Great Depression. Around the turn of the century, there had been eight glass and crystal companies operating in Crystalton. All that remained of that once-booming industry were a few slag dumps, the stone foundation of the Brilliant Glass Works, and the Upper Ohio Valley Glass Museum, which was a meager display of fallow photographs, canning jars, and bowls occupying a second-floor room of the village hall. Admission to the Upper Ohio Valley Glass Museum was free, but you had to ask the village clerk for the key, which hung on the wall behind her desk next to those for the public restrooms. Crystalton had about sixteen hundred residents, an electric generating plant just south of town, a sand quarry, and the headquarters of the Belmont Coal & Gas Company. We had a high school that was much beloved by generations of graduates who never left town, a hardware store that sold bunnies and colored peeps at Easter, a drugstore with a marble soda fountain, and the usual assortment of mom-and-pop diners, dry cleaners, and grocery stores. Although we had a name that evoked beauty and style, there was nothing that set Crystalton apart from the other dusty, industrial communities lining the river. However, it was a wonderful place to be a kid. We had ball diamonds, hills to explore, creeks and a quarry to fish, a community swimming pool, and the Big Dipper Ice Cream Shop, where Edna Davis gave you a free double scoop of your choice if you made the honor roll. On grade card day, kids would be lined up to the street, proof in hand, awaiting their rewards.

A heavy fog had rolled off the Ohio River that morning and shrouded Crystalton in a damp cloak that stretched from the water's edge to a hundred feet up the Appalachian foothills that rimmed the town in a huge semicircle. Deak and I cut through the alley behind the drugstore and across the Little League field, where the ground was still soggy from the previous day's rain, to the Lincoln Elementary School playground. Behind the monkey bars, concealed by a row of blue spruce trees planted by the PTO, was the beginning of the hunting path that led to the crest of the encircling hills, known as Chestnut Ridge. Deak and I could hear the voices of our friends float through the fog long before they came into view. Our classmate Adrian Nash and his younger brother Eldon, whom everyone called Pepper, were sitting on the first rung of the monkey bars, their arms wrapped around the second rung, giving the appearance they were strapped to a crucifix. As we walked out of the fog, Pepper said, "Low man buys the Cokes? How about it, Hutch? You in?"

"Sure, works for me," I said.

"How about you, preacher, or is that too close to gambling?"

It was said in fun and Deak took it as such. "I'm in."

Deak's real name was Dale Ray, but he was so devoutly religious that we gave him the nickname, Deacon, which over time had been shortened to Deak. We joked that he was the perfect child—he was a good student, rarely cursed, had earned more merit badges than anyone in the history of the Crystalton Boy Scouts and was well on his way to Eagle Scout, and served as president of the youth group at the Crystalton United Methodist Church. He was a tall, gangly kid, with an angular face and a sharp nose and chin. On both cheeks were patches of acne that stretched like quarter-moon-shaped mountain ranges, purple and red and blue eruptions with pustular snowcaps. The acne also ran across his forehead and on his neck and shoulders. He was so self-conscious that he was never without a T-shirt, even at the swimming pool. Once, just before the opening tip of a freshman basketball game, a kid from Martins Ferry lined up against Deak, pointed at the rash of acne popping out on his neck and shoulders, and asked, "That shit's not contagious, is it?" The question so rattled Deak that he only had two points all night.

It was a half-mile hike up a twisting trail from the playground to Chestnut Ridge. Beneath the canopy of conifers, it was still midnight. The fog saturated the leaves and the condensation dripped to the ground, pelting the carpet of desiccated vegetation with a rhythmic cadence. Soaked limbs hung low over the trail and slapped at our faces. The acrid stench of decay and mold was heavy in our nostrils. A little more than halfway up the trail we walked single file out of the mist and found the sun bright over the West Virginia hills to our east. As always, Adrian led our small troop, quiet as usual, with Pepper following close behind, a dervish of nervous energy, chattering away, throwing stones at trees, tickling the back of Adrian's neck with a length of foxtail. Adrian, Deak, and I had been good friends since we began attending Sunday school together when we were barely out of diapers. In fact, there isn't a moment in my memory when they weren't my pals. Pepper was fourteen and a year younger than the rest of us, but he fit right in. He was as fun-loving as his older brother was somber. Adrian and Deak were both quiet types, so I enjoyed Pepper's constant banter.

We hiked beyond Chestnut Ridge to the Postalakis farm, which stretched more than three hundred rolling acres from the crest of the ridge west to the fertile bottomland on the shores of Little Seneca Creek. Marty Postalakis let us search his fields for Indian relics as long as we didn't trample the crops. When we weren't playing ball, arrowhead hunting was one of our favorite pastimes. There had been a big thunderstorm the previous afternoon and we arranged the hunt while the lightning was still streaking over the hills west of town. Arrowheads were easiest to find after a big storm had washed away a layer of dirt, exposing the shiny pieces of flint.

We had been going on the hunts for years. Deak's collection was neatly arranged in framed, wool-lined cases that he dutifully cataloged, labeled, and displayed on the walls of his bedroom. Mine were kept in several coffee cans, canning jars, cigar boxes, and other miscellaneous containers scattered about my room. I had no idea how many arrowheads I had and getting the collection organized was something I had been promising myself for years, similar to my mother's continual vow to organize the family snapshots in albums. For me, the thrill was in the hunt, not the display.

Adrian and Pepper's artifacts never made it home. They were in it strictly for the money and each hunt ended with a stop at Fats Pennington's cluttered antique shop at the south end of town. The brothers Nash had a pact that called for each hunt's findings to be combined, sold, and the proceeds split. Adrian spent his money as fast as he earned it on records, eight-track tapes, magazines, and condoms; he wanted to project the image that he was having sex with Darcy McGonagle, which he most certainly was not. Pepper banked every dime he made and had a bank account worth more than sixteen hundred dollars, a fortune for a fourteen-year-old in 1971.

The last time Pepper was in my bedroom and saw the numerous cans and jars of arrowheads scattered about, he asked, "Why don't you sell those? You'd get a lot of money for 'em."

"I'm going to wait until I'm older. Then they'll be worth even more."

Pepper shook his head and said, "No, no, no. That's not the way you do it. Sell 'em now, put the money in the bank, and start earning interest. It'll compound and you'll make a lot more money."

How many fourteen-year-olds could explain the intricacies of compound interest? Adrian and Pepper's dad was the president of the Glass Works Bank and Trust Company. Obviously, Pepper had been paying attention to his father's lessons and was way beyond the rest of us in the area of fiscal management. None of us doubted that he would someday be ridiculously rich.

After three hours of exploration in Marty Postalakis's feed-corn fields, we ended our search on the east bank of the Little Seneca Creek, the sun high overhead, our shirts clinging to moist skin, the tang of testosterone in the air. We washed our treasures in the clear stream, compared our finds, bragged a little, then followed a furrow that snaked along the tree line back toward Chestnut Ridge. As we neared the end of the path that cut through a coppice of chestnut trees at the edge of the Postalakis property, Pepper was ragging on Deak, who had found only two points, although one was by far the best point of the day, a gray and maroon flint spear tip in near perfect condition. "I think the spear point should count for more than one, since it's in such good shape," Deak said.

"I agree," Pepper said. "I'll give you one and a half for it."

Deak thought for a minute. "That still makes me the low man."

Pepper grinned. "I know."

I had six arrowheads for the day, Pepper five, and Adrian three, though he also had the prize find, a maul made of red quartzite. The maul was used by Indians as a hammer head. It was about the size of a tennis ball and had a groove worked into the middle so the user could get a solid grip when using it for pounding. It was in pristine condition, without nicks or chips. The fact that it was made of red quartzite, which is not found in eastern Ohio, meant a Mingo Indian had once traded for the maul, probably with a tribe in the northern United States. It was a valuable piece.

As we walked, Adrian was rolling the maul around in his left hand, admiring his find, and said, "Maybe I'll just keep this."

"If you do, you have to pay me half its worth," Pepper quickly chimed in. "We have a deal, remember? We sell everything we find and split the money."

"That's just on arrowheads," Adrian countered.

"Really? Then how about the axe head I found last fall? How come we didn't have an arrowheads-only rule when I sold that?"

You were not going to beat Pepper Nash in an argument about money. Adrian muttered something unintelligible, and I was laughing at the end of our single file line, enjoying the brotherly squabble. I was still grinning when the column emptied into a clearing atop Chestnut Ridge and Adrian abruptly halted, causing a chain-reaction collision of teenage boys. Standing at the side of the clearing under the shade of an oak tree, blocking the path leading back down to the school, was Petey Sanchez.

He spotted us immediately and was yammering before we began walking again. "What are you guys doing up here, huh? Queers. Faggots. You up there jerkin' each other off, huh? Havin' a circle jerk, I bet. Circle jerk. Circle jerk. You're a bunch of fuckin' queers, aren't you? Queers. Queers. Queers." Drool fell from his lips as he spoke, and he spread his legs, bent his knees, and made a masturbating motion with his right hand. "Bunch of faggots, faggots, that's what you are. Faggots."

My stomach knotted up. "Get the hell away, Petey," said Pepper, who among the four of us had the shortest fuse.

"Queers. Cornholers. Cocksuckers. Queers. Bunch of queers."

Petey was nearly eighteen with sparse, prickly hairs sprouting on his upper lip and chin, and growing into a strong, physically mature man. The same mental limitations that made him annoying and scary also made Petey fearless, or perhaps just incapable of understanding danger. We made our way toward the hunting path, a tight, shoulder-to-shoulder phalanx around Adrian, who was a full head taller than the rest of us and offered a modicum of protection. I walked at his right shoulder, not wanting to seem afraid, though I had goose bumps covering both arms. I kept my eyes on the path and avoided looking at Petey, who met us in the middle of the clearing and hovered around our group, cursing and yakking and making bird calls, twice leaning his face close to mine and gagging me with his putrid breath. He was dressed in a sleeveless maroon T-shirt with dark sweat and salt stains under the armpits. His grimy underwear was pulled above his cut-off blue jeans, which drooped low on his hips. A pair of black socks sagged around his ankles, lying in ridges on the tops of his battered tennis shoes. Petey reeked of dirt and sweat and excrement, and as we neared our escape path he screeched and leaned in close to Pepper, who said, "Jesus H. Christ, Petey, when's the last time you took a bath? You smell like horse shit."

"Fuck you, queer. Queer. Faggot," he said, waving his arms in a bird-like motion. When Petey attempted to again lean into Pepper's face, Adrian stepped forward to block the charge, and the bony ridge of Petey's forehead hit him on the chin. It was a glancing blow, but Adrian's jaw muscles tightened, his neck flushed and pulsed. Adrian brought his fisted right hand and the hand holding the maul together in front of his chest, and striking a pose like an offensive lineman, he stepped forward and drove his forearms into Petey's sternum. It was a powerful blow, and Petey looked like a marionette jerked off his feet by a puppeteer, flying backward into the scrub near the path. Pepper and I laughed. Deak said, "Hey, come on, let's not do this."

Petey got on all fours. He was starting to cry, spit flying from his mouth, and then, in a motion quicker than I imagined him capable of, he came up with a dried oak limb with a few brown leaves still clinging to it, and swung at Adrian's face. The dried leaves rattled as the limb arced toward Adrian, who ducked and threw his right arm up to block the attack. He tried to grab the limb, but Petey pulled it back and swung again, this time hitting Adrian first in the upper shoulder and snapping the limb in two off the back of his head. The broken end of the stick helicoptered into the clearing; the business end remained clutched in Petey's hands.

We stopped laughing, and I can tell you for a fact that I knew what was going to happen next. As clear as the noontime sky, I could see it unfolding in my mind's eye. I knew it was going to be tragic, but I could not, or did not, stop it. Years afterward, I would ponder that moment and wonder if my hatred and fear of Petey Sanchez trumped common sense and prevented me from stopping Adrian. I was only three feet away when I saw the muscles twitch in Adrian's forearm and the maul drop from his palm into his fingers, easily sliding into the grip he used for a two-seam fastball. I made no move to stop him. Instead, I looked at Petey. He was enraged, his face crimson, squealing and slobbering. When Petey raised his arm for another attack, Adrian's right foot came off the ground.

As the foot came forward, his left shoulder dropped. Petey's right hand started forward with the stick at the same time Adrian's left hand arced past his ear. The maul came out of his hand and covered the two feet to Petey's forehead in a blur. I never saw it leave his hand and I never saw it hit Petey, but I heard it. Pepper always said the impact sounded sharp, like a walnut cracking or a tree limb snapping in a high wind. That's not the way I remember it. What I heard was a sickening crunch, like the sound of someone stepping on an ice cube.

We sometimes make decisions in a span of time so infinitesimal that it cannot be comprehended by our own minds. Yet the impact of the decision is life-altering. There may be times when people lash out purely on instinct, reacting to fear or pain without regard for the consequences, but I think those instances are few. A decision might be made as the result of fear and rage, but it is still a decision. I have had years now to think about the events that occurred that day on Chestnut Ridge, and I believe that Adrian Nash meant to kill Petey Sanchez.

I had known Adrian a long time. He was the star pitcher on the baseball team and I was his catcher. I had seen Adrian Nash in his zone. I had witnessed firsthand the times his eyes narrowed and he honed in on my catcher's mitt and delivered the ball with such accuracy that I caught it without ever moving my hand. Those were the eyes I saw just before Adrian delivered the maul into the forehead of Petey Sanchez. After the limb broke across the back of his head, the pain seared, the adrenaline surged, and a neuron fired somewhere deep in Adrian's brain. It was during that millisecond that the primal instincts of survival took over and I saw the look flash in Adrian's eyes. They narrowed, the teeth clenched, and the maul slipped into his fingers. The desire to kill Petey only lasted an instant, but it struck while Adrian had a three-pound granite projectile in his throwing hand. When Adrian's right foot strode forward, Petey Sanchez was as good as dead. The maul struck Petey an inch to the right of the bony ridge, directly between his eyebrow and hairline, exactly where Adrian wanted to put it.

The stick dropped from his hand, but Petey didn't go right down. Death had yet to register in his feeble mind. The impact of the maul spun his head toward me, like the head of a boxer that has just taken a vicious left hook. It was an instant after granite had compacted bone and his eyes carried a perplexed look, as though trying to process the electric charge that had ignited in his brain and sent a shower of sparks shooting from the cerebellum to the bottom of his spine. But it was only momentary. The brain that had served Petey so poorly in life was shutting down, his eyes turning blank, mouth agape, jaw slack, blood flowing from the crater of pulp in his forehead. The dim lights inside his head began shutting off in quick succession. Like that same staggered boxer, he stood for a moment, wobbled, then began a slow descent to his back. As he started to topple, Petey looked like a wooden soldier in the throes of death, his arms and legs stiff, hinged only at the shoulders and hips. One leg extended awkwardly to the side and his arms windmilled as he fell backward into the weeds, scaring an animal that moved in the thicket and scattering a flock of starlings from a nearby mulberry tree.

We froze for a long moment, just looking at one another. I fought back the salty bile that flooded my mouth and the urge to run as far and fast as my legs would carry me. The clearing and woods had gone suddenly silent. The only sound I recall was Adrian sucking for air through his mouth, his saliva whistling with each heaving breath. The silence was broken when Deak Coultas, the church acolyte, said, "Holy fucking Christ."

The blood drained from Adrian's face. I watched it. The color dropped like the line of a cooling thermometer, and his face took on the pale, waxy hue of the hot candle drippings that clung like stalactites from the church candelabras. Adrian began walking in circles, his splayed fingers on his hips, sucking for air and fighting back tears. Pepper put a hand on his brother's back and offered consolation in a hushed tone. Deak dropped to one knee and held his face in his hands. I twisted a dark blue felt bag in my hands. It had once contained a bottle of fine Canadian sipping whiskey, but now held my arrowheads, which clacked together as I approached the prone figure of Petey Sanchez.

He had fallen into a patch of high grass, thistles, and milkweed under the low branches of the oak tree that had shed the limb he had used as a weapon. After he fell, the parted grass and weeds drooped back over Petey, creating a tomb of green into which his torso and head had disappeared. I set the velvet bag near his legs, which jerked every few seconds, took the stick that had fallen from Petey's hand,

and slowly parted the vegetation. His left arm lay limp at his side, the right extended over his head as though he were swimming the backstroke. Blood pooled in the crater; the right side of his face was awash in red. A few stems of grass clung to his cheeks, held in place by the sticky blood; a blowfly had already alighted at the rim of the hole. His fingers twitched and his mouth opened and closed in a manner that reminded me of a fish that had been dragged up on shore and struggled for breath. I thought Petey, too, was gasping for air, but later in life learned that it was simply the spasmodic reaction of his muscles after his wiring had been short-circuited. I watched for several minutes, maybe as few as two, or as many as five, I'm really not sure, until his body relaxed and settled hard into the brush. When all movement stopped and two more blowflies lit on the moist side of Petey's face, I moved the stick and allowed the grass to fall back over him. I snatched up my velvet bag and moved away. "He's dead," I said.

"Are you sure?" Pepper asked.

"Positive."

"Fuck, fuck, fuck," Adrian said.

"Did you check for a pulse?" Deak asked.

"I don't need to check for a pulse, Deak. There's a hole in his forehead that I could stick my fist in."

"Maybe we should call for an ambulance."

"Fuck no, we're not calling for an ambulance," Pepper said. "For what? He's dead."

"Why in hell didn't he just leave us alone?" Adrian asked, his eyes glassy with tears. "Why'd he always have to get up in your face like that? Goddamn him."

"It was self-defense, Adrian. You had no choice," I offered. "He was going to club you again with that tree limb. He could have killed you."

I expected Adrian to protect his infallibility and shift the blame to us for not helping, but it didn't come. He just stood there, chewing on his lower lip, shaking his head and fighting back tears. With each breath his chest and stomach rolled in unison.

"I'm just saying, if we ran down the hill and called right now, maybe the paramedics could do something," Deak offered.

"Yeah, they'll do something, all right. They'll declare his retarded ass dead and then call the cops to arrest us," Pepper said.

"But, if we don't do . . ."

"No, Deak," Pepper said, his nostrils flaring as he took a step toward him.

I stepped between them and put a hand on Pepper's chest. "Stop it. Enough. Let's give it a minute." I looked at Adrian, who was our unspoken leader. He was beginning to regain his composure, but offered no help. It was on me. "Look, there's nothing anyone can do for Petey. Deak, if you want to check for a pulse, be my guest, but I'm telling you he's stone dead. If we're standing around here and someone wanders by, we're screwed. I say let's get out of here and go somewhere where we can talk and sort things out."

"Agreed," Pepper said, starting past me to the path that would lead us back to the playground.

I snatched his shirt and said, "No. We can't walk back down that way. If anyone sees us coming down the path they might put two and two together after someone finds him. Let's cut over Hogback Hill and take the path down Riddles Run to the glass works. It will look like we were scouting those fields. We'll come into town from the south, and no one will ever know we were up here."

We looked at Adrian and he nodded his approval. In spite of the situation, I welcomed the nod. It was the first time in my life that I could recall making a decision of significance around Adrian. Usually, we simply deferred to him.

Deak looked back at Petey. "Deak, there's nothing we can do for him," I said. He nodded. As we headed across the clearing, I stopped and used the stick to point back to the brush. "Better pick up that maul, Adrian." He went back, kicked around the weeds, and found it a couple feet from the body. As he emerged into the clearing, he rolled it in his hand and appeared to be examining it for bloodstains.

Pepper led us south along the backside of Hogback Hill, the largest of the foothills that rimmed the southwest corner of Crystalton. It would bring us out of the woods near the old Longstreet Mine No. 8 and along the Little Seneca Creek, a quarter of a mile from where it emptied into the Ohio River near the foundation of the old Brilliant Glass Works. The glass works was more than four decades gone, but its stone foundation remained and we would occasionally dig around the grounds for slag, the large pieces of glass that were formed when leftover molten glass was dumped at the end of a run. The slag was considered trash when glass factories lined the Ohio River in Crystalton, but in 1971 they were treasures of our lost past and people would pay five dollars for clear, brick-sized pieces, which were commonly used as doorstops. Along the east side of the old foundation, sloping several hundred yards toward the river, was another farm field that we sometimes searched for arrowheads. After a big storm the relics could be found in abundance along the lower ridge of the field and in the mouth of the Little Seneca, where we scooped out silt and rock in kitchen colanders, searching for arrowheads like prospectors panning for gold.

We did not run across Hogback Hill, but walked in silence and at a brisk pace. I recalled that I had been thinking about lunch when we walked out of the Postalakis's feed-corn field. I was no longer hungry, the pangs canceled by the clenching of my throat and intestines. As we walked I remembered that I had promised my mother I would cut the grass that afternoon. I thought it odd that in the midst of such chaos I would remember something as seemingly insignificant as mowing the lawn.

As we followed the path around Hogback Hill, I felt oddly euphoric, light in the chest, as though I had just walked away from a plane crash. I had witnessed a horrific event, a young man had died, but there was a modicum of relief in knowing that I had not thrown the stone that ended Petey's life. As bad as things were, I knew that I would never have to shoulder that blame. Was I helping to hide the killer? Absolutely. But I could never be held accountable for the murder. The ground was ablaze and strewn with crushed wings and engines and body parts, but I was walking out of the fuselage virtually unscathed.

Chapter Three

On the hillside farmed by Del Cafferty south of town, an outcropping of sandstone protruded from the soil a hundred feet from the edge of the field, which tumbled toward the river and within a few feet of the New York Central Railroad tracks. During our arrowhead sojourns to the field, we would often pack a lunch and sit on the pitted outcropping as we ate, our feet dangling two feet from the loam below, watching freight trains, barges loaded with coal, clouds, and the muddy river roll by.

To the northwest was Crystalton, though all that could be seen from our low vantage point was a handful of houses built high against the encompassing hills, the spire of the Presbyterian Church, and the white water tower that proudly proclaimed in purple block letters:

Crystalton, Ohio
Home of the Royals

When we emerged from the dense foliage of Hogback Hill into Riddles Run, we walked directly to the outcropping. No one said that is where we should go to talk. Instinctively, we just knew. By the time we arrived at the outcropping the sun had arced past noon, burned off the fog, and begun heating the sandstone, which was warm on the backs of my legs and felt good in spite of the temperature already hitting the low eighties. I had been unable to shake the goose bumps and chills since walking away from Petey's body. I pressed my hands between the rock and my thighs to warm my cold fingers.

We sat in silence for a few minutes, each of us pondering our personal situations and waiting for Adrian to take the lead. During youth, leadership is most often determined as it is in wolf packs or lion prides—by size and strength. Thus, Adrian had always been our leader, first by size, but later by intelligence and natural ability. He was simply one of those people you turned to for leadership. On that day, however, he was silent, nervous, and made no movement to tell us how we would address the dilemma. When he looked over to me, his eyes moist and rimmed in red, I realized that Adrian could not accept a leadership role in this situation because he was now dependent upon us for his survival.

I finally slipped off the rock and said, "Okay, what's the plan? I've got to get the grass cut before my mom gets home from work." It sounded ridiculous under the circumstances, but it was no less a fact.

"I've been thinking," Adrian said, his tone hardly more than a whisper. "If they never found the body, how would anyone know he had been killed?" He looked around at us. "I mean, Petey rode that damn bicycle all over the place, anything could have happened to him. He could have fallen in the river or into an abandoned mine, or run away. Who knows? If they never find a body, it'll just be a missing person, right? Who's going to look for him? Not his parents, and not the Crystalton cops, that's for sure."

"Someone is going to find him eventually," I said.

"Not if we get rid of the body."

A wave of ice ran from my brain stem to my heels.

Adrian continued, "Maybe tonight we camp out, and go back up and drag his body over and throw it in the fly ash pond. They'd never think to look in there."

There were two fly ash ponds built into the hills above Crystalton. They were decades-old craters in the earth left by strip mining companies. As a way of reducing air pollution, the electric generating plant in town pumped a slurry of fly ash captured from the smokestacks to the ponds. They were quicksand-type pits of acid-heavy ash and water. We had found deer tracks leading into the ponds, but never coming out.

"After a couple of months the acid will completely dissolve the body," Adrian said. "It'll eat away everything but the teeth, and they would never find those. The pits are bottomless."

Despite his distressed state of mind, it wouldn't have surprised me if Adrian was conspiring behind the wild eyes, trying to elevate our involvement in the crisis to make us all more culpable. I wanted to help Adrian, but such a move would increase my participation in Petey's death from that of mere witness to co-conspirator, and I was going to have to balk. "You're just thinking out loud, right, Adrian?" I asked.

"It's Petey, goddammit. No one would look for him."

"I can't do that," Deak said. "No way. I'm not throwing him in that pit never to be found and never given a proper funeral."

"A proper funeral?" Adrian asked, flashing Deak a hateful look.

"Look, what if we go back on the hill and come running down behind the playground and say we found Petey up there and he was already dead?" Deak offered. "Then someone could go up and get him and he wouldn't have to lie up there in the weeds in the heat with all the bugs."

"Oh, for the love of Christ," Adrian groaned.

Pepper hopped off the ledge and said, "Look, first of all, the heat and bugs aren't bothering Petey, and why in hell do we need a plan?" He looked around at all of us. "Seriously? Why? This is very simple. Listen to me. Tonight, maybe tomorrow, maybe a week from now, someone is going to walk up to you and ask, 'Hey, did you hear about Petey Sanchez?' When that happens, you say, 'No. What?' They'll say, 'He's dead.' You say, 'No shit, really? How?' That's it. That's all we have to say. Game over."

"Once they find the body the cops will start an investigation. What if they ask us questions?" Deak asked.

"So what if they do? It's the same routine," Pepper said, his voice climbing as his patience with Deak ran short. "If the cops ask you if you've seen Petey in the last week, you say no, not that you recall. If they ask if you have any idea who might have killed him, you say not a clue. If they ask if we were up on Chestnut Ridge, we say no. It was foggy as hell this morning. No one saw us walk up there. We were a mile from the Postalakis house. They didn't see us." He pointed at Deak, then me. "Did either of you guys tell anyone we were going up on Chestnut Ridge?"

"No," Deak said. I shook my head.

"Well, there you have it," Pepper said. "We met at the elementary school and walked down here. We spent the morning hunting for arrowheads. Period. Let's not make this more complicated than it needs to be. We keep our mouths shut, and when someone asks about Petey Sanchez, we don't know a damn thing."

He was right. If no one could put us on Chestnut Ridge and we kept our mouths shut, there was nothing to fear.

"If we get caught, we'll all go to juvenile hall," Adrian said.

I nodded. I wasn't sure that was true, but I was willing to let it hang there for Deak's benefit. It was a little cruel, but necessary. Deak Coultas was a great friend and a very caring kid. He had a kind word for everyone. In the heat of a basketball game, he would be the first one to extend a hand and help a fallen opponent back to his feet. He was the apotheosis of a parent's perfect child. The fact that he had been witness to a murder and part of the cover-up was going to be particularly rough on him.

"I just think we should tell someone," Deak said. "It bothers me that he's dead and his family doesn't even know."

I said, "Deak, let me ask you this: What good is telling someone going to do besides clearing your conscience? If Adrian gets nailed, we do, too. Adrian threw the rock, but we share in the blame because we didn't stop him. We let the retarded kid die. And let's remember this: We didn't start it. Petey was the one who started it. He head-butted Adrian and clubbed him with a tree limb. Adrian was trying to protect us."

We all looked at Deak, the obvious weak link in the chain. "I got it," he said.

"Are we in agreement?" Pepper asked.

Deak and I both nodded. Deak, I knew, believed he was failing in the eyes of God and had just committed his soul to eternal damnation. Pepper couldn't be bothered. He was probably wondering how much Fats Pennington was going to give them for the arrowheads and the maul. He was concerned for his brother, but the fact that Petey Sanchez was lying dead in the weeds would not cost Pepper Nash a minute's sleep. He would give it no more thought than if Adrian had punched Petey in the nose. Petey Sanchez? Fuck him. He got what he deserved. That psycho hit Adrian twice with a tree branch and Adrian punched his ticket, gave him a one-way trip to the big retard school in the sky. Sayonara, crazy boy. I'm glad the goofy sonofabitch is gone. And that would be that. How much for that maul, Fats?

As it became apparent that our business at the rock was complete, Adrian turned and began walking toward the river. Pepper instinctively knew what his brother was going to do and said, "Wait, Adrian, don't throw that away. It's worth a lot of money."

Adrian stopped and looked at Pepper for a long moment, as though contemplating the risk versus the financial gain, then he took a few more steps and hurled the maul far into the Ohio. When it hit, the water plumed up on both sides and for an instant looked like a glass vase before fading into ripples that were soon consumed by the current.

"Dammit," Pepper said.

We walked across the furrowed field, stepping over young corn sprouts, heading for the wooden foot bridge that spanned the Little Seneca below Third Street. When we were halfway across, Adrian turned and asked, "Are you keeping that for a souvenir?"

In my hand was Petey's oak branch. I had taken it to remove any clues from the crime scene, but had been mindlessly using it as a walking stick. I inspected it for a moment, then dropped it over the side of the bridge and into the rushing waters of Little Seneca Creek, which was still running fast from the previous day's rain. We all watched it float downstream until it went through the concrete culvert under the New York Central tracks and made its way to join the maul in the Ohio.

Chapter Four

The front door of Fats Pennington's antique shop could be reached only by traversing a weed- and gravel-covered lot that was cluttered with rusting farm implements, a couple of old-fashioned gasoline pumps, a weathered church pew on which Fats sunned his considerable girth on slow days, several wagon wheels with missing spokes, and a battered wicker gondola from a hot air balloon that Fats swore had been used by troops under the command of Ulysses S. Grant to spy on the Confederates during the Tennessee campaign of 1863. "Only a hundred and twenty dollars to own a piece of history," he once told me.

As we crossed Third Street at the south end of town, Deak extended his hand and gave Pepper his spear point and a smaller white arrowhead. "Add these to your collection to sell Fats," Deak said.

Pepper frowned. "You want the money, don't you?"

"Nah, you keep it."

Pepper shrugged and headed into the antique shop. We stayed outside in the lot amid the rusting farm implements and General Grant's gondola. "That spear point is a prize," I said.

"I don't care. I don't want it in my bedroom. I don't want to have to look at it and be reminded of this day."

Fred Webb, a biology teacher at the high school and the line coach on the football team, drove by in his pickup truck, honked, and waved without taking his hand off the wheel. The bus from

Steubenville went past us going south, blowing exhaust in our faces. It went to the gravel turnaround at the edge of town and came back, pulling up to the sheltered stop in front of the sand quarry to pick up Mrs. Bush, a nearly blind retired schoolteacher who felt her way up the steps with a mahogany cane.

"It's going to be all right," I said.

Deak nodded. "Yeah. I guess."

In another minute the Nashes came out of the shop, Pepper dividing the bills between them.

"Twenty-four bucks with the points Deak gave us," Pepper said. "We'd have gotten a lot more if you hadn't . . ."

"Drop it," Adrian said.

We walked up Third Street, two by two, the Nash brothers in front. I have heard people describe tragic events as surreal, even dreamlike. They say it was like watching a show through a foggy pane of glass. As the tragedy unfolds before them, often in slow motion, they are sure it is simply a dream from which they will awaken. That was never the case with me and the death of Petey Sanchez. From the time we entered the clearing until Petey dropped couldn't have been much more than sixty seconds. Yet, the event still remains crisp in my memory. It is more than three decades past, yet I can recall with vivid clarity the sound of granite crushing bone and brain.

Surreal, however, is a word I would use to describe walking down Third Street after we left Fats Pennington's antique shop as if nothing in the world had changed. The sun was high and the blue sky stretched from the foothills to our west, across the Ohio River and beyond the hills of West Virginia for as far as we could see. And there we were, walking down Third Street, four of Crystalton's favorite sons—All-American-looking kids, clean-cut athletes—enjoying a beautiful summer day. We strolled down the street as though we didn't have a care in the world, smiling, waving at passing cars, and talking about going to the evening swim at the community pool that night. I have thought about that all these years. Petey was dead in the bushes and we were going swimming. When we got to the bottom of Hudson Hill, Adrian and Pepper turned up Gilchrist Street toward their home.

"See ya later," Adrian said.

"Later, 'gator," Pepper added.

"Yeah, see you around," Deak said.

"See ya," I said.

Deak and I walked in silence past the high school and the Big Dipper Ice Cream Shop. He broke the silence. "They're talking about me right now."

"Who's talking about you?" I asked in a hushed tone.

"Adrian and Pepper."

"They're worried that you're not going to be able to hold it together."

"Why do they think that? I've always been a good friend."

"They're just scared, Deak. Put yourself in Adrian's position."

"I would never allow myself to get in that position."

"You don't know that, Deak." I snapped my fingers. "It happened just that fast. I'm sure Adrian would like to have that instant back, but it's water over the dam."

We walked in silence for a few minutes. "How long until someone finds his body?" he asked.

"I don't know. Not long. Couple of days at the most, I'd guess. Someone will find him."

Deak looked at me and frowned, a brow arched in a quizzical manner. "Do you remember seeing his bicycle anywhere?"

"Now that you mention it, no."

"What do you think he was doing up there?"

When we emerged from the path Petey was just standing in the clearing, like he was waiting on a bus, and I recalled wondering the same thing—what is he doing on Chestnut Ridge and where was his bike? However, the ensuing events had erased the question until that minute. "That's a good question. I have no idea."

"The clearing is a half-mile up that steep path. He certainly wasn't hunting arrowheads, and when was the last time you saw Petey Sanchez without his bicycle?"

"Never."

"So, what was he doing up there?"

"It was Petey, Deak. You're asking me to make sense of his actions? Who knows why Petey did the things he did."

"It just seems strange, is all."

"Try not to think too much about it, Deak. It'll make you crazy. We need you to hold it together."

"I will. Don't worry about it." We walked past the community center and Blackie Mehtal's auto repair garage. When we stopped in front of Deak's house, I asked if he wanted to do something after I finished cutting the grass. "You don't have to hang around with me all day, Hutch. I'm okay. I'm not going to say anything."

"It'll get better with every day that passes. We just need to get some time behind us."

"I'll be fine."

"What are you going to do for the rest of the afternoon?"

"I'm going up to my room, close the door and pray for the soul of Petey Sanchez and for our forgiveness."

I thought about that for a moment and said, "Put in an extra word or two for me, will you?"

Chapter Five

The fire whistle, as it was called in Crystalton, began as a slow, tinny whine, grew to a gurgle deep in the throat, and bloomed into a screaming, air raid siren-like blast that lasted a full ten seconds before dying back down into the throat, recycling for another round.

The whistle blew every night at nine o'clock. It was a daily test, but parents called it the "curfew whistle," and anyone under the age of twelve and living in the home of Miriam Van Buren had better be home by the time the single blast settled down. When the whistle blew and it wasn't 9 p.m., the hearts of mothers throughout Crystalton palpitated and they all conducted a quick inventory of their children. Those with children not within eyesight—a teenage son out in the car or a daughter at the swimming pool—could not relax until they had been accounted for.

Unlike police or ambulance sirens that blare all hours of the day and night in big cities, the occasional blast of the whistle in a town of sixteen hundred people signified problems for someone you loved, cared about, or at least knew.

On Tuesday, June 15, we were winning three to one with two outs and none on in the top of the fifth inning of a summer league game against Dillonvale when the whistle began its tinny whine. The umpire suspended the game while the siren blew. I took off my catcher's mask, retrieved the bandana I kept in my hip pocket, and mopped up the sweat captured in the peach fuzz on my upper lip before wiping away the thin line of mud that encircled my face where perspiration and dust from the ball field congealed beneath the pads of my mask. During the second siren blast, I walked to the pitcher's mound. Adrian and Pepper were playing catch just to keep Adrian's arm loose. I held up my catcher's mitt and called for the ball, a tacit sign that I wanted to join their game of catch. Pepper tossed one to me side-arm and it snapped into my mitt. On the fifth blast of the whistle, a Crystalton Police cruiser could be seen climbing New Alexandria Pike, a twisty, two-lane road carved out of the hill just above the water tower, and one that led to Chestnut Ridge. As the tenth and final blast of the whistle began to sound, the rescue squad appeared on the road, its red beacon flashing off the backdrop of foliage.

In centerfield, Deak had his throwing hand and glove on his knees, looking down at the ground so all we could see was the top of his purple cap. "He's going to crack," Adrian said.

"He'll be fine," I said, turning my head from the home crowd. "How are you holding up?"

He responded with silence and a glare, as I knew he would before I asked the question. I never knew what was going on in Adrian's head because he would never let me in. He didn't let anyone in. As the final blast died down, I said to Adrian, "You're up oh and two, keep the next pitch down and out. Make him chase it."

"Shut up and go catch," he said.

I hunkered down and set up on the outside corner, knee-high. Adrian did not have that focused look in his eyes. Rather, he looked scared, maybe angry. He went into his windup and never once looked at my glove. The ball flew high and tight, hitting the Dillonvale batter in the ribs, just below the armpit. Air rushed from his lungs and he twisted and danced his way to first base, wincing the entire ninety feet.

I picked the ball out of the dirt and smoked it back to him. "Throw to the glove," I said. He regained his control, but the game was over as soon as he hit that kid in the ribs. No batter would stand in on him the rest of the night. We won five to one.

As we were leaving the ballpark that evening, the four of us walking out together ahead of our parents, Denny Morelli, a kinky-haired classmate who played the saxophone in the marching band, came pedaling into the parking lot and skidded to a halt, flicking pebbles on our shins. "Hey, did you hear about Petey Sanchez?" he asked.

"No. What?" Pepper asked.

"He's dead. Murdered, maybe. They found him up on Chestnut Ridge. I guess he's got a big hole in his head."

"No shit, really?" Pepper asked. "A hole? What kind of a hole, like a bullet hole?"

"Maybe, I don't know for sure. My aunt heard them talking about it on the police scanner and they said he had a big hole in his head. They were calling for the coroner to look at him."

Denny pedaled off to spread the news like the town crier. When he was out of earshot, Pepper turned to us, a smug little smile on his lips, and said, "That's how it's done, boys. Now we've all been informed that Petey's dead and don't have to act surprised. We just have to act like we don't know a damn thing."

Adrian looked ready to vomit.

★ ★ ★

The maple tree that was wedged between the sidewalk and Second Street near our front porch was over a century old when in May of 1970 a windstorm that snapped telephone poles in two and blew tractor-trailers off Ohio Route 7 uprooted the beast and dropped it into our side yard. While it miraculously missed our house, it stretched from the sidewalk and a root ball the size of a Volkswagen minibus to the back of our property where its whippy top branches dangled in the alley. My mother blanched at the idea of paying someone to cut up a tree. She rented a chain saw for eight dollars a day and we spent an entire weekend turning the saw blade blue with heat and stacking maple logs in the garden, which gave me a virtually unlimited supply of firewood for campfires.

Deak came over to my house after the Dillonvale game and we started a fire in a corner of the property that we called the garden, though we never planted so much as a single tomato plant. We snagged some chips, RC Colas, a package of hot dogs, buns, and a plastic squirt bottle of mustard. As the fire began to grow, I sharpened a pair of sticks with my pocketknife and skewered a hot dog on each, handing one to Deak, who had been quiet most of the evening.

We sat on logs that I had rolled into a rough circle around the fire pit. The flames danced and painted our faces with streaks of flickering orange and yellow light. Deak sat to my right, the bag of chips between us, and we talked in hushed tones. "Are you feeling better now that he's not lying up there in the woods?" I asked.

His head bobbed almost imperceptibly. "A little. At least his family can have a little peace." Petey's family probably didn't even know he had been missing, but I didn't say that. "What the devil was he doing up there?" Deak asked, repeating his question from the previous day.

"You're going to make yourself crazy if you keep this up. Sometimes, Deak, there are no logical answers."

"Why'd Adrian have to do it? Why didn't he just run away?"

"It's not always easy to run, Deak. Sometimes you have to fight, especially if someone's a threat and coming at you."

"Jesus said to turn the other cheek."

"I'm not sure this is the best situation to relate to scripture. Besides, I'll bet Jesus wasn't getting pummeled with an oak branch when he said that."

He stared back into the fire and took a sip of his RC Cola. "My stomach feels like it's on fire, Hutch. I feel like I gotta take a crap all the time, but there's nothing left because I've had diarrhea since yesterday afternoon. I didn't sleep hardly at all last night because I couldn't get my brain to shut down." He wrapped a bun around the hot dog on his stick and slid it off. Holding the stick between his knees, Deak grabbed the mustard with his free hand and squirted a yellow string on the blackened dog. "Do you ever think about the events that led to Petey's death?"

"You mean the constant turmoil he had been causing his entire life?"

"No, I mean what happened yesterday morning, the events that put us and Petey up on Chestnut Ridge at the same time—Petey doing bird calls and Adrian with that chunk of granite in his hand?" I admitted I hadn't. "Think about it. It all started with that storm Sunday afternoon." He looked at me while he worked over a mouthful of hot dog. "God, or a high pressure system, whatever, brought a big storm over eastern Ohio. You, me, Adrian, Pepper, we all got on the phones and started lining up our arrowhead hunting trip. At first, we were going down to the old glass plant, but you said you didn't think there were many good arrowheads left there because we've found so many over the years, so we decided to go to the Postalakis farm." He again looked at me and I nodded, acknowledging my culpability in the decision. "After we were there on the hill for a while, Pepper said he was tired of hunting, but Adrian said he wanted to scout around the field closest to the Little Seneca, and we all said okay."

I chuckled, remembering Pepper's response to Adrian's declaration that he wanted to search longer. Pepper had said, "Well, if that's what the great Adrian Nash wants to do, then by all means let's all stand out here in the scorching sun and sweat our balls off some more."

"When we walked over near the creek, that's when Adrian found the maul, and we all spent another five minutes admiring it and Adrian washed it off in the creek. You and Pepper whizzed in the creek. So, all those events put us in the clearing at the precise moment that Petey was there. If we had gone to the glass house field, or if we had left when Pepper wanted to, or if Adrian hadn't washed the maul off in the stream, we'd probably never have run into Petey and none of this would have happened."

"Maybe it was God's way of taking Petey Sanchez out of the mix before that goofy bastard could hurt someone else. It was only a matter of time before he killed or really hurt some kid, or burned up his entire family."

"You don't know that. Only God knows that."

"Exactly. Maybe that was his way of stopping it."

"He doesn't work that way."

"Well, he should. I know Petey didn't deserve to die, but he brought it on himself when he went after Adrian with that limb. Adrian was trying to protect all of us and he probably saved some little kid in the process."

"I don't think he was trying to protect us. I think his temper got the best of him and he reacted." Deak threw a nub of hot dog bun into the fire. "You know, you've always looked at Adrian not as a friend, but as your hero, like he's bigger than life."

"That's bullshit."

"Is it? Would you be able to justify your silence if it hadn't been Adrian Nash who threw the rock? Would you take a chance like this if it had been some other kid who killed Petey and you saw it happen?" I shrugged. "I'll bet you wouldn't. And what if he hadn't been Petey? What if it was me up there in the weeds that Adrian killed instead of him? Would you tell then?"

"It wasn't you."

"That isn't what I asked."

"Of course I would tell someone."

He went back to staring at the fire and roasting his second hot dog. "I'm not sure I believe that."

We had just finished our hot dogs and thrown our roasting sticks into the flames when my mother and her friend Walter Deshay came out the back door and walked toward the fire. Walter was a widower who worked at an automobile parts store in Steubenville and kept a fishing boat on Catawba Island in Lake Erie. He had a round belly and thinning hair, and was forever pushing his wire-rim glasses up on his nose. They weren't dating, my mother stressed on several occasions. Rather, they were just "seeing each other." They had been playing bingo at the Knights of Columbus Hall in Mingo Junction and probably stopped for a beer or two at Foggy's Tavern on the way home, as was their usual Tuesday night routine. "What's this I hear about Petey Sanchez?" she asked when she got close enough that I could see her face illuminated by the flames.

I shrugged. "They found him dead up on Chestnut Ridge, I guess."

"It's all over the radio. How'd he die?"

"I don't know." I was grateful for the orange glow the fire threw upon my face, camouflaging the red I felt creeping up around my ears, a common side effect when I lied.

"Denny Morelli told us about it after the game. He said someone might have shot him in the head," Deak offered with a tone of surprising sincerity.

"Good heavens," Walter said, pushing up his glasses.

"Why are you two out here?" my mom asked.

I didn't understand the question. "Where am I supposed to be?" I asked.

"Inside. You don't know who killed Petey. There might be some nutcase running around."

"Mom, really?"

"Don't you 'Mom, really' me, mister. Clear up your stuff and get in the house. Dale Ray, you get in the car. I'll give you a ride home."

"You don't have to do that, Mrs. Van Buren."

"I'm well aware of what I have and don't have to do, Dale Ray. Get your butt in the car."

Mom and Walter walked back into the house while we picked up our trash and scattered the still-burning ashes with an old spade that I kept in the garden for that purpose.

"Reverend Timlinson called me this afternoon. They need another counselor at the fourth- and fifth-grade church camp out at Bergholz," Deak said. "I think I'm going to go over and help them out for the rest of the week and get away from this."

"I think that's a good idea. What about Saturday? Will you be back? We have a double-header against Mount Pleasant."

The engine on the Plymouth turned over and the headlights came on, illuminating the red brick street. He nodded. "I'll be back Friday evening, but I'm amazed that with everything flying around us you're still concerned about a baseball game."

"It's two baseball games," I said, offering some levity.

He walked to the car, shoulders stooped, without looking back.

Chapter Six

You didn't sleep late in the home of Miriam Van Buren. Mom had grown up on a dairy farm and believed sleeping until 5 a.m. was a luxury. She didn't have to be at the post office until 7 a.m., and it was only a two-minute walk from our house, but she would get up, shower, eat, read the paper, and work around the house until it was time to leave. She would call up the stairs at a quarter before seven. If I wasn't in the kitchen by ten 'til, she would march upstairs, building a little froth with each step, grab hold of the little toe on my left foot, and twist it until my right foot was on the floor and I was hopping and yelping.

When she called up the morning after the body of Petey Sanchez had been discovered, I was already awake and awaiting her call. Spread on the kitchen table was the morning Wheeling *Intelligencer.* I was anxious to see what had been written about Petey, but I stuck to my morning routine and poured a bowl of raisin bran cereal and snagged the sports page. I feigned interest in the baseball box scores until she put fifteen dollars on the table with a list printed on an index card of groceries she wanted from Connell's Market, reminded me to clean the gutters, and headed out the door. When I heard the front door close, I waited a few minutes, then began flipping through the *Intelligencer*'s local news section. The story was on page five, a four-paragraph brief under a one-column headline:

Boy's Body Found; Foul Play Suspected

The body of a 17-year-old mentally retarded boy was discovered in a wooded area west of Crystalton yesterday afternoon by a woman picking berries, according to Jefferson County Sheriff Sky Kelso.

Kelso identified the boy as Peter Eugene Sanchez of 117 River Street, Crystalton. Kelso said relatives had not seen the boy since late Sunday, but had not reported him missing.

Kelso said Sanchez died of head trauma and "not the type you receive from a fall." When asked if Sanchez had been murdered, Kelso said, "It's not much of a stretch to suspect foul play," but he would not release further details. The boy appeared to have been dead "at least 24 hours, but we'll know more after the autopsy," Kelso said.

The body was sent to the Allegheny County Coroner's Office in Pittsburgh for the autopsy. Kelso said the Jefferson County Sheriff's Department is working on the case in conjunction with the Crystalton Police Department.

My ass puckered at the thought of the sheriff's department investigating the case. The Crystalton Police Department consisted of Errol Durkin and two full-time patrolmen—Errol's brother Flip and Bobby Joe Wyatt—and seven or eight auxiliary officers who worked a couple shifts a month. The thought of them solving a murder case was laughable, but I didn't find the sheriff's department as humorous. Sky Kelso was a former U.S. Army military policeman who liked to see his photograph in the paper and personally showed up at every big crime scene in the county. Kelso had a capable staff and full-time detectives that he would turn loose and ride herd over, because he knew that solved crimes made for happy voters.

Connell's Market opened at eight. Before I left the house I reminded myself that just because someone looked at me didn't mean they were thinking that I was part of a murder conspiracy. I walked into the store about twenty after eight to find my third-grade teacher, Florence "Bulldog" Kearns, standing at the checkout counter with her usual scowl, from which she earned her nickname, chatting with Jewel Connell. As I neared the counter, Miss Kearns halted her conversation with Jewel in mid-sentence and zeroed in on me with the cold, gray eyes that had terrified Crystalton third-graders for generations. "What do you know about this affair with Pete Sanchez?" she asked.

I was prepared. This was little Crystalton, and I knew that all anyone would be talking about was Petey's death. I had steeled myself against acting paranoid. I shrugged and said, "I guess he died of some kind of head injury."

"Well, I know that much," Miss Kearns said. "Have you heard anything else?"

"Just what I read in the morning paper."

When it was apparent that I could contribute no additional information about Petey, she dismissed me as quickly as she had in the third grade when I became stumped on a multiplication problem.

I had Artie Connell slice me a half-pound of turkey breast and an equal amount of mild cheddar at the deli counter, then pushed a little shopping cart around the store, picking up the milk, eggs, bread, and the other odds and ends on the list while I eavesdropped on the conversation at the counter. According to Mrs. Connell, Gladys Hoefer had driven out to Overlook Park on Chestnut Ridge to pick blackberries and raspberries to make preserves. Overlook Park is a small township park with a few picnic tables on the north side of New Alexandria Pike where the road crosses over Chestnut Ridge, just before the bridge that spans the Little Seneca Creek. Mrs. Connell said Mrs. Hoefer had a bad hip and had "absolutely no business" climbing those hills and looking for berries when she could buy a nice size bag of frozen berries right there at the market for only sixty-nine cents.

"Gladys never uses frozen berries in her preserves," Miss Kearns said.

Be that as it may, Mrs. Connell said that Mrs. Hoefer pulled her car into an area of the Overlook shaded by a grove of shagbark hickories, tied the string of her big straw hat under her chin, and went to the clearing on the south side of New Alexandria Pike to pick the wild berries. She made her way around the edge of the clearing where the berries are the most plentiful and noticed a cloud of blowflies swarming near the path that empties out behind the elementary school. Mrs. Hoefer assumed there was a dead animal in the weeds—the place is loaded with groundhog holes and it's no place for someone with a bad hip—and she stayed clear of the swarm. She had been up there several hours and her bucket was nearly three-quarters full and she was getting tired—Mrs. Connell assumed her hip was hurting her, too, but of course Gladys would never admit that—so she headed back toward her car. That's when she saw the tennis shoes protruding from the weeds. At first, it didn't register that the shoes were attached to legs, which were directly under the swarming flies. She crept closer, and when she got a glimpse of a swollen, pale hand lying alongside a pair of cut-off blue jeans and a slight whiff of rotting flesh, she ran for her car.

"She ran?" Miss Kearns questioned.

"That's what she said, but I don't think she could with that bad hip and all."

By the time I made my way back to the counter, the tale of Gladys Hoefer's discovery had ceased and the two women had been joined by a young man who did not look a lot older than me. He was carrying a pad and pencil and had a startled look on his face after having been told, "Don't you even think about putting my name in that newspaper," by the humorless Miss Kearns.

He looked at me and asked, "Did you know the Sanchez boy?"

"Why do you want to know?" I asked.

He pulled a laminated badge from his shirt pocket and held it out for my inspection. "I'm Reggie Fuschea. I'm a reporter for the *Steubenville Herald-Star*. I'm writing a story about the murder and I'm looking for a little color, you know, someone who can tell me a little bit about this Peter Sanchez. Can I ask you a few questions?"

"I guess."

This earned another hateful stare from Miss Kearns, who wrapped her bag of groceries in a chubby arm and headed for the door. Mrs. Connell rang up my purchases.

"Did you know Peter?"

"We all called him Petey. Crystalton's a small town; everyone knew Petey."

"You were close friends with him?"

"No, I just knew him. He was older than me—a couple of years, maybe three. We weren't friends or anything. I just knew who he was."

"So, a young, mentally retarded boy is murdered in a small town. I'll bet Crystalton is pretty broken up over this, huh?"

"I don't really know, Mr. Fuschea. I haven't talked to anyone. But, you're right, this is a small town and everyone knows everyone else. We all know the Sanchez family, and I'm sure there's a lot of sympathy for them right now."

"Great," he said, and got my name and age. He tucked his pad and pencil into his hip pocket and fetched a bottle of chocolate milk from the stand-up cooler. As I paid for my groceries, Fuschea asked, "Who did this Sanchez kid chum around with? Can you point me to some of his friends who might talk to me?"

"To be real honest, Petey was kind of a loner. He didn't have a lot of friends, at least none that I knew of. I don't remember ever seeing him pal around with anyone, so I don't think I can help you with that."

"Okay, thanks," he said as I left the store to begin cleaning our gutters. I spent most of the day on the roof, cleaning fly ash, maple saplings, and two dried-up starlings out of the gutters. I did a particularly fine job, wanting to stay busy and avoid conversations about Petey.

I received a valuable lesson that day in talking to newspaper reporters. Don't say anything around them that you don't want to see in print. When he put his pad and pencil away, I assumed the interview was over. It wasn't. When that afternoon's *Herald-Star* landed on the doorstep, the headline read:

Friendless "Loner" Killed in Crystalton

Other than Sheriff Kelso, I was the only one interviewed for the story.

The Nash brothers walked over late that evening. I was lifting weights in the workout room I had constructed in half of our two-car garage. "What the hell are you doing talking to a newspaper reporter?" Adrian asked.

"He surprised me over at Connell's. Hell, I didn't know he was going to put all that in the paper."

"We're supposed to be keeping a low profile. Remember?"

"Yeah, Adrian, I remember."

Pepper started laughing. "It's a good cover."

★ ★ ★

It took about two days before people in town, mostly the same mothers who had treated Petey like a raccoon in the trash, began referring to him as "that poor Sanchez boy." In death, Petey was transformed into a pitiable character. Mostly, I think it was out of sympathy for his mother, who posed for a photographer from the *Herald-Star* holding a photo of Petey, her sunken eyes moist with tears. Women took casseroles and hams and baked bread and desserts to the Sanchez house. They offered them used but good clothing so the kids would have something decent to wear to the funeral home. The Catholic Women's Club took up a collection and purchased a cheap fiberboard casket.

It was all well intentioned, but a goodly number of the women who were outwardly mourning Lila and Earl Sanchez's loss were secretly glad Petey was gone. In a part of their heart where they never wanted another human being to peek, they were happy that the Lord took Petey before he could hurt one of their children. They said things like, "Perhaps it was for the best as he would never have had a good quality of life." But what they were thinking was, "Thank God, I don't have to worry about that crazy bastard hurting one of my kids."

I understood their sentiments. Never had I walked the streets or ridden my bicycle when, in the back of my mind, I wasn't worried about an encounter with Petey. And I wasn't any different from other kids. I understood that he had problems that were beyond his control, but to us he was crazy and aggressive, and I was glad he was dead, though I greatly wished I had not had a front-row seat to his demise.

Chapter Seven

There was no shortage of things to worry about. I worried about Sky Kelso and his brush cut showing up at my door, the possibility of Deak cracking, going to juvenile hall, and not getting to play sports. Mostly, however, I was worried about my mother. Our family was not something from a Norman Rockwell painting, and she did not need one more problem. I sometimes looked at myself as the last chance for someone in the family not to disappoint her.

My mother was the first female letter carrier in Crystalton. She took the position when it was largely a male job, and the *Steubenville Herald-Star* wrote a story about her that ran with a photo of her standing in front of the post office, austere in shorts stretched against her wide hips, black walking shoes, and a heavy leather bag hanging from her shoulder.

She was a good mother who, when at age eight I came home crying after being told that I was the "suckiest" player on my baseball team, took me to the field every evening after dinner and hit me grounders and pitched batting practice until she could no longer lift her arm above her shoulder. She also taught me how to bait a hook, pound a nail, and say "Yes, sir" and "No, ma'am." And she would not hesitate to pin me against the wall if I needed it. When I was in the fourth grade she gave me a slap up the back of the head for an infraction that I can no longer recall, and I threatened to call the police. "Really?" she said in a very calm voice. She pointed to the phone on the end table near the couch. "There's the phone. Go ahead and call them. They can have whatever's left of you by the time they get here." That was the end of my threats.

I don't remember my dad. His name was David, but everyone knew him by the nickname of "Mugs." He left home when I was still in diapers and Mom didn't talk about him. There were a few photographs of him in the shoeboxes of snapshots in the hall closet, and he appeared to be a man of insignificance, thin, with a hairline that began at the top of his skull, stooped shoulders, and a belt cinched up so tight that his pants bunched up around his waist. When I was in kindergarten, I asked Mom if I had a father.

"Everyone has a father," Mom said.

"Where's mine?"

"I don't know."

"Why?"

"He left."

"Why?"

"I don't know."

"Why?"

"He didn't say and I didn't care to ask."

"Where did he go?"

"Away from here."

"Is he coming back?"

"It's highly unlikely."

That, as I recall, was the only conversation we ever had about the old man. Simply, he was not there, not a factor in our lives, and not someone she wanted to waste time or words discussing.

My brother was twenty-three, eight years older than I was, and had no dominion over his life. Responsibility overwhelmed Steven. Discipline was just another word he could not spell. He caved under the slightest pressure and was so bereft of confidence that he could barely make eye contact with you. A few times each season, he would take the bus from Steubenville to watch me play. He would stand alone, hands in his pockets, and sometimes leave without ever speaking to me. My mother, having raised three children alone while working full time, had long before lost patience with him. His solution was to be a shadow, have little contact with us, and stay high or drunk as much as possible.

My sister, Virginia, was six when I was born. As a high school girl, she was not particularly attractive, but she was heavy in the chest and starved for attention, which is a dangerous combination around hormonally enraged teenage boys. At seventeen she was impregnated by Nick Simpson, a nineteen-year-old dropout from Riddles Run who at the time was the only one of the four Simpson brothers not in prison, a point my sister noted with considerable pride. Nick showed up at the house with a cigarette tucked behind one ear and grease caked under his fingernails, and said he intended to "make things right and marry Virginia Sue." My mother vetoed the offer, and we never saw Nick again. Virginia's son was just over a year old when she got pregnant by a guy named Lou Nicoletti from Mingo Junction. He had stringy hair and a nervous laugh. By the summer of 1971, she had a three-year-old son and a fourteen-month-old daughter and lived in a trailer park near Empire, getting heavier and angrier by the day. I'm sure Lou Nicoletti rued the day he ever crawled on top of her.

I didn't like Virginia. She was vocal in her belief that I was spoiled and Mom's favorite. To this day I don't believe I was ever spoiled, but I was probably Mom's favorite. That distinction was not an especially difficult echelon to reach considering the competition.

I had lived a carefree life until the moment I witnessed one of my best friends drop a mentally retarded kid with an Indian hammer. I visualized us getting arrested and going to court in handcuffs, newspaper photographers' flashbulbs popping in our eyes. Consoling each other behind the rail are Mr. and Mrs. Nash and Mr. and Mrs. Coultas. Off to the side, forgotten in the moment, is my mother, standing alone and dabbing a tissue to her eyes. Her last child, the one for which she had such hopes, has also disappointed her. As the vision replayed over and over in my head, I became even more resolved to stifle the events of Monday morning.

It was important, I believed, to get more time behind us, more hours and days separating us from the events on Chestnut Ridge. I became consumed by the clock. On the wall behind the kitchen table hung a clock in the shape of a black cat. White numbers encircled its round stomach. With each passing second its curled tail swung like a metronome and its eyes moved back and forth in the opposite direction of the tail. During breakfast and lunch, or whenever I had a spare minute, I watched as the sweep hand made its circuit. The tail swished, the eyes rolled, and the seconds beat slowly into minutes, the minutes into hours. Its workings made a hollow tick-tock that I had never noticed before the passage of time became so critical. Long after I had left the kitchen the noise thumped in my ears like a song that gets hung up in your brain and won't release its grip, playing over and over again. Time had never moved so slowly.

The previous fall, we had a career day at school and a detective from the Ohio Bureau of Criminal Identification and Investigation was one of the guest speakers. He had a no-nonsense demeanor, a Marine haircut, and condescendingly referred to us as "all you little darlings." At one point, he opened a window and fired up a cigarette, holding it outside as he talked, bringing it in for an occasional drag. He continued to talk even as he rolled the corner of his mouth and expelled smoke in the general direction of the window. In the hours after we left Petey in the weeds I thought of two points the detective had made during his talk.

One was that the first twenty-four hours after a crime were the most critical in any investigation. That is the period of time when witnesses are most likely to come forward and volunteer information. If an investigator doesn't have a solid lead in that first day, the odds of solving the crime drop exponentially. After a week, it becomes nearly impossible, especially if other crimes begin tugging at investigators' time.

The first twenty-four hours after Petey was killed passed without his body being discovered. The clock didn't start running, I assumed, until the emergency squad members pulled Petey out of the bushes and the sheriff's detectives began scribbling notes while milling around the crime scene. That was about 7:30 p.m. on Tuesday. That's when the clock started to run.

The second point the detective made was that after a case grows cold, it is rarely solved by science or good detective work, but by criminal stupidity and the inability of the perpetrator to keep his mouth shut. The detective said, "They always tell someone—a girlfriend, a buddy, or another perp. I don't know why, maybe it feels good to get it off their chest, maybe they're bragging, but they always talk, and when they do, that's when things start to unravel. He breaks up with the girlfriend and she calls us, or he doesn't pay his buddy back some money he borrowed, and then it comes out."

I thought of Deak. At first, I thought it was a good idea that Deak had gone off to church camp. I thought getting him out of Crystalton was a good idea. While I was up on the roof cleaning the gutters, however, I started worrying about him being at church camp. I was afraid that he would be so moved by the spirit that he would feel compelled to tell someone about Petey. I was grateful, however, that we United Methodists did not have confessionals.

⋆ ⋆ ⋆

The autopsy on Petey Sanchez was completed on Wednesday afternoon. Early Thursday morning, Ralphie Ketchum, who was a crane operator at Weirton Steel and worked part-time at the Williamson & Keller Funeral Home, drove the station wagon up to Pittsburgh to pick up the body. Visiting hours were scheduled for Friday evening, the funeral for 11 a.m. Saturday.

As she was heading out the door Friday morning, Mom said, "What are you doing tonight?"

"Nothing," I said.

"Good. When I get home from work we'll eat, then get cleaned up and go to the funeral home."

Dammit! She had feinted with her right, then blindsided me with a thunderous left hook. I staggered; my legs felt like jelly and I could see the lines of black closing in from both sides. Saliva pooled in my mouth. I backed into a corner, my hands covering my face for protection, trying to clear my head and regain my balance. "The funeral home—why?" I knew why, of course, but I was stalling, trying to come up with an excuse not to go. She was crafty like that, casually asking about my plans for the evening as though she had no real interest, allowing me to drop my guard and walk right into the punch.

I heard her coming back through the sunroom and into the kitchen. "What do you mean, 'Why?' The calling hours for Petey Sanchez are tonight."

"I don't really want to go."

"It would be nice if you did."

"But I don't like funeral homes and I didn't like Petey Sanchez. He gave me a traffic ticket that time when I was six." I lifted my chin and pointed to the "J" scar. "And he did this to me when I was ten, remember?"

It made her smile. "That was a long time ago. I was not endeared to him, either, but I see his mother every day on the route and she's a sweet lady. I doubt many people will go and I want to make an appearance. It'll mean a lot to her. Besides, his sister is in your class. It will be nice to pay your respects. "

"Yeah, but I never talk to her. I hardly know her."

"It'll take ten minutes, and I don't want to go alone."

"But, Mom . . ."

She started for the door. "We'll go right after dinner. Be ready."

I almost wished she had just surprised me with the plan at dinner, rather than giving me the entire day to let my stomach stew on it. The cat's tail and eyes moved in rhythm. The door clicked shut behind Mom. Tick-tock, tick-tock, tick-tock. The hollow beating echoed through my head. There was no follow-up story in the morning paper, just the paid obituary. *Peter Eugene Sanchez . . . a loving son . . . Earl and Lila . . . taken from us by the hands of someone unknown . . . preceded in death by his grandparents . . . brothers Earl Jr., Wayne, Johnny, Gary, Bill . . . Sisters Ruth, Wilma, Susan . . . services to be held . . . Interment at New Alexandria Cemetery . . . Rev. Clark A. Loakes presiding.* Tick-tock. I fetched my transistor radio from my top dresser drawer and went out back to clean the garage, my work assignment for the day.

While I was cleaning and stressing alone about the funeral home visit, Pepper was out jogging and stopped by the garage when he saw a plume of dust energized by my push broom billowing like a miniature storm cloud through the bay door opening and into the alley.

"How's Adrian?" I asked.

"Moody as hell, just like always."

"He's got a lot on his mind right now."

Pepper waved at the air. "Petey Sanchez has nothing to do with it. Adrian spends half his life in a foul mood. I told him if a woman was on the rag as much as him, she'd bleed to death."

"How'd he take that?"

"Like you'd expect. He smacked me up the back of the head." He grinned. "Hard, too." He looked around the garage at the mound of trash I was piling near the door. "Does your mom ever give you a day off?"

"Not too often. She says it keeps me out of trouble. You saw what happened the last time she gave me the morning off."

Pepper rolled his eyes. "I hear that." He walked across the garage and sat down on the weight-lifting bench. "Are you going to the night swim tonight?"

"Maybe. I've got to go to the funeral home first."

His eyes widened. "For Petey?"

"Yep."

"You're shitting me?"

"I shit thee not."

"Why?"

"Because my mom thinks I should go and pay my respects. It's not so much about Petey as it is being nice to Mrs. Sanchez. Mom feels sorry for her with all those kids and no money."

"Well, whose fault is that? She's like a damn Pez dispenser for ugly, squash-faced babies."

"Christ, Pepper!"

"Tell me it's not so. Every one of those kids except Petey has a face like the top of a pumpkin."

I had to choke back a grin. "Are your folks going?"

Pepper shook his head. "Dad said the only contact he ever had with them was the time old man Sanchez came to him for a car loan. He needed eight hundred bucks to buy a used station wagon to haul all those kids around."

"Did your dad give it to him?"

""Yeah, he said Mr. Sanchez had more fingers than he had dollars in the bank, but he was driving those kids around in an old car that had rusted through the floorboards, so he gave it to him."

"He ever pay it back?"

"Every dime, on time."

I worked a broom under the bench and pulled out some dirt and mouse turds. "Are you supposed to know that kind of stuff?"

"Probably not." He leaned back on the bench and pounded out a set of eight. "I hear Dad talking to Mom when he thinks I'm not listening. I know every bad loan risk in town and who's late on their mortgage payments." Pepper stood for a minute and stared into space, lost in his thoughts, then said, "I don't think I could do that, Hutch."

"Give Mr. Sanchez a car loan?"

"Smart ass. Go to the funeral home."

"Haven't you ever been to the funeral home?"

"Sure, but you know what I mean—being up there with Petey and his family."

"They don't know anything."

"That's just the point. You're going to be standing around all his family. They're going to be all teary and wanting answers and you're one of the few people who has them. You know, it was one thing to leave Petey up in the woods and just walk away. I mean, we all walk away from problems, and that's exactly what we did. There wasn't anything we could do for him, so we just wiped our hands and left. But, going to the funeral home?" He shook his head and whistled. "I couldn't do that. If I don't have to look at them, or be around them, or hear them cry, then I can deal with this. I can justify it in my mind by saying that I'm doing it for my brother. But I couldn't go to the funeral home knowing what I know."

"I'll be all right."

"Don't get weak."

I shook my head. "I won't." But I wish he had not planted that seed of doubt.

* * *

The Williamson & Keller Funeral Home was just half a block up Ohio Avenue from my house, catty-corner from the post office, and clearly visible from our sunroom. Ralphie Ketchum opened the front door and greeted us as we stepped onto the porch.

The viewing room was full of Sanchez kids and kin. Five of the tiny-faced older siblings were married and had kids of their own, several of whom ran around the visitation room, squealing and smearing snot across their faces with the backs of their hands. Uncles, aunts, and cousins also filled the room, creating a humming maze around the casket. The men and boys had clean white shirts and dirty dress shoes, their hair held into place with cream that smelled of antiseptic. They stooped at the shoulders and shoved their hands deep into their pants pockets, and greeted you with soft, limp handshakes. Some women wore stretch pants and white shirts that stretched at the bosom, while others wore sleeveless dresses that exposed thin, milky arms and dark moles. The women all hovered around Mrs. Sanchez, who sat with a framed school photograph of Petey on her lap and worked a soggy, balled up wad of tissue into the corners of her eyes. Mr. Sanchez stood in the back of the room, talking to his brother and clamping a paper coffee cup between his thumb and ring finger, which were the only digits remaining on that hand.

When Mrs. Sanchez saw my mother, I could see her say, "Oh, there's Mrs. Van Buren," and she immediately stood, propped the photo of Petey on the chair, and came across the room. She began sobbing before she reached us and threw her arms around my mother's neck. "It was so nice of you to come," Mrs. Sanchez said, a tear running around the edge of her nose and into her mouth. She put her hand on the small of my mother's back and, as if on cue, the sea of Sanchezes parted and opened a clear channel to the casket.

Petey was laid out in a white shirt with an open collar and a brown sport coat that funeral director Bernard Williamson had donated from a collection of clothing he kept for indigents. The skin was stretched taut over his horrific overbite and the lips were so bent around the teeth that only a sliver of pink appeared. The hole in his forehead had been filled with putty and the skin stitched together and covered with makeup.

"Mr. Williamson did a nice job of covering up the hole in his forehead," Lila said, speaking with the matter-of-fact casualness of someone explaining a repair to a dented fender. "You can hardly tell where it was." She had to be kidding, I thought. It looked like it had been patched up by a second-grader. "I guess he put some kind of clay in there and then smoothed it out real nice and covered it with makeup." As she spoke, Lila ran the back of her index finger gently down the length of the scar. "Mr. Williamson said if he'd been out in that heat much longer they wouldn't have been able to show him.

I'm glad they could, otherwise I'd never gotten to say goodbye to my boy." She looked at me and smiled. "Don't you think he did a good job on him?"

I nodded my agreement and muttered, "Very nice."

"Do they have any idea what happened?" Mom asked.

Lila shook her head. "Not yet. The coroner said he got hit right where he died. He said Petey didn't last no time at all after he got hit, which I guess was a blessing."

As they continued to talk, I stood at attention before the casket and recalled that, including this visit, the last two times I had looked at Petey he had been lying on his back. As I tried to block the image of Petey lying in the high grass and weeds, my mind locked in on that moment after Petey had been struck, but before he fell, and his head had swiveled toward me. His eyes had been blank, the lids drooping like a young child fighting sleep, and I wondered if there had been a flicker of life in them yet. I wondered if the last snapshot they took before the lights went out was of me standing wide-eyed, mouth agape, a blue felt liquor bag in my hand. Was that image permanently etched on the back of Petey Sanchez's eyelids for him to stare at for all eternity?

Lila's crying and sniffling snapped me out of my trance. "Poor thing. He had a tough life, that one," she said. "God knows he had his problems, but he didn't deserve this." She dabbed at her eyes with her left hand and extended her right to touch his right, which rested atop the left. "I love all my babies, even this one."

It was an odd thing to say, but I understood the intent. A parent never wants to bury a child, even one who went through life making bird calls and who twice tried to roast the family alive. Lila began sobbing and my mother hugged her. Eyes turned toward the casket; I stepped away and moved toward the back of the room. I avoided Earl Sanchez. I wasn't afraid of approaching him and offering my condolences, but I wasn't sure of the protocol of shaking the hand of a man with no thumb or index finger on his right hand, and to tell the honest truth, the thought of it creeped me out. Susan Sanchez, my classmate, was sitting in the corner of the room, bouncing a little boy of about three on her lap, and I made my way toward her.

I was not kidding when I told my mother that I didn't know Susan very well. Our class had fewer than a hundred students, but she was one of those kids who seemed to materialize during first period and vanish after the final bell. I never saw her walking the street, or at the store, the firemen's street fair, or a sporting event. If she had any friends, I didn't know who they were because I don't recall ever seeing her talking to anyone.

She was wearing a green dress and the same aqua-colored cat eyeglasses that she had worn since the sixth grade, and which squeezed the sides of her round head. A homemade wooden cross the dimensions of a playing card hung from around her neck with a piece of rawhide that looked like it came from a dirty work boot.

"Hi, Susan. I'm very sorry for your loss."

"Thank you," she said, continuing to bounce the boy, who had one hand pushed into his mouth to the knuckles and a purple stripe from a grape lollipop running down his chin and neck. She looked at me, a faint smile on her lips, but offered nothing else. I struggled to think of something else to say, and as I did her lips and jaw began to quiver. Her head tilted back and as her eyes rolled into the top of her head she said, "He's in a better place, and I . . . hope . . . he's . . . riding . . . his bicycle." And with the last syllable she burst into uncontrollable sobs.

I stepped back. Various Sanchez clan members charged over as if I had slapped her. A girl came over and hugged her. Someone else lifted the boy off her lap. As this commotion took center stage, I turned and slipped back into the protection of the maze.

As we walked back down Ohio Avenue, Mom asked, "Now, don't you feel better about going?"

"Not really. I'm not crazy about funeral homes to begin with, and then I had to listen to Lila talk about Petey like he'd just come out of an auto body shop."

"Well, it was nice of you to pay your respects. I know Mrs. Sanchez appreciated it and I'm sure Susan did, too."

"Yes, did you notice how appreciative she was when I offered my condolences and she burst into tears?"

"It was still nice that you went. I just hope they find out who killed him."

"Do you think they will?" I asked, deliberately responding with another question to avoid concurring. I could feel a wave of heat starting under my collar.

"I don't know. It's a crazy world out there."

By the time we returned to the house, the cat on the wall showed seven thirty.

Three days were behind us.

Tick-tock.

★ ★ ★

At 11 p.m., I was ready for bed. Mom and Walter Deshay were at the kitchen table playing dominos for a dime a point and drinking Iron City beer from longneck bottles. I said goodnight and started up the stairs when Mom asked, "What are your plans for tomorrow?"

"I've got practice for my summer league basketball team at ten." It was a lie. There was no practice. "Why?"

"No reason. G'night."

I took two steps up the stairs, stopped and squeezed my eyes closed for a few seconds. "Crap," I muttered under my breath. I turned and walked back down and into the kitchen. "Did you want to go to Petey's funeral? I can skip practice if you do."

"Oh, no," she said, playing a double-five. "I have to work in the morning. I was just wondering what you had going."

Miriam Van Buren kept me on my toes.

We had no air-conditioning and summer nights upstairs were oppressive. An old box fan sat atop the desk on the far side of the room, and I always turned it on before hopping into bed. Its housing was slightly off center and it whined like a prop plane struggling in a high wind. The fan didn't make my room any cooler, but at least it kept the hot air circulating. I wore only my boxers and stretched out on top of the sheets.

I was glad the day was over. Relieved, actually.

The fan strained and the moving air tickled my chest. For the first time since the night Petey was killed, my mind shut down and I quickly drifted off to sleep.

Chapter Eight

Mom didn't have to be at work until eight on Saturdays, so I got to sleep in an extra hour. When she yelled up the steps, I sat up in my bed, stretched, and rubbed at my eyes. As Mom headed out the door, I fixed myself a bowl of cereal, poured a glass of orange juice, and flipped through the morning paper. In a one-column story on page four of the local section, wedged between the crease and an advertisement for Big Phil's Tires summer blowout sale, was a brief article under the headline:

Murder Victim's Bicycle Found

The bicycle belonging to Peter Eugene Sanchez was found yesterday on a hillside near Overlook Park west of Crystalton, about a quarter-mile from where the body of the 17-year-old mentally retarded boy was discovered Tuesday, according to Jefferson County Sheriff Sky Kelso.

Kelso said detectives and auxiliary officers from the Crystalton Police Department had been searching the area for the bicycle, hoping it would reveal clues in the boy's death. It will be dusted for fingerprints and examined for other evidence, Kelso said.

Sanchez died from a blow to the head and his death is being investigated as a homicide.

Kelso said deputies are following several leads in the case, but declined to say if investigators have any suspects.

I scanned the rest of the local section hoping to find reports of other crimes that would distract detectives from the investigation into Petey's death. A woman near Hopedale had been charged with domestic abuse after striking her husband in the side of the head with a cake mixer. Someone was shooting out car windows with a .22-caliber handgun near Richmond. There had been a series of burglaries in Knoxville. Nothing, I thought, interesting enough to keep them away from an unsolved homicide.

At nine forty-five I pulled the back door shut and headed down the alley, dribbling my basketball around the puddles left by the overnight rain. Each bounce echoed off the phalanx of garages that lined the alley, eaves to eaves. Basketball was my least favorite sport, but going to the basketball court alone was one of my favorite pastimes. No coaches, no opponents, no whistles, no clock. I could get lost in myself, mindlessly shooting or playing games against invisible opponents, which always fell victim to my last-second heroics.

As I emerged from the alley onto Kennedy Avenue, the Clemens twins, blonde pixies of about ten, were heading to the swimming pool on a bicycle—the sister in front standing up and pedaling and the second sitting on the seat, her legs splayed to keep her toes away from the turning spokes while holding on to her sister's shoulders. Two boys—one in a blue-trimmed uniform with block-lettered "Indians" across the chest, the other in red with "Cardinals" written in script—walked toward the Little League field, gloves in one hand, rubber cleats in the other. Two other girls had drawn a hopscotch grid on the sidewalk with yellow chalk and were yelling at a grinning little brother, who was taking delight in interrupting their game by tossing pebbles onto their grid. At the playground, the swings, merry-go-round, and monkey bars were all in use.

It dawned on me at that moment that not all of Crystalton was consumed by panic over the death of Petey Sanchez. In fact, my own mother's admonition and insistence on giving Deak a ride home the night Petey's body had been discovered was the only sense of concern that I had witnessed. I had anticipated parents reacting with more alarm. When I was in the second grade, a man attempted to abduct a girl walking to school in Tiltonsville, the next town south of Crystalton. For weeks afterward, mothers, my own included, walked their kids to school. At the final bell, cars were lined up in front of the school and a conclave of unsmiling mothers waited near the front door. There was a sense that the randomness of the attempted abduction could strike their child, as well. But that wasn't the case with Petey's death. It seemed that people did not believe it was a random act of violence.

At noon on Friday I took a break from cleaning the garage and went to Connell's Market for a bottle of RC Cola. Jack Vukovich was standing near the front counter, a carton of Kool Filter Kings in his hand and a giant ring of keys hanging on his belt, talking demonstratively to Denny Morelli and Jewel Connell, pointing at them and himself with two fingers that were pinching a lit cigarette. Jack was Deak's ne'er-do-well uncle who drove around in a beat-up Valiant and worked as a janitor at the junior high. I tried to stay away from Jack. There was no topic on which he did not consider himself an expert, and he was happy to espouse opinions and offer advice ad nauseum. Of Jack, my mother was fond of saying, "He'll tell you everything you don't want to know about everything you don't want to hear about." People in Crystalton would listen to him, nod as though they found him fascinating, then walk away rolling their eyes. That was only part of the reason I distanced myself from Jack. He also liked to lean in close when he talked and his breath usually smelled of cheap gin, and his right eye was permanently rolled into the lower outside corner of the socket, and I couldn't help but stare at the fraction of exposed pupil.

When I approached the counter they were talking about Petey.

"I think it was just an accident," Jewel said. "I think he fell or something."

Denny moved aside so I could pay for my pop.

Jack shook his head. "It wasn't an accident."

"You don't think?" Denny asked, always anxious for any snippet of gossip that he could repeat as gospel.

"I'll tell you what happened. That simple kid crossed the wrong person." I looked up and Jack's good eye was honed in on me. It gave me chills. "That's all there was to this, I guarantee it. Petey Sanchez went up to the wrong person and started making bird sounds or got up in their grill, and that was all it took." He winked at me with his one good eye. "What do you think, Mr. Van Buren?"

I shook my head. "I don't really have an opinion."

"Really? Well, you'd be the only one in town." He turned back to Jewel and Denny. "Someone didn't want to put up with any more of that kid's bullshit, and they popped him—simple as that."

I thought my knees were going to buckle. Jack Vukovich was spouting off in his usual know-all blather and he didn't know how eerily on target he was. They were still speculating when I left. It seemed that most people in town shared Jack's opinion, believing that Petey was somehow responsible for his own murder.

I dribbled to where Second Street came to a dead end at the high school parking lot and cut behind the school to the courts that overlooked the sand quarry. The sky was clear and the smoke from the electric plant drifted to the east, dissipating before it reached the West Virginia hills. I set my water jug on one of the green wooden benches along the side of the court and began shooting. It was only fifteen minutes before I saw Deak walking up the gravel road between the courts and the quarry.

When he got to the court I asked, "How was church camp?"

"It was nice to get away from here for a few days."

"I'll bet."

"What are you doing down here? It's going to be eighty-some degrees this afternoon and you've got to catch a double-header. You ought to be saving your energy."

"I just wanted to burn off a little steam."

Deak nodded. "And you didn't want to be at your house when Petey's funeral procession went past."

He had me. "That, too."

He grabbed a rebound and hit me near the free throw line with a bounce pass. I took a dribble to the left and launched a fade-away jumper that skipped off the front of the rim. "So, what's happened since I left?"

I shook my head and shrugged. "Nothing, best I can tell. No one has asked me anything. I've read the stories in the papers and listened to some of the gossip at Connell's Market, but that's it. Everyone thinks Petey's lunatic behavior led to him getting killed, which it did. I went to the funeral home with Mom last night. Mrs. Sanchez gave us all the details on how they fixed the hole in Petey's head so they could show him in the casket, but she didn't say much about the investigation. If the detectives had told Mrs. Sanchez anything about a suspect, I guarantee she would have told my mom about it, but she didn't say anything."

We replayed the events of Monday morning several times. Deak shook his head, and with each passing minute looked more like someone had gut punched him. He chewed at his lip and looked to be fighting off tears. After about thirty minutes of talking and feeding me bounce passes, Deak said, "I don't know how much longer I can keep this up, Hutch."

"You'll be okay. We're through the worst of it."

He grabbed a rebound. I held out a hand, waiting for the pass, but he held the ball, tucking it under his arm, wedging it between his elbow and waist. "I've been giving it a lot of thought, Hutch, and I really think we need to tell the sheriff what happened. I don't care if we tell him it was self-defense or an accident, but we have to tell him. The Sanchez family will never have peace until they know what happened. It's the right thing to do."

"What makes you think that it's the right thing to do?"

"Come on, Hutch, don't play this game with me. It's just the right thing to do and you know it."

"No, I don't, Deak. And if you rat out Adrian, we all go down. We all get our names in the paper and end up in juvenile court. Is that what you want?"

"I want to do what's right. You, Pepper, and I, we didn't do anything wrong."

"And neither did Adrian. Why can't you get that through your head? Petey's the one who's at fault." I waved my fingers at him and he bounce-passed me the ball. "I think you want to tell the cops so you can relieve your conscience, and you want me to back you up. Well, I'm not going to tell you that it's okay. And if you go to the cops, you go alone. I'm certainly not going to stand behind you and applaud your bravery."

"How can you talk like that? You don't know what that family is going through."

"You're absolutely right. I don't. I know it's terrible because I went to the funeral home and saw it. But going to the police isn't going to make it any easier on them. I thought we talked about this?"

"Adrian needs to step up and take responsibility for his actions, and you need to quit protecting him."

"You're starting to piss me off, Deak. What do you want Adrian to take responsibility for? He didn't go out looking for Petey. He didn't say, 'Hey, let's go out and throw rocks at the retarded kid.' All we were doing was minding our own business and walking down off the hill. I know Petey had a lot of mental problems, and in some ways couldn't help himself, but Adrian didn't start it, and he wasn't out looking for trouble. None of us were. Adrian was protecting himself and us, and I don't think he deserves to get fried for that." I walked over to the bench and got a drink. As I did, I saw the flashing red lights of the police motorcycle escorting the funeral procession up New Alexandria Pike. "Come on, let's go."

We cut behind the high school and hadn't gotten as far as the parking lot when Denny Morelli again came pedaling up on his bike. "Did you hear the news?"

"News about what?" I asked.

"The sheriff has a suspect in Petey Sanchez's murder. It's someone in his own family."

"Denny, where do you get this stuff?" Deak asked.

I said, "I know where he gets it. He spends too much time stocking shelves at Connell's Market and listening to Jewel and those other busybodies yak all day. You're starting to gossip like those old women, Denny."

"No, seriously, they're . . ."

Deak cut Denny off. "That's a heck of a thing to say about someone, that they killed their own son or brother. You ought to be more careful about spreading nonsense like that around."

"It's true, I tell ya! The sheriff is searching their house right now," Denny said, pointing to the north end of town. "I saw 'em.

It's all over town. The sheriff showed up with a search warrant about the time they were getting ready to leave for the funeral. Earl Junior told the sheriff he wasn't getting in the house. He called 'em a bunch of cocksuckers and he got into a fight with one of the deputies. Earl Junior took a swing at one of 'em and three of the deputies whipped on him with their nightsticks. They threw him down on the porch and handcuffed him behind the back. They arrested him and he didn't get to go to the funeral. I saw them drive off with him in the back of a sheriff's car and he had blood running all down his face."

We stopped in our path. Frozen pinpricks covered my body, and I felt Deak's eyes boring in on me.

"You saw Earl Junior in the back of the sheriff's car?" Deak asked.

"Yeah, he was crying and cussing and screaming and kicking the doors. Mrs. Sanchez and all the girls were crying. The sheriff was barking at the old man, telling him he better get his family under control. I saw it with my own eyes. It was a circus."

"That's terrible," Deak said.

"Irene Kopinksi, her husband's a dispatcher for the sheriff, and she stopped in the store yesterday afternoon and said that the detectives told her husband that none of them Sanchezes were upset about Petey getting killed except the mom. The dad hardly talked when the sheriff's detectives were up there, and one or two of the brothers said it was probably for the best because the parents couldn't control Petey anymore. That's why they're searching the house, I'll bet."

"What are they looking for?" I asked.

"I don't know. Maybe the murder weapon?" Denny rode around in a semicircle and came up alongside of me. "Did you see they found Petey's bike up on the hill near Chestnut Ridge? It makes sense if you think about it."

"Why does that make sense?" I asked.

"Because if someone in his family killed him, they might have taken the bike up on the hill to make it look like he'd been abducted or something."

"Maybe he was abducted," I said.

"I'll bet not. You know how much trouble Petey always caused. Maybe the dad got tired of it, or maybe the brothers were afraid he was going to hurt one of their kids. He tried to burn up their house twice. They might have killed him right there in the house and dragged him up on the hill to make it look like someone else murdered him. You never know."

"That's the point, Denny. Nobody knows for sure, especially you, so you shouldn't be spreading around rumors," Deak said. "No one in the Sanchez family killed Petey. I'm positive."

I puckered up a bit, wondering how far Deak was going to take his admonition.

Denny started to pedal away on his bike, looking for others to inform of the breaking news. He looked back over his shoulder and said, "I'll betcha anything one of 'em gets charged with murder. You watch and see."

When Denny was out of earshot Deak turned to me and asked, "Well, that's just great. Are you happy now?"

"What'd I do? I didn't send the sheriff up there. Besides, it's no big deal. They'll never charge anyone. There's no evidence."

"No big deal? The Sanchezes lose a child, have no explanation for the loss, the sheriff does a search warrant on their house, so obviously they're suspects and will have to live with that stigma, and now one of their kids is in jail and missed his own brother's funeral. The whole family has been thrown into turmoil because of us."

"No, Deak, their lives have been thrown into turmoil because their crazy-ass son stirred the shit with the wrong person. They're in turmoil because they let him roam like a wild animal for years. It's not our fault."

He shook his head. "You know, Hutch, your level of compassion is simply overwhelming. I hope to God that you or no one in your family ever has to go through life looking at the world the way Petey had to look at it. You have no idea what the world looked like through his eyes."

I wanted to punch Deak in his smug, self-righteous mouth.

We were in the alley behind my house. "This is sickening," he said. "I'm telling you this, Hutch, if they charge someone in the

Sanchez family with Petey's death, I'm calling the sheriff, and I'm going to spill my guts. I don't care if I do go to juvenile hall, and I really don't care if Adrian Nash spends the rest of his life in a juvenile detention center or prison or wherever else they want to send him, and I don't care if he throws another touchdown pass as long as he lives. This is wrong and you know it." He spun and continued down the alley.

"Deak . . ."

He waved an arm in the air and didn't look back.

★ ★ ★

We were at the diamond at one that afternoon to begin warming up for the first game against Mount Pleasant. Adrian and I, the pitcher and catcher, sat in the dugout, staying out of the heat until it was time for him to get loose. When Deak showed up and put on his cleats, Pepper asked him, "Want to throw?"

Deak just glared, walked past him, and ran up the steps of the dugout. "What's the matter with you, Coultas, are your ovaries hurting again?" Pepper asked. Deak ignored the comment and ran to the outfield to stretch. Pepper looked at me and shrugged. "What's up his ass?"

"He's just having a bad day," I said. "He'll be all right."

★ ★ ★

The headline stared at me through the screen door, and the knot that had been locked in my intestines for nearly a week winched up tighter. The morning paper had landed neatly on our doormat and the bold headline stretched across the top of the front page.

Sheriff Searches Home of Murdered Crystalton Boy

A photo that covered three columns was inset under the headline and showed Sheriff Sky Kelso and a deputy leading a handcuffed Earl Sanchez Junior to a cruiser while Lila Sanchez bawled in the background, one spindly hand clutching her breast while the other reached out for her son. I made no pretense of being interested in the sports page and began reading the article as I walked back to the kitchen.

> As the family of Peter Sanchez prepared to bury their youngest son yesterday morning, Jefferson County Sheriff Sky Kelso and a team of four deputies swarmed over their home in the north end of Crystalton in an apparent search for a murder weapon.
>
> According to the search warrant, deputies were searching for "a ball-peen hammer or mallet with a rounded end, a ball bearing, or implement of similar size."

Or roughly, I thought, the size of a granite Indian maul.

Mom was fixing breakfast. The kitchen smelled of coffee and fried bacon and eggs. I poured myself a glass of orange juice and sat down at the table.

> Although the search warrant clearly indicated that deputies were looking for a murder weapon, Kelso refused to comment when asked if a member of the Sanchez family was considered a suspect in the boy's death. "We're just trying to cover all our bases and eliminate all possibilities," the sheriff said.
>
> One member of the Sanchez family, Earl Sanchez Jr., 27, of Steubenville, was arrested and charged with obstructing official business and assault after he attempted to stop deputies from entering the house and scuffled with the law officers. The charges were later dropped and Sanchez Jr. was released from jail late yesterday.
>
> "It was an unfortunate encounter in the midst of a terrible situation," Kelso said. "There's no reason to make things worse for the family."

Hearing about the search warrant from Denny Morelli was one thing, but to see details of it spread across the top of the Sunday morning paper took things to a different dimension. It was, as Deak said, sickening.

Kelso would not reveal what had been removed from the house, but said that deputies found several "items of interest."

Sanchez, 17, was found dead Tuesday in a wooded area west of Crystalton. He died of a massive head injury and his death is being investigated as a homicide.

Mom slid a plate of bacon and over-easy eggs in front of me. The headline caught her attention and she began reading over my shoulder while she waited for my toast to pop up. She set the toast on the side of my plate and shook her head, saying, "I just can't believe that it could be Earl or one of those boys."

"It says they were just trying to eliminate all possibilities," I said.

"They wouldn't waste their time searching the house if they didn't think the murder weapon might be there." She sipped her coffee. "That's terrible, just terrible."

I faked a stomachache and didn't go to church. I didn't want to face Deak.

Chapter Nine

It stormed Monday night and Deak called about nine to see if I wanted to search for arrowheads Tuesday morning. It was the first time that I had spoken with him since our ugly departure in the alley Saturday. He had managed to play both ends of a double-header against Mount Pleasant without uttering a word to Adrian, Pepper, or me. But when he called Monday night, all seemed well. I was anxious to go and glad to have the uncomfortable silence behind us. He said, "Great. I'll pick you up at eight." Adrian and Pepper were out at the family cabin at Clendening Lake, so it was just Deak and me hiking up to search Marty Postalakis's corn field again. I asked if he wanted to search the glass house field, figuring he wouldn't want to walk past the place where Petey had died, but he said no, that there were more and better arrowheads on the hill.

For most of my life I had always associated Chestnut Ridge with the smell of cherry blossoms. As a young boy, I spent untold hours exploring every square foot of the hills west of town, enjoying the solitude and my imagination. On one of these sojourns, I discovered a pathway, a narrow trail though a mazy thicket of briars that only a nine-year-old could slip through. On the other side of the thicket I found stone foundations protruding from the rocky earth like the bones of long-dead animals. When I described the find to my mother, she said it was likely the remains of the mining community of East Berlin, a turn-of-the-century coal town of German immigrants that disappeared after the Hudson Mining Company's nearby deep shaft mine was closed in the 1920s. "You didn't go in there, did you?" she asked.

"No," I said, a quick, defensive lie.

"Don't let me hear you've been up there running around. It's dangerous. There are old mine shafts and sinkholes everywhere."

"I won't," I said.

I returned often to my new hillside discovery. I climbed the foundations and searched for bottles and coins and other traces of East Berlin, and told none of my friends about the lost society. On a graceful slope east of the community, there was a cherry tree that I would climb, wedge myself into a bough near the top, and scan the valley far below. I imagined that after creating the world, God had stood at this very site and surveyed his magnificent work of hills and river, watching the water as it turned the bend north of Crystalton and flowed south to Hopewell Island, where barges hugged the West Virginia side to avoid shallows near the Ohio banks. In the spring I would sit in the tree and breathe in the heavy scent of the cherry blossoms, an aroma so wonderful and thick that it stayed with me long after I had walked off the ridge. Lying in my bed at night, I could close my eyes and imagine myself back up on the hill, sitting in the tree, the sunshine warm on my face, and the aroma of those blossoms would mysteriously fill my nostrils.

Chestnut Ridge would never again evoke thoughts of cherry blossoms. I could no longer go to bed and conjure up images of my tree, nor would the sweet smell of blossoms come to my nostrils. Chestnut Ridge now evoked a different memory, one of blowflies dancing around a cratered wound.

All morning, Deak didn't say a word about Petey, even when we walked within a few feet of the spot where he had fallen, and where a strand of yellow crime scene tape remained dangling from the branches of a mulberry tree. It was a good hunt. I found six excellent pieces and Deak found nine. When we came out on the path at the elementary school playground, Deak said, "I still haven't made up my mind about going to the sheriff."

"You're killing me, Deak."

He shrugged. "I know what God wants me to do, and I know what you, Pepper, and Adrian want me to do. I'm praying on it."

I didn't want to argue about it. I said, "Let me know when God gets back to you."

"You'll be the first to know."

That evening, I was catching a game at Harrisville. At the end of the fourth inning, I asked our coach for the time. He frowned and asked, "What the hell, you got a date tonight, Van Buren? Don't worry about the time. Get your head in the game." When I went out to catch the bottom of the fifth, I sneaked a peak at the umpire's watch. It was seven thirty-two. The first week was behind us.

Tick-tock.

★ ★ ★

On Wednesday morning, the Wheeling *Intelligencer* blared a story that a family of four had been shotgunned to death in their home in Dunglen, a decrepit coal-mining town that lined an orange sulfur creek in the southern end of the county. I am not so coldhearted as to say that I was delighted to see a family slaughtered. However, I was glad that the sheriff's department would have more to worry about than Petey Sanchez.

When the sheriff's detectives hadn't shown up on my doorstep within the first week, I was sure that no one had seen us heading up the path to Chestnut Ridge. No one could place us at the scene of Petey's death. Without that bit of information, there was no reason to suspect that we had any involvement. If that was the case, then it was simply a matter of continuing to keep our mouths shut.

Chapter Ten

There were four basketball courts in Crystalton—two at Community Park overlooking the quarry, one behind the Lincoln Elementary School, and one built into the asphalt parking lot at the side of the junior high school. The court at the elementary was laced with cracks that played havoc with ankles and occasionally caused a dribbled ball to bounce sideways. The steel backboards at the park were rusty and the rims loose. The favored court was the one at the junior high, which stood on the northwest corner of Ohio Avenue and Third Street. South of the school building there was a smooth asphalt parking lot where a basketball court had been laid out. It was in the center of town, across the street from the Big Dipper Ice Cream Shop, where you could get a fountain Coke between games.

On days when we didn't have summer league baseball, the junior high court was full of kids playing shirts and skins, sweating, arguing, and playing for hours at a time. Guys from other communities up and down the river knew they could usually find a game at the junior high and would often show up in a couple of cars with six or seven players. Two weeks and two days after Petey's death, we were playing at the junior high against some guys who had driven down from Mingo Junction.

Our third game was stopped by first the whine and then the roar of wide-open engines coming from the east. The din echoed off the hills and between the store fronts. Within a few seconds a sheriff's car—a black, 1970 Plymouth Fury with a 440-cubic-inch V8—led a cavalry charge of cop cars through the intersection on Ohio Avenue, red lights flashing, its grill lifting as it roared toward the junior high parking lot. Another sheriff's car followed, then another, and then two Crystalton police cruisers. Pedestrians froze in mid-step to watch; red lights bounced off the walls and windows of Nero's Barber Shop, Connell's Market, and Mehtal's Auto Motors. When the lead car hit the edge of the parking lot, the others fanned out and crossed the empty asphalt like a squadron of fighter planes forming up. They squealed to a stop, forming a semicircle barrier beyond the court, entrapping us between the cars and the school.

My heartbeat sounded like thunder in my ears. I looked at Deak. He was getting teary-eyed and his lower lip was starting to quiver. Pepper, too, was looking at Deak. I wondered if he had gone to the sheriff. Adrian appeared to be in survival mode. His eyes darted from side to side as he sought an escape route.

Two lawmen emerged from each sheriff's car, and one each from the Crystalton cruisers. As they exited their cars they holstered their nightsticks and unholstered their service revolvers. Two unmarked cars sped down the alley behind the school, spitting gravel into the basketball court and throwing up a plume of dust. Following the squadron onto the parking lot was a fleet of news vehicles—a van adorned with a giant peacock from the Steubenville television station and two sedans, from which emerged photographers and reporters, including Reggie Fuschea, from the Steubenville *Herald-Star*, and a television reporter named Don Redley.

Sheriff Sky Kelso slid from behind the driver's door of the lead car and held a pistol in the air, a tacit signal of restraint, as though holding back the attack while his troops at the flanks fell into line. Actually, he was posturing, waiting for the television cameraman and the news photographers to catch up with the officers. Sheriff Kelso was never one to miss a good photo opportunity. When they were in position and the television camera was rolling, he surveyed the landscape before him, smoothed his black moustache with the webbing between a thumb and index finger, then pointed his pistol toward the school, like a Union general aiming a saber toward enemy lines, and eight armed law enforcement officers charged toward the basketball courts.

A cluster of sweaty teenage boys splintered in all directions. Adrian jumped over the benches and ran toward the fence. I pushed Deak to get him to the side of the court. One of the Crystalton cops, Flip Durkin, the brother of the chief, was running right toward me. And then, he kept running. Four of the officers charged through the side door while four others ran to the front.

I looked at Adrian, who also looked like he was near tears. They hadn't been after us after all. I had no idea what they were looking for, but I didn't care so long as it wasn't us. I had to sit down. That moment of abject terror had left me spent, my knees wobbly and drained by the adrenaline surge that had ramped up my heartbeat. It was a relief not unlike being jolted awake from a dream to learn that you were not actually falling off a cliff, or that you were not standing naked at the chalkboard struggling to diagram a complex sentence in Mrs. Hesske's English class.

As soon as the officers disappeared into the school, the Mingo Junction boys ran to their cars. We Crystalton boys sat on the benches next to the court and waited to see what the excitement was about. Four of us were just relieved, grateful that we were not the center of attention. Adrian, Pepper, and Deak joined me on the bench, elbows resting on our knees, sweat rolling down our faces and dripping from our noses, leaving a pattern of bright dots on the asphalt. People living along Third Street began streaming out of their houses, some talking in small clusters in front yards, others congregating in the shade of the Big Dipper's overhang. Within a few minutes, Denny Morelli came running over from Connell's Market, dressed in a white butcher's apron, a T-shirt, cut-off blue jeans, and leather work boots. "That's a good look you've got going there, Denny," Pepper said.

"What's going on?" Denny asked.

"Holy shit! You mean the town crier doesn't already know?" Pepper asked.

"There's a switch," Deak said.

"Seriously, what's going on?" Denny asked again.

"Don't know," I said. "We were in the middle of a game when the light brigade showed up."

"Are they going to arrest someone?"

"It certainly doesn't look like a damn social call, does it?" Pepper asked.

"Who are they after?"

Deak said, "Denny, are you deaf, or just stupid? We already told you that we don't know."

"I'm just asking. Who do you think it is?"

I could see the top of Deak's jaw tighten. "What part of 'We don't know' don't you understand?" Deak asked.

He looked at Deak and said, "Your uncle's in there, isn't he? Are they after him? What do you think he did?"

Deak stood and fired a two-hand chest pass, drilling Denny in the face with my basketball. It ricocheted back into Deak hands. "Get out of here, Denny. You make me sick. Go back and gossip with the old women at the grocery store."

It was the first time in my life that I ever saw Deak Coultas show any degree of aggression. Denny ran his tongue around the inside of his mouth, then wiped his lips and inspected his fingers for blood. "Goddammit, you dick. I was just trying to find out . . ."

Deak again hit him in the face with the ball, harder than the first time. It slammed off Denny's forehead and sent him stumbling backward. He reeled for several steps, trying in vain to regain his balance before momentum claimed victory. He sprawled, his tailbone hitting just before the back of his head bounced with a dull thud on the asphalt. Deak said, "Get out of here." Denny teared up and a stream of blood ran from his left nostril. Several drops fell from his lip and stained the front of the white apron. "Don't say another word, Denny, just go away. I mean it."

When Denny got to the edge of the parking lot, cupping the lump that was sprouting on the back of his head, Deak turned and bounced the ball hard against the court, catching it with both hands.

Pepper grinned and said, "Well, that was certainly out of character for you, preacher."

The muscles in Deak's forearms strained as he dug his fingertips into the ball. "That guy really rubs me the wrong way."

"Apparently," Pepper added.

Deak sat back down on the bench, and we all stared at the side door, where the news crews congregated. Our relief at not being the targets of the invasion was tempered, but only a little, by the fact that Deak's uncle—One-Eyed Jack, as we called him—was the only one in the school. The indicator was his sky blue, first-generation Plymouth Valiant, which sat across Third Street, rust eating away at its doors and wheel wells.

Jack Vukovich was Deak's mother's only surviving brother. An older brother, Paul, who had been an All-Ohio halfback at Crystalton High, was killed in the Korean War. A black-and-white photograph of Paul Vukovich stiff-arming an imaginary opponent hangs in the Crystalton High School Athletic Hall of Fame. The American Legion Post is named in his honor.

As Paul Vukovich was revered in Crystalton, Jack was looked upon as the underachieving younger brother of the war hero—the piteous janitor. He was two years younger than Paul, worked a few menial jobs after graduating from high school, and disappeared from Crystalton for more than a decade, during which he had very little contact with his family. When he resurfaced in the mid-sixties, it was the first time Deak had ever seen him. Jack moved into a garage apartment down the alley from our house and took a job as janitor at the junior high school. During his second winter on the job, Jack put a cot in the subbasement so he could sleep between rounds of stoking the coal-fired furnace and watching over the boiler. Over time, he slowly began moving furniture into the subbasement until he had a dungeon-like, two-room apartment forty feet below Third Street, where he lived year-round. He showered in the locker room, used the restrooms for other business, and seemed quite content with the accommodations. The school board thought it odd, but then Jack was a little odd, so they shrugged off any concern, joking that it gave them an unpaid security guard. It was the sort of small-town arrangement that was usually overlooked as harmless, so why cause waves?

He wore white T-shirts with an omnipresent pack of Kools wrapped in the sleeve. His salt-and-pepper hair was greased back in a fifties-style ducktail. During his absence from Crystalton he had gotten into a bar fight and taken a beer bottle to the right side of his head, causing the eye to permanently roll into the southwest corner of the socket, which led to the nickname of One-Eyed Jack. Deak rarely spoke about his uncle, which didn't strike me as particularly unusual since he smelled of cheap booze and lived in the subbasement of the school.

One of the reporters said, "Here they come," and the cameraman and photographers spread out and began shooting the instant the door opened. An erect, stone-faced Sky Kelso emerged with his right hand grasping the elbow of Jack Vukovich, who was handcuffed behind his back, his shoulders hunched, the hair of his signature ducktail falling forward over his bowed head. The photographers walked backward across the lot, dragging their shoes against the asphalt and clicking away. Two deputies wrapped yellow crime scene tape around the Valiant. The remaining officers filed in behind the sheriff. Watching from the sidewalk across Third Street, women in housecoats and bedroom slippers nodded to each other in agreement that they always knew Jack Vukovich to be no good. Certainly, he was nothing like his brother.

Deak put his face in his hands and groaned, "Oh, not again."

"What do you mean, 'again?'" Pepper asked.

"He was in all kind of trouble before he moved back to Crystalton. Mom and my granddad helped get him out of a couple of messes. He's kept his nose pretty clean since he came back. This is bad."

"Not to play Denny Morelli, but what kind of trouble was he in?" I asked.

"I don't know. They would never talk about it. They just said he made some bad decisions and needed a fresh start." He stood up. "I better hustle over to the house and tell Mom before she hears it from someone else."

Chapter Eleven

The fire whistle blew at five twenty that evening and the emergency squad went past our house a few minutes later, disappearing onto Third Street, heading south from Ohio Avenue. When the whistle first sounded I knew it would only be a few minutes before one of my mother's friends who owned a scanner or spotted the emergency squad within their purview would call with an update. We were finishing our dinner when the phone rang about ten minutes later. Normally, Mom enforced a strict no-phone-calls-during-dinner rule. This rule, however, was null and void if the call arrived within a few minutes of the fire whistle. I walked into the family room where the phone sat on an end table between the couch and Mom's recliner.

It was Pepper, who began talking without introduction. "Hey, the emergency squad is down the street at Deak's granddad's house. His mom and dad are standing in the front yard; his mom's crying." Deak's grandfather lived a few doors down and across the street from the Nashes. "Okay, they're hauling him out of the house on a stretcher."

"Is he alive?"

"Must be. He's got an oxygen mask over his face and they're hurrying. Have you heard anything about his uncle?"

"No."

"Okay, I'll talk to you later."

And the phone went dead.

"It's Deak's granddad."

Mom's face puckered up, her lips squeezing into a ball and deep furrows lining up between her eyes. "That's not good. He's had heart problems," she said. "I'm sure that whatever is going on with that worthless Jack triggered it again."

"Maybe I should go over and see how Deak's doing?"

"I think that would be good. If Deak or the girls haven't eaten, bring them back and I'll fix them something."

As I walked up Labelle Avenue to Deak's, I watched the emergency squad carrying his grandfather speed north on Route 7, its siren and lights bouncing off the hills as it raced for Ohio Valley Hospital in Steubenville. The echoes died before I reached his porch, where I could hear the television in the Coultases' front room. I cupped my hands around my eyes and leaned close to the screen to see if Deak was in view. His three younger sisters were playing school in the front room, the eldest, seven-year-old Katie, standing in front of the two younger ones and using a ruler to point to words she had written on a little chalkboard. Deak was in the kitchen cleaning up paper plates on which were a few bun stubs, all that remained from the dinner of hot dogs and potato chips he had prepared. I let myself in. The girls ignored me. Deak peeked around the corner. "Not a good day," I said.

"The whistle was for my granddad."

"I know. Pepper called. Is he going to be all right?"

Deak shrugged. "Mom called the power plant and had Dad meet her at Grandpa's to tell him about Uncle Jack. I guess Grandpa started crying and having chest pains, so she called the squad. She said she'd call me later from the hospital. That's all I know."

"Heard anything about your uncle?"

"Nothing."

"I wonder what he did."

Deak looked at his watch. It was five fifty. "We'll find out in ten minutes. Whatever it was, it was enough to bring five cruisers, two unmarked cars, and three news crews to Crystalton."

"Drugs?" I offered.

He shook his head. "Don't know."

Sometimes I wasn't happy about my own selfishness. Deak was my best friend and for more than two weeks had been trying to deal with what he believed to be a morally corrupt decision, leaving the Sanchez family to wonder why their son had been murdered and who was responsible. Now his entire family was in crisis. His uncle was in jail and his grandfather on his way to intensive care. But I was not thinking about the plight of Deak and his family. Rather, I was thinking that Jack Vukovich's arrest was an excellent diversion. Whatever he had done was causing a major distraction for the sheriff's office, eating up valuable hours that prevented detectives from searching for Petey's killer, and allowing the case to grow colder still. It was undeniably selfish, but that's what I was thinking—thank you, Jack Vukovich.

We stood in front of the television, watching the credits roll on a game show, when the screen went black for an instant, then lit up with Don Redley, the reporter we had seen at the school earlier in the day, staring hard into the camera. "A Crystalton man is being held at the Jefferson County Jail tonight being questioned in connection with the murder of a seventeen-year-old mentally retarded boy earlier this month. Channel Nine was on the scene when he was arrested this afternoon. This story, coming up next."

My gut seized up with such ferocity that a backwash of city chicken, gravy, fried potatoes, succotash, and stomach acid surged into my throat and mouth. The vacuum sucked my balls into my chest cavity and every molecule of air escaped from my lungs in a death groan. I was almost afraid to look at Deak, who continued to stare at the television as the intro to the news rolled. When I caught my breath I said, "Holy shit."

"How can that be?" he whispered.

"Beats me."

As the anchors began to introduce the lead story, a video of Jack Vukovich being led from the school to the cruiser ran across the screen. Katie began leading her sisters in the ABC song. "Katie, hush for a minute. I need to hear this," Deak said.

This got their attention as the video continued to roll and Lucy, the five-year-old, squealed and pointed at the screen, "Lookie, Uncle Jack's on the telebision."

"You can't talk out in class," Katie said, pointing her ruler at young Lucy. "Sit down."

"Girls, quiet," Deak yelled.

Don Redley read from the narrow notebook he held in one hand. "The suspect has been identified as Jack C. Vukovich, a thirty-five-year-old custodian at Crystalton Junior High School. What we know is this: Sheriff's deputies, armed with a search warrant, swarmed over the school this afternoon, taking Vukovich into custody and impounding his car." The video showed the blue Valiant in a lot surrounded by the chain-link fence of the police impound lot. The doors were open and deputies in rubber gloves were seen dropping items into paper evidence bags. "Sheriff Sky Kelso said Vukovich is being held in connection with the Sanchez boy's death, but he has not released specific information pertaining to the charges."

Kelso, standing in front of the courthouse in Steubenville, appeared on the screen, saying, "We have physical evidence linking Mr. Vukovich to the crime scene. He is currently being questioned by our detectives. As of yet, no charges have been filed. As soon as I'm able to release additional information, I will."

"Have any idea when that will be?" the reporter asked.

"No, I don't."

The reporter appeared back on the camera. "According to our sources, Vukovich grew up in Crystalton and has worked at the junior high there for at least the past five years. We'll continue to follow this story as it unfolds and update you at eleven. Reporting for Channel Nine news, I'm Don Redley."

"Why's Uncle Jack on television?" Katie asked.

Deak ignored the question.

"I don't get it," I whispered. "How can they charge him with the murder?"

"They haven't, yet. All they said is he's being held in connection with the death. They never said anything about charging him with the murder."

"So, what's that mean?"

"Beats me. Lord in heaven, I hope my mother was busy with my grandfather and didn't see that." No sooner were the words out of his mouth than the telephone rang. All Deak said was, "Okay, okay, okay. I will. I will. I'll be fine. How's Grandpa? Okay. Love you, too. Bye." He looked at me and said, "She saw it in the waiting room at the hospital. It's his heart. She said if they can get him stabilized they're going to transfer him to Allegheny Hospital in Pittsburgh. Girls, go upstairs and get your toothbrushes, pajamas, and some clean clothes for tomorrow. You're going to go down and spend the night at Aunt Sissy's." The three girls cheered and tore up the steps on all fours. "I wish I was five and oblivious to all this; then I wouldn't have to put up with the humiliation."

I called my mother, updated her on the situation, and told her that I would spend the night with Deak. Aunt Sissy, his father's sister, arrived from Martins Ferry forty-five minutes later and took the delighted girls for the night. Mom came up a few hours later to check on us and brought some ham sandwiches, chips, and RC Colas, although Deak said his stomach was too upset to eat.

A three-alarm fire had broken out in a restaurant in downtown Weirton, West Virginia, and Don Redley was reporting live from the scene for the eleven o'clock news. The story on Deak's Uncle Jack followed the fire, but it was simply a repackaged version of the early report and contained no additional information. Deak and I talked into the night, mostly asking each other the same question over and over: How could Jack Vukovich be linked to the murder? Despite the number of times we each asked the question, we had no logical answer. We fell asleep downstairs, Deak on the couch, me on the love seat, my legs draped over the end.

I awoke when the July 1 edition of the Wheeling *Intelligencer* bounced off the screen door. The banner headline across the top of the front page left nothing to the imagination.

Crystalton Man Charged with Molesting Murdered Boy

Jack C. Vukovich, 35, a junior high school janitor with a history of sex-related crimes, has been charged with rape and gross sexual imposition in connection with the molestation of a mentally retarded boy who was found dead of a head injury in a wooded area west of Crystalton last month.

Vukovich was arrested at Crystalton Junior High yesterday afternoon and is being held in the Jefferson County Jail pending arraignment tomorrow.

Jefferson County Sheriff Sky Kelso said Vukovich admitted to having sexual relations with Peter Eugene Sanchez, 17, of 117 River Street, Crystalton. However, Vukovich denied having any connection with Sanchez' death, Kelso said.

Kelso said detectives received a tip that Vukovich was in the area where Sanchez was killed on June 14, a day before the boy's body was discovered. The witness, who Kelso refused to identify, said Vukovich was spotted running out of an area known as Chestnut Ridge to his car, which was parked in Overlook Park on New Alexandria Pike just west of Crystalton. The park is about a quarter of a mile from where Sanchez' body was found.

A sheriff's department investigation revealed that Vukovich was convicted on a sodomy charge in Texas in 1961, and spent two years in a Texas penitentiary. In 1964, he was charged with the molestation of a minor and contributing to the delinquency of a minor in California. Those charges were dropped for unspecified reasons.

Kelso said an autopsy performed on Sanchez' body revealed that the boy had been molested and tests indicated that the assailant was someone with Vukovich's blood type. Kelso also said Vukovich's fingerprints were found on a ten-dollar bill that authorities recovered from Sanchez' pocket.

Presented with this evidence, Vukovich confessed to paying $10 to Sanchez, who has been described as having severe emotional and mental problems, in exchange for sexual relations. Kelso said Vukovich confessed to meeting Sanchez in the woods to have sexual contact "at least a half-dozen times" in the past.

"Mr. Vukovich is a predator," Kelso said late last night. "He has a history of sodomy and preying on boys with mental retardation."

Kelso said his department is continuing to investigate Sanchez' death. Asked if Vukovich was a suspect in the boy's death, Kelso said, "We can place Mr. Vukovich in the area and with Peter Sanchez about the time he was killed. It's not a stretch to consider him a suspect in the death."

The rest of the story was background on Petey's death.

How close, I wondered, had we come to crossing paths with Jack Vukovich on Chestnut Ridge? It gave me chills.

"What's the paper say?" Deak asked, stretching his arms over his head.

"Nothing that you're going to want to read."

His eyes widened and he reached for the paper, which I handed him story-side up. He read in surprising silence, showing no emotion other than a slow shaking of his head. "Well, at least this answers my question," he said.

"What question?"

"Remember my question: What was Petey doing up on that hill?" He slapped twice at the paper. "That's what he was doing. God, this is sick."

"We dodged a bullet," I said.

"I guess," he said, staring off. "This is going to just kill Mom and Grandpa."

"When you said that your uncle had some problems before moving back to Crystalton, I'm assuming this is what you were talking about?"

"No one ever told me what it was about. All they said was that he had some problems and had to move back. I always knew he was no good. What kind of man sodomizes mentally retarded kids?" He dropped the paper on the floor. "I hope he burns in hell."

"That's a little harsh."

"It's a sin, Hutch. It's a sin against man and a sin against God." He sat up quickly on the couch, both hands gripping the seam of the maroon cushion, and looked hard into my eyes. "'But the men of Sodom were very wicked, and sinners before the face of the Lord, exceedingly.' Genesis thirteen-thirteen."

I put my hands up, palms facing Deak. "Okay, okay, Deak, I don't want to tangle with you or God about this."

★ ★ ★

Adrian didn't show up for that night's game against Adena. I overheard Pepper tell our manager that his brother had some kind of stomach virus.

"Where is he?"

"Home. He's a fuckin' basket case. This whole thing with One-Eyed Jack has got him so rattled he hasn't been out of bed all day except to shit and throw up."

In my short life, I had never known Adrian Nash to miss a ball game. I had seen him show up for baseball games covered with poison ivy, play basketball with a 102-degree fever, and play the last quarter of a football game with a broken finger on his throwing hand. He was a warrior. The assault on his conscience was apparently more disabling than any physical ailment.

"You don't look so good yourself."

He grabbed a baseball out of the milk carton on the bench and we started jogging toward the outfield grass to throw. "I gotta admit it, Hutch, when I saw those cop cars coming across the playground, I about pissed myself. It's got me rattled. I thought that if we just kept our mouths shut this would all go away in a couple of days, a week at the most, but Mother of Christ, it just keeps getting worse. I thought we were home free, then One-Eyed Jack gets his ass arrested for buggerin' Petey and now that's all everyone's talking about again. I just want it to go away." He looked over at Deak, who was stretched out in the centerfield grass, pulling his right foot toward the small of his back. "How's the preacher holding up?"

"About as well as can be expected for someone whose uncle was just exposed as a sexual deviant—embarrassed, pissed off, worried about his grandfather—and all that got heaped on top of the fact that he still thinks we should go to the cops."

"Is he going to crack?"

"I don't know. Right now he's focused on hating his uncle."

"That gives us some time."

I nodded. "Tick-tock."

"What?"

I lobbed the ball to him. "Nothing."

Chapter Twelve

As a young boy sitting in the congregation of the Crystalton United Methodist Church and looking up at the Reverend Forest P. Timlinson in the pulpit, I thought I was staring into the face of God. He was a distinguished Tennessean with a light drawl, an oval face creased deep at the eyes and across the forehead, hair like snow, pale blue eyes, and a slight smile. He had grown up in the backwoods of Tennessee and played offensive tackle for the Vanderbilt University football team. He was broad across the shoulders and stood six-foot-five, and when he grabbed the sides of the pulpit with his massive hands and leaned toward the congregation to emphasize a point, he was a most imposing sight.

The Yankee congregation was a little suspect of Reverend Timlinson when he arrived in Crystalton shortly after World War II. They appreciated the fact that he had been a Marine and had a Purple Heart and a Bronze Star that he earned fighting his way across several South Pacific beachheads, including Guadalcanal and Iwo Jima, but they were leery of his Southern twang and the way he answered their questions with questions of his own. However, he ingratiated himself to them for life in March of 1949 when an explosion ripped through the Belmont Coal Company's No. 3 mine in Little Salt Run. The slope mine caved in a half-mile below the surface, trapping forty men in the rubble. As rescue workers made their way down the shaft, Reverend Timlinson donned a miner's hat and followed them in, struggling to squeeze his giant frame under the busted timbers. He prayed over the dying and comforted the injured. The most repeated story from that day was of Reverend Timlinson praying over Joe Grabowski, whose two legs were pinned beneath a slab of stone the size of a station wagon. As he prayed, an injured miner named Eddie Barone was being hauled out of the chaos on a stretcher. As he passed the kneeling Reverend Timlinson, Eddie reached out and touched the preacher's arm and said, "Reverend, please include me in that prayer."

Reverend Timlinson raised his head, saw that Eddie's injuries were not life-threatening, and said, "I'll get to you later, Eddie. Right now I want God's full attention focused on Joe."

Joe Grabowski lost his left leg below the knee and the ankle on the right never bent again, but he swore it was the work of Reverend Timlinson that saved his life. Twenty years later, when the United Methodists tried to move Reverend Timlinson to a church in Youngstown, there was such a revolt in Crystalton that they never tried it again.

He didn't yell from the pulpit, or pound his fists, or threaten us with eternal damnation. Rather, he talked about life, personal responsibility, service, and following the "spirit of the law" that the Bible presented. He never claimed to have all the answers and was fond of saying that he didn't think God was in heaven with a tally book, keeping track of the number of things we did to please Him. Rather, he believed God kept track of the things we did to help our fellow man. That did not absolve those down on their luck from helping themselves, he was quick to point out. It was a message that resonated with his blue-collar congregation. Reverend Timlinson talked often of his family and his father, who plowed his land behind a mule and worked part-time at a local sawmill. The old man had struggled to hold on to his farm through the Great Depression, but still saved enough money to send his boy to Vanderbilt. His blue-collar roots helped him to understand the working men in his congregation and how they thought, worked, and lived.

On the Sunday after Jack Vukovich was arrested, Reverend Timlinson came out of the back room, placed his Bible on the pulpit, grabbed one of the heavy oak chairs that sat at either side of the altar, and carried it to the riser in front of his congregation. He was wearing a black cassock and a purple stole with gold satin tassels. He sat down and leaned forward, resting his elbows on his thighs and interlocking his fingers, which hung limp between his knees, and said, "Let's all talk a little bit." He asked the organist and members of the choir to leave the risers at the front of the church and join the congregation. When they were seated, he smiled and said, "Did you ever get a bad splinter?" He held his left hand up and squinted at his index finger, as though examining an imaginary splinter. For a moment he kept his eyes focused on the end of his finger as he spoke. "You know, you're working out in the yard or in the basement and you grab a piece of wood and a splinter gets you." He dropped his hand and looked at his congregation. "I hate those little devils, and if you're like me, you sometimes want to leave them buried under the skin instead of digging them out because when you dig and dump peroxide on them, they hurt like the dickens. Right?" The congregation gave a collective nod. "But, we all know what happens if you don't dig a splinter out right away, don't we? It gets infected and festers. Well, my friends, I feel like we've all got a splinter under our skin and we're not digging it out. We've decided to let it sit there and fester. This has been a difficult week for us, and I know you're all stinging this morning. I know you've been stinging most of the week. You're feeling deceived and you're angry. I understand all that. But, folks, what we can't do is let the events of the past week tear apart friendships that have stood for years. If we allow that to occur, it's going to be just like leaving that splinter under the skin, but when it's done festering, we're not going to be able to clean it up with a little peroxide. You see, if we don't dig that splinter out today, it's going to tear the heart out of our community, and I'm not about to let that happen. I love this town and I love you people, so let's get some things out on the table."

Nobody said a word. Some parishioners stared at the minister; others looked down at their hands. It was uncomfortably silent. The school superintendent, a retired army colonel named Cletus T. Brubaker, and three members of the school board were sitting in the congregation. Amidst them were steel workers, coal miners, a few railroaders, and a steam turbine operator from the electric generating plant, all parents who had fumed all week and craved the opportunity to dispense their own form of justice upon Jack Vukovich. They were angry. Their kids were attending the junior high or had passed through its halls. Why would the superintendent, the principal, and the school board put their children in harm's way, allowing them to walk the same halls as that predator, a convicted child molester?

At first, the townspeople were surprised and saddened when they heard the news about Jack Vukovich. But after a while, after they had time to think and allow the potential ramifications to settle in, an anger began to climb through their spines and ribs. They wanted revenge, but Jack Vukovich was in jail and there was no way it could be exacted. Instead, they turned their venom on the superintendent and the principal, lambasting them for allowing One-Eyed Jack to work at the school. Didn't they know he had been convicted of sodomy? No? Why the hell not? Didn't they do criminal background checks on employees? No? Well, they damn well better start. They were just lucky he never touched *their* kids. They were sorry that Deak's grandfather was in the hospital, but he certainly knew his son's sordid past. Why in God's name did he bring him back to Crystalton and near their children?

Beyond being scared, the people also were embarrassed for Crystalton. They loved their town and they loved their school, and now they had to live with this humiliation. Petey's death, sad though it was, did not reflect poorly on Crystalton. This, however, was an indictment of the entire community. The *Town Talk Bread Show* on the AM radio station in Steubenville was overwhelmed with callers wanting to know why the people of Crystalton allowed a pedophile not only to work in the school, but actually to live in the basement. The *Herald-Star* wrote an editorial stating that allowing Jack Vukovich to live in a junior high school was like allowing a fox to take up residence in the henhouse, and then acting outraged when all the chickens had been eaten. There had been no shortage of finger-pointing, and old friendships were being sorely tested. It had been a long week.

After what had to have been a full minute of silence, Reverend Timlinson asked, "No one has anything to say?"

Nellie Jones was the first to stand. He was an iron worker at the Wheeling-Pittsburgh Steel Plant in Yorkville and had forearms that looked like twisted rope. He was wearing a maroon sport coat that stretched taut across his shoulders, a white shirt, and a black clip-on tie. "You're right, preacher, I'm doggone mad about this. I've had three boys go through that school in the past five years, and now I find out that Jack Vukovich is a child molester. I never thought he should be living in the school anyway. As far as I'm concerned, Mr. Brubaker and the whole school board should resign."

He sat back down. I looked over at Mr. Brubaker; blotches of red were populating his neck and cheeks, though he remained impassive. Nick Carwell got up next and reiterated Nellie Jones's thoughts. And then another stood, and another. The tones were civil, but no less hurtful. When six people had stood and said their piece, and sentiments fell just short of lynching Mr. Brubaker and the board members, Reverend Timlinson asked, "Did any of you hear the whispers?" Again, no one spoke. "Did you? Any of you? Did you hear the whispers? Nellie? Nick?" He gave them pause, but the sanctuary was silent. "I heard them. I heard them before Jack Vukovich ever got back to Crystalton. In fact, a man in the congregation today first told me about it, must have been seven, maybe eight years ago. He whispered it to me, even though there was no one else around. He said, 'Jack Vukovich got arrested for having sexual relations with a teenage boy. That's why he went to prison in Texas.' So, if the preacher is hearing these things . . ." He winked. "My guess is you all heard the whispers, too, but chose to ignore them. Perhaps you wanted to give Jack the benefit of the doubt, or perhaps, being good Christians, you wanted to give him another chance. But you heard the whispers. They were like a mysterious noise under the hood of a car that you try to ignore, maybe even turn up the radio, and hope it will fix itself, which it rarely does."

I had never heard such whispers. But I was young and it was the kind of talk reserved for low-speaking adults. Jack's dad, Deak's grandfather, Roy Vukovich, was an elder in the church. He had been president of the Little League and mayor of Crystalton for three terms. It was he who lobbied for the state and federal grants that enabled Crystalton to build a public swimming pool. He was much beloved and it was out of respect for him that much of the talk about his son had been muted.

Nellie Jones stood again, took a breath, and exhaled. "Yep, I heard 'em, I heard 'em before he came back to town."

The preacher nodded. "Can I ask you, Mr. Jones, why you didn't say something about it then?"

"I did. Nellie Junior was going into the seventh grade. So I went over to Jack and I said, 'I don't know if the rumors I've been hearing are true, but I want you to know this, Jack, if you lay a hand on any of my boys, I'll kill you where you stand.'" He lowered his head and chewed on his lip. "That probably isn't the kind of story I should be telling in God's house, but I was concerned. I also didn't want to make a big deal out of it out of respect for Roy."

"I appreciate your honesty, Nellie," Reverend Timlinson said. He put his hands on his knees and pushed himself up, stepped down off the riser, and stood between the first sets of pews. "My friends, it is going to do no good to point fingers at your friends and neighbors. We all heard the whispers, but we did nothing about it, and the consequence has been a terrible wrong against a young boy, a boy with many problems who we were supposed to protect. But what's done is done. We can only hope that there are no other children out there who have suffered because we—all of us who heard the whispers—didn't speak up, didn't take action." He took a minute to scan his flock, seemingly trying to make eye contact with everyone in the church. "You will notice that the Vukovich and Coultas families are not here today. I asked them not to attend the service because I planned to talk about their son and brother and uncle. It would not be an easy thing to hear. We cannot change what has been done. They are our brothers and our sisters, and they are hurting mightily this day. If you are embarrassed as a community, think of how they must feel as a family. They knew the whispers to be true, but this was their son and brother. He promised he would change and they believed him. They wanted desperately to believe him. So their hurt runs deep. If we feel betrayed, imagine their pain. It has been a dagger to the heart of people we care deeply about. Embrace them. Love them. We could all stay home and pray by ourselves. But we don't. We come together in worship because we need one other, we rely on one other. So, when you leave today, remember that we all heard the whispers, and point no more fingers."

He took the chair in his massive hands and returned it to the altar. People in the congregation were crying, trying to muffle their staccato bursts of breath with handkerchiefs. Reverend Timlinson returned to the pulpit, led us in prayer, then smiled at the congregation and said, "That's all for today. Let's all be good to each other."

They weren't upset about Petey's death. It had never been about Petey. They all believed he had brought about his own death, even if it was at the hands of Jack Vukovich. The anger was over what could have happened to their own kids. They were angry with the school and angry with themselves for not acting when Vukovich was first hired. They had left a loaded revolver in the silverware drawer and were fortunate that their kids hadn't found it. If Petey hadn't been murdered, they reasoned, it was only a matter of time until one of their kids became a victim. The very thought paralyzed them with waves of fear and the anger followed.

The next morning, the janitors from the high school were at the junior high, moving One-Eyed Jack's apartment furnishings to the trash bin.

★ ★ ★

I was committed to silence. At least I was until five o'clock the following afternoon. I was putting the finishing touches on a fresh coat of slate gray enamel on the floor of the back porch, and Mom was sitting on a little wooden stool at the edge of the porch, husking corn and waiting for the charcoal to heat before placing some chicken breasts on the grill. I could hear the AM radio station out of Steubenville through the screen door. The musical intro to the news came on, followed by the baritone voice of the reporter.

A man charged with sexually molesting a seventeen-year-old Crystalton youth has now been indicted for his murder.

My mother and I looked up, staring at the screen door as though it were a television.

Just an hour ago, a Jefferson County grand jury indicted Jack C. Vukovich, a thirty-five-year-old junior high school janitor, for the murder of Peter Eugene Sanchez, who was found slain on a hillside west of Crystalton on June fifteenth. Jefferson County Prosecutor Alfred Botticelli said Vukovich was indicted on a charge of first-degree murder with death penalty specifications. Vukovich was charged with rape and gross sexual imposition last week. While admitting he had sexual relations with the teen, Vukovich has steadfastly denied that he was responsible for Sanchez's murder.

The tightness returned to my gut, the fire to my chest. My mother looked at me and asked, "He never tried any funny business with you, did he?"

"Never."

"Good damn thing."

I ate, forcing down every bite. She was going to be devastated when she learned the truth. It was best that she hear it from me, but not just yet. It would take me a while to summon the courage. I wouldn't get to play football for the Royals. I would always be looked upon with suspicion. People would talk. Decades from now, when my name came up in simple conversation around Crystalton, they would say, "Wasn't he with that bunch of boys who killed that retarded Sanchez kid?" I would stand before Juvenile Court Judge Rayford P. Simmons, a dour man with bushy eyebrows and a reputation for harsh penalties, and he would make me apologize to the Sanchezes, Earl without his fingers and Lila with those huge stitches running across her neck, then he would body slam me for my cowardice in not coming forward immediately.

After I had helped clear the table and dried the dishes, I told Mom that I was going over to Deak's to see how he was doing. She said that was a good idea. She was going bowling with Walter and would be home late. When I got to Deak's, he was sitting on the railing of his back porch, picking at his fingernails. He had just returned from three days working at church camp, which was becoming his refuge.

He nodded when he saw me walking across the yard. "My mother is hysterical," he said. "She and Dad took the girls down to Aunt Sissy's. They're on their way to Pittsburgh to tell my grandpa. How'd you like to have that job?"

"No thanks." I leaned against the rail to Deak's right. "If you're ready to go to the sheriff, I'll go with you," I said. "And, if you want, I'll talk with the Sanchezes, too."

Deak's eyebrows knotted up in the middle of his forehead. "What? No. Absolutely not."

The stabbing pain in my heart, which had been like an electric shock with each beat since hearing the radio news report, subsided a bit. I stared at Deak for a long moment, then asked, "Aren't you the same guy who said . . ."

"The guy's a deviant, a pervert," he said. "He deserves to burn in hell, but if the state of Ohio would like to fry his ass in the meantime, all the better."

"You remember that he didn't really kill Petey, right?"

Deak's eyes were ablaze, his jaw stretched taut and a dozen tiny dimples covered his chin. "He put his own father in the hospital. If the poor guy ever gets out, he'll never be the same. My uncle might as well have put a gun to his father's head and pulled the trigger. He's embarrassed my mother and our family. He was molesting a retarded kid. He's a pedophile. It's a sin against God and it is so friggin' embarrassing that I don't ever want to show my face in this town again. The Sanchezes have an answer. It's not the right one, but they don't know that. They'll believe it's true and it will give them some peace of mind."

I blinked. "This, uh, this is a bit of a turnaround in your attitude."

"What he did to Petey is worse than murder."

"I'm not sure I agree with that."

"He's not your uncle."

"So, just so I'm clear, now you don't want to go to the sheriff?"

"Jack Vukovich should be put away so he can never hurt another kid."

"What's the Bible say about this?"

"The Bible is open to interpretation."

Chapter Thirteen

It was just after dark when I left Deak's house. I didn't know whether to be disappointed or relieved. I had mentally girded myself for a meeting with Sheriff Sky Kelso. I was ready for him to stare me down with those icy blue eyes and shake his head in disgust, but I would stand tall, accept responsibility for my part in the cover-up, and take my punishment without complaint. As Coach McHugh said before every big game, it was time to "man up."

I needed time to think. I walked down Labelle Avenue to where it emptied into the parking lot at Community Park. To the south the red warning lights blinked on the smokestacks at the power plant. Between the two stacks, a hazy full moon appeared to rest atop the West Virginia hills. A Pennsylvania Railroad coal train sent vibrations across the earth. I stretched out on a picnic table, interlocked my fingers behind my head, and stared at a starry sky. I smelled of nervous sweat, which soaked the pits of my gray T-shirt.

How in God's name did this get so screwed up? How? I awoke that fateful morning a virtually carefree fifteen-year-old. My biggest worry was whether I would get enough time on the field to earn a varsity letter in football. Before noon, I was involved in covering up the murder of a retarded kid who mimicked raptors. I wasn't so naïve as to say that some of the mess wasn't of my own devising, but it still seemed like a heavy load to throw on the shoulders of a fifteen-year-old.

I couldn't believe that Deak didn't jump at the opportunity to go to the sheriff with an ally. I had kept quiet to protect Adrian—to protect all of us. Deak had stayed quiet because he was terrified of the ramifications. His reticence in approaching the sheriff stemmed only from the potential fallout. He would not be hailed as a hero who told the truth, who did what was right, but as a pariah who took down the starting quarterback. Deak was not a mentally tough kid, and he knew that ratting out Adrian would cause a backlash that he was ill equipped to handle. If Deak thought the pressure from the community was intense just because his uncle was accused of molesting and murdering a seventeen-year-old retarded boy, wait until it became known that he was the one who cost Crystalton a chance for a state championship because he went to the sheriff and our quarterback went to juvenile hall.

In spite of Deak's silence, I didn't feel I had been given a reprieve. I had vowed silence to keep the true identity of Petey's killer a secret. I couldn't, wouldn't, stand back and let someone go to the electric chair for a crime he didn't commit. I would be the pariah, but at least I wouldn't be burdened with that terrible secret. Somewhere in my future, there was going to be a meeting with Sky Kelso. I didn't know when, but eventually I was going to have to man up and make that trip.

★ ★ ★

As I walked back up Second Street toward the house, I spotted the red 1964 Buick Wildcat parked across from our house. There were only two cars like that in Crystalton. Carson Nash owned one and Dan Benton owned the other. But Dan didn't smoke cigars, and through the open driver's side window I could see the bright, orange ember of Mr. Nash's cigar and in the cast of the yellow streetlight I watched the gray smoke snake out of the window. The harsh aroma of the tobacco wafted across the street.

The gas lamp in front of our house stretched my shadow across the red bricks of Second Street. Adrian got out when he saw me approaching. "What's up?" I asked.

"I need to talk to you for a minute."

"Is your dad coming in?"

"No." He put a hand on my spine and nudged me between the overgrown and sagging spirea bushes that guarded the entry to our front porch.

"Is something wrong?"

"Is your mom home?"

"No."

"Let's talk inside."

I turned the key and pushed open the door to the sunroom. Before I could get the key out of the lock, Adrian grabbed me by the tender deltoid muscle and squeezed, pushing me inside. A streak of fire raced up my neck; the pain was nearly paralyzing. I whirled on a heel, knocking his hand away with a forearm. My fists went up, ready to protect myself. "What the hell's your problem?"

The streetlight cast a faint glow into the room, and Adrian's imposing silhouette was outlined against the windows of the sunroom. "You're going to the sheriff?"

He made no attempt to move closer and I slowly lowered my fists. "Who told you that?" Of course, I knew, but it was one of those questions you instinctively ask in a tight situation.

"Deak. Who do you think?"

"He called you and said I was going to the sheriff?"

"No, I heard about his uncle getting charged and I stopped by to see how he was doing. He told me you had been there and were talking about going to the sheriff."

My eyes narrowed. That was a lie. Adrian didn't concern himself with the difficulties of others unless they directly involved him. "That's bullshit, Adrian. You went to see if *he* was going to the sheriff and he told you I offered to go with him. Since it's not Deak's style to run his mouth, I assume you put the squeeze on him, too."

He pointed at me and said, "We're in this together, or did you forget?"

"What I haven't forgotten, Adrian, is that one of us is in a lot deeper than the rest."

He wanted to knock me out; I could see it in the way his nostrils flared. "So, are you going to the sheriff, or not?" Adrian barked, angry at the accuracy of my assessment.

"I haven't decided."

"What the fuck! I thought you were supposed to be my friend."

"Are you kidding me, Adrian? I am your friend, which is why I've been protecting your ass."

"It doesn't sound like you're protecting me now. If you go to the sheriff, I'm screwed. I'll be sitting in juvenile hall instead of playing football. You can't say anything, Hutch. We had a deal."

I put my hands on my hips and took a long breath. "Look, Adrian, our agreement was to keep quiet about what happened to Petey. It didn't involve sending Jack Vukovich to the electric chair. We can't allow that to happen to an innocent guy!"

"Innocent? He's not innocent. He's already admitted that he's a child molester."

"Yeah, he's a child molester, but he didn't kill Petey, remember? And now, that's what everyone thinks."

"They ought to put him in the electric chair. In my book, child molesters are worse than killers."

"You're not going to get much of an argument from me there, but Ohio doesn't give child molesters the electric chair."

"Oh, but it would be okay if I went to juvenile hall, huh?"

"There's a big difference between juvie hall and the electric chair, Adrian. The electric chair is a little more permanent. You know, I would very much like not to have this on my conscience for the rest of my life. It's already eating a hole in my stomach." I looked outside. The ember on Mr. Nash's cigar still glowed. "Does your dad know why you're here?"

"No. I told him I needed to talk to you for a minute. Hutch, look, you can't go to the sheriff. Jack's not going to get the death penalty."

"How do you know?"

"My dad was talking about it. He's big with the Republican Party and he talks to all those guys up at the courthouse. He said they'll probably give him some kind of plea deal."

"What's that mean?"

"If he pleads guilty to something else, they won't give him the death penalty."

"I don't know, Adrian, this is making me really nervous."

"Look, if you go to the sheriff, it'll be in all the papers. I'll be screwed. I'll never get a scholarship to play football."

"This might surprise you, but the entire universe does not revolve around Adrian Nash."

"I can't play football if I'm sitting in juvie hall. What about the team? Are you willing to sacrifice a shot at a state championship?"

"That's not fair, Adrian. You can't compare someone's life to football."

"Even if he did get the death penalty, which he won't, it's not going to happen tomorrow. Just don't call the sheriff."

There was a modicum of relief in agreeing not to call the sheriff. I nodded. "Okay, I won't."

"Promise?"

"I said I wouldn't, Adrian."

He nodded. "Okay, good. Sorry for the . . ." His voice trailed off. Adrian Nash wasn't used to apologizing or being sorry for anything.

"No problem."

After the door shut, I sat in the wicker chair and watched the Wildcat's headlights come on as it started down the brick-lined street. I sat for several more minutes, staring into my reflection in a sunroom window. I wasn't completely happy with the young man looking back at me. Coach McHugh always talked about the man in the mirror. "You can never fool the man in the mirror," he said, usually talking about our adherence to an off-season conditioning program, but it seemed appropriate now. I could not fool myself. I was protecting Adrian while another man sat accused of Petey's murder, and yet I was doing nothing to change what I knew to be a terrible wrong.

Chapter Fourteen

We played the Cadiz Colts on the last Wednesday in July for the championship of the Eastern Ohio Hot Stove League. Adrian was magnificent. He threw a two-hitter; I hit a three-run homer in the first inning, and we won six to nothing.

In the instant after we won, I saw the dichotomy between the brothers Nash. It has remained etched in my brain, a snapshot lost to time to everyone but me. When the final strike, a fastball on the outside corner, snapped into my mitt, Pepper leapt and threw both arms up, his glove sailing off his hand. At that same instant, as Pepper reached the apex of his jump, his mouth and eyes wide, Adrian bent at the waist, his gloved hand and left palm resting on bent knees. He sucked air like a distance runner trying to catch his breath after crossing the finish line.

While that mental image remains firm in my memory, more tangible proof rests in a wooden frame on a shelf in my office. It is a black-and-white team photo taken after the game by one of the parents. Pepper is in the front row on one knee, smiling broadly, his arms draped around the shoulders of two teammates, a trophy in one hand and the index finger of the other held in the air. Adrian is standing next to me in the back row, impassive, staring at the camera with a tired look in his eyes.

I treasure that photograph, not because of the championship, but because I enjoy the memory of being a gritty ballplayer, playing on skinned infields with hard-nosed sons of steel workers, coal miners, and railroaders. We were a tough bunch of kids who did not enjoy lives of privilege. Our status was not determined by the clothes we wore, but by our accomplishments on the athletic field. Most of our mothers stayed home and the dads toiled in jobs that both dirtied and blistered their hands.

The exception was Carson Nash. Other dads came to our games right from work, salt stains on their shirts and dirt under their fingernails. Carson was always freshly scrubbed, usually dressed in Bermuda shorts, sockless with oxblood penny loafers, and a golf shirt. Other dads smelled of sweat and dust; Carson smelled heavily of aftershave and suntan lotion. Carson was a little heavy through the girth, but he had broad, solid shoulders. If you shook his hand and didn't give it a firm grip and look him in the eye, he would reprimand you and make you practice until you performed it to his satisfaction.

Carson was, by far, the wealthiest and most influential man in Crystalton, a member of the Masonic Lodge and the unapologetic chairman of the Jefferson County Republican Party in a Democrat-dominated, blue-collar valley. He was a shrewd businessman and it was commonly said that if you angered him, he would put your head on a stake, go eat breakfast, and never give it a second thought. If he saw a bank customer with a new automobile, obviously having secured a loan from somewhere other than the Glass Works Bank and Trust Company, he would patiently wait for their next visit to the bank. He would invite them into his office and deliver a standard speech that evoked the memory of our founding fathers and their collective interest in banking. Why, did they know that George Washington himself, the father of our country, signed the charter for America's first bank? It was a fact. The founding fathers understood that if our country was to grow, we needed strong banks. Well, the same principle applies for communities. Small, locally owned banks are the economic bedrock of every community in this great country. Did they know why? Because small banks cared about the community and its citizens. After all, would a bank president sitting in Cleveland or Columbus give a hoot in hell if little Johnny needed braces or if the Joneses needed a new addition for their new addition? Of course he wouldn't. By God, I bet he couldn't even find Crystalton on a map.

By the time most of those people walked out of his office they believed it was their civic and patriotic duty to do all their banking at the Glass Works Bank and Trust Company. It was a soft-spoken talk, but the message was implicit. He would forgive them that one transgression, but if they did it a second time, they better hope they never needed money for a life-saving operation, because if it depended on a loan from the Glass Works Bank and Trust Company, they would just have to die.

While we milled around and accepted congratulations from our parents and friends after the game, I spotted Carson Nash talking to my mother near the concession stand. He was all smiles and animated as, I assumed, he recounted one of Adrian's highlights. Adrian, Deak, Pepper, and I posed for a photo for Deak's dad. After the shutter clicked, Mr. Nash placed a hand on my shoulder, the other on Deak's. "We're going to have a cookout at the house to celebrate and I want you two boys to come on up." He gave our shoulders a jiggle. It sounded more like an order than an invitation.

"I'll need to check with my mom," I said.

"It's already taken care of. I talked to both of your moms, and they're good with it."

We changed out of our cleats and tied the shoestrings together so they would drape over our shoulders and headed out with the Nashes. It was a two-block hike up Hudson Hill to the Georgian colonial that sat behind a manicured lawn and a semicircular driveway that arced in front of the house. As we walked, Pepper and Mr. Nash recounted the game. Adrian walked without comment, and Mrs. Nash wheezed, straining to get her ample behind up the grade.

The Nashes had a housekeeper, a Lithuanian woman named Ella who was all of about four-foot-nine, kept her hair wrapped in a red bandana that she tied in a tiny bow at the hairline, and ran in high gear all the time. When we arrived at the house, the charcoal in the brick barbeque pit was lit and the picnic table on the patio was set with china nicer than the plates we used only on Christmas and Easter Sunday. Ella brought Carson a tumbler of ice and whiskey and a platter piled high with T-bone steaks. Mrs. Nash and Ella carted out large bowls of tossed salad, potato salad, steaming corn on the cob, and a carrot cake.

"Quite a feast," Deak noted.

I washed my hands, arms, and face in the outside spigot and sat down. The patio was rimmed by the same wooded hillside that led up to Chestnut Ridge. Thousands of fireflies danced along the tree line. Crickets chirped and blue bug lights hissed with the corpses of dive-bombing insects. The dinner conversation was cordial and focused mostly on the championship game and the approaching football season. Conditioning was scheduled to begin the following Monday and Mr. Nash was excited about the prospects of the coming season. He told some stories of his playing days with the Royals and, touching the tip of a slightly twisted nose, described them as, "the days before facemasks were popular."

When the carrot cake was mostly gone, Adrian and Pepper got up and helped Mrs. Nash clear the table. I started to do the same, but was waved back into my seat by Carson. He pulled a dark brown cigar from a breast pocket, snipped off the end with a silver cutter, and rolled it in his mouth for several seconds before striking a match and drawing the flame into the tobacco. He talked a little more about football, quoted Winston Churchill concerning the pleasure of a good cigar, and said he had high hopes that President Nixon would end the mess we had gotten ourselves into in Vietnam. As he spoke, the engine of the Buick Wildcat roared to life and Mrs. Nash, Adrian, and Pepper pulled away.

When I saw the lights disappear down the hill I asked, "Where are they going?"

"Oh, they've got a few errands to run."

"At nine forty-five at night?" Deak asked.

"I wanted to talk to you boys for a few minutes, anyways," Carson said, dispelling a laser of blue smoke over the table. "So, how's your grandpa doing?" he asked Deak.

"Pretty good. He's back home. Weak, but coming along."

"Good. He's a good man—done a lot for this community, I can tell you that for a fact. I imagine this mess with your uncle hasn't done him a lot of good."

"Mr. Nash, it hasn't done any of us any good."

Carson nodded, the cigar wedged between two fingers and dangling in front of his chin. "I heard some good news today up at the courthouse. At least, I expect you'd think it was good news. I heard from a pretty reliable source that the county prosecutor is going to let your uncle plead out."

"What's that mean?" Deak asked.

"The prosecutor is going to drop the first-degree murder charges and death penalty specifications, and your uncle will plead guilty to a lesser charge in Petey's murder and the sexual assault charges. He'll still do some considerable time, but he'll avoid the death penalty and the time he'll spend in prison won't be much longer than if he was convicted of the original sexual assault charges."

Deak's face took on the confused, slack jaw of a third-grader trying to comprehend the realities of procreation.

"So, he's going to plead guilty to killing Petey?" Deak asked.

"It'll all be wrapped up in one neat plea agreement. You hadn't heard this?"

Deak shook his head. "No, not a word."

"Well, maybe I was a little out of line for telling you before it's been made official, but I thought you'd like to know. I imagine it's been weighing heavy on your mind. I mean, for your grandfather's sake we don't want your uncle going to the electric chair."

"When is all this going to happen?"

"I was told within the week."

"Who told you about this?"

"Just a friend of mine up at the court. You wouldn't know him."

"I don't understand how this works. He won't go to trial?"

"No, everything will be settled before he walks into court. The judge will ask him if he agrees to the reduced charges, he'll say yes, and the judge will give him a sentence that your uncle and his lawyer and the prosecutor have agreed to. It'll be all cut and dried." He rolled his cigar on the edge of his dessert dish, sharpening the end of the ash on the glaze. "I know this has been difficult on your family, Deak, but it's also been difficult on the entire community. This plea arrangement that your uncle has agreed to is a good thing for all of us. It's important for Crystalton to put this in the past. The

Sanchez family will be able to put a face with the evil that took their son, and we'll be able to get this ugliness behind us. Once he pleads guilty we'll all be able to get on with our lives. We can start concentrating on football, huh?" He smiled, and drained the last of his whiskey. "The thing I wanted to talk to you boys about was your futures." He let those words hang in the air for a minute, spinning the ice in his tumbler. "You boys have been great friends to my sons, and I appreciate that. Friendship, true friendship, is rare and should be treasured. It does my heart good to have seen you boys grow up together, and now you're becoming young men and playing ball together for the Royals. I get a great joy out of that; so does Mrs. Nash. So, what are you boys thinking about doing when you're out of high school?"

He looked at me, shrugged, and held out an open palm, a tacit signal to start talking. "I don't know, Mr. Nash. I'll probably pick up a trade, go up to the tech school and study welding or plumbing, or something like that."

"You're not interested in going to a four-year school?"

"I am, but Mom doesn't have that kind of money. She can't afford to send me to college."

Carson nodded and looked at Deak. "I'm thinking about seminary school. Maybe college. I haven't decided."

Carson scratched his chin with the thumb of his cigar hand. "Well, what I want you boys to know is that I'm in a position to help you out with college, both financially and from an admissions standpoint." He paused, tilted his head back, and looked over the bridge of his nose at me, then Deak. "You're both good boys, so I'd like to make sure you get the same opportunities as other kids. I'm going to be talking to my board of directors about setting up some funding for scholarships. Two bright boys like you would make excellent candidates. And, I sit on the board of trustees at East Liberty University, and I know many influential people who could get you into a good school and possibly find some scholarship money. You'd be surprised how creative some schools can be if they want a student bad enough." He winked, struck a match, and put a fresh flame to his cigar. "I want you fellas to keep that in mind, and don't ever hesitate to ask me for help. Glad to do it. I know you've been good friends to Adrian and Pepper and I want you to know how much I appreciate it."

We both said, "Yes, sir," as though on cue. Then Carson Nash said, "Thanks for stopping over, boys. That was a nice win tonight." It was our signal to leave.

We walked down Hudson Hill, watching our shadows overtake our bodies and sprint ahead in the glow of the streetlights. "What just happened up there?" I asked. Deak shrugged, but said nothing. "Do you think he knows what happened with Petey and now he's trying to buy our silence?"

Deak said, "I don't know, and I don't care. Maybe it was coincidence, maybe not. But if that's what he's trying to do, congratulations, Mr. Nash, you succeeded. I'm never saying a word. I'm glad they're going to put Uncle Jack away, and I hope it's for a long, long time, so I wasn't going to say anything, anyway. If he wants to think he's buying my silence and help me pay for my college, that's fine with me. But I'm not the one they're concerned about anymore. You're the wild card, now. You're the one who's suddenly developed a conscience."

"Excuse me for not wanting to see someone go to the electric chair for a crime he didn't commit."

Deak looked at me, his brows knit together in the middle of his forehead, and said, "I heard my grandfather and mother discussing my uncle the other night. My grandfather said he hoped that something could be arranged—I'm assuming it was the plea bargain Mr. Nash was talking about—so that my uncle could someday get out of prison and make a new life for himself. My mother said, 'You mean get out and molest another child? I hope he rots in prison for the rest of his life.' You see, Hutch, you were okay with hiding the truth when it meant protecting Adrian. I'm okay with hiding the truth if it means protecting some kid from being molested twenty years from now."

Chapter Fifteen

The Pennsylvania Railroad tracks ran through the coal yards of the power plant south of town, then angled up a grade toward the foundation of the old glass house and Del Cafferty's field before crossing over a graffiti-covered steel bridge that spanned the Little Seneca Creek and passing the loading shoots at the sand quarry. It continued through town on the western edge of the flood plain, running a tight squeeze between Labelle Avenue and the lumberyard. The tracks came within a hundred feet of my bedroom, where with each passing freight the windows hummed like a nest of angry hornets. Near the lumberyard, the tracks angled by the old headquarters of the Redhead Oil Company and back to the river flats, where they straightened out and headed north toward Mingo Junction.

At the final curve in Crystalton, between the gravel ballast and the muddy riverbanks, there was a natural amphitheater of sandstone, the remains of a once-proud hill scoured down by millions of years of wind and rain. Surrounding the rock was a covering of towering sycamores and shagbark hickories, warriors in their own right, having survived decades of Ohio River floods. Hidden in the middle of this covering was an area of the softest, greenest grass I have ever known. The little enclosure was called Hobo Camp, a name that had survived since the days of the Great Depression when tramps would hop off the trains and start cook fires in the protection of the rock and trees. They could drift to sleep on the sandstone boulders, feeling the quake of passing barges and listening to their wakes slap against the muddy shoals.

My youth was not filled with the traditional fears of childhood—vampires, witches, or monsters. Rather, I grew up terrified of hobos. The days of hobos riding into Crystalton on the rails had long passed, but parents still told stories of evil, cannibalistic hobos who lingered near the rails seeking succulent children on which to dine. They all told a similar story, a tale of a young boy, a wispy image of a lad whose name no one could quite remember, who one day disobeyed his parents and wandered down by the railroad tracks where he was captured and eaten by the hobos. Want to be eaten by the hobos? Fine, young man, just you wander down by those railroad tracks and see what happens. It didn't matter that I had never seen a single hobo in Crystalton, I was certain they were down there, a campfire ready under a boiling cauldron, just waiting for a tasty seven-year-old to parboil and serve over wild onions and stolen potatoes.

By the age of eighteen, however, I had lost my fear of hobos. Hobo Camp was a secluded refuge where I could go to be alone with my thoughts. On this day, I stretched out on the sandstone, which was still warm from the afternoon sun. Barges passed on the river; a single train of a hundred coal hoppers headed north out of town. I loved the sounds and smells and vibrations of the Ohio Valley, but I was ready to leave. It was an hour before dusk on August 16, 1974. At six o'clock the next morning I would leave for football camp at the University of the Laurel Highlands. I would drive out of town, leaving behind Crystalton, my youth, my friends, and my secret.

It had been nearly three years since Jack C. Vukovich was led from the Jefferson County Jail across the third-floor skywalk to the courtroom of the Honorable Harvey T. Fitzmorgan, judge of the court of common pleas. After Prosecutor Alfred Botticelli and Vukovich's court-appointed attorney conversed in whispers in front of the judge's bench for several minutes, the courtroom was called to order. Judge Fitzmorgan, looking down over a pair of half-reader glasses, pointed at the accused with the handle of his gavel and asked, "Mr. Vukovich, do you understand the terms of the plea agreement that has been entered on your behalf?"

Seated at the defendant's table, his head bowed, Jack said, "Yes, sir."

"You will plead guilty to the charges of second-degree murder, rape, and gross sexual imposition with a minor. Do you agree with the terms of the plea agreement?"

Jack nodded, but still didn't look up. "Yes, sir."

Judge Fitzmorgan made a few laps around the inside of his mouth with his tongue, then signed the documents that had been placed before him and handed them to his bailiff. Judge Fitzmorgan was a dour-looking former prosecutor who was known to be lenient on offenders of what he considered victimless crimes, such as gambling and prostitution, which led to wide speculation that he was taking kickbacks from the Youngstown mob. However, that didn't mean he couldn't rev up some disgust for a child molester and murderer, particularly when the courtroom was full of reporters. He took off the glasses and let them dangle against his robe by a gold-link chain. "Do you have anything to say before I pass sentencing?" he asked.

Jack said no and again avoided eye contact.

"Well, Mr. Vukovich, let me tell you that I am normally not inclined to accept a plea agreement for such an egregious act, and I am not bound to this plea agreement as far as sentencing is concerned." He held up a copy of the agreement, shook it twice, then let it fall from his hand. "I could sentence you here today to whatever term I deem appropriate. However, I am told by the prosecutor, and I must admit that I am a little perplexed by the agreement, that your actions have put the entire village of Crystalton under great duress. In fact, those actions have pitted neighbor against neighbor, friend against friend. I guess some people take exception to a child molester living in the basement of a school, and I can't say that I blame them. The prosecutor states that the agreement will enable Crystalton to begin healing by permanently removing you from its citizenry without further delay. Therefore, I am inclined to accept this agreement. You understand, sir, that by this agreement, should a day come when you are eligible to be released from prison, that you are never to return to Crystalton?"

"I understand," Vukovich said.

"Good. You should also know this. It is my fervent hope that you never again take a single breath of free air and if there's anything I can do to make that happen within the next twenty-two to thirty-eight years, you can rest assured, sir, that I will do it. Mr. Vukovich, I am sentencing you to a term of not less than twenty-two years and not more than thirty-eight years in the state penitentiary." He stood and pointed to a deputy standing behind the defense table and said, "Get him out of my courtroom."

Jack Vukovich never totally disappeared from my memory, but he didn't linger on the fringes either. Once he was in the state penitentiary, my memory of him was like an image on an old photograph exposed to the sun, slowly fading, lighter and lighter. My confidence that we would never be caught grew with the passing weeks and months.

A lot of people might think that such an event would have traumatized me to the point where the remainder of my teenage years were fraught with despair and nightmares, but that wasn't so. The smaller Petey Sanchez and Jack Vukovich got in my rearview mirror, the more I slid back into the routine of being a teenager. I worried about girls, acne, geometry, and the next big game. Maybe that says something not very flattering about my psyche. I don't know, but that's the way it was.

As for Adrian, Deak, Pepper, and me, we didn't talk much about Petey or One-Eyed Jack. Adrian wanted to pretend it had never happened. Deak believed God's work had been done. Pepper was Pepper. He believed that Petey Sanchez had gotten what he deserved for messing with Adrian, and that Jack Vukovich got what he deserved for messing with Petey. As far as he was concerned, the world was spinning on its axis and all was well.

One of the reasons we didn't discuss that day was that the tight friendship we had enjoyed began to slowly erode after Vukovich went to prison. Adrian was never social to begin with, and he became even less so in the waning days of that summer. He grew more distant and difficult to talk to. My friendship with Adrian was like a loose strand on a wool sweater that began to unravel. Clipping it or tying it off just delayed the inevitable. It was only a matter of time until there was a gap in the material that could never be mended. We were still classmates and teammates, still hunted arrowheads together, and were still pals, but there wasn't that closeness, that tight-knit feeling that we once had, confident that nothing in the world could disrupt our bond. Obviously, that wasn't so. Petey Sanchez had done it. Things change. Sometimes that's all you can say.

As the last of the evening's rays spread over the Ohio River, I left Hobo Camp, crossed the railroad tracks, and followed the gravel path past the old Redhead offices and back to Market Street. I had a very keen sense of who I was in Crystalton, and I felt very much part of the community. When I left the following morning, I knew that would change forever. Some freshman would be wearing my number fourteen on the football team and my accomplishments would be relegated to yellowing pages in a scrapbook. I would come home between semesters and for vacations, but in time those visits would become fewer and fewer. Like the images of Petey and Jack, the friendships that were so dear to me were about to fade and fall into distant memory.

I wouldn't admit it to myself, not at the time, as I was eighteen and full of testosterone and false bravado, but the truth was I had been running away from Petey Sanchez since the day he died. I projected years down the road—the black cat clock on the kitchen wall clicking off the seconds of my life—awaiting the day when I could put years and miles between myself, Petey, and Crystalton, Ohio.

PART II

Chapter Sixteen

For those who decry the death penalty and believe that all human life is sacred, allow me to introduce you to Richard Terrance Buchanan Junior, who for two decades was arguably the most feared man in Akron, Ohio. He was more commonly known by his street name, Ricky Blood, and was suspected in at least six homicides that to this day remain unsolved in Summit County. But let's not deal with conjecture. I'll give Ricky the benefit of the doubt on the six unsolved murders and just stick to his official criminal record.

At age ten, Ricky was sent to a state juvenile detention center for mental evaluation after he was caught burying neighborhood cats to their necks in his backyard and decapitating them with a lawn mower. He was expelled from the eighth grade after presenting a classmate with a beautifully wrapped Christmas gift exchange package containing a dead sewer rat. At fifteen, Ricky was convicted on a juvenile count for the felonious assault of his court-appointed mental health counselor. He was released from the juvenile detention center on his twenty-first birthday. At age twenty-one and twelve days, he was arrested for aggravated assault and attempted rape of a woman he met in a bar, lured into an alley with promises of cocaine, then head-butted into unconsciousness. Only a chance encounter by a passing Akron police car saved her from being raped and murdered. Some might consider that conjecture on my part, but he was standing over her naked body with a full erection, his pants around his ankles and a switchblade in his right hand. You do the math. Over the next seventeen years Ricky Blood was in and out of prison three times for assault, selling crack cocaine, and violating his parole. A prison psychologist wrote of him, "This is one of the most profoundly disturbed human beings I have encountered in my forty years as a prison psychologist. He is wholly without conscience."

Early in my career as a Summit County assistant prosecutor, I stood behind a two-way mirror and watched police interrogate a career drug dealer and local badass named Tyrone Whittaker, who had tattooed biceps the size of whole hams and was himself a feared man on the streets. As police questioned Tyrone about a drug-related shooting to which he had purportedly been a witness, he was flip and smug and cocky until the investigator said, "Word is Ricky Blood did the deed and you were there." The instant Ricky Blood's name came up, Tyrone's attitude suddenly improved, as did his memory. He said, "It weren't Ricky. I'll tell you who it was, but it weren't Ricky. I don't want nothin' to do with that boy. He'll kill you, he'll take his time, and he'll enjoy every minute of it."

Thus, I was aware of Ricky Blood long before our lives became intimately connected. Some might find the word "intimate" a little unusual in this context, but when you send a man to his death, there is no other way to describe the relationship.

After dinner on Monday, November 15, 1999, Tina Westmoreland, a twenty-year-old single mother and the daughter of Nick Westmoreland, a detective for the Akron Police Department, dropped off her eighteen-month-old son with her father en route to the local junior college where she was taking an accounting class. Tina was a beautiful girl with a wide smile and hair the color of a garnet. She never returned.

Late that night police found her car parked on a side street near the school, locked, her books on the passenger seat. She had attended her class and a security video captured her walking across the parking lot at seven fifty-five. It was the last time anyone ever saw her alive. Nineteen days later, a charred corpse was found in Cuyahoga Valley National Park. It took the coroner another day to make official what everyone already knew—the body was that of Tina Westmoreland.

Nick Westmoreland was a personal friend and I was heartsick for his loss. A memorial service was held and as stories in the paper about the abduction and murder waned, I remembered that day long past during my freshman year in high school when the detective from the Ohio Bureau of Criminal Identification and Investigation spoke at career day. Twenty-four hours, he said. You better have a break in the case within twenty-four hours or you're in trouble. After a week—kiss it goodbye. I feared that we would never find Tina's Westmoreland's killer.

Thanksgiving passed; so did Christmas and New Year's, and detectives were still without the first solid clue in the case. As Valentine's Day neared, on a day when the snow swirled and the sky had been gray and sunless for a month, a telephone call came in to the detective bureau from an antique dealer in Cuyahoga Falls.

He said, "I don't know if this is anything important, and in the holy name of Christ I can't explain why it's taken me so long to think of it, but sometime in early or mid-November, I'm not really sure of the date but it was a piece before Thanksgiving, I remember that much, this fella with wide-set eyes stopped by my antique store and asked to borrow a five-gallon gas can to get some gas for a friend who had run out down the road somewheres. I had this Sohio gas can for sale for thirty dollars, which was a very good price because they're hard to find, particularly in good condition, which this one is. Anyways, I tell this fella with the wide-set eyes that I'd sell it to him. He just stared at me with those eyes, and I swear to Jesus they were looking right through me. He said, just like this, he said, 'I just want to *borrow* it, not *buy* it,' like he thought I was retarded or something, and then he pulled it off the shelf. Well, let me tell you, I'm not as young as I used to be, and I didn't want no trouble, and I figured he was going to take it anyway and better that he just leave than beat me with it first, so I told him it was okay to borrow it, but bring it back when he was done. He said much obliged and left. I figured that was the last I was ever going to see that can, but, sure enough, he showed up a couple of hours later and put the can on the shelf and said much obliged again. I figured he might at least give me a couple of bucks for using it, but he didn't and I was just glad to get the can back anyway. So, like I said, I don't know why it took me so long to think about this, but I'll bet that was right about the time that little girl from Akron got burned up, the one whose body they found in the national park. That's only about five or six miles from here, and maybe he borrowed that gas can to start the fire."

A homicide detective named Homer Malesky asked the antique dealer if he would mind coming down and looking through some books of mug shots. The dealer said his business was really slow and he could certainly take the time to do that the following morning. Homer called me over to the detective bureau about ten-thirty after the antique dealer picked Ricky Blood's mug shot out of books containing more than a thousand photographs. "Are you sure that's the guy?" Malesky asked.

The antique dealer tapped the mug shot with a yellowed fingernail. "I remember those wide-set eyes. I'm positive."

"Really positive?" I asked.

"That's him. No doubt about it."

We booked the antique dealer and his wife into a Pittsburgh hotel for safekeeping and went looking for Ricky Blood. The physical evidence was overwhelming. Police searched Ricky Blood's Chrysler and found Tina Westmoreland's student identification card wedged into the passenger seat. They found hair samples in the trunk of the car, and bloodstains and more hair in the basement of his house. The Sohio gas can was still on the shelf at the antique store and Ricky Blood's fingerprints were all over it.

Ricky was picked up on suspicion of kidnapping and murder and brought to police headquarters. Detectives interrogated a belligerent Ricky Blood for four hours without success. When the police were ready to give up, I went into the interrogation room, a small, rectangular space not much larger than the rectangular table that occupied its center. I pulled out a chair in front of the two-way mirror and sat down across the wooden table from Ricky Blood. He had pale blue eyes, a strong, pronounced chin, and the straightest, most perfect set of teeth I had ever seen on a career criminal. He sneered, "Well, well, well. Look who's here—the Button Man. What happened? The fucksticks with the clip-on ties weren't getting the information they wanted so they called in the big gun, huh, Mr. Prosecutor?"

"They said you're not being particularly talkative, Ricky."

He looked around the room. "You fucks ever feed anyone around here?"

"Once in a while. It depends on how cooperative they're being."

He blew air from his mouth, then made an obvious point of looking over my suit. I never appeared in public without a suit, starched white shirt, the tie snug under my chin, and cuff links that showed below the cuffs of my jacket. When he finished eyeing me over he said, "I eat prissy little pricks like you for breakfast."

"Is that a fact?"

"You don't know who I am?"

I leaned in closer, my forearms resting on the table, my fingers interlocked. "Of course I know who you are; I'm just not impressed. This will probably strike you as unusual, Ricky, but I'm not afraid of you, not even a little bit."

There was a tightening of his jaws that made his ears twitch. "Well, you're stupid then, because you ought to be."

"Why is that?"

He lifted his wrists for my inspection. "If you were out on the street and I wasn't wearing these handcuffs and shackles, you'd be afraid."

I sat up straight and nodded, tapped twice on the rough table with an index finger, then pointed it at Ricky Blood. "You make a very good point, Ricky. If we were out on the street, in some dark alley, and you weren't wearing handcuffs and shackles, I probably would be afraid." I leaned in toward the table and in a calm, slow voice said, "But, here's the rub, Ricky; we're not on the street. We're in an interrogation room at police headquarters, you're in deep shit, and you *are* wearing handcuffs and shackles. And, here's another factor in my favor, there are some extremely angry police officers standing behind that two-way mirror with some very big guns who would like nothing better than the opportunity to unload them on you. So, you see, I have no reason to be afraid."

Ricky Blood looked at me for a long moment, as though processing my words, before he tilted his head and laughed and shook both index fingers at me. "You . . . you son of a bitch . . . I like you. You get it. You're dealing from a position of power and you understand that. You understand power." He laughed and put both arms on the table. "Those other sons of bitches, they come in here pretending to be my friend, telling me I need to confess to get things off my conscience." He looked up at the mirror. "Fuck you, you cocksuckers." He leveled his head to me. "So, tell me, how can I help you, Mr. Van Buren? What is it that you want to talk about?"

"Tina Westmoreland."

His eyes widened. "Oh, yeah, Tina . . ." He closed his eyes and smiled, as though recalling a fond dream. "That was one fine piece of ass." As the words left his mouth, there was a scuffle in the hall and a thump against the door. I heard one cop say, "No, Nick, no." Ricky again looked up at the two-way mirror, smiled, and said, "Oh-oh, Daddy must be one of the cops watching from behind the mirror." He wiggled the fingers on his right hand. "Hi, Daddy."

And then he began talking; it was the most repulsive two hours of my professional career. He told me in sickening, graphic detail of the final week of Tina Westmoreland's life. He just happened to be driving down the road when he saw her grinding her starter and lowering her forehead to the steering wheel in exasperation. It was an opportunity. He smiled and asked if he could help. She said thanks. Her car wouldn't start and her cell phone battery was dead. He thought, Ricky Blood, it's your lucky day. Would he mind giving her a ride to her father's house? Why, precious thing, he didn't mind at all. He didn't know she was the daughter of a cop. That was just a bonus. He hated cops. Tina was so grateful and happy that she didn't have to stand out in the cold and she thanked him several times before he turned in the opposite direction of her father's house. Where was he going? He just needed to make a quick stop by his house, then they would go. She must have known at that moment that she was going to die.

Ricky had me where he wanted me, dangling the critical information in front of me, when he stopped the narrative and said, "What the fuck, am I going to get something to eat, or what? I ain't sayin' nothin' else until I get some food."

I stepped out of the room and a uniformed cop was sent for twenty dollars worth of burgers, French fries, root beer, and deep-fried cherry desserts. Ricky Blood tore into the grease-stained bag and began stuffing food in his mouth. "Where'd I leave off?" he asked.

"You said Tina knew she was going to die."

He nodded. "Oh, yeah."

When he pulled into the dark alley behind his house, he hammered her face against the dashboard until she slumped in the front seat. He carried her unconscious to the basement and strapped her down with rope, duct tape, plastic ties, and handcuffs, just like the ones those cocksucking cops use. Then he raped and sodomized her, over and over again. When he left during the day, he taped her mouth. When he heard on the news that she was the daughter of a cop, he cut her with razor blades and tortured her with a cigarette lighter and rubbing alcohol. He put a revolver to her temple and clicked on empty chambers. He cut off her ears and bit her. When her once beautiful face became so battered and disfigured that he couldn't stand the look of it, he wrapped it in gauze and duct tape, leaving only her nostrils to keep her alive so he could continue raping her. At first she pleaded for her life to be spared, then for days she pleaded for death, but he only laughed. He attended a candlelight vigil outside the Our Lady of Fatima Catholic Church and snickered to himself as hundreds around him prayed for her safe return. After a week, he wrapped her in a tarp, threw her in the trunk of his car, drove to the national park, doused the bitch in gasoline, and torched her.

"Ricky, the coroner's report states there were more than three hundred razor blade cuts on her body."

He thought about this for a minute, nodded slowly, and said, "Yeah, that's probably about right."

By the time I had extrapolated every detail that I thought possible, I was exhausted and beyond rage. When the uniformed officers entered the room to take him to his cell, he smiled and extended a cuffed hand and said, "This was fun, Mr. Van Buren. I liked talking to you. You're a straight-up guy. You come back sometime and we'll chat some more."

Ricky Blood—proof that we spend way too much time preserving the lives of those who have repeatedly proven themselves unfit for our society.

★ ★ ★

On Wednesday, September 15, 2004, I awoke at 3:45 a.m. Despite the ungodly hour, I ran on the treadmill in my basement for thirty minutes because I knew it would be my only opportunity of the day to work out. I ate breakfast while standing at the kitchen counter and watching the Weather Channel. I had a bowl of shredded wheat and strawberries, a toasted English muffin dry, a splash of orange juice, and a cup of black coffee, which I finished while I showered and shaved. I tossed my briefcase in the back seat of my 2004 Chrysler Pacifica and before inserting the key in the ignition I pulled my digital recorder from my suit coat pocket and set it in the cup holder. The recorder had become more of a crutch than my cell phone. Six months earlier I had been driving south on Interstate 77 while talking on the cell phone and scribbling notes on a notepad in my lap, totally unaware of the traffic congestion in front of me. I came within inches of rear-ending a family in a minivan. Since then, I used the recorder religiously to leave myself verbal notes and reminders.

With the dew heavy on the grass of my lawn, I nosed the Pacifica out of the garage and headed for the Southern Ohio Correctional Facility in Lucasville to witness the execution of Richard Terrance Buchanan Junior. As the county prosecutor, I believed it was my duty to attend the executions of the men I sent to death row. If you stand in front of a jury and ask them to sentence a man to death, then you should have enough guts to look the condemned in the eye before he dies.

It is a three-and-a-half-hour drive from Akron to the southern Ohio community of Lucasville in Scioto County, and I planned to arrive an hour before the 10 a.m. execution. Officially, my presence was simply as a witness, a requested guest of Nick Westmoreland. There was little chance of a last-minute appeal or stay of execution, so I felt no obligation to arrive at the death house any earlier than was absolutely necessary. I stopped by an all-night hamburger joint and bought a large black coffee in a Styrofoam cup, requested a dollar of my change in silver to buy a *Beacon Journal* and a *Plain Dealer* from the metal boxes by the front door, then continued along the darkened streets on the short drive to the entry ramp to westbound Interstate 76.

The road was empty and I cruised along the interstate at seven miles over the speed limit, nothing but the hum of the tires in my ears. Unlike in my teen and early adult years, I rarely played the radio in the car. Occasionally, I listened to an audio book, but mostly I drove in silence. I enjoyed the silence. It was a time to think, plan my day, or just daydream, and I was grateful for the solitude. I was a little surprised that the political reporter from the *Beacon Journal* hadn't asked to ride with me to the execution. Barbara Zeffiro had been shadowing my every move since I announced my candidacy for attorney general, and the conviction and death sentence of Ricky Blood had been big news locally. I was glad she hadn't asked. It was an execution, and I didn't want to turn it into a political campaign sideshow.

My time was rarely my own and the Pacifica was my one sanctuary. The exception to this rule was the tether that is my cell phone. I had been careful not to freely distribute the number. My secretary, Margaret, would not call unless it was an emergency. My campaign manager, Shelly Dennison, however, didn't give me the same consideration. When she got up, even if there was no urgent need to talk to me, she would hit my speed dial number before she sat down on the toilet. That was one of the downfalls of sleeping with my campaign manager.

Shelly pleaded with me not to attend Ricky Blood's execution. With less than two months before election day, some polls had me up by as many as eighteen points. She was a savvy strategist and wanted me to sit on the ball and run out the clock. "This one's in the bag," she said. "Don't get careless." She fretted that by attending the execution I was setting myself up for an ambush question from some reporter and it would cost me serious points. She didn't care about my moral or professional obligations to attend Ricky Blood's execution. I believed I owed it to Nick Westmoreland, Tina Westmoreland, the voters, and in an odd way, Ricky Blood. She refused to listen to my reasoning. Her eye was on the prize—the November election—and Shelly was infinitely more concerned about votes than my obligation to justice.

Given my past history with the Petey Sanchez affair, the irony was not lost on me that I was the Summit County Prosecuting Attorney, a proponent of the death penalty, and a man sworn to uphold the law. Petey Sanchez represented a part of my life that was long past and, I hoped, forgotten by all but a few. Looking back, it was easy for me to justify my actions as youthful indiscretion. For God's sake, I was only fifteen at the time; I would be forty-nine in a month. As you would expect, I had never been able to totally suppress the memory of that June morning, but I certainly didn't dwell on it. I moved on with my life. I had a job to do, which occasionally involved sending violent criminals to death row. I never lost much sleep over sending those men to their deaths, and I certainly hadn't lost any over the impending execution of Ricky Blood. I was elected by the voters of Summit County, Ohio, to uphold the law, keep the bad guys off the street, and put the really bad ones to death. That is exactly what I did and usually with great proficiency.

Ricky Blood's conviction had been a foregone conclusion. We had Ricky's confession on tape and he did nothing to refute the story. He was convicted in thirty-five minutes. Before the jury left to deliberate the penalty phase of the trial, the defense attorney paraded in a cast of characters who testified to Ricky's abusive childhood, and to his good heart, and how his life should be spared. My remarks were simple. I reminded the jury that the man sitting at the defense table had raped and tortured an innocent girl for an entire week before dousing her with gasoline and burning her alive. I told them that pure evil had a face, and it was that of Richard Terrance Buchanan Junior, and the only just punishment was death.

The jury concurred.

★ ★ ★

Just north of the village of Lucasville, U.S. Route 23 intersects with Lucasville-Minford Road. Turning east, you pass a ball field and a few houses before you see the glint of razor wire that caps the fencing around the sprawling campus of the Southern Ohio Correctional Facility. As the main parking lot came into view, I could see the marching circle of chanting, dour-faced protesters carrying signs and decrying the cruelty and inhumanity of the death penalty. In one corner of the lot a victim's advocacy group had set up a card table with brochures about their group and a clock with the ten and twelve painted red, signifying the time at which Ricky Blood would die. From the front of their table hung a banner with a scanned and digitally reproduced photo of Tina Westmoreland with her infant son, and the simple words, "Remember Tina." This group was having coffee, eating donuts, and smiling.

I introduced myself and shook hands with the two men and three women at the victim's advocacy table, told them I appreciated their efforts, then walked over to where Nick Westmoreland and the oldest of his two sons were sitting in a Ford sedan that was backed into a parking space in front of the protestors. "How ya doing, boss?" I asked.

"I'll be a lot better in about an hour," he said.

I had been through enough of these to know that Nick Westmoreland was not going to find peace of mind with the death of Ricky Blood. It is a misconception that the death of the perpetrator brings peace to those who loved the victim. It doesn't. It helps bring some closure, but never peace. The solace Nick Westmoreland was seeking would not be found in this world. He would carry to the grave the emptiness in his heart.

As we started across the parking lot toward the administration building where we would fill out the appropriate paperwork to be allowed inside the prison and then searched, an Associated Press reporter approached me and asked, "Mr. Van Buren, can we talk for a few minutes after the execution?" I nodded. My talking points were already prepared. I would talk about Tina Westmoreland and her father and her brothers and a son who would grow up never knowing his mother because of Richard Terrance Buchanan Junior. One of them would doubtlessly ask if I thought the death penalty was a deterrent, and I would shrug and say, "It's certainly going to deter Richard Buchanan from ever hurting another person."

The protestors paid no attention to me, with one notable exception. As we neared the administration building, a nun of about four-foot-eight stepped out of the protest circle and stood in my path. She was carrying a white placard with red lettering that read, "Stop State-Sanctioned Murder." It was Sister Bernadine, who headed the Ohio Catholic Council on Human Rights, an organization that opposed the death penalty and was a general pain in my ass. You couldn't not like Sister Bernadine. She, on the other hand, thought I was the devil incarnate.

"Here to witness the murder of another of God's children, Mr. Van Buren?" she asked.

"No, Sister, I'm here to witness the execution of a vile, heartless predator. Would you like to meet the father of the victim?"

She ignored my offer, saying, "'Vengeance is mine; I will repay, saith the Lord,' Romans . . ."

"Romans, twelve-nineteen. I know the verse, Sister. But I prefer Genesis nine-six, 'Whoever sheds the blood of man, by man shall his blood be shed.'" Growing up with Deak Coultas had taught me a few things about the Bible. I winked and kept moving. "Have a good day, Sister."

A prison guard who walked like he was chafed and had a bulldog's jowls and disposition led us to the Death House, a tan brick structure just across the courtyard from the administration building. I sat in silence with the Westmorelands and six newspaper and television reporters in a witness area that was separated from the execution room by a large picture window. At about ten minutes before ten, Ricky Blood walked into the execution room, looking atrophied, smaller, less intimidating than in the days when he had worked out and done pushups by the hundreds to make himself more intimidating. I could see the jaw muscles of Nick Westmoreland tighten. He looked at me and I nodded. No words were exchanged.

Ricky Blood turned backward and hoisted himself onto the table without assistance. He was strapped down and an intravenous line inserted in his arm. The tube ran from his arm into another room where, out of sight, the lethal drugs awaited their ride into the veins of Ricky Blood. The warden asked Ricky if he had any last statements. He shook his head and said, "Nope. Let's do it." At the warden's signal, sodium thiopental was injected into the tubes. Within a few minutes, Ricky Blood's eyes closed for the final time. Once he was unconscious and his brain activity depressed, the intravenous line was flushed with saline and pancuronium bromide was injected into the line. A neuromuscular blocker, pancuronium bromide prevents the nerves from communicating with the muscles and causes paralysis of the lungs and respiratory arrest. Following another saline flush, potassium chloride was injected into the line, interrupting the heart's electrical mechanism. In seconds, it stopped beating.

When it became apparent that Ricky had not taken a breath for several minutes, a curtain was pulled across the windows of the viewing rooms. After the prison physician declared him dead, the curtains were again opened and the warden announced the time of death—10:11 a.m.

Chapter Seventeen

My cell phone service returned when I got just north of Chillicothe and away from the barrier hills. There were four missed calls, all from Shelly Dennison. I erased them in rapid order without listening. She had a habit of calling my cell while she was driving and left long, rambling messages that had no purpose, other than to sate her boredom. If the allotted time for leaving a message on my phone ran out, she simply called back and continued from that point. If any of the messages were important, she would call again. My first call was to Margaret, who dispensed with hello and asked, "Is that son of Satan dead?"

"Yes, he is."

"Good. He made the world a better place by leaving. Umm-umm-umm-umm-umm, now maybe that poor little girl can rest in peace."

"Umm-umm-umm-umm-umm" was Margaret's all-encompassing expression for a variety of emotions—joy, sadness, disbelief, anger. I had heard it uttered many times outside my office when someone wanted to get past her to me. "Umm-umm-umm-umm-umm. That is not going to happen." You could sooner get past a momma grizzly protecting her den than you could get past Margaret and into my office without an appointment. This included one monumental confrontation with Shelly, who shortly after becoming my campaign manager tried to brush by Margaret and into my office. I heard Margaret say, and could visualize that chubby index finger swaying back and forth in front of Shelly's nose, "You remember this, missy, you may run his campaign, but I run this office. You want to see Mr. Van Buren, you come to me first."

By the time I opened the door they were nose to nose, Shelly's eyes had turned to slits, and the venom was about to pour from her mouth. "Ladies, this is no place for a cage match," I said. "Please step in here." After twenty minutes of mediation, Shelly agreed to try to call ahead for appointments, and Margaret agreed that Shelly was due some scheduling latitude in light of the complexities of running a statewide political campaign. However, the truce was tenuous at best, and Margaret refused to refer to Shelly as anything but "the girl," and Shelly pretended not to be able to remember Margaret's name, calling her "that large black woman who sits outside your office."

Margaret Benning was fifty-two, highly intelligent, and profoundly religious, had skin the color of obsidian, the sense of humor of a military policeman, a rear end the size of a truck, and was the most intensely loyal human being I have ever known. She kept me on schedule, guarded my office with the ferocity of a Rottweiler, smelled heavily of lilac, and adored floral neckerchiefs, making Christmas shopping for her easy.

After I was elected Summit County prosecutor in 1996, Margaret was one of the hundreds of applicants to be my executive assistant. She was one of the few who didn't have some connection to the Republican Party seeking a return for favors so slight that they weren't worth mentioning. To be brutally honest, she got the interview because she was black. I had narrowed the field to a half-dozen candidates when my chief of staff brought to my attention that I had not one person of color on the list of finalists. I didn't think that was important, but at his insistence I selected three minority candidates, of which Margaret appeared to be the least qualified. She had not been employed for ten years while she was home raising three babies to two different husbands. She was fresh off the second divorce and desperate for employment. We hit it off immediately and I offered her the job on the spot; she kissed me full on the lips and danced around my office like she had just won the grand prize on a television game show. It remains the only expression of uncontrolled exuberance I have seen from Margaret Benning since that day.

The previous year we had to trim five percent out of our budget and I teasingly told Margaret that she had better shape up or she might be one of the casualties. She planted two fists on her ample hips and said, "Mr. Van Buren, I'm a black, fifty-two-year-old single mother. I know you ain't messing with me." I thought about that comment the day Ricky Blood told me that I understood dealing from a position of power. Maybe I did, but no one understood it better than Margaret.

"So, what's going on back there?" I asked.

"Oh, it's all sunshine and kittens here, Mr. Van Buren. You leave town in the middle of a campaign and miraculously everything gets nice and quiet."

"You're kidding."

She drew in a breath and I knew she was rolling her eyes at me. "Of course I'm kidding. The phone hasn't stopping ringing today since I parked myself in this chair." I choked back the urge to laugh, listening to her flip through the pages of the spiral pad she kept on her desk. "Let's see, I've had five calls from folks wanting you to speak to their group; calls from a couple of very annoying, very persistent people who want jobs if you win the election, a request for an interview by a newspaper reporter in Zanesville, and a call from a lovely woman named Gladys Pickleseimer, who is about ninety-six and deaf as a haddock, who asked if you would consider being the grand marshal of the Obetz Zucchini Festival parade. It took me fifteen minutes of screaming into the phone to get her to understand that I couldn't make that decision. I'm still not sure that she understood, but I had to hang up on the poor thing before I went completely hoarse."

"Busy morning," I offered.

"Well, that was just the campaign. Then, of course, there's this annoying little daytime job you have. Let's see what occurred here. The secretary for the county commissioners called for the third time in the past week wanting to know why you haven't called to schedule a meeting with the commissioners to discuss next year's budget. Detective Guilivo of Akron P. D. called in with his shorts in a bunch because the West Akron Rapist case goes to the grand jury next week and you two have yet to meet to prepare. And you apparently told Joe Steele that you would help him with his opening statement in the Jimmy Knox murder case. He's been back here three times looking for you this morning. He's the nicest man I know, but I'm going to snap his neck if he comes back here one more time."

"I'm waving the white flag, Margaret. I give." I started laughing. "I'm sorry, really."

"Oh yeah, you sound sorry, all right."

"Okay, are you ready?"

"Pencil in hand."

"Send the speaking requests and the zucchini lady to Shelly."

"With pleasure."

"Tell anyone looking for a job that I won't even consider filling positions until after the election."

"Uh-hum, that's a lie."

Margaret hated lies on any level. She knew I'd already had discussions with several people about filling posts in the attorney general's office, but I couldn't be bothered with every request for every secretary's position. "I know, but it's just a little lie and it will give you an easy out when they call back. Give the reporter in Zanesville my cell phone number and tell him . . . him or her?

"Him. Cal Kapral."

"Tell Cal he can call me any time after three o'clock. Schedule my meeting with the commissioners—sometime late next week. Call Detective Guilivo and tell him to relax; the rape case is a slam dunk indictment. I'll give Joe a call in a few minutes to go over his opening remarks. Anything else, Margaret?"

"The girl called twice wanting to know if I'd heard from you."

"I'll give her a call."

"You do that, so she'll quit bothering me."

"Anything else?"

"Nope. Now, you're sure that boy's dead, right?"

"Quite."

"My other line is ringing. I've got to go."

And with that, the line went dead.

★ ★ ★

In part, I relayed the story of Ricky Blood because it gives a good snapshot of what I have been doing with my life for the past thirty years. Oddly, there is a direct tie between Ricky Blood and my current political aspirations. It was Ricky, or more accurately, his lawyer, who unwittingly launched me on my quest to be Ohio's next attorney general. It occurred two years earlier when one of Ricky's attorneys filed an appeal stating the death penalty was cruel and unusual and the state couldn't guarantee Ricky a painless death. A reporter from the Associated Press called me and asked for a comment. It was the first time I had heard about the appeal and it hit such a nerve that I was unable to censor myself. I said, "Painful, compared to what—keeping an innocent girl tied up in the basement for a week while he raped and tortured her before burning her alive? Any pain he feels will be a fraction of what Tina Westmoreland went through, not to mention her family, so quite frankly I'm not too concerned with the amount of pain Mr. Buchanan feels from an intravenous needle."

The article and my comments went out over the national wire. I was inundated with letters and e-mails, a few of which chastised me for being so cavalier about the death penalty, but an overwhelming majority supported my comments and said it was about time someone stood up for the victims of these crimes. Three days after the Associated Press interview, the chairman of the Ohio Republican Party navigated his way past Margaret and was sitting in my office, attempting to recruit me to run for state attorney general. He said the Republicans had not a single viable candidate and just when it looked like they would have to concede the office, I had "arisen like a Phoenix from the ashes." Part of me thought it sounded a little hokey, but I liked the mental image and I accepted his invitation. He suggested that I hire Shelly Dennison as my campaign manager, saying, "she has a real taste for the jugular. You'll love her."

Until that moment, I had no lofty political aspirations. However, it came at a time in my life when I was again watching the clock on the wall. I knew my days as a prosecutor were numbered.

I had a great job putting bad guys in jail and on death row. I liked it, and I was good at it. Many of my law school compatriots were making a lot more money in corporate law or as defense attorneys, whom, in the case of the latter, I routinely pounded in the courtroom. I brought a swaggering, tin-badge-and-six-shooter mentality to the office. I was slow to negotiate plea bargains, particularly when I believed the accused deserved a harsh penalty. This was the central theme to my campaigns, and the public seemed to appreciate my take-no-prisoners approach.

Although I loved my job, I knew it was time to move on. I had known this for a while. The job was consuming me. It absorbed most of my waking hours and I seemed unable or, sadly, powerless to change. Being the Summit County Prosecuting Attorney was the overriding passion in my life. It was how I identified myself. I thrived on the ego surge and adrenaline rush that coursed through my veins when I won in the courtroom. It was my drug, and it was every bit as addictive as crack cocaine.

A few years back, I realized the job was getting the best of me as I planned for the trial of Jimbo Mull, a habitual drunk who returned to a Twinsburg automobile repair shop a few hours after being fired and emptied a .38 Special into the torso of his former boss. The wife of the victim opposed the death penalty and did not want to be subjected to a lengthy court battle. She asked that I accept an offer from Mull's attorney for a guilty plea in exchange for a sentence of life in prison without a chance of parole. I refused her request. I wanted to send the bastard to the death chamber as I believed it was the only penalty that fit the crime.

The lead detective on the case was Andy Esposito, as soft-spoken a man as I have ever met. During a pre-trial meeting, Esposito spent twenty minutes trying to persuade me to accept the plea deal. Finally, exasperated, he rubbed at his eyes with his fingertips and said, "Let me tell you a story, boss. When I was in Vietnam we hopped on a chopper and made a run somewhere in Quang Tri Province to pick up some Viet Cong prisoners. There were four of them. We landed, loaded them up, and headed south. We hadn't been in the air a minute when one of them starts acting up, he's yelling in Vietnamese to the other three, looking at us, gesturing with his head, sneering, yelling, spitting, looking back at his buddies, more yelling. I knew just enough Vietnamese to understand that he wanted to try to overtake us. Their hands were tied behind their backs, but there were still four of them and I certainly didn't want to start shooting inside a helicopter. I start yelling at the guy, telling him to knock it off, but he didn't understand anything I was saying. I get close to him and yell and he spits in my face. He starts yelling again and tries to get up. I push him down with my foot, then a couple of the others start to get up. Me and my buddy, we didn't discuss it or think about it, we each grabbed an arm, walked him to the open door and pitched him out."

"How high up were you?"

"High enough that it was his last landing. As soon as we did that, the rest of them settled down real quick. The next time it happened, we didn't wait for it to get out of control. As soon as one of them started giving us trouble, out he went. After a while, I couldn't wait for one of them to act up so I could pitch his ass out of the chopper. In fact, I liked it; I wanted one of them to act up. You know what we used to say about them?" I shook my head. "Charlie flies real good, but he can't land for shit."

"Sounds like the war was getting to you."

"That's the point. Things had gotten real personal for me. You drop off some buddies and go to pick them up a few hours later and find their mutilated bodies in a fox hole with their testicles sewn in their mouths, it gets personal."

I leaned back in my chair, crossed my arms, and asked, "How does this pertain to Mr. Mull and his trial?"

"This has all gotten too personal for you, Mr. Van Buren. You've been around the bad guys a long time, maybe seen too many of them get away with murder, and now it's gotten inside your head. You're going to disregard the wishes of the victim's family in order to extract your pound of flesh."

"I'm not sure I concur with that assessment."

Esposito slowly nodded. "Then why are you seeking the death penalty when no one else wants it? If you accept the plea, Jimbo Mull will spend the rest of his life in a state penitentiary, but that's not good enough for you. You want to throw Mr. Mull out of the helicopter. You want the pleasure of sending him to his death. You need to back off. A long time ago I refused to back off, and after I got back to the states it took a lot of years looking at the bottoms of whiskey tumblers to get my life back in order."

I relented and accepted Mull's plea offer. Of course, Esposito was right. His revelations weren't a surprise to me. The job was no longer about justice. It hadn't been for a while. It was about winning. Or rather, it was about never losing. I was driven more by a fear of failure than a need for victory. The victories in my life had never been as sweet as the defeats were bitter.

In many respects, I was not happy with the man I had become. I had insulated myself and protected my feelings like they were an exposed nerve. I had few close friends and I had been unable to sustain a relationship with a woman for more than a few months. I was considered one of the most eligible bachelors in Summit County and I had plenty of relationships, but most of the women left saying they didn't feel needed, or that I would never love them as much as I loved my job. I'm not sure I was in total agreement, but I was smart enough not to live in denial.

When a constant parade of women roll in and out of your life, changing with the seasons, and all tell you the same thing, any rational person would have to believe there's some truth to the matter. I'm not happy that I've fumbled relationships with some terrific women, but I haven't made any real attempts to change, either.

Could I ever discount the potential psychological damage that had occurred while covering up Petey's death and trying to smother it in my psyche? Of course not, but I never blamed the events that occurred on Chestnut Ridge for the man that I had become—a loner consumed with his job. It was a self-imposed exile.

★ ★ ★

At times, it seemed nearly unfathomable to me that a man with little or no political aspirations could stumble out of blue-collar Crystalton, Ohio, and end up as the Republican candidate for state attorney general. I often think of the movements in the universe that put into motion events that change our lives. Why, for example, was Ricky Blood driving near the community college at the moment that Tina Westmoreland's starter broke? Why did those two paths cross? How did I end up running for Ohio attorney general and not working the graveyard shift in a steel mill?

In my case, it was individuals, not events, that set the ball in motion. The first was my high school baseball coach, Andrew Suranovich. Along with coaching the baseball team, he was the guidance counselor at the high school. He was short—about five-six—and short-tempered. Although I never heard him say anything worse than "dag gummit," he could give you a look of exasperation that made you feel like the dumbest human being ever to walk God's earth. He was not a particularly warm person and was tough to get close to, but he lived four doors down from us and we would occasionally walk to school together. He always asked about my grades and seemed to take a particular interest in my well-being. I'm not exactly sure why, and I imagine pity played into the equation since I was fatherless, but I couldn't discount the fact that I was a hell of a catcher and they don't grow on trees in small high schools.

On the second day of school my senior year, Mr. Suranovich walked into the metal shop where I was arc welding. He reached up under my shop coat, grabbed the back of my jeans and lifted, smashing everything of vital importance to me, and marched me whining and on tiptoes back to his office. The pressure had set my entrails ablaze and I sat for a moment sucking air and blinking away tears, wondering what infraction I had committed in barely more than one day of school. When I was finally able to speak, I asked, "What'd I do?"

"Don't you want to go to college?" he asked. I did. "Then why are you taking auto body repair instead of literature?"

I had no answer. Well, I had no good answer. "I wanted to learn to weld."

He leaned over his desk and I could smell the bacon he had eaten for breakfast. "Yes, Mr. Van Buren, the question that's on the lips of college admissions officers everywhere: How are his welding skills?" He took a breath and filled out a drop-add form. "Tomorrow morning you report to Mrs. Siebert's literature class. Now, what are your plans for college?"

"I was thinking about attending the East Liverpool branch of Kent State. If I commute, take two classes a term, and go year-round, I can keep the costs down and graduate, I'm guessing, in about six years, maybe a little longer."

I thought it was a good choice, but soon learned otherwise. Mr. Suranovich rubbed at his temples in a circular motion for a few moments before looking up, giving me that exasperated look. Then he flicked the back of his hand toward his door. "Please, be gone," he said.

The following week I was summoned to his office where sat an erect, broad-shouldered man with a high forehead and the nose of a boxer who took more punches than he landed. When he stood, the man towered over me; he extended a hand that looked like it could have encircled mine twice. His name was Landis Jacoby and he was the head baseball coach and an assistant football coach at the University of the Laurel Highlands outside of Latrobe, Pennsylvania. He also had been Mr. Suranovich's college roommate. He had a hint of a West Virginia twang, and said, "Mr. Suranovich tells me that you're a pretty fair baseball and football player. He said you're the type of quality student-athlete we're looking for at the University of the Laurel Highlands, and frankly, I'm in desperate need of a catcher for next season. Think you might be interested?" I was apoplectic. The high school had given Adrian his own mailbox because he received so much mail from college coaches. This was the first time any college coach had shown any interest in me. Before I could answer he continued. "I've seen your grades. They're good enough for an academic scholarship. I could get you some money for baseball, add a little for football, and it'll be pretty close to a full ride."

He started saying something about the beauty of the Laurel Highlands, trying to sell the school, but I cut him off. "You can quit selling now, coach, I'm in. I'll come play for you."

He frowned. "Don't you want to come see the campus first?"

I shook my head. "No, sir. No need for that. I'm sure it's a fine campus."

"You should probably talk it over with your parents."

"That's not necessary. It's just my mom and she'll be real excited about this. Do I need to sign something?"

That was it. Landis Jacoby offered me a chance to go to college on a scholarship and I snatched it on the spot. I didn't step onto the campus until the two-day freshman orientation the following July.

The second person of influence was my ex-wife, Marie, who was actually a graduate student at the University of the Laurel Highlands and my speech instructor my sophomore year. Halfway through the semester, before we became lovers, she said, "Your oratory skills are exceptional. You should consider going to law school."

It was the first time in my life that anyone ever told me I was exceptional at anything. With all the forethought that I had given my college selection, I asked, "Okay, how do I do that?" The next semester I enrolled in a debate class and found that, indeed, I was quite good at public speaking and debating. I changed my major to pre-law and following graduation was accepted to law school at the University of Akron.

Marie and I were married the summer after my first year of law school and divorced before the third summer. After eighteen months of marriage, while I was downtown clerking at the Ninth District Court of Appeals, she packed up her bags and left. The marriage had gone on the rocks quickly and I knew a split-up was coming, but I officially found out we were getting divorced when a classmate called and said he had read it on the statistics page of the *Beacon Journal* under the heading of "Divorces Requested." I haven't spoken to Marie since the day our divorce was final. I never remarried.

After law school I clerked for a municipal court judge who recommended me for hire to the prosecuting attorney. It was 1982, and I became the youngest assistant prosecutor on the staff of Summit County Prosecuting Attorney T. Ambrose Livingston, who was the third person who dramatically influenced my life.

I rose through the ranks to the position of chief assistant prosecutor, which meant I supervised all the felony cases and personally prosecuted the death penalty cases. I was undefeated—four for four—in such cases when in January of 1995 T. Ambrose walked into my office, sat alone at the conference table, balanced a pair of black wingtips on the lacquered surface, and scratched his testicles, an annoying habit that he was loath to stop because he was T. Ambrose Livingston, goddammit, and no one told him what he could and couldn't do, including scratching himself in public and sneaking cigarettes in his office. The county's chief law enforcement officer burned through a pack and a half of non-filtered cigarettes each day in a non-smoking building.

T. Ambrose interlocked his fingers behind his head and said, "My boy, I've decided to run for the United States Congress."

"Congratulations, sir," I said. "You'll make a fine congressman."

He winked. "I know that. I think you'd make a fine prosecuting attorney."

I nodded and said, "So do I."

For a change it wasn't a rash decision. I knew T. Ambrose was considering a run for Congress, and I had been contemplating running for his vacated office for several months. With T. Ambrose's endorsement, I ran unopposed in the primary and easily won the general election. I was reelected in 2000. It was during that campaign that I became known as "The Button Man."

Two days after Christmas in 1992, Gerald Riddick broke into the Barberton home of his ex-wife and shotgunned her to death. He then got a beer from the fridge, made himself a ham and cheese sandwich, and watched the Cleveland Browns game on television until her boyfriend came home from his job as a department store security guard. He walked into the house, said, "What the fu . . ." then met the same fate as his girlfriend. Gerald stepped over the boyfriend's corpse, got another beer, watched the last quarter of the Browns loss to the Steelers, threw his beer bottle through the television screen in disgust, then called the police to report the murders. I tried the case and secured a death penalty.

In 1999, the *Beacon Journal* did an article about Summit Countians on death row. During their interview with Riddick, he said he didn't think he deserved the death penalty because the murders had been crimes of passion. "The Button Man knew I didn't deserve the death penalty, but he nailed me with it anyways," Riddick said.

When the reporter questioned the term "Button Man," Riddick explained that on death row I was known as "The Button Man," because I enjoyed seeing the button—the top of the plunger—drop on a syringe delivering the cocktail of deadly chemicals into a convict's arm. "If he could push the button himself, he would," Riddick continued. "He enjoys watching men die."

That was not true, but Riddick's nickname for me stuck. For better or worse, I became known as "The Button Man." I believe it helped secure my reelection in 2000, and it certainly didn't hurt my name recognition in my run to be Ohio's attorney general.

★ ★ ★

Every male elected official in Summit County had receptionist envy over Justine Lundquist. She was a former college volleyball player who was six-foot-four in her heels, had legs that connected just below her rib cage, long blonde hair, blue-green eyes, and a smile that melted the heart of every man who walked into my lobby. During her first two weeks of employment, I had three talks with Justine about appropriate dress—skirt too short, top too revealing, skirt and top too tight. After the first two talks, I asked Margaret to handle the third. She said, "Umm-umm-umm-umm-umm, that is not my job. You hired little Miss Sugar Britches, so you go tell her your own self."

Although it had been a patronage job—Justine was the niece of one of my biggest contributors—she had done an excellent job of running a smooth lobby, which at any moment could contain a half-dozen edgy men on the brink of indictment. She was intelligent and had an elementary education degree, but her primary motivation seemed to be husband hunting. She was in the midst of a steamy affair with Ben Brandt, chief of my civil division. Ordinarily, I would have nipped that in a hurry. But, with an eighteen-point lead in the polls and less than two months until the election, I was content to feign ignorance and hope that Mrs. Brandt didn't find out about the affair until I was sitting comfortably in Columbus.

Although she was not my secretary, I used Justine as my first line of defense. She always knew if there was trouble brewing back in the offices. When I returned from Ricky Blood's execution, I stopped by her desk and asked, "Anything going on that I need to know about?"

"It's been pretty quiet out here," she said. "However, the rock star in the corner has been waiting for you for two hours."

I looked over my shoulder to where a silver-haired man slouched in an orange fake leather and chrome chair, his arms crossed at the chest, a thin smile creasing his lips. He was wearing dark, wraparound sunglasses that pinched his forehead so that little ripples of skin puffed up around his temples. I turned back to Justine and asked, "Who is he?"

She shrugged. "He wouldn't give me his name. He said he needed to talk to you in person. I asked what it was in regard to, and he said it was very important, something about helping you win the election. He's been sitting there with that stupid-ass smirk on his face. He gives me the creeps."

The man had a greasy, unwashed look to him and a yellow tinge to his skin, like a long-time smoker or someone losing a battle to a cirrhotic liver. His hair was a dingy, gunmetal gray, heavy with gel and combed neatly off his face. While his face and hair appeared to need a good scrubbing, he was neatly attired, his khakis and blue dress shirt cleaned and pressed, his brown dress shoes buffed and shiny. He smelled heavily of tobacco smoke and cheap aftershave. His smile revealed dull, graying teeth, and the smug look of a poker player holding a royal flush in a winner-take-all pot.

I walked up to him and asked, "Are you waiting to see me?"

"I am, at that."

I extended my hand and said, "Hutchinson Van Buren."

In a condescending tone he said, "Why, I know who you are, Mr. Van Buren. Everyone knows the Button Man. Why, I feel as though I am in the presence of greatness."

He made no effort to extend his hand and I could feel a wave of heat racing up around my neck. I withdrew my hand. "Is there something I can help you with?" I asked.

"No, not at all." He nodded toward Justine. "You heard the lady at the desk, the one I give the creeps. I'm here to help you. I'm going to help you win the election. In fact, what I have to say is critical to your campaign."

"Really? How's that, seeing that I'm already up eighteen points in the polls?"

He smiled. "Ah, but polls are just opinions of the electorate, Mr. Van Buren, and as we know they can be fickle animals. The momentum in an election can change quickly. Maybe we should go to your office and talk in private."

"Whatever it is you have to say, why don't you just tell me here? I have a full schedule the rest of the afternoon."

The playful smile turned evil. "Oh, I think you'll be able to carve out a little time for me, Mr. Van Buren." Slowly, he took off his sunglasses; the eyes were tired and yellow, and his right pupil was lying dead in the corner of the socket, staring at his shoes. Tens of thousands of frozen needles peppered my skin. The heat raced up from my neck, engulfing my ears and forehead. "Is it all coming back to you now, prosecutor?"

"You're Jack Vukovich."

"I can excuse you for not recognizing me at first. I've changed quite a bit since you last saw me, but thirty years in a penitentiary will age a man before his time."

"What is it that I can do for you, Mr. Vukovich?"

"See, we're still having a communications problem. It's not what you can do for me; I'm here to help you."

"I don't see how that's possible."

"Oh, but it is. You see, I'm not blind in both eyes." He pointed to the left. "I see real good out of this one. And I saw some things up on Chestnut Ridge thirty-three years ago that a smart man running for state attorney general might want to discuss."

I choked down the tennis ball that was lodged in my throat; I was struggling not to look panicked, but felt I was failing. "I can't imagine that, but I'll hear you out. Come on back."

Jack Vukovich smiled as he arose and followed me to my office. Along the way he asked, "So, how was the execution? Everything you'd hoped for?" I didn't answer. "Nasty bit of a human being, that Buchanan fella. I can't say I'm a big fan of the death penalty, given my past experience, but he was particularly anti-social, don't you think, torching that young girl the way he did?"

"I'd like not to be disturbed, Margaret," I said without breaking stride.

She looked up and stared hard at Vukovich, who danced his fingers across her desk as he passed and said, "Good afternoon, madam." She just frowned.

As I took off my suit jacket and situated myself behind my desk, Vukovich walked to the corner window and stared out over the downtown. "Ah, the once-majestic city of Akron, the has-been, never-will-be-again rubber capital of the world. Now it looks like Beirut." He shook his head. "I just can't believe the way this country has allowed its industrial complex to crumble."

"Really? I find it interesting that a man such as yourself would be concerned about our country's industrial demise."

"Why, I am, indeed. In spite of the injustices that have been heaped upon me, I am a proud American, Mr. Van Buren." He continued to smile.

"How about we get to the point? What is it that you want, Mr. Vukovich?"

"What say we keep it friendly? Call me Jack. Or, if you like, call me by the nickname you and your buddies used when you didn't think I could hear you. What was that name? Oh yeah, 'One-Eyed Jack.' Just call me that."

"That was a long time ago, Mr. Vukovich. I'd prefer to keep this formal. Again, what do you want?"

He ignored me, walking across the room to a wall adorned by my college and law school diplomas, two state prosecutor of the year plaques, and framed certificates of commendation. "My, my, look at all the little boy from Crystalton has accomplished." He rocked from heel to toe, his hands shoved into his pants pockets. "Why, you've got your own little hall of fame here. It's very impressive." Again, the tone was condescending. He had retained his Ohio Valley twang, though his voice had a faint feminine quality that I didn't recall from my younger years. He walked over to my desk, reached into the glass dish, and plucked out a piece of chocolate candy. As he sat in the chair directly in front of my desk, he skinned the chocolate of its aluminum foil wrapper, popped it in his mouth, and casually dropped the wrapper on the floor.

"You mentioned Chestnut Ridge," I said. "Why would I care about anything that happened up there?" Jack Vukovich rolled his tongue around the inside of his mouth, working it between his lips and gums, skimming the chocolate off his teeth before he swallowed and said, "You wouldn't have brought me back to your office if you didn't know what I was talking about, so how about we dispense with the bullshit, Mr. Van Buren? Here's what happened that morning on Chestnut Ridge. Yeah, I was in the weeds with that Sanchez boy. Guilty as charged. I didn't kill him and you know that. However, I was still in the woods when you and your little Boy Scout troop came into the clearing and ran into that retard. I saw everything." Again he pointed to his good eye. "I saw Petey bump the Nash kid with his head. I saw the Nash kid push him, and I saw Petey come up with the stick. Then I watched as Adrian Nash took that rock and crushed the retarded kid's skull. That poor bastard was dead before he hit the ground."

For a long moment I sat in silence. My mind raced back through the decades to that morning on the hill. Bits and pieces flashed through my mind—the fog, the burn in my thighs as we climbed the steep path, Pepper's incessant chatter, Adrian finding the maul and washing it off in the high-running Little Seneca Creek, the hunger pangs before we made the clearing, the chilling sight of Petey in the bright sunshine, the awful instant that stone hit bone. The memories, however, did not end there. I distinctly recalled the sound of an animal crashing through the brush after Petey dropped. At least I always assumed it to have been an animal. I felt light in the head, woozy, a combination of panic and nervous energy. It felt like the aftermath of an Adrian Nash fastball to the temple, a pain so intense that your mouth fills with salty bile and your guts erupt in fire while you choke back the urge to vomit. Moisture soaked my armpits and the heat of a tropic sun pounded on the back of my neck. Still, I was careful not to give any verbal confirmation of the veracity of his comments because of the possibility, though remote, that he was wired. "That's a very interesting tale, Mr. Vukovich, especially when you consider the fact that you pleaded guilty to that murder."

For the first time, the smug smile disappeared from his lips. "You'd be surprised what a man will confess to when someone is threatening him with the electric chair and he's been stupid enough to leave physical evidence at the scene of a murder. By the way . . ." He pointed to a spot an inch above his right eye. "That Nash boy hit him right here."

"That's something you could have learned from detectives or an autopsy report."

"You're right. I could have. But I didn't. I know it because I saw it happen."

"If you saw it happen, why didn't you tell the sheriff?"

"Maybe I did. Maybe they didn't want to keep young mister Nash from earning a football scholarship. Or, maybe I didn't want to drag my nephew into the mess."

"It doesn't seem like you're having any problems with that right now."

"Three decades in prison will change your perspective on things. My heart's not as soft as it used to be."

"I'll ask you this one more time, Mr. Vukovich, then I want you to get the hell out of here. What is it that you want?"

"Well, I would hate to see ill come to a small-town boy, someone with such great potential as you, Mr. Van Buren, but I'm afraid I'm being pushed into a corner where I might be forced to reveal to the world what really happened that day up on Chestnut Ridge."

"I see. So, this is a shakedown."

He recoiled and said, "Oh," pressing his hands to his chest like a cowboy pierced by an arrow in an old western. "'Shakedown' is such an ugly word. No, no, no. That's not it at all. I'm just here asking for a little . . ." He paused, looking upward as though in deep contemplation, " . . . consideration."

"What kind of consideration?"

"I'm having an issue with the police department in Portage Township."

"What kind of issue?"

He brought his fingertips together just below his chin. "Let's just say it's a little misunderstanding, some accusations that are going around. Totally untrue, you understand?"

"I see. These accusations, they wouldn't have anything to do with you messing around with some little boy, would they?" The question hung in the air for several silent, tense moments. I sensed his discomfort and added to it. "Is he mentally retarded, too, Jack?"

The salvo hit home. His nostrils flared and the jaw clenched under the flaccid skin, and I thought for a moment he was going to come over the desk at me. It took a moment for him to regain his composure. The forced smile slowly returned to the lips of Jack Vukovich as he pushed himself upright with his elbows. "Here's the deal, Mr. Van Buren. You make this go away and I'll go away. I'll leave the county and never be a problem to you again. We'll all go on with our lives."

"What about the boy, the victim of this alleged misunderstanding? Will he just go on with his life, too?"

"I don't know how much clearer I can make this. There's nothing to it. This is just the imagination of an overzealous cop, the kind of guy who gives law enforcement a bad name, if you know what I mean. Just be a good prosecutor and make it go away. Do that, and you and me are good."

"And if I don't?"

"If you don't, then my memory is going to get a whole lot better. I'll give the information to every newspaper in the state and your opponent. I'll tell them everything I know."

"Do you really think that will hurt me? No one will believe an ex-con."

"Ordinarily, that might be true, but I've already gone to the trouble of taking a polygraph test." He reached into his jacket and produced photocopies of several pages of polygraph results and dropped them on my desk. "I took the liberty of making you a copy, along with the list of pertinent questions that I was asked."

I picked up the paper and scanned the questions.

Were you in the woods on Chestnut Ridge near Crystalton, Ohio, on the morning of June 14, 1971?

Did you kill Peter Sanchez?

Can you identify the killer?

Was a prominent Ohio politician among the group when Sanchez was killed?

He pointed with a grunge-stained index finger at the papers in my hand. "I suggest you have those results reviewed by your own polygraph expert,"Vukovich said. "I'm certain you'll find that I was truthful." I felt a burn deep in my stomach, as though I had been kicked in the balls. I dropped the papers back on my desk without comment. I was trying to disguise my fear, but the heat rising in my ears told me I was failing miserably. He continued, "Look, Mr. Van Buren, I'm an old man and a danger to no one."

"Except for the boys you target."

"See, there you go again with all that ugliness."

I massaged my temples with the tips of my fingers and asked, "This is a big state, Jack. How in God's name did you end up in my jurisdiction?"

It was a rhetorical question, but one that caused Jack Vukovich to snort and laugh out loud. "Well, it wasn't by accident. Hell, once I found out you were the prosecutor, I said, 'Jack, my boy, this is your lucky day. You just found yourself a get-out-of-jail-free card.' That's when I moved to Summit County—been living here a couple of years. I figured if I had any problems, you'd be glad to help me out, considering that I did all those years in the joint for a crime you helped to cover up." He went for my jugular, continuing to smile. I wanted to vomit. "I've got to tell you, Mr. Van Buren, it was almost worth all those years in prison to be able to sit here today and see you with that sick, I'm-so-fucked look on your face."

I hit the little button under my desk that summoned Margaret. She walked in and I said, "Please escort Mr. Vukovich to the lobby."

Margaret stared down at the aluminum foil candy wrapper and her face pinched up like someone had stuck a turd under her nose.

"Well, it has certainly been a pleasure reacquainting myself with you, Mr. Van Buren," he said. "Let me give you my cell phone number in case you want to call me." He held a new phone up for my inspection. "Aren't these the damnedest things?" He tapped a few buttons and held the screen a few feet from my face, holding it steady until I took my pen and scrawled the number on an index card that I kept by my phone for just that reason. When he was satisfied that I had recorded his number, he snapped it shut and said, "Yes, sir, it's the damnedest thing. But then, you miss a lot of interesting things when you're in prison for thirty years." As he stood, he reached into the candy dish and grabbed all but two of the candies and put them in his pocket. "I have a bit of a sweet tooth." He started walking toward the door, then turned back and said, "You have one week, Mr. Van Buren."

"We'll see."

Margaret was holding open the door. "One week," he repeated.

When the door closed, I took the glass dish and dumped it and the remaining pieces of candy in the trash.

Tick-tock.

Chapter Eighteen

Jack Vukovich had one hand firmly around my scrotum and was squeezing for all he was worth, the veins in his forearm erupting through sallow skin like mountain roads. And he was enjoying every minute—twisting and laughing. As a prosecuting attorney I was certainly familiar with such treatment, but I had always been the one doing the squeezing and twisting, and I can tell you for a fact that it was absolutely no fun being on the receiving end. I was panicked. My stomach hadn't roiled so much since that June day in 1971.

As I stated, prior to running for attorney general I had no great political aspirations. But with victory so close and virtually assured, I certainly wanted to grasp it. The revelations that Jack Vukovich could unleash would end not only my statewide political career, but my days as a prosecutor, as well. The fact that I had been present at Petey Sanchez's slaying would not hurt me, but my three-plus decades of silence was a career-ender for someone sworn to uphold justice. Acid gurgled in the back of my throat and I was once again fifteen years old and angry with myself, Adrian Nash, and that damn Petey Sanchez.

There was always the possibility that Jack Vukovich was telling the truth and there was nothing to the Portage Township investigation, but I knew I was just kidding myself. If the allegations were baseless, he wouldn't have wasted his trump card. Rather, he simply spread his cards on the table. It was my move.

I hit my intercom and asked Margaret for the phone number of the Portage Township Police Department. She brought in an index card, the number written neatly on the top line, and set it on my desk. I thanked her without looking up, attempting to avert the steely eyes that I knew were boring into the top of my head. She bent over and snatched the foil candy wrapper off the carpet. "What was that all about?" she finally asked, her fist clenched tight around the foil.

I was forced to raise my head. "No big deal."

"What's that mean?"

"Nothing," I said. I didn't offer up any additional information. She puckered up her lips and raised her brows. Trying to lie to Margaret was like trying to lie to my mother. She knew a shit storm had just rolled through my office. As she grabbed the doorknob, she turned, pointed to the lobe of her left ear with an index finger and said, "You know, when you lie, your ears turn the color of tomatoes." She pointed the finger at me like it was a revolver and left without further comment.

★ ★ ★

The chief of police in Portage Township was Jerry "Amana" Adameyer, a profane former Akron city cop who was never without a cheek full of chewing tobacco and rarely without a caustic remark, to which four former Mrs. Jerry Adameyers could attest. He had been nicknamed Amana by his fellow cops, who said he looked like a refrigerator with arms. While he had a room full of trophies and medals for power lifting, he was better known for his vociferous dislike of lawyers, newspaper reporters, child molesters, and blacks. His days on the Akron force became numbered when women and minorities began to fill the fraternity of white males. The times changed and he didn't, or, more likely, simply refused. He longed for the old days when a little street justice could be dispensed to settle problems, and he didn't have to check over his shoulder every time he wanted to utter the words nigger or cunt.

Racism and sexism were two of Adameyer's more endearing qualities. He had a reputation for extracting "elevator confessions," which were obtained by putting a handcuffed suspect into the old freight elevator in the police station, stopping it between floors, and beating a confession out of a suspect. I always assumed there would come a day when I would end up defending Adameyer on a civil rights violation for his cowboy ways, but it never happened. Despite these reprehensible qualities, he also had a reputation as a solid investigator and his investigative files were always neat, complete, and without holes. But he had a cops-versus-the-world mentality, and there were times when I had to remind him that we were on the same team.

He was a sergeant in the homicide squad when it was announced that the first female captain on the Akron police force had been assigned to the detective bureau. The next day he retired after thirty-two years, seven months and four days of service. He worked as a private investigator for eighteen months before he was named chief of the small Portage Township Police Department.

I called him from my office and asked if he knew if one of his officers was conducting a molestation investigation. I should have known better than to ask Jerry Adameyer such a question, and he rightfully skewered me for it.

"You think I don't know what the hell's going on in my own damned department?"

"It's just a question, chief."

"There's me, two sergeants, and eight patrol officers down here. I know every time one of 'em takes a shit. Of course I know about it. What of it?"

"I need to talk to the investigating officer," I said.

"Why?"

"Because I'm the county prosecutor and I want to know what the hell's going on, that's why. I'll be there in about a half hour." I hung up without giving him a chance to ask me more questions. As I walked past Margaret I said, "I'll see you tomorrow."

"Um-humm," she responded, not looking up.

As I walked to my car I replayed the conversation with Jack Vukovich in my head. He had to be lying, I thought. There was no way Vukovich could have been on Chestnut Ridge that morning. If he had actually seen what he had claimed to have seen, why in God's name did he plead guilty? It made no sense. I dismissed the polygraph results. There were polygraph operators out there with morals only slightly higher than prostitutes, and they operated in the same manner. If you had the money, they would tell you anything you wanted to hear. Unfortunately, if he released the documents to the media they would be taken as gospel, and it would blow my campaign out of the water. It was, however, perplexing that he had such details on Petey's killing, and I suspected the ultimate source of the information was a penitent Deak Coultas.

During the drive to Portage Township, Shelly blew up my cell phone. As soon as one call went to voice mail, she would hang up and hit redial. I turned off my phone ten minutes before I got to the police station, having lost track at eighteen the number of times she had called. Somewhere along Interstate 77 between Cleveland and Akron, she was speeding and cussing into her cell phone. My brain was racing with memories of Petey Sanchez dropping in the weeds. I didn't have the energy or the focus to talk to her.

The Portage Township Police Department was headquartered in an historic, red-brick Gothic Revival house with two pointed-arch windows at the corner of Tallmadge Road and Church Street. A bronze plaque adhered to the brick near the front door noted its inclusion on the National Register of Historic Places as it was a stop on the Underground Railroad and once the home of abolitionists Reverend Josiah and Annebelle Clelland. Jerry Adameyer was working in the former home of Akron's most noted abolitionists. I suppressed a smile as I walked through the door.

The front of the building had been sectioned off so that visitors stood in a five-foot by eight-foot rectangle surrounded by bulletproof glass, observation cameras, and a microphone built into a pane that separated the lobby from the receptionist, a humorless-looking woman who was straining the seams of her gray uniform slacks. "Can I help you?" she asked, her voice tinny through the speakers.

The chief stood behind the receptionist. It had been several years since I had seen Adameyer, but he had not changed much. He still carried a thick paunch that looked like it could stop a bullet and wore the same half-inch-long gray crew cut that he had sported since his army days. He was holding a Styrofoam coffee cup into which he was spitting tobacco juice created by the bulbous wad he carried in his cheek. Years of chewing had stretched his jowls and stained brown a tiny crease that ran from one corner of his mouth down around his jawbone. In his familiar baritone, he said, "Let him in."

She tripped the electronic lock and I entered. Adameyer shook my hand, then pointed toward his office with the index finger that was wrapped around his spit cup. Seated at the chief's conference table was one of the most perfectly sculpted human beings I had ever seen. Officer Clarence Davidson appeared to be about six-foot-four, with broad, square shoulders that tapered down to a narrow waist, and biceps that stretched taut the white material of his uniform shirt. He had a square jaw, light brown skin, and looked as though he had just stepped out of a Marine Corps recruiting poster. I had not expected to find a black man in Adameyer's department and I was afraid my face may have revealed the surprise.

Adameyer did the introductions, identifying me as "Mr. Van Buren, our esteemed prosecuting attorney."

"Mr. Van Buren is interested in your investigation of Jack Vukovich," Adameyer said.

Davidson nodded and one eyebrow crinkled like a caterpillar in mid-stride. "How did you find out about the investigation?" he asked.

"Well, let's just say it's not my first rodeo with Mr. Vukovich," I said. "He saw fit to pay me a visit this afternoon."

"Let me guess," Adameyer interjected. "It's all just a goddamned misunderstanding?"

I grinned and nodded. "Yeah, pretty much." I turned back to Davidson. "What can you tell me?"

Davidson opened a manila folder that had been pressed beneath his long, slender fingers. He handed me a photocopy of the initial police report, the transcribed notes of his subsequent interviews, background information on Vukovich from the Ohio Department of Rehabilitation and Corrections and the Ohio Parole Authority, and an envelope of photographs. Like several of the smaller departments in my jurisdiction, Portage Township had no full-time detectives. The officers who took the initial report were responsible for conducting the investigations. This method produced myriad results, most of them extremely bad. At first glance, however, Davidson's report looked especially thorough, and I assumed it was at least partially due to Adameyer's tutelage.

Davidson began, "The victim is Oscar Francis Gentry—male, white, fifteen. He has Down syndrome, an extreme case, and some physical disabilities. I was alerted to the possible sexual assault by a social worker at Our Lady of Mercy Hospital. A therapist who regularly visits the boy to give him physical therapy noticed he had bled through his pants in the rectal area and called the emergency squad. An examination revealed gross tears of the rectum." He pointed to the envelope in my packet of information. "The social worker took those photographs at the emergency room."

My gut roiled as I flipped through the photographs of the boy's torn rectum, recalling a day long past when Deak Coultas said he never wanted his uncle to hurt another kid. "Parents?" I asked.

"Single mom—Delores Gentry."

"How'd you get on to Vukovich?"

"According to the mother, Mr. Vukovich showed up at the door one day claiming to be from a church-related group that provides respite care to parents with mentally retarded or developmentally disabled children."

"Did she ask for any identification?" I asked.

"What the fuck do you think?" Adameyer interjected. "Of course not. She's a dipshit."

"No," Davidson said, ignoring his superior's outburst. "She said he was dressed neatly and had a clipboard. He conducted an interview with the mother and returned a few days later and said she qualified for the services. She said Vukovich began showing up at the house two or three times a week for up to six hours at a time while she went out. This occurred over a three-month period."

"And she never asked any questions?" Davidson shook his head. "What about the blood in his pants?"

Davidson flipped through the report until he found a passage. He read: "I asked Mrs. Gentry if she had seen the blood in her son's pants prior to him being taken to the emergency room. She responded, 'Oh, yeah, there's been blood in his diaper for a month or so. Oscar has a lot of health issues and I didn't think it was a big deal.'"

I had been a prosecutor for more than twenty years and privy to some astoundingly stupid remarks, but those words stunned me. "How does a mom think blood in her fifteen-year-old's diaper is no big deal?"

"Apparently, Mr. Vukovich began making social calls on Mrs. Gentry. He started coming over to the house from time to time, bringing donuts and coffee, or hamburgers or groceries. Supposedly he took Mrs. Gentry shopping for clothes. She believes Mr. Vukovich is in love with her and in no way believes he is capable of such an assault."

"Did you tell her that Vukovich spent thirty years in prison after pleading guilty to sexually assaulting a retarded boy about the same age as her son?"

"Jumpin' Mother of Christ," Adameyer moaned. "He killed the kid."

No he didn't, I thought.

"The chief's early assessment of Mrs. Gentry was not off target," Davidson said. "She's . . . " his voice trailed off.

"Not the sharpest knife in the drawer?" I asked.

Davidson nodded. "That would be a kind way of phrasing it. I would also say she's a bit delusional."

"She's a fuckin' loon," Adameyer said.

"Where's the boy?" I asked.

"Foster care. We removed him from the house; children services has temporary custody."

"Did they do a swab at the hospital?"

"Yeah. We sent it to Columbus to the state crime lab. They found what they believe are trace amounts of blood that don't match the boy's. They also found another matter that may or may not be semen."

"Not much to go on."

"No. They're sending the samples to an FBI lab in Virginia. Supposedly, they have a process that enables them to separate mixed fluids and analyze them to a greater degree. They said they've had good luck with this process in the past. We'll see."

"Is the boy able to testify?"

Davidson closed the manila folder. "No. He's not verbal and has only very basic communication skills, much like an infant, cries and grunts. He also has some physical challenges—cerebral palsy, I believe—and spends most of his days in bed or a wheelchair."

"Did you talk to Vukovich?"

"Not much. He wouldn't talk other than to deny any involvement and say he was insulted at my accusations. Then he told me to call his lawyer."

"Is he working anywhere?"

"Not that I can tell."

"How's he living? Where's he getting his money?"

He shrugged. "I don't know. He's living in a house out in the Thimble Lakes area." He looked down at the report. "Twelve eighty-eight Little Thimble Lake Drive."

I removed a leather-bound pad from my jacket pocket and scribbled down the address. I stood to shake Davidson's hand. "I appreciate your time," I said.

"What do you think?"

"Based on what you've told me so far, it's not looking very good. There's no physical evidence, the victim can't testify, and the mother won't testify. You know he did it and I know he did it, but that doesn't mean we're going to get a jury to convict."

Davidson frowned, creating neatly spaced ridges between his brows and hairline. "So, you know this guy, huh?"

"I'm familiar with him, yes."

"How's someone like this get back out on the street?"

I had no answer. "Keep me posted on any progress in your investigation."

After Officer Davidson had disappeared through the glassed lobby, I said, "Good officer."

"Damned good," Adameyer said. His left eye squeezed shut, a sharpshooter honing in on his target, and he slowly tapped the eraser of a pencil on the conference table. After a moment's silence, he asked, "What's going on here, sport?"

"What do you mean?"

"Come on, don't blow smoke up my ass. You didn't drive all the way down here just because you were curious. You've got a reason. I've worked with you enough to know this is ordinarily the kind of case you'd be jumping all over. Hell, you're running for state attorney general. This would be great publicity. Something's eating at you about this, something personal, I bet."

Jerry Adameyer was a good cop, a good observer. He had watched me during the interview and I wondered what my demeanor had revealed. I shook my head, but again felt the burn creeping up my neck. "No, I just have a lot on my mind."

"Uh-huh. I don't think I'm buying that one, sport." He stared at me for a moment. "I'll figure it out."

I shook my head. "No, you won't."

★ ★ ★

When rubber was king of Akron, the Thimble Lakes were the playground for wealthy executives. Situated in the southeastern corner of Summit County, the lakes were actually flooded rock quarries formerly owned by the Portage Sand & Gravel Works. When the quarries were mined out in 1952, a developer bought the property—fifty-two acres—for three thousand dollars. He planted pine trees around the perimeter of the grounds, renamed it Thimble Lakes, and began selling what he generously advertised as "exclusive lakefront property." The wealthy began building weekend homes on Thimble Lakes and until the decline of Akron's rubber industry in the early seventies it was considered a sign of considerable prestige to have "a place at Thimble Lakes." Most of the homes were now occupied year-round and it had recently enjoyed a revitalization as people bought up two or three adjoining lots, tore down the existing houses, and built larger, modern homes. This created an awkward lakefront array of mammoth, glass-encased homes next to modest cabins. Although Thimble Lakes was no longer considered one of Akron's most elite addresses, it was still a very nice area.

Little Thimble Lake Drive was a two-mile asphalt road that snaked between the old quarries. I drove slowly along until I found the numbers 1288 on a mailbox next to a gravel driveway that disappeared into a grove of pine and ash trees. Through the stand of tree trunks I could see a light burning on the screened-in front porch of a cedar-sided ranch home. Beyond the house a wooden dock extended into Little Thimble Lake. I drove down the road, turned the car around in a cul-de-sac, and crept back along the blacktop, searching for a better vantage point to view the house. On my third pass I spotted a home under construction on a bluff above Vukovich's place. It seemed the ideal spot as it was nearly hidden by a thicket of pines and there was no sign of construction workers or the owner. I pulled into the empty garage, then backed out and pointed the Pacifica toward the driveway, giving me a clear view of the ranch house.

The shades were drawn, but I could detect a faint light burning in a back room. I don't know what I hoped to accomplish by watching the house, but I felt compelled to see where Jack Vukovich was living. The visit created more questions than answers. Did he own the house? I made a mental note to check property records at the county auditor's office in the morning. Where would Jack Vukovich get that kind of money? Even if it wasn't his, where was he getting the money for rent? A three-bedroom ranch in Thimble Lakes was not cheap. He had to be paying at least twelve hundred a month in rent. Parked in a carport was a gleaming, late-model black Saab. More questions.

In the moments just after dusk when darkness began to envelop the Thimble Lakes and the house behind me cast a dark shadow across my windshield, the dome light on the Pacifica flickered with the metallic click of the passenger door handle. I about pissed myself.

"Well, good evening, Mr. Van Buren," said Jack Vukovich, opening the door and sliding uninvited into the passenger seat. "What a nice surprise. What brings you to the Thimble Lakes? Did you come to pay me a visit, or are you just doing a little spying?" He let the question hang for a moment while he surveyed the inside of the SUV, massaging the dashboard and whistling. "Nice ride, Mr. Prosecutor. Did the taxpayers buy this for you?" He played with the electric window, rolling it up and down several times.

While he played with the window and the automatic door locks, I took a few deep breaths and tried to slow my racing heart. "You've managed to achieve a new low, Mr. Vukovich—sexually assaulting a mentally retarded and developmentally disabled boy who can't talk or fight off your attacks."

He rolled his good eye toward me, but kept facing forward. "It would seem to me, Mr. Van Buren, that you are in no position to be talking to me about new lows, considering your continued silence for the entire duration of my incarceration."

"I would argue that you spent thirty years in prison for the crime you *did* commit. Now, get out of my car."

He made no move to leave. "Did you know that the house I'm renting used to be owned by a member of the Firestone family? It has cherry floors and an oversized fireplace made of limestone that was quarried right here in the Thimble Lakes. Don't you find that fascinating?"

"Get out of my car, Jack."

When he turned toward me the corners of his lips turned down, the tension in his face puckering the skin around his nose. "So, what did that spook tell you?"

"Officer Davidson told me nothing that I didn't already know—that you're a sick animal who preys on the defenseless."

He swallowed, his Adam's apple bulging between his shirt collar as he struggled to control his anger. "I do believe I am losing my patience with you, Mr. Van Buren, so it might be best if I bid you adieu." He got out of the car, slammed the door, and leaned down into the open window. "You have a good day, Mr. Prosecutor. And don't forget, you've got one week."

Chapter Nineteen

As a young boy, I surrounded myself with the comfort of the familiar. My bedroom was a refuge where I kept my prized possessions close to me—my record albums, trophies, school awards, arrowheads, favorite books, Civil War figurines. Sitting at a diagonal in the corner of my room was an old oak desk that my mother had scavenged from the trash heap at the post office. It was a beast and had taken three of her male co-workers and me to maneuver it up the stairs and into my bedroom. It was scuffed with age and had a leprous coating of yellowed shellac, chipped and thinned by years of neglect. From my desk, I could look out one bedroom window to the northwest and see the water tower and the ridge of the hills that rimmed Crystalton. The window to the east revealed the train tracks as they turned toward the Redhead Oil Company, the Ohio River, and the banks of the West Virginia shore where the cobblestone wharf and old ferry landing in Wellsburg materialized from the brown water and climbed up to Eighth Street. From the comfort of my room, behind the fortress of a desk, I surrounded myself with my favorite possessions and created views that were familiar and home.

Subsequently, I spent most of my time at home in my room. On several occasions my mother asked, "Why are you always up in your room living like a hermit?" I wasn't a hermit, but I liked having a place where I could retreat and be alone with my thoughts. This extended into my adult life.

Shortly after I was elected Summit County prosecutor I purchased a Queen Anne–style home in the Fairlawn Heights section of Akron. A young couple had bought the home in disrepair with the romanticized notion of rehabilitating it while they lived there. About the time they ran out of money for the project, they apparently ran out of patience for each other. She filed for divorce and left with everything that wasn't nailed down. When I went to look at the house, the ex-husband was months behind on the mortgage and living there with his clothes, a television, a blow-up mattress, and a three-legged cocker spaniel. I offered what he owed the bank and he snatched it up, glad to be out from under the mortgage and the bad memories.

Before I moved in I hired a contractor to finish the renovation, which included converting the third-floor attic space into my den. The showpiece of the room was the old post office desk, which I had painstakingly stripped and restored. The room occupied the entire top floor and my home office occupied one end of the room. A ceiling fan with three fluted lights hung in the middle of the room, directly over a pool table. An oxblood leather couch and two overstuffed chairs surrounded a wood coffee table with blue and white sodalite inlays in a living area just beyond the top of the stairs. When home, this is where I spent most of my waking hours.

The walls were adorned with black-and-white family photographs, plaques and photographs from my high school and college days, and framed prints of Forbes Field, the long-ago demolished home of the Pittsburgh Pirates. In the corner of my office was a trophy case and an old steamer trunk that I had rescued from the basement of my mom's house. Inside the trunk was a lifetime of memories from my youth, including my Civil War figurines, my college varsity jacket, scrapbooks, and a half-dozen cigar boxes of arrowheads, which I continued to vow that I was going to organize someday. While I spent virtually no time going through old scrapbooks and reminiscing, I still found comfort in surrounding myself with the familiar.

I once dated a psychologist who said my "man cave," as she called it, was my subconscious compensating for a missing facet in my life. She speculated that I was seeking security for the lack of a father figure. "Don't be alarmed," she said (I wasn't). "This is a very common malady in men who feel compelled to spend exorbitant amounts of money on fancy garages with sports cars or convert basements into shrines to particular sports teams. Yours is simply a shrine to yourself."

I told her she was full of shit and never saw her again. I'm not saying there wasn't some degree of truth in what she said, but I didn't want to hear it.

At ten fifteen that night I was slouched in one of the overstuffed chairs on the third floor, the floor lamp behind me casting a pale light over my shoulder, sipping from a tall glass of Jack Daniel's, pondering Jack Vukovich and my next move. The whiskey had been in a kitchen cabinet for four years, a Christmas gift from one of my assistant prosecutors. I rarely drank hard liquor, and I had been tempted to regift the bottle a couple of times, but this particular evening called for something a little stronger than merlot. I was acclimating well to the kick. The liquid burned all the way down, leaving my eyes moist and a tingling numbness in my lips.

Spread on the coffee table was the investigative report Officer Davidson had given me. There was little in the report that he hadn't told me. The background from the Ohio Department of Rehabilitation and Corrections and the Ohio Parole Authority, however, brought me up to date on Jack Vukovich.

Jackson Carter Vukovich; Male/Caucasian; DOB: 03-12-1932; Place of birth: Wheeling, W.Va.; Crime/Conviction: Second-degree murder, rape, and gross sexual imposition with a minor; Date, Place of Crime: On or about June 15, 1971, near Crystalton, Ohio; County: Jefferson; Victim: Peter Eugene Sanchez; Age: 17; Sentencing Date: Sept. 13, 1971; Admitted to Institution: Sept. 15, 1971; Release Date: Oct. 24, 2001; Time served: 30 years and 39 days. Ohio Parole Authority Case No. 71-CR-0201-8; Case Manager: Rita Ann Dayton. Summary: Mr. Vukovich served more than 30 years for the murder and rape of a 17-year-old boy. Most of that time was served at the North Central Correctional Institution in Marion, Ohio. He was incarcerated at the Montgomery Education and Pre-Release Center at the time of his release. Mr. Vukovich's incarceration was without major infractions. He is currently residing in Portage Township, Summit County, Ohio.

Earlier that evening I had given an uninspired talk at a meeting of the Medina County Republican Party, having arrived fifteen minutes late after my encounter with Jack Vukovich. I spoke in detail of the execution of Ricky Blood and of my goals for the attorney general's office, and feigned interest in the few questions from the floor. All I wanted was for it to be over. I hadn't shaved since four thirty that morning and hoped to God I didn't look as tired as I felt, though I suspected I did.

Ordinarily, I wasn't one to try to mask my problems with alcohol, but I began thinking about the bottle of Jack Daniel's long before I hit Fairlawn Heights. As the effects of the alcohol took hold, I began to fantasize about killing Jack Vukovich. I thought about Elmer Glick and something he had said to me several years earlier. Glick was a drug dealer who early in my career was charged with first-degree murder for allegedly bashing in a rival's brains with a shock absorber. Glick was not as crazy as Ricky Blood, but he was just as mean. While I believed Glick was guilty of the murder, there was not a shred of physical evidence implicating him and the only witness was a jailhouse snitch whose testimony was shaky at best. I dropped the charges before it went to the grand jury. In a meeting with Glick and his lawyer, I said, "Personally, I think you killed him, Elmer, but I've got nothing to give a jury."

He grinned and said, "I certainly do appreciate that, Mr. Van Buren. You're a stand-up guy, and I want you to know that if I can ever do anything for you . . ." He squinted with his right eye, ". . . anything at all, you just let me know."

I daydreamed of calling in the marker and having Glick take out Jack Vukovich. I wasn't seriously considering it, but it was fun to fantasize. Like Ricky Blood, the loss of Jack Vukovich would only benefit society. However, I had been around the criminal justice system long enough to know that such a request, no matter the precautions taken, would simply set into motion a series of events that would culminate in me going to prison.

I took a sip of my whiskey and allowed one of the ice cubes to slide into my mouth. The letter was tucked into an old scrapbook in the wooden steamer trunk in which my great grandfather Van Buren had brought over his every possession when he'd immigrated from Holland. I had only read it once in my life. It had been like a knife to the heart, and I hoped that by hiding it the memory would dull, which it had not. Petey Sanchez was never far from my memory. I didn't think about him every day, and I imagine there were times when weeks passed without my memory venturing into that space, but he was always there, floating on the periphery of my psyche, circling my brain as he had circled the streets of Crystalton on his bicycle.

Earl Sanchez died during my first year of law school. His obituary arrived in a packet of newspaper clippings that my mother sent me about once a month in an effort to keep me apprised of local happenings. The next time I talked to Mom, I asked what had caused Earl's death. Mom said, simply, "He died of being Earl Sanchez."

Lila died in the fall of 1999. I don't remember the date and Mom had moved to Florida, so I didn't get the obituary. However, I received the letter the previous June. I had been forewarned of its arrival by my mother, who said Lila had called to get my address.

"What's she want?" I asked.

"She said she wanted to send you a letter. I didn't pry."

It arrived on the last Saturday of the month. I was working in the yard and wiped the sweat and dirt off my hands on my shorts before taking the stack of envelopes from the mail carrier. It was mostly junk mail, a few bills, and a small envelope with shaky script. I read it, then tucked it into the scrapbook.

The lid to the trunk squeaked as I raised it and allowed the arched top to rest against the wall. I didn't need to search for the envelope. It was pressed between yellowed clippings of the long-past heroics of the Crystalton Royals. The air whooshed out of the seat cushion as I flopped back down in the chair. It was written on a sheet of yellow legal paper and folded several times to fit into the envelope. I slipped it out and unfolded the sharp creases, exposing it to my bloodshot eyes. Like the script on the envelope, the letter was written in the weak and jittery hand of a dying woman.

Dear Mr. Van Buren:

It has been many years since I last saw you and you have no cause to remember me, but my name is Lila Sanchez. I am a friend of your dear mother and the mother of Peter Sanchez, who was murdered by Jack Vukovich in the summer of 1971.

As you remember, Mr. Vukovich was sent to prison for up to 38 years for killing my boy. Twice in the past eight years I have gone to Columbus to testify in front of the parole board about how that animal sexually molested Petey before he murdered him. I asked them both times to please not let Mr. Vukovich out of prison and they didn't.

That is why I am writing you this letter. My husband Earl died in 1979. I was recently diagnosed with lung cancer and the doctors say I need to get my affairs in order as it is unlikely that I will live to see Christmas. I am very concerned that when I'm gone no one will fight to keep him in prison. My children think I should just let go and not waste my last days worrying about trash like Jack Vukovich. But, I cannot let go, not when he took my boy.

Your mother calls me from Florida every few weeks to see how I am doing. She talks about you often and is quite proud of you and your work as a prosecutor. She says you are a respected and honorable man. I have been receiving end-of-life counseling from my minister and he also said it would be a good idea to ask for your help.

For those reasons, I am asking you to please, please not forget my son.

Mr. Vukovich will come up for parole in two years. I am asking you as a man of authority to do all you can to make sure he never gets out of jail. He is evil and vile, and if he gets out he will hurt someone else. Please tell the parole board to keep him in prison.

I hope that I can count on you to do what is right and keep this murderer of my son in prison for the full extent of his sentence.

I pray that you will be my voice when I am gone.

May God bless you and keep you.

Lila Sanchez

The following Monday morning I typed a letter to Lila. I did it myself, rather than dictate it for Margaret to transcribe, in part because I knew I would never follow through on my promise. I am not particularly proud of the fact that I told Lila I would do what I could to keep Jack Vukovich in prison, all the while knowing it was a lie. I justified it by telling myself that I was simply trying to ease the mind of a woman who had only a few months to live. That doesn't make it right, but what could I do? Jack Vukovich was sentenced to prison for a murder he did not commit. I couldn't in good conscience testify to keep him in prison. Therefore, I elected not to attend Jack Vukovich's parole hearing in August of 2001.

I heard the deadbolt in the front door retract and click. It echoed through the foyer and made its way throughout the house. It was Shelly. I listened as her footfalls—the clack of each angry heel slapping the hardwood—crossed the foyer and started up the stairs to the second floor. I was familiar with the cadence of her footfalls; she was pissed and on a mission. She marched down the hall to the steps leading to the third floor. The single bulb in the stairwell cast a stark light on the wall at the top of the steps and the bobbing shadow of her head preceded her into the room. "Well, it's my most beautiful lover come to see me," I said.

She did not respond in kind. "Is your cell phone broken?"

"I don't think so."

Her jaw tightened. "I've tried to call you at least twenty times today."

"Don't be modest. It was at least forty times." I sipped at my booze and set the glass on the coffee table. "It's been a busy day, love. I was witness to the state of Ohio ridding itself of one of God's mistakes, had to give a speech in Medina County, and had some other chaos to attend to."

"You couldn't find two minutes to pick up the phone?"

I shrugged. "When was the last time we had a conversation that lasted only two minutes?"

She ignored my remark, walked into the room, and picked up the drink, held the glass under her nose and took a light sniff. "Whiskey? What's the occasion?"

"It seemed to be the only thing that would answer the call." It was nearly ten thirty. "Where've you been?"

She sat down on the couch and began speaking without making eye contact. "I had dinner with Dirk Baker and his wife."

"Who's Dirk Baker?"

She waved it off. "A minor player. He's running for Cuyahoga County commissioner and wanted to pick my brain on some campaign strategies." Shelly's ash-blonde hair was done in soft curls that hung to her shoulders, and she was wearing a cornflower blue cocktail dress that revealed a hint of cleavage. A black satin clutch purse was in her right hand. In her closet were dozens of power suits and matching purses; she certainly wasn't dressed for a business meeting. She smelled of expensive perfume and lies, but I didn't press it.

Shelly Dennison was thirty-seven and the complete package—stunningly beautiful, smart, and witty. Our first meeting had been at the Tangier Restaurant in Akron. I hired her as my campaign manager before dessert and was sleeping with her inside of a week. I could not get her out of my mind. Despite my unbridled attraction to her, I realized early in the relationship that it was doomed. I was simply occupying a spot on her dance ticket until someone better, more powerful, came along. She had been dating a state representative from Ashtabula County when I came along. He lost her to me, and I would lose her to someone else, and they would in turn lose her to someone else. She was a political animal and I lacked the political drive to sate her lust for power.

As she sat on the couch, her legs crossed at the knees, brushing hair from her face with her fingers, my loins jumped. I wanted her and for a moment contemplated playing to her weakness. Since the talk of politics and power seemed to be the only aphrodisiac that worked on her, I toyed with the idea of telling her that after one term as state attorney general I planned to run for the U.S. House of Representatives and then chart a course to the presidency. She would have been immediately moist and wouldn't have been able to shimmy out of her panties fast enough. In seconds she would have straddled me, arched her back, and moaned, "Oh yes, oh yes, fuck me, Mr. President, fuck me." That's all it would have taken, but I didn't have the energy for the post-coital strategy session that would have lasted until dawn as she planned my ascendancy to the Oval Office.

"So, what was all the chaos about?" she finally asked.

Because I knew the clock was running on our relationship, I had always been somewhat cautious about what I told Shelly. I didn't want her falling for a political rival and suddenly in possession of my secrets and weaknesses. I took another sip of my Jack, then cradled the glass between my hands in my lap. "A guy who used to live in Crystalton came into my office today. He got out of prison a couple years ago after doing thirty years for the rape and murder of a seventeen-year-old mentally retarded kid named Petey Sanchez. He committed the rape, but he didn't commit the murder."

"That's what he says."

"Yes, but I have a strong reason to believe that it's true."

"How do you know?"

I took a deep breath and exhaled slowly before continuing, carefully choosing my words. "Crystalton is a small town. There was some suspicion that he didn't commit the murder. He had a lot of time to sit in prison and think, and he's come up with a conspiracy theory. He thinks one of my friends killed the boy and he suspects I knew the truth."

"How old were you?"

I squinted, as though trying to retrace the years. "Probably fifteen, or so."

"Even if you did, you were a juvenile. You can't be held responsible for that. You would have had to have been an eyewitness to the murder to have any culpability."

Again, the heat started up my neck. "Maybe so, but it doesn't do my political future any good if he takes this to the newspaper."

"Why have you never told me this?"

"It wasn't important until now."

"Is he blackmailing you? What does he want? Money?"

I shook my head. "No, not money. He's back to his old tricks, molesting a fifteen-year-old severely disabled kid in Portage Township. He's under investigation and the cop who's after his ass is top-notch, and Vukovich is starting to sweat. Essentially, he says he'll slip into the night and forget about his conspiracy theory if I make this problem go away."

"How strong is the case against him?"

"It's virtually nonexistent. No physical evidence, no witnesses."

She frowned, puzzled by my inability to grasp the obvious answer. "Then do it, for God's sake. If the state of Ohio found out he had served time for a crime he didn't commit, they'd give him a cash settlement. Instead, you cut him a break on this investigation. Everything's even. Justice served."

"Justice? From whose perspective? I'm not sure that fifteen-year-old boy down in Portage County would see it that way."

"Hutchinson, this is a no-brainer. Let him go. What are your options? If he takes this cock-and-bull story to the papers, we'll be swimming upstream for the next two months. That certainly doesn't serve the best interests of the people of the state of Ohio when you're not elected attorney general. Cut this guy loose. He'll leave town and be away from the kid."

"He'll go somewhere else and molest some other kid."

"Not your problem." Shelly could only look at it from a political perspective. To her, fifteen-year-old Oscar Gentry was expendable, collateral damage in our march to Columbus. "Look, you're the victim. Protect yourself. Give him what he wants and make him go away. If this screwball goes public we could see our eighteen-point lead disappear overnight."

I pondered countering her argument with one of my own about truth and justice, but then thought of the hypocrisy, given my three decades of silence in Petey's death, and the fact that I had just given Shelly a distorted version of history. I had been hoping for some calming, reassuring words from her. Instead, my guts were in more of an uproar, part from the stress, part from the booze.

She arose and walked over to where the overstuffed chair was consuming my tired and limp body. "Are you staying tonight?" I asked.

"No, not tonight." She kissed me on the top of the forehead. "I've got an early day tomorrow." She ran the back of a hand down the side of my face. "Don't let this upset you; it's going to be fine. Just get the mess cleared up in Portage Township. If there's scant evidence against him, you have no reason to seek an indictment. Case closed."

I nodded. "You're probably right."

In the haze before sleep, I listened as she traversed the stairs and let herself out. Case closed. Forget about Oscar Gentry. Just go to sleep and it will all be better in the morning. Hutchinson Van Buren. Prosecutor. The future attorney general of the great state of Ohio. The Button Man. Lila Sanchez's last hope for justice. Keeper of a thirty-year secret.

I was such a fraud.

Chapter Twenty

The sun was filling the third-floor room when I awoke the next morning at six fifteen, still slumped in the chair. My mouth was parched and my clothes were damp with sweat. My back and neck ached, but they were in the minor leagues of pain compared to my head, which throbbed so badly my right eye had a heartbeat. I covered my eyes with my right hand and used my left as a guide, feeling my way to the second-floor bathroom. Fighting off the urge to vomit, I turned the shower on as hot as I could stand it. Wedging my back into a corner of the tile shower, I slowly lowered myself to the floor and allowed the water to pound on my head. In my fist I clutched three aspirin that I washed down with a stream of hot shower water.

It was nearly seven when I made my way to the kitchen, wrapped in a red and yellow striped terrycloth bathrobe, my hair wet and uncombed, and began scavenging for something to eat. Most days I would have been at the office for an hour already. I called Margaret to check in. "I'm running a little late," I said.

"I'd say. Are you okay? You don't sound so good."

"I don't feel so good."

"Maybe you shouldn't come in at all."

"I'll take that under advisement." I snapped closed my cell phone and dropped it into my robe pocket.

I made some coffee and found a half a cantaloupe in the refrigerator. The aspirin was beginning to work its magic. I took a few hard swigs of orange juice from the half-gallon jug before pouring myself a glass and walking to the table on the patio, a semicircle of stamped concrete that was shielded from the neighbors by rows of emerald green arborvitaes that lined the border of my lot. I picked a few soggy leaves off the table and dug into the cantaloupe. There was a reason, I recalled at that moment, why I didn't normally drink hard liquor, and my quivering hands were a present reminder. My stomach emitted a cacophony of noises as it wrapped around the cantaloupe. The thumping in my eye had started to ebb, but not much. Somewhere on the front lawn was the *Beacon Journal*, which I enjoyed reading on the rare mornings that it arrived before I left for work, but I didn't have the energy to get up from the chair.

"Howdy-doo, Mr. Prosecutor," came a voice from behind me. It startled me and I jumped, spilling coffee on the table. I turned to find a smiling Jack Vukovich standing at the wooden gate under a rose-filled trellis, the entry to my backyard. "Beautiful place you got here."

"What are you doing here, Jack?"

He reached over the fence and flipped open the hook-and-eye latch, entering without invitation. "Oh, just socializing a bit." He held up my *Beacon Journal*. "Brought you your paper."

"This is my house, Jack, and it's off limits to you."

"That's not very hospitable," he said, dropping the paper on the table and sliding out a chair across from me. He sat down, not the least bit concerned about my admonition. His sunglasses were resting on the top of his head and, like I did back in junior high, I found it difficult not to stare at his sunken right eye. He grinned and said, "Besides, I thought since you were kind enough to pay me a visit last night, I ought to return the favor." He scanned the yard as the morning sun grew stronger. Squinting, he pulled his shades back down on his nose, for which I was grateful. "Yes, this is a beautiful place you have here." He put his fingertips on the table and leaned in toward me. "And speaking of beautiful, that blonde who was visiting you last night is certainly a looker, isn't she?"

Jack Vukovich continued to lean in, grinning, waiting for me to flinch. I stared at my reflection in his sunglasses and took a sip of my coffee, fighting the urge to rake the mug across his skull. "You're starting to concern me, Jack."

He feigned shock. "Why is that? I'm just being neighborly is all, and you haven't even offered me a cup of coffee."

"And I'm not going to. What do you want?" I pulled my cell phone out of my bathrobe pocket. "And make it fast, because I'm losing patience with you and I'm about two seconds away from calling the police."

He shrugged. "Go ahead and call them. When they go to fill out the police report, I'll simply tell them that I wanted to discuss your role in the cover-up of the Petey Sanchez murder. We'll see what happens after we put that in a police report, which I'm sure I don't need to remind you, Mr. Prosecutor, is public record." He crossed his arms and leaned back in the chair, looking down at the cell phone with that annoying smirk. "So, where are we on our present issue? Are things all cleared up?"

"You know I haven't had time to make that decision. We're waiting for some lab results to come back." I tried to harness my angst with some false bravado of my own. "The preliminary results indicate you've been a bad boy, Jack."

"I don't think you should be worrying about lab tests, or my behavior, Mr. Van Buren. I think you should be finding a way to make this all go away. You can sit there and pretend you're not concerned, but I know better. I was in prison for a long time. I know what fear looks like on a man, and I know what it smells like. And right now, it's all over you, son. You reek of fear."

"Is that why you stopped by, Jack? Did you just want to jerk my chain?"

He stood and stretched. "Yes, yes, it's a beautiful place you have here," he repeated, ignoring my question. "Since you're not in a hospitable mood, I guess I'll be tootlin' down the road. I've got a busy calendar today. You have a good day, Mr. Van Buren. I'll be in touch."

I said nothing as he went through the gate, leaving it open behind him. I pushed myself out of my chair and walked to relatch the gate. From the shade of the trellis, I watched Vukovich cross the westbound lane in front of my neighbor's house, tromp through the marigolds that the Junior Women's Club had planted in the island dividing Middlesex Boulevard, and continue onto the far sidewalk, turning east. I crept behind the holly bushes at the side of my neighbor's house, watching to see where he was heading. As he continued to walk, I slipped along the front of the neighbor's house, seeking the shrubberies as cover for my garish bathrobe. Middlesex Boulevard bends slightly to the north, which allowed me the cover of homes and trees as I tailed him for two blocks until he made a right on Algonquin Avenue. When he disappeared around the corner, I sprinted across westbound Middlesex, dodging a car, tiptoed through the marigolds, waited for a garbage truck to pass, avoiding eye contact with the driver, and crossed the eastbound lanes. My hair had fallen into my eyes; I was unshaven and looking positively ridiculous in my robe and slippers, which were soaked by the morning dew. From the backyards of the houses that faced Algonquin, I could stay hidden, dashing from yard to yard, watching between the houses as he strolled down the sidewalk, hands in his pockets, seeming to be whistling. The Saab was parked in front of the sixth house from the corner. I could see the license plate number and tapped it into my cell phone for future reference.

After the car disappeared down Algonquin, I started back across the backyards, hoping that no one had called the police. "Where in the hell is he getting his money?" I said aloud. Jack Vukovich was living in an upscale neighborhood and driving an expensive car, all with no visible means of support.

I crossed back over Middlesex and headed back to my house, walking, head down. A car that pulled up behind me on Middlesex rolled along behind me for several moments. I actually hoped it was the cops, but my luck had not been running that way lately. It pulled up alongside me, and I heard the hum of the window motor as the passenger side glass dropped. He took off his sunglasses and stared, his one good eye boring into me. "You must think this is all some kind of game, Mr. Van Buren, or you wouldn't be following me around the neighborhood in your pajamas," Vukovich said.

It was embarrassing on a number of levels, not the least of which was standing along Middlesex Boulevard in my robe being lectured by an ex-convict. To a lesser degree, I had been busted by Jack Vukovich, whom I didn't believe to be particularly intelligent.

"You better stick to prosecuting, because you're a piss-poor spy. I've caught you twice in two days."

I walked over to the car and leaned down into the open window. There was a faint odor of bourbon in the air, which I hadn't noticed on the patio. "Nice wheels, Jack. Just out of curiosity, where'd you get the money for a car like this? You're not working, but you drive a nice car and live in a nice house. What's up with that?"

"Let's just say I have a benevolent benefactor, not that it's any of your concern. You better just concentrate on making sure no charges get filed." He stomped on the gas, and I jerked my head out of the opening just ahead of the oncoming rear window.

★ ★ ★

It was just after ten o'clock when I arrived at the office. Margaret looked up for only a moment. "Couldn't stay away?" she asked.

"It's just a touch-and-go. I'll be out of here in ten minutes."

She murmured in a tone of disbelief.

While my computer ramped up, I put two fresh batteries into my digital recorder. I signed on to my computer, logged into the Ohio Parole Authority website, and printed out Jack Vukovich's criminal and prison record, and a prison mug shot that came out a little grainy on my black-and-white printer, but was still recognizable. I tucked the recorder and my laptop into my briefcase and locked my office on the way out. "I'm going to be out for a few days," I told Margaret.

"How many is a few?"

"I don't know—two, maybe three."

She frowned. "You're going to take a vacation in the middle of the biggest campaign of your life?"

"I need to get out of here for a while. Just a couple of days."

"I'm not sure I believe that, but good for you. You need it."

"I sent Barry an e-mail telling him I was going to be gone for a couple of days. Anything short of a crisis, let him handle it." Barry Lanihan was my chief assistant prosecutor and heir apparent, a former cop who had attended law school at night to earn his degree.

"Enjoy yourself."

"I'm supposed to give a talk tomorrow night to the Youngstown Chamber of Commerce. Would you . . ."

"Cancel it for you?"

"Please."

"I'd be delighted."

"Tell them . . ."

"Something of an urgent nature has come up. You're terribly sorry but it's unavoidable. You hope to make it up to them in the near future."

I grinned. "Perfect. Thanks."

"It's my pleasure."

I drove over to the Mercantile Building, ignoring Shelly's first call of the day on the way. I parked the Pacifica in a surface lot next to the building and took the elevator to the ninth floor and the offices of the Judith Norris Investigative Agency. I'd met Judy more than two decades earlier when she was an investigator with the Summit County Juvenile Court. In those days she was known as "the frenetic woman," because she was always wired with caffeine—never without a Coca-Cola or a coffee—and multitasking—talking on the phone while typing on the computer while searching through the mountain of papers on her desk that seemed to defy physics by not collapsing. She was beautiful, wore her skirts short, and was perpetually brushing long brown hair out of her eyes. I teased her that she had an unfair advantage in the business world because the cover of her company brochure featured a full-length photo of her leaning against a desk, arms crossed, with a come-hither look, and there wasn't a male CEO alive who wouldn't invite her in after receiving it. Her response was to call me a pig, but she knew it was true.

Judy had an eighteen-month-old daughter and was four months pregnant when she quit her job as an investigator with the juvenile court and started her private investigative agency in a spare bedroom of the home she shared with her now-ex-husband. She hired a secretary who didn't mind changing diapers and began building her business by spying on errant spouses, conducting background checks for government agencies, and traveling the state for the bureau of worker's compensation, secretly videotaping men who were supposedly disabled but miraculously able to hoist a V8 engine from a car. I frequently farmed out work to Judy, who interviewed witnesses for pending criminal cases.

In the twenty years since that modest beginning, The Judith Norris Investigative Agency had grown to fifteen full-time employees and a statewide reputation for business merger and acquisition due diligence. Corporations hired her to investigate other companies before a merger or acquisition, making sure there were no major obstacles to the plan, such as pending lawsuits, cooked financial records, or that the headquarters of the company to be acquired wasn't built over an abandoned nuclear waste dump. Judy now shunned government work and the mundane investigations that got her started, unless it was me asking. While she disdained criminal investigations, she also knew that I never questioned an invoice and she never had to hound the county to get paid.

When I walked into her office, she was standing at the copy machine. She smiled and said, "Oh, I was just thinking about you. I was going to call you this afternoon and see if you wanted to get coffee."

"You say that every time you see me, but my phone has yet to ring," I said.

"I know. It's very disingenuous, too. I promise to be much more sincere if you get elected attorney general." She smiled and laughed, waving the papers in her hands toward her office. "Come on back. How's the campaign?"

"Good, if you believe the polls. I'm up by eighteen points."

"That's huge. You've got my vote."

"That may be the one that puts me over the top."

"I hope so—then you'll owe me. Want some coffee?"

"I'm good."

She pulled the door shut behind us. "Your eyes are all bloodshot."

"Thanks for noticing. It was a rough night."

She grinned. "So, what's up?"

"I've got a mission for you, but you can't farm it out to one of the twentysomethings out there. I need you on this."

"God. I'm swamped right now."

"I'll make it worth your while." I pulled the print of Jack Vukovich's mug shot from my briefcase and pushed it across the desk. "This is Jack C. Vukovich. Ex-con, did thirty years for murder and rape, likes mentally retarded teenage boys."

"Nice guy."

"Unfortunately, he's currently my headache. He's living in Portage Township and under investigation for a sexual assault on another kid, mentally retarded and non-communicative."

She nodded, jotting down notes in a yellow legal pad. "Do you have witnesses you want me to interview?"

I pulled the rap sheet from the briefcase and handed it to her. "No. I want you to find out where he's getting his money."

Frown lines stretched across her forehead. "What's that got to do with the sexual assault?"

"Absolutely nothing. That's why I want you on this. I don't want anyone else knowing what I'm looking for. This guy doesn't work, has no visible means of support, but he's driving around in a late-model Saab, living in a house out on Thimble Lakes, and unless I miss my guess he's got a hefty alcohol bill. I want to know how much he's spending every month and see if you can locate the source of his income."

She scanned over the rap sheet. "His DOB and social are here. Shouldn't be a problem."

"He's dangerous. Be careful."

She waved me off and rolled her eyes. "Please. I've been doing this for a while. Who do I invoice?"

She was a businesswoman at heart. "I don't know yet."

If we filed charges against Jack Vukovich, I would pay for it out of prosecutor funds. If we didn't, I would justify it as a campaign expense and pay for it out of my war chest. I was dancing on the ridgeline of ethics, but that was the least of my concerns.

"When do you need it?"

"Yesterday."

"Of course you do."

"Don't send anything to the office. Give me a call on my cell and let me know what you find."

Chapter Twenty-One

I had a dream about Petey Sanchez the summer after he was killed. It occurred on a steamy July night when I was tossing in my sleep, drifting in and out, trying to get comfortable in a house without air-conditioning and a bed that was soaked with my own sweat. I dreamed that I was sitting on the side of my bed, the light of a full moon and a warm breeze filtering through the curtains, floating them into the room and exposing the West Virginia hills and a shimmering river.

Like the escaping light of a receding eclipse, the moonlight rolled across the room and lit up the side of Petey's face. He was sitting at my desk chair, impassive, unblinking, wearing the same clothes in which he had died, though they were neat and clean. His hair was combed and face scrubbed, without the little stubble that always dotted his chin, and there was a calmness in his eyes that I had never seen in life. The light exposed the crater in his forehead and the streaks of dried blood that ran down the side of his face and disappeared into the collar of his shirt. Although he appeared clean, Petey still smelled strongly of urine and dirt. We stared at each other for a few minutes before I asked, "What are you doing here, Petey?" He didn't respond. "Why are you here? What do you want?"

He slowly shook his head. "Nothing." In death, his voice was clear and soft, perhaps the tenor he would have possessed had his temples not been crushed by the doctor's forceps.

"If you don't want anything, why are you in my bedroom?"

He waited a moment before speaking. "I wanted you to know that I'm still around. I'm still here."

"What do you mean?"

There was, perhaps, a slight shrug of his shoulders. "That's all. You can't see me all the time, but I'm still here. I'm never leaving."

"Don't you want to go to heaven?"

"I like it here."

I kept expecting him to tell me to do the right thing, to tell the truth, go to the police and turn in Adrian Nash, but he didn't. I thought it was the spirit of Petey Sanchez communicating through my subconscious, prodding me to tell someone what really had occurred, but there was no such message. I said, "I don't want you in my room, Petey. You need to leave."

He began repeating, "I'm never going. I'm never going. I'm never going." With each repetition his voice climbed higher, and soon the old Petey began to emerge; his eyes turned wild and the squawking, barking voice returned. "I'm never going," he screamed, rising out of the chair and sending it backward into the desk, the skin stretching taut across his twisted face.

I awoke with a jerk, sucking for air and afraid to look at the desk chair for fear it might actually be occupied by the ghost of Petey Sanchez. Sweat collected in the crease of my neck before releasing streams of warm rivulets down my chest. Imagined or otherwise, the smell of urine and dirt was heavy in my nostrils. I turned my pillow over, trying to find a cool, dry spot to rest my head, and rolled on to my side, my moist back facing the chair. It was a long time before I drifted back to sleep. My brain would not shut down, fearful that Petey had taken up permanent residence in my subconscious.

The dream had been so real, so vivid, that for weeks afterward I hated going into my room at night, and I continued to hear his voice in my head. "I'm never going. I'm never going. I'm never going." I didn't understand the message and wanted to ask Adrian, Pepper, and Deak if any of them had experienced a similar dream. If they had, perhaps it was Petey trying to contact us from the spirit world. Ultimately, I never said anything to anyone, but too, I was never convinced that Petey Sanchez had left Crystalton.

I recalled the dream just before dusk as I pointed the Pacifica east on Route 250, cruising along the north shore of Tappan Lake, the large, man-made reservoir that stretches for miles though Harrison County, Ohio. Bass fishermen stood in their boats near the shoreline, sending lures into the reeds and lily pads as the last rays of sun painted the lake with a million diamonds. There were times when I longed for such a simple life.

Soon, I would snake through Hopedale and Smithfield and begin the descent out of the foothills and into the Ohio River Valley and the town in which I had grown up. West of Crystalton on New Alexandria Pike, I would round Tarr's Hill and head into the tunnel of maples and oaks that formed a hundred-yard-long natural tunnel over the two-lane asphalt road. Just beyond the tunnel was a nameless hill that cut off moonlight, and on nights when the foliage was on the trees it was like driving into a giant cave. When the leaves were gone, the naked limbs reached over the road like so many bony fingers.

The tunnel is less than a half-mile from where Petey Sanchez dropped. When I was in high school and dating Veronica Strausbaugh from Smithfield, I had to drive through the tunnel on my way home. After the dream that Petey had invaded my bedroom, my imagination assured me that he was still lurking in the area, and what better place for a ghost to hover than the tunnel? On moonlit nights I would round Tarr's Hill to see the pale yellow cast lighting up the approach to the cave; chills percolated in my ribs and spine as my headlights bore in on the darkness. I would turn my rearview mirror upward so that I would not look and see the reflection of Petey Sanchez sitting in the back seat. My eyes focused on the asphalt ahead, fearful that lifting them would reveal Petey Sanchez standing alongside the road.

As I drove back to Crystalton that evening, I no longer feared the ghost of Petey Sanchez. After more than three decades, I had grown somewhat immune to his hauntings. Still, I got goose bumps at the sight of the tunnel and the memory of long-past fears. I drove into the north end of town, where New Alexandria Pike pulls hard to the right, emptying onto High Street, and a part of me lamented the years away. I was sure that beyond the darkness, Crystalton was badly showing its age, and the little town of my youth had disappeared. The years since I had left had not been kind to the entire Upper Ohio River Valley, and like the other towns that lined the river, Crystalton was sagging under its own weight. The steel mills were dying a slow death, employing a small fraction of the people they had twenty years earlier, coal mines had closed, and the domino effect pounded the railroads and suppliers up and down the river.

Although I had left Crystalton at the first opportunity, I must admit that in the years since, I never felt as though I knew and understood my place in the world as when I lived there. I was Miriam's son and a varsity letterman for the Crystalton Royals. In my world, that was sufficient. Crystalton had been the cocoon that shielded me from the harsh realities of the outside world, and with one stark exception, my memories were grand. But as an adult, I avoided returning. No class reunions, no homecomings, no firemen's festival. I treated my hometown like poison ivy. I felt that by going back, I was somehow tempting fate. It was like walking along the edge of a cliff and hoping that a gust of wind didn't come along. Petey, as he had said in my dream, was still there.

I loved the memories that Crystalton provided, but I had virtually abandoned my relationships with its people, even those who had once been my closest friends. My years in Crystalton seemed like a slice from another lifetime.

I had made an occasional holiday visit to see Mom, though I was always in and out on the same day. My last trip to Crystalton had been ten years earlier when I went down to help her close up the house and move to Florida. She and Walter Deshay had moved to Apalachee Bay and opened a charter boat deep-sea fishing business. They had never married, though their relationship had progressed quite a bit from my mother's previous contention of simply "seeing each other." I went down to Florida at least once a year to visit and I would usually find them at work on the deck, tanned, gray-haired, and spry. In Walter, Mom had found someone she could rely on; he had become the focal point of her life.

The summer before my senior year in college, two Steubenville police officers broke into my brother's apartment when neighbors complained of the emanating stench. Steven had been dead at least a week. Drug paraphernalia was scattered on the coffee table next to his body and his death was ruled an accidental overdose. I took the urn containing his ashes from Mom's closet shelf and boxed it up for her move to Florida.

I had seen my sister only once in thirty years. The last I knew, Virginia Sue was living in a trailer park outside of Las Vegas, Nevada, with Lou and a grandson she was raising for a daughter who was doing seven to twelve in the Florence McClure Women's Correctional Center on a methamphetamine rap. I was in Las Vegas for a prosecuting attorney conference and went out to visit her. She had grown quite round—a bowling-ball figure that pressed against a dirty pink housecoat and was supported by spindly legs that were eaten up with twisted cords of purple varicose veins. Her flabby tits hung to her waist and her breath had the stale odor of yesterday's beer. Virginia Sue's hair was oily and her teeth were rotten, and I suspected that the daughter wasn't the only one with a meth habit. Virginia complained about Lou, who was working as a janitor in a hospital, and talked constantly about her dire financial situation. She chain-smoked and had a voice like a transmission straining to find a gear. I gave her a hundred dollars and was glad to be gone.

A few years earlier I'd received a call from the Brooke County, West Virginia, prosecutor, who was working on an extradition case concerning an inmate in our jail. We were chatting a bit and I asked him if he knew of David Van Buren.

"You mean Mugs Van Buren?"

I recalled that "Mugs" was my father's nickname. "I think that's his nickname."

"Yeah, I know him; he's the town drunk. What a pathetic character. I'll bet he's been in my drunk tank a hundred times." He paused, realizing after the words were out of his mouth that we shared a last name. "He's not related to you, is he?"

"Distantly. He's a cousin a couple of times removed. I knew he was living in Wellsburg a while back, but I had lost touch with him."

"I wouldn't go out of my way to get in touch with him. He's trouble."

Under the cover of darkness, I took a nostalgic lap through Crystalton, driving past the old homestead, which was occupied by a family whose name was lost to me; a light burned in my old bedroom. Across the street from the post office, two boys in Crystalton Royals varsity jackets stood talking under a streetlight, duffel bags slung over their shoulders. All was quiet as I drove south on Third Street, past the drugstore, the Glass Works Bank and Trust Company, the stadium, the sand quarry, and the Danduran Insurance Agency, which had converted Fats Pennington's antique shop into a neat, vinyl-sided office. It had cleaned up the corner, but sacrificed much of its former character.

I drove out of Crystalton, headed north on Ohio Route 7, and picked up Route 22 in Steubenville. The spotlight on a passing barge lit up the Fort Steuben Bridge as I crossed the Ohio River and headed east toward Pittsburgh. The visual of Jack Vukovich sitting behind the wheel of his car, glaring at me with his one good eye, the other sagging deep in the socket, continued to invade my psyche. He wasn't kidding. I knew that. I also knew that if I made this particular problem disappear, it would not be the last I saw of him. He held the upper hand. Why wouldn't he continue to blackmail me? Today it was a professional favor, tomorrow it would be money.

If the evidence wasn't there and I didn't pursue an indictment, Vukovich would still win. He would be convinced that his pressure had prompted me to collapse and meet his demands. His promise to leave the county was hollow. He might stay low for a while, but he would be back with his same threats. I was certain that it was only a matter of time until Jack Vukovich's story of our involvement in the death of Petey Sanchez would be made public. That would be hastened if the FBI crime lab found evidence enough to indict him.

For that reason, I needed to confer with my co-conspirators. I was Vukovich's target, but when he dropped the bomb they would certainly be peppered with shrapnel, victims of collateral damage. As I pondered my predicament, the absurdity of my current mission seemed even more immense—reconvene the old gang to reconfirm our commitment to silence. With a renewed commitment from the old gang, I could indict Vukovich, then feign outrage when he went public with his claims. I could find a polygraph expert of my own to dispute the results. Such allegations would create a cloud of doubt over my campaign, but not one that I couldn't buffer with an eighteen-point lead in the polls.

There would, however, be a major difference this time around. When we were fifteen, we were juveniles committed to silence. We never told any lies because we were never questioned. Now, we were adults. Questions would be asked. Lies would be told. Reputations were at stake.

It was a long shot. A lie grows like frost on a window. It extends in all directions and efforts to rein it in are futile. The more people who know the truth, the more the lie grows and branches in nearly incalculable directions. The challenge was heightened by pure logistics. The four of us had not been in a room together since before high school graduation. I at least knew how to find Deak and Pepper; I had no idea of Adrian's whereabouts. From what I last heard, he might be living under a bridge somewhere. The last time I had spoken to him was when our paths crossed in Connell's Market during Christmas break of our sophomore years in college. I was wearing my Laurel Highlands varsity jacket. I'd heard he was dropping out of the University of Iowa after sitting the bench for two years. He didn't want to talk. Jewel Connell handed him his change, and he muttered, "See ya," and walked out the door. That was the last time I laid eyes on him.

Traffic was sparse when I got onto the Parkway, the freeway that connects Greater Pittsburgh International Airport with downtown. A mile onto the Parkway, high on the hillside to the north, was a large, blue and gold neon sign stretching over a four-story glass and stainless steel building built hard into the hillside. The top of the sign was a blue "22" in block letters. Beneath the numerals, in gold neon script, was "Double Deuce Enterprises." It was the headquarters for the corporate conglomerate that operated the Double Deuce Car Wash franchise, Double Deuce Food Distributors, Beast of the East Fitness Centers, Beast of the East Vitamin & Supplement Shops, and a myriad of other businesses that included a vending company, a steel scrap yard, an excavation and construction business, and the Homestead, Duquesne & Glassport Railroad, a short line that ran along the banks of the Monongahela River. The president, CEO, and sole owner of Double Deuce Enterprises was Eldon "Pepper" Nash.

Years earlier, when I stated that Pepper was destined to be rich, I had underestimated his potential. After graduating high school, Pepper earned a bachelor's degree in business from the University of Pittsburgh, where he played on the 1976 national championship football team, started three years, was named the team's defensive MVP his senior year, and was second-team All-American, wearing number twenty-two. After graduation, he bought a small car wash in Mt. Oliver and played on his popularity as a member of the Pitt football team, naming it Pepper Nash's Double Deuce Car Wash.

From that single car wash, Pepper Nash launched an avaricious climb that would make him a multimillionaire. Within a year he had opened car washes in Dormont and Castle Shannon. Within three years he had sixteen facilities stretching from Monroeville to Sewickley. He opened the first Beast of the East Fitness Center in Cranberry Township in 1985. Beyond that, I could never keep up with his business ventures. He was a popular figure in Pittsburgh and was frequently asked to be a ceremonial chair for a variety of business and charitable events, as having Pepper Nash's name associated with an event was gold.

Jutting from the hillside on the ground floor of the headquarters building was the Double Deuce Steak House, a high-end restaurant and bar that was popular with professional male athletes and business leaders and the women who followed them. Of all his successful business ventures, Pepper most loved the restaurant, where he was always the center of attention, except when some of the more popular Steelers showed up. It also kept him in contact with the city's other power brokers, and a steady, seemingly endless string of women.

Although it was late on a Tuesday night, the lot encircling the building was full, and I parked in a remote corner. At the instant I pulled the key from the ignition, my cell phone rang. It was Shelly. I waited for the call to roll to voice mail, then sent her a text message: *All is well. Will call soon.* I turned the phone off before she could respond and tossed it in the center console.

There was an open stool at the end of the bar nearest the kitchen. I sat down, ordered a merlot, and scanned the restaurant. A piano player swayed and rolled through slow versions of American classics; a bubbling tank of lobsters awaited their fate on a wall behind me; the restaurant hosted an extraordinary number of fake breasts and bad toupees, often at the same table; a trim, muscular man with a quick smile, a receding hairline, and the cuffs of his white, tailored dress shirt rolled up to his forearms strode from table to table, shaking hands and slapping backs. It was the old double deuce himself—Pepper Nash—and he was working the crowd like a career politician.

I ordered dinner—a small Greek salad and Castellane pasta with sausage, peppers, cherry tomatoes, and marjoram. It was excellent. I was finishing my dinner—the first food I had eaten since the cantaloupe earlier that morning—when Pepper walked past. He slapped me on the back and asked, "How was the Castellane?"

"Excellent," I said. "The sausage had just enough bite."

"Isn't that great sausage? I get that made-to-order at a little butcher shop in the North Hills. It's got a little cayenne, some crushed chili peppers, and fennel seed. They do a terrific job." He patted my back again. "Glad you liked it." He kept walking to the computer behind the bar and seemed to be punching in an order when the picture his eyes had taken finally registered in his brain. He jerked like he had grabbed a hot electric wire, then slowly turned back toward me. I winked. "Son of a bitch," he said, already in full stride back toward me, laughing, arms spread wide. "I don't believe it," he practically yelled, causing everyone at the bar to look his way. I stood to greet him and he wrapped me up in a bear hug. "What the hell are you doing here?" He laughed and hugged me again. He turned to a couple sitting at the bar who had absolutely no interest in the encounter and said, "You see this guy?" He pointed at my chest. "He's going to be the next attorney general of the state of Ohio." They could not have been less impressed. He hugged me again. "Why didn't you tell me you were going to be in town?"

"I didn't know myself until a couple of hours ago."

"Christ, I can't believe it. How long's it been?"

I shrugged. "Seven, maybe nine, maybe ten years. The last time I saw you was when I was in town for the prosecutor's conference."

"Damn, it's been way too long." He pointed up and behind me. "Let's go up to my office and catch up. You want some dessert?"

"Just some coffee, black."

Pepper's office was on the second floor of the building, but had been built with a one-way window that allowed him to look down over the first-floor restaurant. We sat in chairs around a round, granite coffee table. A young woman with her hair pulled back in a ponytail came up with a pot of coffee and cups. Pepper peeled off a ten-dollar bill and thanked her. "Good kid," he said. "She's an engineering major at Carnegie-Mellon."

I turned and watched as her tight hips disappeared out the door. "Uh-huh. And . . . "

"And nothing. I don't mess with the help, especially the ones who are younger than my daughters. It's bad for business."

I smiled and poured myself a cup of coffee as Pepper crossed his arms and leaned back in his chair. "So, what brings you to Pittsburgh? You're not campaigning in Pennsylvania, are you?"

"In a manner of speaking, I guess I am." I took a sip of my coffee and he frowned. "I'm trying to keep my campaign from running against the rocks."

"What's up? The last time I talked to Deak he said you had a big lead in the polls. You need money?"

I shook my head. "No, nothing like that. My lead is solid, but there's a chance it could collapse pretty quickly."

"Why's that?"

"Well, someone from our mutual past paid me a disturbing visit yesterday."

He shook his head and shrugged. "I give."

"One-Eyed Jack."

He frowned for a moment, the old nickname not immediately registering, then his mouth dropped and eyes widened in unison. "Holy shit, Jack Vukovich?" I nodded. "You're kidding me? He's still alive?"

"Very much so."

"Wow, I figured he would have died a long time ago."

"No, we couldn't be that lucky."

"What did he want?"

"He's blackmailing me, Pepper. He's been living in Summit County and taking liberties with a severely mentally retarded boy. He's under investigation for the assaults and wants me to ignore it in exchange for his continued silence on what he knows about how Petey Sanchez really died."

"I'm not sure I'm following you."

"Vukovich says he was still in the brush when Adrian threw the maul. He claims he saw the whole thing. In fact, he described it in pretty convincing detail. He said he passed a polygraph test, but that doesn't mean anything. The bottom line is, he knows what happened up there. I'm not sure he was really in the brush. I'm guessing Deak got weak at some point and decided to clear his conscience by telling his uncle what really happened up on Chestnut Ridge."

Pepper swallowed and rubbed his eyes. "Deak didn't say anything, Hutch. Vukovich was there." He sat up on the edge of his chair, rested his forearms on his knees and interlocked his fingers. "Goddammit." He was silent for a moment longer, collecting his thoughts. "Let me tell you something you don't know. The night after they arrested Vukovich, it was real late, dark out, I remember, and I see this car coming up Gilchrist Street. I was already in bed, but I could see out my bedroom window and I watched it pull up to the curb at the side of the house. I couldn't tell that it was a cop car until he turned off the headlights, and I about shit. Sky Kelso and a deputy got out of the car and started toward the house. I ran into Adrian's room; he was working on a model car and listening to records. He turned off the stereo and we put our heads down by the register so we could hear what was going on; they were in the room right below us. The sheriff and my dad had known each other for years; they both belonged to the Mingo Sportsman Club. Dad had no idea why they were there and he's acting like it's some kind of social call. Then Sky says, 'I received some disturbing information this evening, Carson.' My Dad tells him to sit down, but Sky says he would rather not. He says he wants to talk to Adrian. He says that Jack Vukovich had admitted to sodomizing Petey Sanchez, but claimed he didn't kill him. Sky tells Dad that Vukovich was hiding in the scrub and he saw Adrian throw a rock and kill Petey. You can about imagine how that went over with the old man. An admitted child molester had fingered the anointed one with a murder. He tells Sky that he can talk to our attorney, but he isn't getting anywhere near Adrian without an arrest warrant. Then, they start arguing. It got ugly and loud. Sky told Dad that Vukovich said it was total self-defense. Vukovich told the cops that Petey was attacking Adrian with a tree limb and that he was just defending himself. Sky told him that if it was really self-defense, Adrian wouldn't do any time. Probably wouldn't even get charged with anything. But Dad didn't want to hear any more. He told Sky to fuck off. Sky said he had information that there were other boys with Adrian, but that Vukovich said he didn't really get a good look at them."

"He didn't want to implicate his nephew," I offered.

"I suspect. Dad said Jack Vukovich was nothing more than a child rapist and he was just trying to save his sorry ass at the expense of a good kid. Dad told the sheriff to leave and not to come back unless he had a warrant. Dad asked Sky if he had a murder weapon. He didn't. Did he have any collaborating witnesses? No, he didn't. He said, you've no physical evidence and no witnesses, just the word of an admitted rapist. If all you've got is Jack Vukovich's word, then you've got nothing. We watched the sheriff's car pull into the drive, back out, and leave. About the same time the taillights disappeared down the street, the old man started up the steps. We were both sitting in Adrian's room in our underwear when he came in. He sat down on the edge of Adrian's bed and said, 'Okay, let's hear it.'

"We told him everything. We laid it out, including throwing that maul in the river and our agreement to keep quiet. Dad sat there for a few minutes, absorbing everything we'd said, then he said, "Get some rest," and went back downstairs. You know what I remember most about that night? Adrian was an absolute basket case. He was sobbing so hard he could hardly get his breath. Hell, he was only fifteen and I thought he was going to have a heart attack. The old man never gave him a hug, never told him things were going to be okay, gave no reassurance at all. It was all business. He was working on a plan to get Adrian out of trouble, but he didn't show the first bit of compassion. After he went downstairs, I heard him talking on the phone. I couldn't hear what he was saying, but when we came downstairs the next morning there was a defense attorney from Pittsburgh sitting at the kitchen table talking to Dad. His name was Frank Guyton and I remember thinking that he smiled and laughed a lot for a defense attorney. He gave us each a business card, and on the back was this paragraph we were supposed to read to a cop if he tried to question us. Basically, it said we're not talking and you need to call our attorney."

"Was that it?"

"No, Guyton came back later that day. He and Dad talked in whispers out on the patio. I don't know what all was said, but I saw Dad exhale, like he was relieved about something, then he pumped Guyton's hand and told him how grateful he was for everything Guyton had done. That was it. Before Guyton left he told Dad, 'Make sure you take care of the other two.'"

"Deak and me?"

He nodded. "Remember when you and Deak came over to the house for the cookout after that baseball game against Cadiz? We ate, then Adrian and I left with Mom. That was all arranged so Dad could have some private time to talk to you two and make sure you were going to keep quiet."

"Where did Guyton go after he left the house that morning? Up to talk to the sheriff?"

"Beats the hell out of me, Hutch. I honestly don't know what happened, and I never asked. Can I guess? Sure. I'd say someone got a big, fat payoff to stay away from Adrian, but I don't know that for sure. They charged Vukovich with the murder and even though I knew he didn't do it, I was just grateful that Adrian was off the hook and it wasn't our problem anymore. I figured once that bastard went to prison we were home free."

I pinched the bridge of my nose and pondered the story I had just heard. It didn't dramatically change the situation, as far as I could tell. "I hate to ask this, Pepper, but is your dad still alive?"

"Yeah, he had a bout with lung cancer a few years ago. No surprise, I guess, considering he smoked cigars the way most people smoke cigarettes. He went through chemo and radiation and it's in remission. He's plugging away, too damn mean to die. He's at the bank every day at six in the morning, and he's never at home before six at night."

"What about Adrian?"

He shrugged. "Believe it or not, I haven't seen him in about four years. He doesn't come around. He's living on a little dirt farm that Dad bought for him somewhere out around Bergholz."

"Adrian's a farmer?"

Pepper shook his head. "No. I think that was the original idea, but he just lives there. I think he leases out the land to a farmer down the road. Adrian doesn't do much of anything these days except drink, smoke dope, and mooch off the old man. He's a fuckin' embarrassment. You know, I can remember sitting at the dinner table and Adrian said his long-term plan was to go off to college, win the Heisman Trophy, and come back and be president of the bank after his career in the pros was over. Obviously, that didn't work out quite the way he planned."

"Was the knee injury the start of the problems?"

"Knee injury?" Pepper scoffed, spitting like he had a mouthful of dog piss. "You know what Adrian's problem was? He got to the University of Iowa and found out that no one there gave a rat's ass that he was the great Adrian Nash, or that his dad was the bank president. He also found out there is a great big world outside of Crystalton, Ohio, and there are lot of guys out there who can play the game, and a whole bunch of them were anxious to take his head off. He thought he was simply going to walk on the field and take over, and it didn't happen like that. Some other freshman beat him out and was the starting varsity quarterback. It zonked Adrian's mind. They moved him to fullback, tight end, wide receiver. He was a fish out of water. He dropped out of school after fall semester of his sophomore year. My dad said it was because Adrian had a bad knee, but the only thing wrong with Adrian was this." Pepper pointed to his forehead. "He was a damn head case."

"Why didn't he at least stay and get his education?"

"Because he was the great Adrian Nash. He couldn't stand the fact that he had failed. In his defense, my dad put so much pressure on him it was ridiculous. He couldn't stand it that Adrian wasn't a star, either. After the seventy-six season, the year Pitt won the national championship, we had a big banquet and I invited Mom and Dad. I earned a varsity letter as a redshirt freshman. I mostly played special teams and mop-up work at safety, but what the hell? It was a varsity letter on a national championship team. You know what the old man talked about all night? He wanted me to talk to the coach about getting Adrian a scholarship to Pitt." Pepper got up and went to the window overlooking the restaurant. He ran his hands through his thinning hair and locked them atop his head, taking a couple of deep breaths. "That was just about the beginning of the end of any civil relationship with the old man." He walked back to his chair and sat down, slouching, his legs extended and crossed on the granite table. "This mess with Vukovich is not a good thing for either of us."

"Agreed."

"Not for Deak, either. He's built up a nice church just outside of Steubenville. Have you seen it?"

"No."

"Heck of an operation. He has a Christian school and some kind of social outreach program that's gotten a lot of attention for helping the poor."

"What about Adrian?"

"It's not going to bother him. Legally, could they do anything to him?"

"No. He was a juvenile. They won't pursue it." I took the last sip of my coffee and set the empty cup back in the saucer. "Hard to believe that we did this to protect Adrian and now he has less to lose than any of us."

"True, but not in the eyes of our old man. He's the most realistic person I know, except when it comes to my brother. You bring up Adrian's name around Dad and his eyes light up and he starts doing a play-by-play of Adrian Nash heroics. You'd think it was still nineteen seventy-three and Adrian was leading us to the state championship. Trust me on this—Carson Nash will have a stroke if this gets out and bruises the precious memory of his eldest son."

"How do I get in touch with Adrian?"

He shook his head. "I don't know, Hutch. I don't think he even has a telephone. The last time I asked Dad about him he said Adrian was spending most of his time at a place called the Crazy Horse Bar, somewhere out between Jewett and Scio."

"I want to get everybody together and talk this over."

"What's to talk about? Are you going to go after Vukovich?"

"Maybe. I'm waiting on some lab results to come back."

"Christ, Hutch. That'll open up a shit storm. We've all got an awful lot to lose, and you're at the front of the line."

"True. But I've got a fifteen-year-old mentally retarded boy who Vukovich has been molesting. I don't know that I can sit back and ignore it."

"Can you wait until after the election? If this comes out it will kill your chances to be attorney general."

I grinned. "Sounds like you've been talking to my campaign manager. Are you going to be around town for a while?"

"No travel plans."

"Let me see if I can track down Adrian. I want to talk to Deak, too. If nothing else, I need to let them know what's coming down the pike. If Vukovich goes public with the information, I'd like to know if everyone will recommit to our continued silence."

"I'm in. The solution's as simple today as it was then. We don't know anything, and we feign outrage of being wrongfully accused." Pepper shook his head. "What year did that happen?"

"Nineteen seventy-one."

"Thirty-three years, and it still hasn't gone away."

I smiled and we walked toward the door. As I reached for the handle he slapped me across the shoulder with a backhand. He pointed to a photo propped on a bookshelf—a high school football team dressed in white pants and purple jerseys with gold trim. Printed across the bottom of the photo were the words "State Champs."

"Remember those guys?" he asked.

"Every day," I said.

Pepper walked me out to the car, gave me a business card with his cell phone number, and told me to keep him in the loop. I promised I would. Before I left the parking lot, I turned on my cell phone. There was a terse message from Shelly.

"Where the hell are you?"

Chapter Twenty-Two

At six fifteen Friday morning I called Shelly. I knew that she would be in the shower; I left a brief message, promising to call later, and hung up. This would infuriate her because she would know that I timed my call to avoid talking to her. I was in the shower when she called me back ten minutes later, and the call rolled to voice mail, which I'm sure made her eyes bleed.

I had spent the night at the Stoney Hollow Motel in Steubenville. As soon as I finished my shower I caught up on some work in my room, answered some e-mails, and drank several cups of harsh coffee that I made from the pot in my room. I ignored two more calls from Shelly and read the Wheeling *Intelligencer* for the first time in years. It was pushing eight by the time I called Margaret on my cell phone. "Just touching base," I said.

"Have you talked to the girl?" she asked.

"No, not yet. I tried earlier but couldn't get a hold of her."

"Uh-huh. You're not trying too hard, because she called here four times yesterday—that's *three* times after I told her you weren't here and I didn't know where you were—and she's already called twice this morning. And just so you know, I am about out of graciousness and good nature."

"Okay, I'll call her in a little bit."

"Please do. You also had two calls from a man named Jack. He said it was important that you contact him."

"Did he leave a number?"

"No, he said you knew how to get a hold of him. Is this Jack the saggy-eyed creep that was in here the other day?"

"Uh-huh."

She waited for me to offer an explanation, but I didn't.

My original plan was to drive to Jewett that morning and track down Adrian. However, I was disturbed by the story Pepper had told me the previous night. Vukovich had fingered Adrian as the killer, so why did Sky Kelso stop investigating? I had always assumed that with the physical evidence against him, Vukovich was without alibi and took a plea deal to avoid the death penalty. But that obviously wasn't the case. Vukovich told the authorities who killed Petey. So, why had the information died somewhere along the trail?

With the help of a phone book and the Internet map function on my laptop computer, I left the hotel at eight thirty and headed to nearby Wintersville and a story-and-a-half bungalow on Nimitz Avenue. I stopped by a fast food restaurant and bought a breakfast sandwich and a large black coffee. A girl who looked like she was twelve handed me my bag of food and gave me change for my twenty without comment. I wrapped the grease-stained receipt inside the bills and dropped the wad into a cup holder, then ate my breakfast on the way.

The brick house was modest but immaculate, all edged in white. The yard was lush and cut on a diagonal, the sidewalk trimmed, the flower beds stripped of their summer residents. A man who appeared to be in his mid-seventies sat on a porch swing, a pair of reading glasses low on his nose, whittling a piece of basswood with a pocketknife. He was unshaven, his white hair thin and brushed back on his head. Wood chips were sprinkled across the belly of his dull white T-shirt, and a wooden cane was hooked over the back of the swing. "Good morning," I said.

He nodded. "Mornin'."

"Whatcha whittlin'?" I asked.

He held it up for inspection. "It's a whistle for my great grandson. He likes trains and this'll sound like the whistle on a steam engine when I get it done." He grinned. "It'll drive his parents crazy. What can I do for you?"

"Are you Sheriff Kelso?"

He shook his head. "Nope. I quit being Sheriff Kelso twelve years ago." He worked his knife into a crevice of the wood and for a moment seemed to forget I was there. When he looked up he said, "I'm just Sky now."

There appeared to be the outline of a .22-caliber pistol in his front pants pocket. I nodded toward it and said, "Is that just a habit or are you worried about old grudges?"

As he continued to work, he said, "Mister, there are a hell of a lot of crazy people in Jefferson County, and I suspect most saw the inside of my jail at one time or another. I see no cause to take chances."

"Mr. Kelso, I'm doing some research on a case that you investigated back in nineteen seventy-one, and I wanted to see if I could ask you a few questions."

"You got a name?"

"I do. It's Van Buren. Hutchinson Van Buren."

His right eye closed to a slit and his left brow arched as he chewed on the name, which probably sounded familiar from my campaign ads, but he didn't seem to make the connection. "You a newspaper reporter?"

I shook my head. "No, sir. Actually I'm the Summit County prosecuting attorney."

He let this information settle for a moment, then drew his knife down the wood, creating a thin scrap that curled up in front of the moving blade. "Now, what could possibly be so interesting about a . . ." He paused while he did the math. " . . . thirty-three-year-old case in Jefferson County that the Summit County prosecutor would personally show up at my door to ask me about it?"

I grinned. "The man who went to jail for rape and murder in Jefferson County is now living in Summit County and he's causing me some degree of heartburn."

"Don't you have any investigators?"

"This is kind of personal."

"I see. So, this fella who's causing your indigestion, what's his name?"

"Jack Vukovich."

Sky Kelso slowly shook his head, sucked on his teeth, and made a few other facial gyrations, before saying, "That's not ringing any bells, partner. What case is it?"

"It was a rape-murder case. The victim's name was Petey Sanchez."

He continued to squint. "Petey Sanchez," he repeated, again drawing the knife down though the wood. "The name's familiar, but you're going to have to help me out. I investigated a lot of murders in my day."

"He was seventeen years old and was found dead up on Chestnut Ridge, west of Crystalton. He had been raped and killed with a rock."

A look of recognition consumed his face, and he appeared a little surprised that it had come to him so quickly. He nodded twice. "Oh yeah, yeah, I remember that one." He tapped his forehead with the second knuckle of the index finger that was wrapped around his knife. "Retarded kid—took a rock to the head. What was his name again?"

"Petey Sanchez."

He frowned. "No, the perp."

"Vukovich. Jack Vukovich."

"Yeah, Vukovich, he was a janitor down at a school in Crystalton, wasn't he?"

"He was, at the junior high. In fact, you arrested him at the school."

"I remember that now, but how did you know that?"

I had been exposed early in the game. "I was there."

"You're from Crystalton?" I nodded. "Well, that makes this conversation a lot more interesting. So, you were there the day Vukovich got arrested and now you're the prosecutor in the county where he's living?" I nodded. "That's an odd coincidence, isn't it?"

"Not as much as you might think. Mind if I sit down?"

He pointed with the knife to an empty rocker across the porch. "Help yourself. You got my curiosity up now. What kind of issues are you dealing with?"

"The kind I'm not at liberty to talk about just yet, but I can tell you that a leopard doesn't change his spots, and neither do child molesters."

He nodded. "No big surprise there. So, what is it that you want to know?"

"You didn't believe that Vukovich killed Petey Sanchez, did you?"

He looked down at his wood and knife, debating, I assume, whether to answer the question. "That's an interesting question, but I'm not sure things are adding up. Just how does my opinion on an old murder case figure into your current investigation?" He was on his guard and trying to turn the tables on me. It was evident that he was not going to give up anything easily, especially when he still didn't know my motivation. "Let's say, just for the sake of argument, that I didn't believe this Vukovich was guilty of the murder. How would you know that?"

"I've been doing some research, talking to some people."

"Uh-huh. You done blowin' smoke up my ass?"

I laughed. "The night after Vukovich was arrested on the rape charge, you went down to Crystalton to talk to a kid that Vukovich said threw the rock that killed Petey Sanchez, but you never got to talk to him. His dad wouldn't let you near him. I'm just curious what happened."

He squinted at me again. "Were you that kid?"

"No, I wasn't."

"What's your name again?"

"Hutchinson Van Buren."

He squinted. "That wasn't it."

"Was it Adrian Nash?"

His brow crinkled above his left eye and he nodded. "Yeah, that's it. Nash. He was a good ballplayer, as I recall. His dad is the banker. Yeah, that was him. I went down to try to talk to him, but I couldn't get past the old man. Me and the old man, we knew each other, talked once in a while, but he wouldn't come near me after that night."

"Okay, so that you won't think I'm blowing smoke up your ass, here's what I really came to ask: If you believed Vukovich and thought Adrian Nash killed Petey Sanchez, why didn't you pursue it?"

"What makes you think I didn't?" he said, his voice, tinged with anger, rising for the first time.

"He was never charged and Jack Vukovich went to prison for the murder."

He took a long breath, brought the whistle up near his face and eyed it down his nose, then commenced whittling. "Vukovich admitted to the rape, but said he didn't kill the kid. I believed him. It wasn't like he said the murder was committed by some kid he didn't know—he was real specific about who did it and how it happened. Vukovich said it was the Nash boy and, as I recall, he said some of Nash's buddies were up there with him. When old man Nash wouldn't let me near his son, I was going to track down his compatriots and squeeze their balls. It wouldn't have been too difficult to figure it out. Kids get scared and talk, especially if they weren't the one who threw the rock." He lifted his head from his work. "And, unless I miss my guess, you're one of the ones whose balls I'd have been squeezing."

It was a guess, but a damn good one. "What happened? How did you go from believing Adrian Nash killed him to sending Vukovich to prison?"

"If this ever comes back on me, I'll deny it to my dying breath."

"Understood."

"I was told, in no uncertain terms, that the Nash boy would not be charged. He was off limits."

"By who?"

"Who do you think? The goddamn prosecutor. I hadn't even talked to him about it, but I got a call one day and was told not to bring up the Nash kid's name under any circumstances. I told him that was horse shit. Vukovich's story was too detailed to ignore and we needed to give the kid a look, but he said I was wasting my time because there would never be an indictment; he wouldn't even think about taking it to the grand jury unless I had a photograph of the Nash kid throwing the rock. He said even if it was true, we were not going to ruin a kid's life when we had a chance to get a pervert like Vukovich off the streets. He said he didn't care if the murder conviction was bogus, Vukovich was a sick fuck and he'd be off the streets. Don't get me wrong, I can't say that I disagreed with his assessment of Vukovich, but I wasn't thrilled about having a guy go to prison for a crime he didn't commit. The next thing I know, they indict the son of a bitch for murder with death penalty specs."

"Why didn't Vukovich fight it?"

Kelso snorted. "Fight it! With what? We had a dead retarded kid that he admitted to molesting. It wouldn't be much of a leap to convince a jury that he killed him. The possibility of going to the electric chair will take the fight out of most men. He was going to prison for a long time for the rape, anyway, and as I recall the time was all rolled in together as part of the deal. Basically, if he wanted to avoid the electric chair, he had to keep his mouth shut and take the fall."

"Alfred Botticelli was the prosecutor, wasn't he?"

"Yeah, the fucking hypocrite. He put on a big show about sending Vukovich to prison while he knew all along he didn't do it." He skinned the train whistle, the muscles and tendons in his forearms tightening. "His kid took over as prosecutor when the old man got elected to Congress. Alfred Junior. He's a weasel, and the little prick is cut from the same piece of cloth as the old man."

"Why didn't you take your story to the newspaper?"

"Yeah, I could have just slit my wrists, too. It would have been the same result. My political career would have been over. You ever play football?"

"Sure."

"Then you understand the importance of working within a system. The same rules pertain to the Democratic Party in Jefferson County. You want their support, you play by their rules. Botticelli held a lot of sway with the head of the party."

I rocked for a moment while he used the tip of his knife to hollow out a hole. "So, Botticelli didn't want to ruin a young kid's life and wanted to make sure a child molester stayed put away for a long time. There are probably a lot of people around Steubenville who would have considered his motives somewhat noble."

"Noble?" He said it like he wanted to spit. "Alfred Botticelli never did a noble deed in his entire, pathetic life. He would put on a big show in the courtroom, pretending to be this goddamn monument to justice, then put his hand out behind his back and expect someone to fill it."

"What's that mean?"

He tooted twice into the whistle and it produced a shrill noise. He chuckled to himself. "Oh, you strike me as a pretty smart boy. I'm sure you can figure that out."

"I appreciate your time, Mr. Kelso."

I started to push myself out of the chair when he said, "I've got a couple questions I'd like to ask you."

"Shoot," I said, lowering myself back into the chair.

"I'm not sure what you're up to, or what you're up against, but unless I miss my guess, either you want to clean your conscience, or you're concerned that this is all going to come out anyway, and I'm betting on the latter. This Vukovich, is he squeezing someone?"

"He is. How'd you figure that out?"

"Doesn't take a genius. A guy goes to prison for a crime he didn't commit and knows who the real perpetrator was, he spends a long time in there with his wick doing the slow burn. It gives him a lot of time to think, a lot of time to plot revenge. Can't say that I blame him. Is he after Nash and his family?"

"Why would you think that?"

"The old man's still president of the bank, isn't he? He's got the money."

He reached around his shoulder and grabbed his cane, using it to help steady himself as he stood. "I have a young man waiting for a train whistle." He extended his hand. "Nice meeting you Mr. . . . damn, I forgot your name again."

"Hutchinson Van Buren."

"Yeah, Mr. Van Buren. Why is that name familiar to me?"

"You've probably heard it around. I'm the Republican candidate for attorney general."

He snapped his fingers. "That's it." He thought about that for a moment, then started laughing. He pointed at me with his cane and laughed harder. Finally, he said, "Now I get it. *You're* the one getting squeezed." He opened the front door, laughing and shaking his head. "It's the perfect storm, isn't it? He knows you were up on that hill; he knows you kept quiet about the truth for thirty-some years, and now you're running for attorney general. Now, that's sweet justice."

Chapter Twenty-Three

Driving down Sunset Boulevard, I passed the Hollywood Shopping Plaza, where I worked weekends in high school at the Mr. Wiggs department store, and Harding Stadium, home of the Steubenville Big Red. The exit to Market Street, the main east-west corridor through downtown, branches off to the right. I slowed to allow a woman hunched with age and pushing a shopping cart to cross Market Street just east of the railroad tracks, and was stopped at the light at Fifth Street. The once-proud downtown business section lay crumbling before me, and I tried to remember what stores had filled the empty lots and shuttered buildings. It was a far cry from the bustling steel city I had known as a boy. Mom and I went to Steubenville nearly every Saturday morning. She would get her hair done, or shop, or meet a friend at the Green Mill Restaurant on Fourth Street. To me, it was a great adventure as I was allowed to roam through the stores and look for items on which to squander my allowance. The Hub department store, the Paramount Theatre, the five-and-dimes—S. S. Kresge Company, McCrory's, W.T. Grant—were gone, as was the bakery where the aroma of fresh-baked donuts had wafted through the streets. In my youth the sidewalks were always full, but on this morning only a few old men shuffled along the streets. Smoke once billowed out of steel mill smokestacks at such a rate that it choked the sky and blocked the West Virginia hills, evidence that the mills were strong, men were at work, and all was well in the Ohio Valley. The sky was now clear and azure, unemployment was rampant, and the mills were on life support. The light turned green and I cruised slowly down Market Street. It was just sad. I turned right on South Court Street, pulling into a parking space on the street.

Before I could turn off the ignition my cell phone hummed. It was Shelly. There was no use putting if off any longer. I flipped open the phone and said, "Good morning, my love."

"Where the hell are you and what are you doing?"

The tone was more anger than worry. Whether Shelly Dennison was acting in the capacity of campaign manager or girlfriend, her modus operandi was one of total control. If she could cajole me into a speaking engagement that I didn't want to do, good. If she could decline my invitation to spend the night, better. Once I left town unannounced, the strings to her marionette had been snipped and it was no doubt driving her to the point of a rash.

"I'm out of town for a couple of days working on a case," I said.

"Where, exactly, is out of town?"

"Steubenville."

"You know that you're supposed to speak at the Youngstown Chamber of Commerce tonight?"

"I know. I had Margaret cancel it."

"What? Why would you do that?"

"Because at the moment I have more pressing matters."

"More pressing than winning this election?"

"Christ Almighty, Shelly, I'm up eighteen points in the polls and it's the Youngstown Chamber of Commerce." My voice climbed. "How many businesses are left in Youngstown? A couple dozen? I'll make it up to them; I'll pay each one of them a personal visit."

She ignored my flippant response. "Does this have to do with that guy? The rapist?"

"Yes, it does."

She cleared her lungs into the phone, a cleansing breath of exasperation. "Just let it go, Hutchinson. Please, just . . . let . . . it . . . go."

"What if I do, Shelly? What if I let it go just this one time? Do you honestly think that he won't come at me again, especially if I'm elected attorney general? Of course he will. That's what people like Jack Vukovich do. They find a weakness and they hammer away at it. He'll blackmail me again at the first opportunity."

"We'll cross that bridge when we come to it."

It was pointless to argue. She had her eye on the prize and would not be distracted. "I've got to get some work done, Shelly. I'll try to call you later."

"I want you back in town tomorrow."

The line went dead.

As I walked to the courthouse I passed the statue of Edwin M. Stanton, Lincoln's secretary of war, which dominates the southeast corner of the square. The right arm of Stanton's statue is held near the chest and in such a manner that the hand can hold a beer bottle, which it does several times a year. This causes a flood of letters to the editor about the disrespect for the man who had been Steubenville's favorite son until he was unseated by Dino Crocetti, a local club singer who became known to the world as Dean Martin.

The Jefferson County Board of Elections is on the third floor of the courthouse, where, upon entering the room, I was greeted by the blank stares of two obese women who lapped over the seats of their chairs. They blinked in unison, like a pair of curious owls wondering if the stranger was going to upset their morning routine and force them to uproot from their chairs before lunchtime.

"Good morning," I said.

The closest one said, barely audibly, "morning." The one nearest the window just continued to blink, her eyes magnified through a pair of heavy glasses that rested on puffy cheeks.

"I'm interested in researching some old records of campaign contributions."

"How old?"

"About thirty-five years."

"Oh, my," gasped the woman nearest the window, snapping out of her trance. She put a pair of flabby forearms on the desk and frowned. "Do we even keep records going back thirty-five years?"

The closest owl spun slowly in her chair, turning away from me, and said, "We're supposed to keep them forever. If we have them, they'd be over at the warehouse." She grabbed the corner of the desk and spun herself back toward me. "I suppose you want to look at them?"

"I do, please."

"Do you want me to take him over?" asked the woman near the window, as insincere an offer as ever I've heard.

"No, I'll do it," said the closest one. Over the next several minutes, she dug through her desk for a key, groaned as she pushed herself out of her chair, and slowly walked around the counter, her upper body rocking from side to side with each step. I followed her to the elevator, which we took to the first floor, then headed out a back door. She struggled down the concrete stairs, taking them one at a time. By the time we walked a couple hundred feet to a three-story brick-and-mortar building built hard against the alley north of the courthouse square, she was crimson-faced and puffing for breath. Little beads of sweat appeared on her upper lip and brow.

She unlocked the door and flipped on the light switch. The room smelled heavily of dirt and mold. A patina of dust covered the hundreds of cardboard boxes and accordion folders that were stacked on steel shelves, many of which were starting to list. The majority of boxes appeared not to have been touched in many years. "Have at it," she said. "The second and third floors are full of files, too. There's a ladder in the corner if you need it. Try not to break your neck. Are you going to need copies?"

"I might."

"Bring them up to the office." She quit talking momentarily to catch her breath. "It's a dime a page. Let me know when you're done and I'll come lock up."

"Do you just want to leave the key? I'll lock up and bring it back to you." She pondered my offer, seeming to weigh leaving the key with a stranger, which probably violated county rules, and having to make another trip down the alley. "I'm very trustworthy," I assured her.

"Be sure to turn off the lights," she said, dropping the brass key in my hand.

The boxes containing the records of campaign contributions were surprisingly easy to find. The section of the warehouse dedicated to the board of elections was tucked into a far corner of the first floor that was so far from the glass block windows facing the alley it was like searching a room at dusk. A cardboard placard held to the side of the steel shelves with brittle tape bore the words, "Campaign Contributions," printed neatly in block letters with a black marker. Each box on the shelf was labeled by year, also with a black marker. They were in order by year, and I slid the one marked 1971 off a high shelf, sending decades of dust into the air and onto my head. The box was closed only by the top flaps being lapped over one another. Inside were cloth-covered ledger books, in no particular order. Alfred Botticelli's was in the middle of the box. The yellowing ledger sheets were separated by month. I found July, and a few days after the arrest of Jack Vukovich were two notable entries:

Carson Nash—$10,000
Crystalton Business Association Political Action Committee—$10,000

Why would Crystalton's staunchest Republican donate ten grand to a Democratic prosecutor? I had never in my life heard of the Crystalton Business Association, and did not believe it ever existed. Even if it had, why would a village with a handful of businesses need a political action committee? My guess was it was a committee of one—Carson Nash—and a way to funnel money into Alfred Botticelli's campaign fund without drawing the attention of federal banking investigators.

I pulled down the 1972 records. Carson Nash donated another ten thousand dollars in March. The political action committee made a similar contribution in July. This pattern occurred again in 1973, 1974, and 1975. Afterward, there was simply a ten-thousand-dollar contribution from Carson Nash until 1982, when Botticelli Junior became the prosecutor. The contributions were made to the son each year until 2001, the last year I could find in the warehouse. The more recent records were probably in the office with the owl ladies, but I didn't need any more proof that Carson Nash had been steadily paying off a debt for three decades. Just to make sure my suspicions were correct, I pulled down the 1968, 1969, and 1970 boxes. Not surprisingly, there were no contributions from Carson Nash or the political action committee prior to the arrest of Jack Vukovich.

Over the next hour, I removed the ledger pages showing the thirty years of Carson Nash's contributions, locked up the warehouse, and took the pages to Linn's Office Supply on North Fifth Street to have copies made. It would have been easier to take them up to the board of elections, but I didn't want one of the women to nib into what I was doing and call Botticelli's office. A tiny woman with several pencils stuck into the bun of her gray hair made the copies at Linn's, smiled, and told me to come back. I picked up a stray rubber band on the counter and rolled my copies into a tube while I made a detour on my way back to the warehouse, stopping by the Pacifica to drop the copies on the floor of the back seat. Having grown up in the area, I was no stranger to Jefferson County politics, and with a Botticelli still in office I didn't want to be caught with incriminating documents. It was just after noon when I returned to reassemble the books and restock the dusty boxes.

As I was headed back down the center aisle of the warehouse toward the door to the alley, I passed a series of shelves on my right marked, "Prosecuting Attorney." Out of curiosity, I walked back into the row and on a low shelf found three boxes inscribed with, "1971—Capital Cases." In the second box I examined, I found a prosecutorial file labeled:

Victim: Peter Eugene Sanchez
Defendant: Jack Carter Vukovich

Inside a thick accordion file were the original sheriff's report, black-and-white photographs of the crime scene, crumbling newspaper clippings, investigative files that included interviews with Vukovich, court documents, and a plea agreement signed by Vukovich and the senior Botticelli. Toward the back of the file was a manila folder with "Children Services" printed neatly on the tab.

Inside I found a cover letter on Jefferson County Children Services letterhead. It was addressed to the prosecutor and an emboldened subject line read: "Vukovich molestation victims." When I turned to page two, my groan was audible. The header read:

"Interview with Dale Ray Coultas, Age 15." I scanned through several typewritten pages of a transcript of a recorded interview. On page two the interviewer got to the heart of the matter.

Dale, did your uncle ever touch you or do anything improper?

(No response. The tape recorder is shut off at 10:12 a.m. The interview was resumed at 10:23 a.m.)

We are now resuming the interview with Dale Ray Coultas. Dale Ray, did your uncle ever touch you in an improper manner?

Yes.

In what way?

He made me touch his penis and put it in my mouth, and he put it in my rear end.

How many times?

I don't know. A lot. Many times.

More than ten?

Yes.

More than twenty?

Yes.

More than thirty?

Maybe. Probably.

More than forty?

I don't know.

Over what period of time did this happen?

You mean dates?

No, did this happen over the past couple of weeks, months, years?

Almost since he came back to Crystalton. A couple of years, I guess.

Why didn't you tell someone?

I was ashamed, and he said he would hurt me if I did. He also said he would tell my parents that I liked it and they would be embarrassed that they had raised a queer.

Being molested doesn't make you a homosexual.

I was scared. I didn't know who to talk to.

The interview went on for six more pages, the interviewer attempting to extract specific information on the attacks. As I read the transcript, my heart ached for Deak. I wondered why he hadn't revealed the attacks to his parents. However, I knew it was impossible to view the scenes of our youth through adult eyes. As we age, youthful scenes suffer from a distortion of perspective as we become more acutely aware of the realities and frailties of life.

I was eleven and helping Mom replace the linoleum in the kitchen. As she worked on her hands and knees with a putty knife, scraping off two layers of old flooring, I hauled the pieces to the garage and burned them in the cast iron stove. I had overloaded the fire pit and the flame had seemingly died and a heavy gray smoke rolled inside the stove. Believing the fire needed assistance, I poured a quart of gasoline into a plastic pitcher that was sitting on the workbench. At first I stood in front of the furnace, but for an inexplicable reason—divine intervention, perhaps—I moved to the side before throwing it into the stove. Instantaneously, the flames roared and leapt from the stove, following the fuel back into the pitcher. The flames singed the hairs on my wrist and forearm. I dropped the pitcher as I sprinted across the garage, and the pitcher melted into the concrete. It terrified me at the moment, but I forgot the incident in the days that passed. As an adult looking back on the moment, I realize how perilously close I came to disfigurement and even death.

Had I known when I was fifteen years old that Deak had been molested by his uncle, I would have felt a passing sadness and pity. I would have been embarrassed for him, but without appreciation for his own embarrassment and pain. I had not experienced enough of life to understand fully the psychological impact of such repeated violations. Like the flames leaping into the pitcher, I would have been jolted at the moment, but it would have faded in my memory as I went about the business of adolescence.

But as an adult, and one with decades of experience in dealing with pedophiles and sexual deviants who made it their cause to ruin the lives of the innocent, my gut burned, and I seethed with anger at Jack Vukovich. My own ignorance pained me. For decades Deak had endured in silence, and never once had I suspected that he had been a molestation victim. After reading the report, it seemed so obvious. I thought back on the days after Vukovich's arrest, and Deak's refusal to support his uncle and his vehemence in keeping him in jail. *Jack Vukovich should be put away so he can never hurt another kid.*

I was squatting on my haunches, ready to tuck the documents back into the file, when the door opened, filling the aisle with light and temporarily blinding me. Two shadows walked into the warehouse, the door slamming behind them. The first man stood in the aisle, nattily attired in a custom gray suit with thin black pinstripes. As I considered him, I remembered the words of the former sheriff, who had called Botticelli Junior a weasel. He had been accurate in his assessment. Alfred Botticelli Junior was of slight build, chinless, with a large ski-slope nose and a weak moustache, the kind often sported by pubescent ninth-graders. Behind him stood a sheriff's deputy of considerable size, sporting a no-nonsense brush cut and thick arms covered with tufted blond hairs that resembled lamb's wool.

The smaller man had his hands in his pockets, rocking from heel to toe. Although he was small in stature, he carried himself as a man of imperious authority. His eyes were dark, dispassionate, intimidating. Some of his strength was no doubt garnered from the large, well-armed deputy standing behind him, but he was a man used to getting his own way. In a smug voice he asked, "So, what do we have here?"

I, too, was used to getting my way. I feigned reading a document to show I wasn't intimidated.

"Are you talking to me?"

"I don't see anyone else here, do you?"

"In that case, I don't understand the question," I said, hovering over the document for another moment before standing, knowing that I was at least seven inches taller than the little man.

"I find it a little disconcerting that you're in here rummaging through records that are the purview of my office."

"'Purview,'" I repeated. "That's an impressive word. While it's true these records are the purview of your office, let's remember that they are still *public* records. That means they're open to the public, of which I am a member. So, I'm not sure why you would find that disconcerting."

He grinned. "Looks like we've got us a smart guy here, deputy. What's your purpose here? You were asking about old campaign records, now you're in here snooping around old prosecution files."

"How would you know what I was looking for?"

"It's a small town. My aunt Audra over at Linn's called and said there was a well-dressed man in there making copies of old campaign contributions. The good ladies at the board of elections guided me down here. Not much happens around here without me knowing about it, Mr. . . ." I stood in silence, which reddened his neck just above the collar. He took the toe of a finely buffed black wingtip and flipped over the accordion file. When he saw which case I had been examining, a little color slipped from his face. He swallowed. It was hardly noticeable, but I saw it. It was a nervous response to the name on the folder, not unlike a second-grader being caught with chewing gum. "Why are you looking through the Vukovich file?" he sneered.

"Vukovich?" I frowned and looked down at the documents. "I thought it was the Sanchez file."

"Answer my question."

"I'm just an interested citizen."

For a long moment, Botticelli stared at me, the sneer replaced by puzzlement, his brain whirling as he tried to put a name with the face. "I know you from somewhere."

"You want some help?" He gave the slightest of nods. "You've probably seen me at the Ohio Prosecuting Attorney Association meetings."

His brows arched. "Hutchinson Van Buren. Well, deputy, it looks like we are in the presence of a real celebrity."

"He doesn't look so important to me," the deputy grumbled, his first words.

"Oh, but he is. This is Hutchinson Van Buren, the Summit County prosecuting attorney. But more importantly, he's going to be our next attorney general, if you believe the polls. But the perplexing question remains: What are you doing here?" He took the children services folder from my hand and examined the interview document. "My, my, but isn't this interesting. I had never actually read this file. I didn't realize the good preacher had a connection to Mr. Vukovich. Is that why you're here?"

"I think the question is, why did your face go suddenly white when you saw that I was looking at this file? Does it have anything to do with the campaign contribution records I saw?"

He forced a slight smile. "I can assure you, Mr. Van Buren, that anything you found in those records strictly adheres to state law, but the question remains, why do you care? If this is official prosecutor's business, wouldn't you at least give your counterpart the courtesy of a phone call?"

"Not if I think the prosecutor in question is dirty."

Botticelli's jaws tightened. He was not used to being challenged.

"Maybe you ought to be moving on down the road," he said.

I dug into my pocket and produced the brass key and dropped it in his hand. "Lock up when you leave, and don't forget to turn out the lights."

Chapter Twenty-Four

The campus for the Cathedral of Peace sat on the sandstone bluff of Buttermaker Hill, just south of Steubenville, overlooking the rusting hulk that was the Wheeling-Pittsburgh Steel Corporation and the Ohio River beyond. It covered the same grounds that was once the campus of St. Brendan's College for Women, a Catholic school founded shortly after the Civil War to train schoolteachers and nurses. As more colleges became coeducational, St. Brendan's withered and died in the waning days of the Great Depression, just before the start of World War II. The buildings were claimed by the Sisters of Bonaventure, a Franciscan order that created a hospital and nursing home for the poor, which disappeared when the last members of the order died off in the early seventies. After it sat in disrepair and became a party place for teenagers, and a general nuisance for the sheriff's department, the Reverend Dale Ray Coultas bought the property for one dollar in 1988 with the promise of resurrecting it for his church and Christian school. Everyone except the partying teenagers was thrilled.

Dale Ray had started his ministry shortly after graduating from college. He had been a devout United Methodist, but didn't want the constraints of an established church. Rather, he rented out the boarded-up shoe store in downtown Steubenville where we had purchased our PF Flyers as kids and opened up River of Peace Ministries. He established a strong children's program and ministered to the infirm in their homes and in nursing homes.

Word spread of his church and his mission of charity. Within a year he had to move his Sunday services to the auditorium at the high school to handle the growing congregation. A year after that, he bought the old United Brethren Church and renamed it the Cathedral of Peace, which housed his ministries until the new church on Buttermaker Hill was completed in the spring of 1990. He was well known for his charitable foundation and was currently serving as chairman of the Governor's Council on Inter-Faith Initiatives.

The new church sat at the apex of the hill and was constructed from stone that had been recycled from the college buildings. It's facade was square and traditional, with two sets of curved stairways approaching the double doors from either side and a towering spire and cross made of stainless steel that was lit up at night and could be seen for miles up and down the river. Two wings with glass fronts curved off from the main building, giving the impression that the church's two arms were embracing the campus. I parked in the arched driveway near the front door and I found my way inside. The sanctuary had a high cathedral ceiling and cushioned chairs instead of pews, which I thought odd in light of its traditional look. It was, however, a spectacular piece of architecture and I marveled at Deak's ability to raise enough money to build such a structure in a depressed area.

From the sanctuary I could see the hallway leading to the church offices. I walked to the rear of the church and found a polished oak door with a plastic placard that read, "Pastor Coultas." I knocked and pushed open the door. The lights were off, but the room was illuminated by the two skylights in the cathedral ceiling. One wall was adorned with a mural of Jesus praying in the Garden of Gethsemane. Another wall held six shadow boxes containing neatly arranged arrowheads, and behind his desk was a large portrait of the Coultas family—Deak, Carolyn, the college sweetheart who later became his wife, a daughter, and two sons who looked like clones of the boy I knew in my youth. They were posed in front of a fake fireplace wearing beige slacks and red sweaters. The ideal family, I thought. The portrait appeared to be several years old. The oldest boy, Caleb, looked to be in his mid-teens in the photo, and I was pretty sure Deak's kids were out of college by now. Time continued to run away from me. I stared at the portrait for a long minute, a little jealous of his family.

I heard voices in the basement and followed them down the stairs to where four women stood amid a small mountain of clothing, separating it into smaller piles for adults and children, male and female. A lean woman with a spray of wild, orange hair saw my look of puzzlement and offered, "They're for our secondhand store downtown."

"Looks like quite a job," I said.

"It's a small pile. You should see the mountain of clothes that comes in before Christmas."

I nodded. "I'm looking for Reverend Coultas. Is he around?"

A squat woman with a seemingly permanent frown who was standing in the middle of the pile looked up and said, "He ain't here. He's at a conference, or something, out in Columbus and won't be back until late this afternoon or evening. He might not stop by."

She seemed to be in charge, so I walked over and handed her my business card and said, "If he does, would you please give him my card and ask him to give me a call?"

She took my card and swallowed, which was not an uncommon reaction to someone seeing that I was a prosecuting attorney. "What do you want to talk to him about?"

None of your damn business, I wanted to tell her, but refrained. "If you could, just ask him to call my cell phone. I'll be up late."

As I left she was passing the card around for all to see. I drove to the bottom of Coal Hill Road and was ready to turn onto Lincoln Avenue when my cell phone rang. I didn't recognize the number and answered in a formal tone, "Hutchinson Van Buren."

The female voice said, "You know, this morning was another wonderful reminder of why I don't like working for you. You send me out to get you a cup of coffee, and the next thing I know I'm fighting drug lords in Colombia."

Judy Norris never identified herself at the onset of telephone conversations, assuming the person on the other end of the line intuitively knew it was her. It had taken me years to get used to the practice. "What's up?"

"Oh, not much, other than I was trying to track down some information at the bank on this Vukovich character, and I was greeted by two humorless men in black suits, with badges and I assume large guns, and all of a sudden I was the one getting interrogated."

"Holy shit. Who were they?"

"Two sweethearts from the Main Street Task Force."

My jaw tightened. The Main Street Task Force was a special unit of the Ohio Bureau of Criminal Identification and Investigation, a division of the Ohio Attorney General. It was originally formed with noble intentions. It would assist county sheriffs and prosecutors with complex, white-collar crimes, particularly in rural and poor counties where expertise in such matters was at a premium. However, most sheriffs were reluctant to utilize the task force for fear that it would wrestle control of the investigation and make them look weak to their voters, and prosecutors never want the state niggling in county matters. Finding the task force underutilized, the attorney general had redirected the unit to begin conducting its own investigations, using state banking and finance laws to investigate criminal activity in local governments, banks, and nonprofits. I thought the task force routinely overstepped the authority of the office of the attorney general, and I had said so during my campaign and planned to abolish it when I got elected. On a personal note, I was no different than any other county prosecutor and I didn't like state investigators snooping in my county without first contacting my office.

"What the hell were they doing there?" I asked

"I don't know, Hutch, I didn't get much out of them. Frankly, they were the ones asking most of the questions. I went to the recorder's office and found that Vukovich bought the car from Ross Maddox Imports in Tallmadge. It's a used two thousand, and he paid thirteen thousand, five hundred dollars for it—cash."

"A check?"

"No. Cash. Green money. I spoke to the salesman who distinctly remembered selling him the car. He said Vukovich walked into the used car lot, pointed to the Saab, and asked, 'What's your best price out the door?' They dickered a bit, but when they arrived at a price Vukovich could live with, he reached into a briefcase and peeled off a hundred and thirty-five hundred-dollar bills and dropped them on the salesman's desk."

"Christ, where's he getting that kind of money?"

"Don't know, chief. I checked the county auditor's records on the house. It's owned by Farmwald Realty Investors. I called them, and they directed me to a company on Copley Road, the Blatz Property Management Company. I went over to their offices and the woman there knew Vukovich. She called him 'the guy with the bad eye.' She said he comes in every month and pays on time, sometimes with cash, but sometimes with a bank cashier's check, always made out to him, and he signs it over. She didn't remember what bank the cashier's check was drawn on, but the management company does its banking at Summit Credit and Trust. So, I went over to the local bank branch, talked to the manager, figuring I was going to get nowhere, and he says, "Come on back. This Vukovich is a popular guy, huh?"

"I said, 'What do you mean?' and he gave me this odd look. He must have thought I was a member of the Main Street Task Force because he led me into a back room where the two men in black suits were sitting at a conference table looking over records. The bank manager announces, 'Here's one of your folks,' and they immediately stood up and flashed their badges. I about peed my pants."

"What were they doing?"

"I don't know. I walked into a damn hornet's nest on your behalf, thank you very much. They were real interested to know why I was there."

"What did you tell them?"

"I told them I was working on your behalf and I wasn't told anything beyond the scope of my particular assignment, which was the truth. They're investigating someone connected to the checks, but I don't think Vukovich is the target of their investigation."

"Why do you say that?"

"One of them said it was an investigation into the misappropriation of funds. I asked by who and he said it wasn't any of my business because it didn't occur in your jurisdiction. I asked them if I could see the checks and they just laughed. Is it possible they were investigating whoever sent him the money?"

I wondered just how committed Carson Nash was to suffocating events so long past. "Very possible. I was going through some old campaign records in Jefferson County this morning and found a decades-long series of payoffs to the county prosecutor."

"Why would they be looking at records in Summit County?"

"I don't know. Maybe money is being funneled through the prosecutor's office to Vukovich."

"Hush money?"

"It's just a guess, but it wouldn't surprise me. Why else would the Main Street Task Force get involved? The prosecutor here is a guy name Botticelli and he's as slimy as they come."

"Well, that's all I have."

"Good job. If you find out anything else, give me a buzz."

"Will do, boss."

I disconnected from Judy Norris and hit the voice mail, picking up a message that had come in during the call. It was another of what seemed to be a steady stream of events designed solely to twist my intestines in knots. "Mr. Van Buren, it's Barbara Zeffiro with the *Beacon Journal*. I'm interested in talking to you about Peter Sanchez. Would you please return my call at your earliest convenience. Thank you."

My groan was audible, and that familiar salty bile filled the top of my throat. I made it my policy to always return phone calls, and return them promptly if the call was from a reporter. While I didn't want to return this one, I was afraid not to. I highlighted her number and hit the talk button. She picked up on the first ring.

"Newsroom, Barbara Zeffiro."

"Barbara, it's Hutchinson Van Buren."

"Oh, Mr. Van Buren, thanks for calling back. I wanted to ask you about Peter Sanchez."

I had been around reporters long enough to know that when they had the goods on you, they clobbered you with the information right from the get-go. Opened-ended questions usually signaled a fishing expedition. "Peter Sanchez? You need to help me out a little here, Barbara. What about him?"

"Uh, well, quite frankly, I was hoping you could tell me."

"I'm not sure what that means."

"I received an anonymous phone call this morning. The caller said that if I wanted a good story I should ask you about Peter Sanchez."

"That's all he told you?"

"Pretty much."

"I don't think I can help you out, Barbara."

"Is he a target of an investigation?"

"If he was . . ."

"You wouldn't be able to tell me anyway."

"Correct."

"Okay, if there comes a point where you can talk about this . . ."

"You'll be the first to know. I always honor a scoop, Barbara."

"Great, thanks, appreciate it. I've got to run."

I breathed with relief, the tightness in my chest leaving with my breath. Vukovich had launched one over my bow, letting me know he was serious. I had not for one second believed he wasn't.

I called Margaret. "Any calls?"

"Mr. Van Buren, do you enjoy asking me questions that you already know the answer to? You know what this office is like. It's a fire fight, just like always, but I've got it under control."

"That guy who was in my office Wednesday . . . ?"

"You mean Jack?"

"Yes, Jack. Have you heard from him today?"

"Only about eight times. One time he's angry, the next time he tries to charm me. He's a very strange bird."

After disconnecting from Margaret, I pulled the index card from my wallet and alternately watched the road while punching in Vukovich's phone number. "What's the deal, Jack?" I asked.

"Where are you?"

"None of your damn business. What are you doing calling Barbara Zeffiro? You said I had a week; it's been two days."

"When I call your office, I expect you to get back to me, pronto. I'm not screwing around. I was letting you know I'm serious."

"So, do I have a week or not?"

"I want to know where things are, right now."

"I'm still mulling over my options."

"What options?" he yelled. "What are you using for evidence, fairy dust? If that cop had anything solid I'd already be in jail."

"If that's true, why did you show up in my office?" I enjoyed his moment of silence. "Just so there is no misunderstanding, Jack, the next sound you hear is going to be me hanging up on you." I pushed the end call button. I had made a tactical error, however, by calling him on my cell phone. He had my number and it took all of about twenty seconds for my phone to ring again. I let it roll to voice mail. I was starting to hate my life. Every time I took a step it was on a land mine—Shelly, Vukovich, Botticelli Junior.

Before I went back to the Stoney Hollow Motel, I stopped by the drugstore for shaving cream, went to the post office to get a package in the mail, and ran the Pacifica through the car wash. All along I was talking into my digital recorder, making verbal notations of ideas, to-dos, and general housekeeping items at the office that I needed to attend to once I finished dealing with the chaos created by the ghost of Petey Sanchez. As the spinning brushes of the car wash rolled over my hood, I dug through my briefcase until I found a black folder containing business cards. I tapped out the number of Darrell Tubbs, who was the director of the Main Street Task Force, a caustic former Cleveland police captain whose days were numbered if I won the election. His secretary answered the phone and I was put on hold for nearly five minutes. The Pacifica was getting a hot carnauba wax when the canned music began playing in my ear, and I was driving toward the Stoney Hollow Motel on Dean Martin Boulevard when he finally picked up the phone.

"Tubbs speaking," he said.

"Mr. Tubbs, this is Hutchinson Van Buren in Summit County."

There was an uncomfortable pause as he refused to acknowledge the statement. It was an intimidation tactic, but one with which I was familiar. He wanted me to keep talking. I said nothing, and after several seconds he asked, "Is there something I can do for you, Mr. Van Buren?"

"You could tell me what members of your task force are doing snooping around in Summit County."

"Mr. Van Buren, you know how this game works. I'm not at liberty to discuss ongoing investigations, even with someone who might be my future boss."

"This has nothing to do with politics. Your investigators are working in my county and I'm the goddamn prosecutor. When you go into another agency's jurisdiction it's considered professional courtesy to contact them."

"Sounds like you found out on your own."

If I won the election, I was going to personally fire his ass and take great pleasure in doing so. "Your men told my investigator it was a misappropriation of funds investigation. I know who received the money. Is the sender of the funds the target of your investigation?"

"Again, I'm not at liberty to discuss specifics. However, I can tell you this. When we pull this guy down, it's going to be big news."

"I'll be talking to you, Tubbs." I hung up, hoping he knew he was in my crosshairs. "Big news," I thought. For all their talk of fraternity, cops loved nothing more than to take down one of their brethren, or an elected official. The most frequent targets of the Main Street Task Force were elected officials. Perhaps there was more to the Botticelli-Nash connection than I realized.

Chapter Twenty-Five

There was a man who used to eat at the horseshoe dining counter at S.S. Kresge in Steubenville who was missing the left half of his face. It looked as though his face had been made of wax and he stood too close to a flame, the skin dissolving into a convex mass between his skull and a thin jaw line, taking with it his eye, ear, and a part of his nose. The pink of the left side of his lips slid into a swirl of crumpled flesh. His name was Kilpatrick and I had heard two stories, one that he was disfigured by a German grenade in World War II, and another in which molten slag slopped out of a thimble car in the mill and splattered on his face. He was a Civil War reenactor and I saw him squatting near a cook fire at an encampment at Community Park in Crystalton one Fourth of July and he winked at me.

He was one of the many characters of my youth. The valley was full of hardy men who wore hard hats and sleeveless shirts and carried metal lunch buckets to work. But there also was a slew of characters that would have seemed out of place anywhere else in the world. There was Rooster Man, who pushed a wobbling grocery cart loaded with his possessions through the streets of Steubenville, stopping periodically to flap his arms and crow. Box Man, who lived in a maze of cardboard refrigerator and appliance boxes that he wove together with duct tape and clothes hangers under the Market Street Bridge. We got to know The Troll, a foul-smelling, low-level mob courier who hung around the Federal Restaurant and collected numbers and sports spot sheet wagers for the Antonelli crime family in Pittsburgh. Boon Bachman was a millwright at Weirton Steel who opened beer bottles with his eye socket and claimed to have once knocked out the great Rocky Marciano in an amateur boxing match.

They were a lively bunch who I embraced as my own when I was growing up in the Upper Ohio River Valley. I was thinking about Rooster Man, Box Man, and The Troll as I pulled into the gravel parking lot of the Crazy Horse Bar. A muscular man with Confederate flag tattoos on both biceps and a skinny guy with a ponytail and filthy blue jeans leaned against the side of a pickup truck and gave me wary eyes as I got out of the Pacifica and made my way to the front door. These were no longer my people. Or rather, I was no longer one of them. I had long ago left the valley and was now the interloper. Although I hadn't lived there for years, I had always felt my roots were still in the valley. Now, it was painfully obvious that I was every bit the outsider.

The Crazy Horse Bar was barely visible from Jewett Germano Road, tucked into a hollow in a one-story cement block building with white paint chips the size of a man's hand peeling off the exterior walls. Neon beer signs clogged the small windows that were cut close to the roofline. An aluminum storm door was bent back on its hinges; the wooden exterior door skidded across worn linoleum as I pushed and walked in behind it. The inside was dark and smelled of cigarettes, marijuana, and beer-soaked carpet. Not every set of eyes turned to look when I walked in, but enough did to make me uncomfortable.

I took a seat on a vinyl stool around the corner of the bar from a man whose ass could have covered three stools. He had scraggly brown hair that hung to his shoulders and a beard to match; his face had such rolls of fat that he looked like a giant insect dressed in bib overalls. I was wearing khaki slacks and a blue dress shirt with pink pinstripes. It had not been a wise wardrobe decision. As he drank a draft beer, the man stared at me without subtlety, trying to play the role of the badass. There are men in this world that it takes just one look to realize they are not to be toyed with, men like Ricky Blood or Elmer Glick. It's not their arms or chest or the way they talk; rather, you see it in their eyes. Their eyes look like those of a shark, cold and dark. The slob at the bar had no such look. I had prosecuted enough men to know the difference. He was fat and soft, flab rolling down around his belly. Having said that, he was still six inches taller and a hundred and fifty pounds heavier than I was.

The bartender was trim, in a clean white T-shirt, with a ducktail haircut and a cigarette tucked behind an ear. He nodded, not a hello nod, but a what-do-you-want nod. I ordered a bottle of Budweiser. I kept my eyes on the bartender, but could feel the eyes of the big man boring into the side of my head. When the bartender set the beer in front of me, I slid a five across the bar and said, "I'm looking for an old friend of mine. I was told he hangs here."

He looked at me for a moment, then said, "Is that a question?"

"His name's Adrian Nash."

He crossed his arms. "What do you want him for?"

"I just need to talk to him."

"You a cop?"

"Do I look like a cop?'"

"That isn't what I asked you." The giant insect got up and walked behind me, but off to the left enough that I could see him out of the corner of my eye, and close enough that I could smell his breath, a mixture of beer and the rancid odor of rotting teeth. The bartender's eyes darted between me and the insect. "Want to try this again? You a cop?"

I took a sip of my beer and tried not to act rattled, though I could feel the burn of anger and fear creeping up around my collar. "Who I am doesn't matter, but who I'm going to be in two months does. In two months I'm going to be the attorney general of the state of Ohio." I pulled out a business card and pushed it across the bar; it landed near the five-dollar bill. The bartender looked at it, but didn't pick it up. "There are four girls over at that table and I'd bet my mortgage that at least three of them are underage. I smelled marijuana the minute I walked in this shit hole, and I'll bet there are more health code violations and cockroaches in that kitchen than one man could count in a lifetime. If you want to give me a hard way to go, trust me that I won't forget this after I'm elected. So, tell the big grasshopper behind me to quit breathing down my neck and answer my question. Is Adrian Nash around?"

He motioned with his head and the big man slid back onto his stool. "If you're old friends, why don't you recognize him?" He walked to the other end of the bar.

Booths lined the walls of the Crazy Horse in the shape of an L. I scanned the short wall where three men and a woman talking with a cigarette in her mouth were tucked into one corner. I slipped off the stool and walked the longer length of the bar, looking into the booths in search of Adrian. He occupied none of them. I went back to my seat at the bar and gave the bartender a quizzical look. His arms were crossed and he lifted only an index finger and pointed to the foursome in the corner.

I squinted and zeroed in on the corner booth. Only his eyes told me it was Adrian. If I had passed him on the street, I wouldn't have recognized him; the old Adrian was gone. His chiseled, square jaw had been swallowed up by a soft, round face that was covered by a dishwater beard that ran down into the neck of his flannel shirt, which hung untucked, as though trying to hide the belly upon which he was resting a beer bottle. He had the red glow of an alcoholic. His face had grown ruddy across his cheeks and the redness extended across a nose that had spread out and was marred by tiny pit marks and dark blue veins that snaked along both sides.

Adrian Nash, the onetime pride of the Crystalton Royals, was huddled in a corner with two men wearing their ball caps backward and a woman whose teeth—they may have been dentures—were too big for her little mouth, giving the illusion of a deep-sea creature pursuing dinner every time she talked. I took a minute before approaching him, fearing the pity I was feeling would be flashing across my face. When I did approach, only the woman made eye contact. Adrian glanced up, but his eyes did not connect with mine. "Hi, Adrian."

The heads of all three men turned at the same time, as though controlled by a puppeteer. He stared for a long moment before asking, "Am I supposed to know you?"

"Yeah, you know me." He shook his head. I pointed across the bar and said, "Maybe if I pace off sixty feet, six inches, and squat down you'll recognize me."

Sixty feet, six inches was the distance from the pitcher's rubber to the plate. I had caught nearly every game Adrian Nash had ever pitched. It was enough of a hint.

Before he spoke, there was a moment of painful recognition in his eyes, as the decades whirled in fast forward through his brain. From the time we first entered school, Adrian Nash had been the standard by which the rest of us were gauged. At early ages, boys begin comparing themselves to each other—in the classroom, on the field of athletic competition, even in the shower. They are not unlike a pack of wolves, constantly maneuvering to be the alpha male. However, one wolf ultimately separates himself from the pack and establishes supremacy, and that had been Adrian.

Adrian's problems arose after he left the security of the pack. Once he was removed from Crystalton, he was no longer the anointed one, and he learned a painful truth about himself: he had no heart and no taste for real competition. He couldn't take a punch in the nose. When he was no longer Adrian Nash, he lowered his head and went home.

In the ensuing thirty years he watched his brother succeed, and in large order. On the periphery, he knew I was succeeding. The alpha male had been surpassed by less gifted, but more determined members of the pack. And at the instant he recognized me standing at his booth, all those truths hit home.

"Son of a bitch," he said. He made no move to get up and kept his right hand wrapped around his beer. "What the hell are you doing here?"

"I came to see you." I extended my hand and he shook it without conviction. "You're a hard man to track down."

"I heard you were running for governor, or something."

"Attorney general."

The woman was suddenly more interested. "Attorney general for the state?" I nodded. She slapped Adrian's arm with a backhand. "You know him? He's famous. How do you know him?"

Her enthusiasm was making me uncomfortable. "We went to school together," Adrian said. "He was the slowest receiver in the history of Crystalton High School."

It was a lame joke, but it made the two men laugh.

"But he's famous now," she said. "Why didn't you tell me?"

Adrian ignored her query and took a hit on his beer.

"Do you have a minute, Adrian? Maybe we could walk outside and talk?"

He frowned. "How long's it been since I've seen you?"

I knew the answer. "Christmas break our sophomore years in college."

"Oh, my God! You went to college?" the woman asked Adrian. "How come you never told me that?"

"How about shutting up for two minutes," he said. It wasn't a request.

The woman with the big teeth and small mouth lowered her eyes.

"So, when was that, nineteen seventy-five? What could you possibly have to say that you can't say here?"

"We have a little personal issue we need to discuss."

"What issue? These are my friends. You can talk in front of them."

The two men looked up at me in anticipation. "Okay. How about this. One-Eyed Jack is breathing free air and he came to visit me the other day. Apparently, we had company on Chestnut Ridge and now he's anxious to tell the world all about it."

The woman frowned and the man at the end of the booth belched and announced that he had to take a piss, and left. For a long moment Adrian looked like the words hadn't registered. He rolled his bottle of beer between his palms for several more seconds, then got up and walked to an empty booth near the door. The old alpha male was sending a tacit signal for me to follow. I did and slid into the booth across from him.

The soft yellow glow of the parking lot light sifted through the red neon of the beer sign in the window and fell across the prematurely aged face of Adrian Nash that held a familiar look of resignation. His jaw had gone slack and there was a hint of moisture building in his eyes. I had seen the look hundreds of times during my years as a prosecutor. It had appeared on the face of every man I had ever questioned the instant they realized the overwhelming weight of evidence against them offered no escape from conviction. He looked like a man who had just run his last race.

I have questioned men I was going to prosecute who had been on the run for a decade or more before being captured. They talked about never being able to relax, never getting a full night's sleep. The slightest of noises awoke them at night. Every time there was a knock at the door or the phone rang, their guts would tighten. They couldn't make friends because they couldn't trust anyone. They never let down their guard. To a man, they told me they knew there would come a day when the phone would ring and the game would be over. Come out with your hands up.

For Adrian, the clock had been ticking for thirty-three years. Like those convicts, I assume that he believed there would come a day when the death on Chestnut Ridge would be known to the world. Tick-tock. He had known it was coming, but didn't know when. For his entire adult life, it had been a point somewhere on a nebulous horizon that never disappeared.

Adrian was not about to admit he was scared. That was not Adrian Nash, even under these circumstances. In his mind, he was still the alpha male and my superior. He did not want to show weakness, but sometimes a person's eyes give him away. "What the hell's he want?" he asked. "Money?"

"No, at least not yet. He seems to have plenty of money. He's living in my county; he's been molesting a mentally retarded boy and the cops are on to him. If I agree to look the other way, he agrees to keep his mouth shut about what he knows about Chestnut Ridge."

"So, is that why you're here? You're going to arrest him and the shit is going to hit the fan?"

"I don't know what I'm going to do, Adrian. I found out some things today that are making this a lot more complicated. Right now there's not enough evidence to indict him. I'm not too confident that we'll ever get the evidence we need and this may go away. But I know guys like Vukovich. If he dodges this bullet, he'll be back again, and again, and again. He's already called a reporter at the *Beacon Journal* and dropped the name of Petey Sanchez just to screw with me. It's only a matter of time until he leaks something and it gets out."

He shrugged and took a drink of his beer. "I don't give a shit anymore."

"You ought to. You and I aren't the only ones with skin in the game, Adrian. Your brother is a successful businessman. Deak has built up a nice ministry. And . . ." I hesitated for several seconds. "There's another problem and it involves your dad."

"What's he got to do with anything?"

"He's been paying off the Jefferson County prosecutor for the past thirty-three years. I've got the documentation."

"Why would he do that?" Little frown lines appeared across his forehead and I was struck by his naiveté.

"Are you kidding me? The problem didn't disappear for free, Adrian. Your dad made some deal to keep you on the football field and not in the juvenile detention center. At least, that's how it began. Now, who the hell knows. He's probably being blackmailed the way Vukovich is blackmailing me. Making a payoff to the Botticellis is like getting in bed with the mob. Once you're in, you're never getting out."

"So, who's Botticelli going to tell? The prosecutor isn't going to investigate himself, is he?"

"Of course not. But the attorney general will. The A.G.'s office has an investigative unit called the Main Street Task Force. It has the authority to cross county lines and go anywhere in the state to conduct investigations. They've been in Summit County looking into payments made to Vukovich, who has a hell of a lot of money for an ex-con with no job. My guess is the payments are either coming from the prosecutor's office to buy his silence, which I think is unlikely, or from your dad, which I think is highly likely. If that's the case, the only reason the task force would be interested is because they believe the money isn't coming out of your dad's pocket. If he's cooking the books to funnel blackmail payments to the prosecutor, then he could be sending hush money to Vukovich, as well."

He didn't look the least bit surprised. "If this comes out, can I still go to prison?"

And there it was, I thought. The reason he moved to the far booth to talk was to get the answer to that single question. Buried under a scraggly beard and body odor, the old Adrian Nash was alive and well. How does this affect me? "There's no statute of limitations on murder, but you were only fifteen years old and it was self-defense.

No one is going to pursue this from a criminal standpoint. That's one of the reasons I'm here. Regardless of what happens in this particular instance, Vukovich will eventually go to the press. He'll try to make a case for a wrongful conviction and get the state to give him a settlement. If he does, we can't waver from our stories."

He shrugged. "No problem."

"I want to get everyone together and talk about this. I've already talked to Pepper. He's in. I'm going to get ahold of Deak and try to set something up for tomorrow night. How about it?"

"I'll check my social calendar and see if I can work you in."

"How do I get in touch with you?"

"Deak knows how."

I stood to shake his hand, but he walked past me and went back to his friends. The meeting had been anticlimactic. I'm not sure what I had been expecting. I certainly didn't think that Adrian would jump up and hug me and tell me how great it was to see me after so many years. That wasn't Adrian. Truth be told, I had been curious to see just how far Adrian had tumbled. It was the same instinct that causes people to slow down to stare at traffic accidents. As a boy I would sometimes buy a Coke at the Kresge's lunch counter just so I could stare at the gnarled face of Mr. Kilpatrick. I was repulsed, but I couldn't not look.

The parking lot was full of pickup trucks and rusting clunkers when I walked out of the Crazy Horse. Night had overtaken the eastern Ohio hills, silhouetting the trees surrounding the bar against a sky lit by a sliver of moon. In the corner of the lot a couple sat on the tailgate of a pickup truck and passed a joint back and forth. I made a few verbal notes of my meeting with Adrian into my recorder before pulling away. As I eased out of the gravel lot onto a barely two-lane asphalt road, for the first time I was struck by Adrian's reaction to the news. Although scared, he hadn't seemed surprised. Pepper had been genuinely shocked that Jack Vukovich was still alive. Both reactions seemed genuine. A pair of headlights pulled out behind me and I adjusted my rearview mirror to night vision to block the glare.

The headlights of the car stayed behind me as I turned onto Route 151. I wondered if I was being followed or just paranoid. I gunned the Pacifica and moved well ahead and the headlights faded in the distance, making no move to close the gap.

As I crossed over the hill from Hopedale—boyhood home of Clark Gable—it dawned on me that I had not eaten since breakfast. I decided to go to Naples Spaghetti House, a wonderful restaurant on North Street in Steubenville. My mother had taken me to Naples for special nights when I was a kid and it had always been a favorite. I hadn't been there in years. The parking along the street was full, so I drove down the alley behind the restaurant and parked. As soon as I walked into the restaurant, I patted all my pockets and discovered that I had left my cell phone in the car. I didn't want to miss a call from Deak.

The phone was on the passenger seat. I unlocked the door and fetched it. The events that occurred in the minutes that followed are still a bit hazy. When I turned away from the car, standing in the lee of the open door, a figure of considerable size emerged from the shadows of a garage. There was momentary panic as I realized I was about to become a victim. One hand was returning my keys to a pocket; the other was slack at my side, my fingers wrapped around my cell phone. I was defenseless against a fist that was already heading toward my face. I might have tried to dodge the blow by jerking my head to the left. I think I remember doing that. If I did, it was a futile gesture. In the next instant, a set of knuckles found their target.

In late April of 1964, my mother went up to the Sears & Roebuck store in Steubenville and bought me my first new baseball glove, which had Ted Williams's signature branded on the little finger. I had been using a battered glove that I found in the basement, which had belonged to my uncle. I was thrilled to have a new glove and was out in the side yard throwing pop-ups to myself. Mr. Regula, who lived across Ohio Avenue, saw me out in the yard and invited me over to join in a game of catch with him and his son, Del, who was three years my senior. During the game, a ball tipped off Del's glove and went over the chain-link fence into Bertha Lewis's yard. As Del hopped the fence to retrieve the ball, my attention fell back to my new glove. I was enamored with it—golden brown, stiff, and smelling of rawhide. I was still looking down at it, patting the webbing with the fist of my right hand, when Del threw the ball to his dad, who threw it at me, probably a little harder than he should have and without first looking to make sure the nine-year-old across the yard was paying attention. The ball had left his hand before he realized my eyes were focused on the glove. "Hutch," he yelled. I looked up and as the ball was about six inches from my face. It is astonishing how much of a third-grader's face a baseball will cover. It hit me square on the side of the nose near my left eye and took me cleanly off my feet. In all of the years I had played football and baseball, fallen out of trees, endured boxing lessons, and gone over the handlebars of my bike when Petey Sanchez shoved his stick in my spokes, I never felt such an incredible impact as I did the day that baseball hit me in the face.

That is, until the rogue fist found home, covering my nose, upper lips, and left cheek.

It was not a sharp, jabbing pain, but a percussion shock, a wave of pressure that rolled over my body, interrupting the electronic impulses between my brain and my legs. My knees buckled and I crumpled, falling back first against the door, then down, smacking my jaw hard on the steel kick plate at the bottom of the door opening. It was as though a huge weight was lying on my head and I could sense the black edges creeping in from the sides and knew I was about to lose consciousness.

I drifted in and out. Warm blood streamed out of my nose and snaked around and into the corner of my mouth, leaving a warm, metallic taste, like I was sucking on a nail. There were, I believe, two men rummaging through my car. I could hear them talking, though I couldn't decipher the words. To my scrambled brain, it seemed as if they were speaking in broken sentences and talking through wax paper. When I became cognizant of my surroundings, the first item to come into focus was the milky haze of the streetlight. I was trying to work my way up on my elbows when the man who was standing over me said, "Just stay down, boy."

It seemed like sage advice. I lowered myself back to the street and was surprised how comfortable the cold gravel and dirt felt. I don't remember losing consciousness again, but I don't remember the men leaving, either. At some point, they were simply not there any longer. The dome light threw a faint glow on the ground where I lay.

I reached for the inside door handle and struggled to pull myself up, wedging my back in the "V" that was created by the open door and car body. Blood dribbled from my face and dotted my blue and pink pinstriped shirt. That's when the phone rang. I ran my hand over the gravel where I sensed it had dropped and miraculously found it.

In a groggy tone I said, "Hello."

There was a moment of silence on the other end. "Hutch?"

"Yeah."

"You don't sound so good. Are you all right?"

I spat away a mouthful of blood and dirt. "No, I'm not."

"Where are you?"

"In the alley."

"What alley?"

"In the alley behind Naples."

The phone went silent. I eased myself onto the passenger seat, keeping my feet hanging out the side of the Pacifica. A few minutes later I heard the sirens of police cars and the emergency squad closing in. By the time the flashing lights filled the alley, I was beginning to think clearly, which also made me more sensitive to my throbbing face. I also was aware that the headlines in tomorrow's papers would be of the Republican candidate for attorney general being found pummeled in an alley in Steubenville.

The paramedics ran up and swarmed over me. One shined a light in my eyes; another wrapped a blood pressure cuff around my arm, then stuffed a cotton wad up my left nostril; a third asked me questions, gauging, I assume, my awareness of my surroundings. None of them had any idea who I was.

One of the cops asked, "Did you get jumped?" I nodded. "Did you get a good look at him?"

I held up two fingers. "Two guys . . . never got a look at either of 'em."

After they saw my condition was not life-threatening, things relaxed. A shadow appeared on the gravel, cast by a man in a clerical collar standing near the open door. "I don't think he's going to need last rites, Reverend," one of the medics said.

"Good thing. I'm not Catholic," said the Reverend Dale Ray "Deak" Coultas. "And neither is he." He looked down and, seeing my face swollen and smeared with blood, asked, "Are you okay?" Without waiting for an answer he turned to the nearest medic. "Is he okay?"

"He'll live. He's going to need some stitches to close up that gash inside his lip."

A cop shined a flashlight inside my car. "Was it a robbery?" he asked.

I shrugged. "Must have been."

He shined his flashlight beam in the cup holder, which held the folded sixteen dollars and change from the fast food breakfast sandwich and coffee earlier that morning. My briefcase was lying on its side on the passenger seat; my laptop computer had slid halfway out.

"Did he take anything on your person?" he asked.

I patted myself down. My money clip was in my pants pocket and the car keys were in the other. My cell phone, which had been lying in the alley in clear sight, had not been touched. "It doesn't appear that anything is missing."

"It's not a robbery if they don't take anything."

"I'm well aware of what constitutes a robbery, officer."

He didn't like my cute remark and shined the light in my eyes. "If it wasn't robbery, smart guy, then what's the motivation?"

"He must not have liked my face." The cop licked a pen and began applying a date to an incident report.

"I don't want to make a report. I can't identify them and they didn't steal anything. Let's just let it go."

The cop clicked his pen and shrugged. "Suit yourself. It makes my life easier."

"Do you want us to take you to the emergency room and get checked out?" asked a paramedic. "You might have a concussion."

I waved him off. "I'll be fine. Appreciate your help."

When the squad and cruiser were gone, Deak stepped closer and pushed up my upper lip, which hurt like hell, and looked inside my mouth. "You've got a pretty hefty gash in there. You're going to need some stitches."

"I don't want to get my name in the paper over this."

"You got mugged. You did nothing wrong."

"It'll just raise a lot of questions that I don't need at this point in the campaign."

"Well, you can't ignore it. The whole inside of your mouth is opened up."

I spat some more blood. "What if we drive across the river to the hospital in Weirton?"

"Hold on a minute," Deak said, pulling his cell phone from his pants pocket and dialing up a number. "Doc, it's Reverend Coultas. Doing well, thanks. Unfortunately, I'm with a friend who's not in such great shape. Yeah, he was downtown and got jumped. He needs some stitches inside his mouth. Uh-huh, I suggested that, but he has a phobia about hospitals and won't go. Yeah, I know. You will? Terrific. Thanks. I'll see you there in about ten minutes." He slipped his phone back into his pocket. "That's one of my parishioners. He's going to meet us at his office."

"He's a doctor?"

"Sort of. He's a veterinarian."

"He's what?"

Deak laughed. "Just kidding. Let's go."

"You're pretty funny for a preacher," I said, locking my car and walking down the alley with Deak to where he had parked, bracing myself with my right hand on his left shoulder.

I was still woozy and he helped me into the car. As he pulled away from the curb, he finally asked, "So, now that the cops aren't here, who did this to you?"

"If I was a betting man, I'd say it was one of the regulars from the Crazy Horse Bar. I had a few words with a couple of them tonight and I think one of them followed me out of there. There's no other explanation for why nothing was taken from my car."

"You went to the Crazy Horse? Why? Are you tired of living?"

"I needed to talk to Adrian; Pepper told me that was his hangout."

Deak nodded. "It is. I've been trying to get him to quit hanging around there for years, but no luck. The last time I talked to him about it he told me to shut up and mind my own business."

"That's our Adrian. A real sweetheart. How often do you talk to him?"

"Not too often. The church has an emergency food pantry and I take him a couple boxes of groceries once a month or so. If he knows it's me he won't come to the door. I think he's embarrassed that he's getting food from the church, so I just leave it on the porch. Pepper sends me money to give his brother—a couple hundred a month. Pepper's been very generous with Adrian and he's asked a couple of times if he should give him more, but I tell him it will just go to Adrian's liver. It's a sad situation. Pepper wants his brother back, but I don't think it's ever going to happen."

"He looks awful."

"Abusing yourself for upwards of thirty years will do that to a person."

Just west of the Hollywood Shopping Plaza we pulled onto Powell Avenue and into the gravel parking lot behind a story-and-a-half bungalow that had been converted into a doctor's office. A pickup truck passed the building, slowing down while we walked to the back door. "Friends of yours?" Deak asked.

I pointed to my swollen mouth. "If this is any indication, I don't have many friends down here."

The back door to the bungalow was unlocked. After we entered the tiny coat room, I slid the deadbolt into the jamb and watched to see if the pickup truck returned. It did not.

Doctor Oliver Judge appeared to be well into his seventies, a little hunched at the shoulders, eyebrows that would need hedge trimmers to control, and a pair of black glasses that sat crookedly on the bridge of his ample nose. I sat on the table in the examining room and he hummed as he worked his fingers around my jaws and poked gently at my nose and cheek. He moved my lips around with a tongue depressor, saying nothing until he asked, "Who did this to you?"

"I don't know."

He pressed his thumbs against my ears and rolled my head around. "You haven't been running around with a wife that isn't your own, have you?"

"I'm not married."

"That isn't what I asked you, but I'll take that as a no."

Deak smiled.

He took a disposable syringe from a drawer and began drawing a clear liquid from a bottle. "This is going to hurt like . . . "

"A bee sting," I said, completing the sentence I had heard from physicians all my life.

He flicked the syringe with an index finger and said, "No, it's going to hurt like the dickens." Without qualm he flipped my lip up and jabbed me, and he wasn't lying. I twitched and closed my eyes while he worked the needle around my mouth. The relief, however, was almost immediate. There were tears in my eyes when he removed the needle and slipped a cotton roll into my lip. "Let's give that a few minutes to take hold," he said, casually slipping the capped syringe into his shirt pocket while he shuffled out of the back room.

He returned a few minutes later and handed me a plastic bag of crushed ice, the top held shut with a green twist tie. "Put this on your nose and hold it there."

"Is it broken?"

He shrugged. "Maybe, maybe not. If you didn't break it, you've missed a wonderful opportunity. You'll have to get it checked out in a couple of days when the swelling goes down." He walked back out.

"Not much for small talk, is he?" I asked.

"He's a good ol' boy. He runs a free clinic for me once a week at my outreach office downtown. He helps a lot of people and asks for little or nothing in return." Deak eased himself into a metal chair with a cracked green seat cover. The years had not been particularly kind to Deak. His nose had become more pointed, but his chin had flattened out and become encased by soft jowls, giving his head the unfortunate shape of a gourd, a look that was exacerbated by his receding hairline. He had a blowzy complexion, his cheeks and neck pitted and scarred by his years-long battle with acne. Brown rings surrounded tired eyes. After he had settled into the chair, he slouched and rested his interlocked fingers across his chest. "So, what's he done?"

"Who?"

"Uncle Jack. That's why you're here, isn't it?"

The comment caught me off guard. I nodded and was about to go into an explanation when Doctor Judge came back into the room, a curved stainless steel needle in his hands with stitching thread hanging from one end. Without comment he began stitching up the inside of my mouth. The numbing agent hadn't fully taken hold and his stitching hurt like hell, but I said nothing. After tying and snipping off the thread, he said, "Be careful what you eat for a couple of days. The stitches will dissolve in time." He reached into his shirt pocket and produced a small envelope. "Take one of these every eight hours. They'll help you forget how bad your face hurts."

"Thanks," I said, swiping at my watering eyes with the back of my hand. "What do I owe you?"

"Just make a donation to Reverend Coultas's foundation and that will cover it."

"Done," I said. "Thank you. I appreciate it."

He was already heading back to his office. "You're welcome. See you Sunday, Reverend."

I washed down one of the pain pills with a drink from the fountain, dribbling water down my numbed chin. We let ourselves out the back door and made our way across the dark lot to Deak's car. He managed to find every pothole in the lot and each bounce sent pain like an electric shock through my face. My lip throbbed with each beat of my heart, and I struggled to make sense of the attack. Was it the jumbo from the Crazy Horse? If so, what had he been after? It made no sense.

As we drove across Pleasant Heights and passed Union Cemetery, I turned my head away from Deak and through my own reflection in the passenger side window I could see the faint glow of downtown and the darkened hulk that had been the Fort Steuben Hotel, once the city's landmark property. I tried to remember what downtown had looked like in its heyday, when all the windows of the grand hotel were alight, the orange glow of the open hearth at Wheeling-Pittsburgh Steel lit up the skies, and the floodlights of the mill reflected off the Ohio's waters, producing a shimmering show in the wake of passing barges. I could re-create the image in my mind and still smell the dirt and taste the sulfur, but it was difficult to believe that something as mighty as the U.S. steel industry—Big Steel—had crumbled in a few short decades. I asked, "So, how did you know this was about your uncle? Do you have some divine power or was it just a lucky guess?"

"Neither," he said. "I talked to Pepper. He told me Uncle Jack was giving you some problems."

It was odd, I thought, that of the four of us, Pepper, the most outgoing and carefree member of our gang, and Deak, the most introspective and serious, and the two who had almost come to blows in the days after Petey Sanchez's death, were the two who stayed in closest contact. "What did he tell you?"

"That Uncle Jack claims to know what happened up on the hill and he's blackmailing you."

"True, but it's a little more complicated than that."

"How so?"

I hated for the words to come out of my mouth. "There's another young boy involved—physically disabled, mentally retarded, unable to speak."

"A new low for Uncle Jack." Deak's hands tightened on the steering wheel; he clenched his teeth and exhaled long and slow, producing a rattling whistle like a heating tea kettle. "What's the connection?"

"The boy lives in my jurisdiction. Your uncle is under investigation for assault, but to date there hasn't been enough information to charge him. Vukovich told me that if I pursue the case he's going to give the story to the papers. He's already called the *Beacon Journal* and gave a reporter Petey's name to research."

"How does this involve us? Oh wait, I bet I know. If he goes to the paper, you want us all to continue the ruse so that it doesn't upset your chances of winning the election?"

"That's kind of a callous remark coming from a man of the cloth."

He kept his eyes focused on the road. From the moment Jack Vukovich said he had an "issue" with the Portage Township Police Department, there was one person who I most dreaded telling, and now I was sitting in a car with him. I recalled very clearly the comment Deak made decades earlier: Jack Vukovich should be put away so he can never hurt another kid.

I took a breath and exhaled slowly. "How come you never told me that your uncle had molested you?"

He glanced briefly at me, then back to the road. "How do you know he did?"

"I'm a prosecutor, Deak. I don't ask questions that I don't already know the answers to."

He nodded. "Uncle Jack tell you about that, too?"

"No, I was doing some research today and happened upon Vukovich's prosecution file. The transcript of your interview with Children Services was part of the packet."

"So, you went ahead and read it?"

"I didn't go looking for it, Deak. It was just there, for Christ's sake. Why didn't you ever say anything about it?"

"You know, it's not exactly a badge of honor for a fifteen-year-old. It's certainly not the kind of thing you want your buddies to know. It was beyond humiliating. It still is."

"You were a victim, Deak. You have nothing to be ashamed of."

"Spare me the sermon, Hutch. I've lived with this all my life. Jack Vukovich is a monster. He should never have been let out of prison. I can't believe you're even weighing this in your mind. You'd ignore a molestation to further your political career? That disgusts me. I thought I knew you better than that."

"I can't charge someone with a crime simply because someone thinks he might have done it. We have a little thing in this country called due process."

"Due process. What a joke. Do his victims get due process?" His forearms again tightened on the steering wheel. "He used to come over to the house; he always smelled like mold, like a damp basement. He would sit at the kitchen table, talking to my mom, stirring his coffee, maybe working the crossword puzzle. Then he would ask what shift Dad was working in the mill. It didn't seem like anything but casual conversation, but he was planning out his next attack. If I knew when he might come around, I tried not to be there, but sometimes I had to stay and babysit. He would come over and bend me over the sink so he could watch the girls playing in the backyard." Deak looked at me, his nostrils flaring like he was fighting back tears, and maybe the urge to spit. "It wasn't something I wanted to discuss then and I don't really want to discuss it now. I've forgiven my uncle. I couldn't do my job if I didn't forgive him. 'For if ye forgive men their trespasses, your heavenly Father will also forgive you: But if ye forgive not men their trespasses, neither will your Father forgive your trespasses.' The gospel of Matthew."

I looked back out the window. "It takes a big man to forgive someone for such an egregious act."

He shrugged. "Anger does nothing but rot your soul. You have to let go of it. I've moved on with my life. He can't help himself. That's the way he's wired, which is exactly why I didn't want him to ever get out of prison. And now my biggest fear has been realized. He's out of prison and he's molested another child."

"I can only do what I can do under the constraints of the law."

"That's fine, if you can live with the possibility—the certainty, actually—that he will molest other children. I work with abused kids every day, Hutch. Come on over and spend some time in my shoes and then make your decision."

"I'm a prosecuting attorney, Deak. I've seen plenty of abused children."

"Then you should have plenty of empathy." We pulled into the hotel parking lot and got out. "I'll walk you to your room. The pain meds must be kicking in. Your eyes are looking a little glassy."

The sound of racing fire trucks echoed in the background. We walked around the back of the Stoney Hollow Motel, which was built on a bluff where the hillside had been sheared away to create the road years earlier. I liked staying on the back side of hotels because it afforded me privacy. Unfortunately, it afforded privacy to others, too. When I opened the door, the room had been torn apart, but in an odd way. The contents of my suitcase had been emptied on the floor and were strewn around the room and my hanging clothes, two suits and three shirts, had been ripped from the closets. But the drawers from the dresser and nightstand were neatly stacked atop one another, and the mattress and box springs had been taken off the bed and stacked against the wall, as though with great care. Deak stepped into the room behind me. "You've had visitors. What's with the neatly stacked drawers?"

"They were trying to be quiet."

"What were they looking for?"

"I imagine the same thing the guys who thumped me were looking for."

"Which was . . . ?"

"I don't know."That was a lie. I knew exactly what they wanted.

"Are you going to call the police?"

"No. I didn't want a police record of getting thumped. I don't need one of my room getting ransacked. My laptop and money were in the car. It doesn't look like they took anything in here, either."

"I'm not sure I would want your life," Deak said. An emergency vehicle flew by the motel, siren blaring, its red and blue lights flashing off the chiseled hillside. "I wonder what's going on?" We walked around the corner of the hotel to see a plume of gray smoke billowing out of the downtown, reminiscent of the days when the steel mills blazed. The reflection of orange and red flares danced off the old Fort Steuben Hotel. "Want to take a ride?"

"Why not?" I said.

Downtown Steubenville was awash with flashing lights, the central two blocks of the city blocked off by police cars. We parked on North Commercial Street and walked down an alley that ran behind the courthouse. I knew what building was burning before we were close enough to see. The three-story, brick warehouse that was the repository for the county's records looked like a giant chimney, the flames and smoke pouring out its roof. It had been an inferno for quite a while before someone noticed the blaze and called the fire department. Fire fighters manning the hoses sent heavy streams of water arcing over the rim of the building, but to little avail.

"Heck of a fire," Deak said. "I wonder what the building's used for?"

"To store old county records."

"How do you know that?"

"I was in there looking around earlier today."

"Is that where you saw the file on Petey Sanchez?" I nodded. "Don't you think it's strange that it would burn the same day you were there?"

"It might not be as strange as you would imagine."

Cutting across the parking lot to the north of the courthouse was Alfred Botticelli Junior, and his goon of a deputy, who was now dressed in jeans and a golf shirt. "Evening, Reverend."

"Hello, Mr. Botticelli."

"A tragic loss for the county," Botticelli said, turning to me. "All those records destroyed. Of course, we'll launch an investigation into the cause. Mr. Van Buren, I understand that you were given a key to the building earlier in the day?"

"You know I was. I put it squarely in your hand."

He shook his head. "I don't know what you're talking about. You didn't give me a key." He turned to the goon. "Deputy, you were there. Did you see Mr. Van Buren give me a key to the warehouse?"

"I have no recollection of that."

"Tsk, tsk," Botticelli said, grinning. "I guess we'll be talking again soon."

Chapter Twenty-Six

The knocking on the door began at 7:15 a.m. The painkilling drugs had knocked me out and it took a few moments to come to my senses. There were dried bloodstains on my pillow; my mouth throbbed; my nose felt as though it stretched from ear to ear. The sun was filtering through the windows. The knocking continued. "Coming," I groaned. It was too early to be housekeeping. This was the deliberate knock of someone demanding attention. I staggered to the door and opened it as far as the safety chain would allow.

Standing tall, trim, smiling, was the dapper chairman of the United States House of Representatives's Ways and Means Committee, Alfred Botticelli Senior. "Are you sleeping away the day?" he asked.

I squinted. There was another man standing behind him, hands folded over his crotch, wearing sunglasses, as erect and nattily attired as the congressman. I said, "I had a bit of a tough night."

"You know who I am?" he asked.

"Of course."

He nodded. "Good. I'd like to talk to you."

I was standing behind the door in nothing but my briefs, and I was not about to allow a U.S. congressman in the room. "Give me fifteen minutes. I'll meet you in the restaurant."

He continued to smile, but his tone was stern. "I'm a busy man, Mr. Van Buren. Make it ten minutes."

Alfred Botticelli was one of the most powerful members of the United States Congress, where he had reigned for twenty-six years. After two terms as the Jefferson County prosecuting attorney, he won the congressional seat in the largely Democratic stronghold of Eastern Ohio. He had been unopposed in Democratic primaries since his first term, and his Republican challengers were little more than sacrificial lambs. He had been the target of numerous ethics investigations, most for questionable financial dealings, but not one of the probes had produced a shred of tangible evidence that he had done anything illegal. He called the investigations "witch hunts" being conducted by his political enemies. The media had dubbed him "Teflon Al" for the way the allegations slid off him.

Despite his challenges within the halls of Congress, he was much beloved in his district. Named in his honor in Jefferson County alone there were no fewer than two baseball fields, three streets, the wing of a hospital, an elementary school, a senior citizens center, a bridge, a heliport, a portion of a highway, and at least three male offspring of loyal Democrats.

His power had been accrued by his longevity and, in part, his ability to collect information on friend and foe. Botticelli had an affable, disarming manner and called those he encountered, particularly freshman congressmen, "my old friend" or "padnah." He would drape an arm around their shoulders and make them feel as though they were the most important person in the world. Ultimately, they would fall prey to his charm, let their guard down, and take him into their confidence. This was their downfall.

In the world of Machiavellian, cutthroat politics, he was an undisputed master. In public, he would smile and joke and pat his fellow representatives on the back. In the confines of his congressional office, he would continue to smile while twisting the balls of anyone who dared oppose him. When one such opponent called him a son of a bitch, Botticelli smiled and said, "I didn't come here to make friends, padnah."

Botticelli charted with amazing accuracy the weaknesses of congressmen, senators, lobbyists, even presidents. And being a member of the Democratic Party did not exempt you from his data base. Botticelli innately understood the fickleness of Washington,

D.C., and national politics. A man who is your ally today could very well be your enemy tomorrow. In his office safe he hid a journal that contained decades of indiscretions by his colleagues. He collected information on their infidelities and with whom, who took bribes, who were tax cheats, and any other scrap of information that he could someday use to his advantage. Once it was known that he craved such information, he became a clearinghouse for the misdeeds of anyone tied to the Washington power scene. Snitches sent him anonymous snippets of information, photographs of congressmen leaving hotel rooms late at night, photocopies of bank receipts from the Cayman Islands. It made him one of the most powerful, feared, and despised men in Washington.

By the time I cleaned up and arrived at the hotel restaurant thirteen minutes later, Botticelli was seated in a corner booth, a newspaper on the corner of his table, a cup of coffee wrapped in his right fingers. The aide was seated at a table in the middle of the room, his eyes drilling me the moment I walked into the room. I slipped into the vinyl bench across from Botticelli. He began speaking, but kept his eyes focused on his newspaper. "I didn't realize we were dealing with a big celebrity," he said. "You're going to be the next attorney general of the state of Ohio."

Botticelli's lips were thin and did a poor job of hiding a mouth full of large teeth that clicked together as he spoke. When he smiled the lips all but disappeared and his mouth took on the perpetual death-grin appearance of a sun-dried corpse. His hair was white and not a strand out of place.

The waitress stopped by, pad in hand. Finally looking up from his paper, Botticelli pointed at me and said, "You should try some biscuits and gravy. They have delicious gravy and biscuits."

"Just some coffee, please." She spun on a heel and was gone. I hadn't eaten in nearly twenty-four hours and was starving, but decided to forgo breakfast until after the encounter.

He folded the newspaper back into its original form, running his finger across the middle to reset the crease "So, back to your old stomping grounds, huh, Mr. Van Buren? You enjoying your stay?"

"Enjoying my stay? Well, let's see. In the last day I've been bullied around by your son and his goon, was jumped and assaulted, had twelve stitches put in my mouth, my room was ransacked, I watched the repository for all county records go up in a fire that was as mysterious as it was spectacular, your son showed up to offer a vague threat of accusing me of starting the fire, and now the chairman of the United States House of Representatives's Ways and Means Committee has invited me to have biscuits and gravy. To say the least, Congressman, it's been a very surreal twenty-four hours. I guess I forgot that you play hardball down here in the valley."

"My son and his associates can be a little overly rambunctious at times." He carved out a pie-shaped piece of biscuit with gravy that was beginning to congeal and shoved it in the corner of his mouth.

"Overly rambunctious? That's one way of putting it, I guess." The waitress set my coffee on the table and dropped two plastic containers of cream beside it. "So, what can I do for you, Congressman?"

"I like a man who cuts to the chase," he said, dabbing at his mouth with a paper napkin. "What's your game, Mr. Van Buren? Why are you hanging around Steubenville in the middle of campaign season, and, more importantly, why were you making copies of my old campaign contribution records?" I started to laugh; it hurt the swollen inside of my mouth. His demeanor turned stern. "Am I missing something funny, Mr. Van Buren? Because I'm failing to see any humor here."

"Last night, I thought some thug from the Crazy Horse Bar had followed me into town and sucker punched me because he didn't like my good looks, because nothing was stolen out of my SUV." I took an index finger and turned up my puffy lip, exposing my stitches. "Then, I got back to my hotel and found my room had been neatly ransacked, and it finally dawned on me that it wasn't the guy from the Crazy Horse, but most likely someone who wanted those contribution records. This was confirmed even more when the warehouse went up in flames. Of course, I thought it was your son behind it all. I didn't realize it was you."

"Where are those copies you had made?"

"Congressman, of all people, you are a man who understands leverage. I'm not sure what the hell's going on here, but I'm certainly not willing to release what might be my only bargaining chip." I gently set the coffee cup in the corner of my mouth that was still of normal size and sipped at my coffee. Despite my best efforts, it still burned the stitched wound inside my mouth.

"What's your interest in the documents?"

"Your son made the connection. That's why he had that goon of a sheriff's deputy sucker punch me in the alley last night. When they couldn't find the documents in my car, they ransacked my hotel room. When they couldn't find the copies, they decided to destroy the originals to eliminate any collaborating evidence, which I assume came at your direction."

He smiled and laughed, a deflective defense mechanism. "Is there more to this fairy tale, Mr. Van Buren? And what does all this have to do with the Vukovich file, which I understand you also were snooping into?"

"Are you familiar with the Main Street Task Force?" He shook his head. "It's a special law enforcement arm of the attorney general. Right now, the task force is investigating payoffs made to Jack Vukovich. I know this for a fact. What I don't know is why they started investigating him, or where the money is coming from. It's certainly hush money, and I suspect it's coming either from you, perhaps your son, or maybe Carson Nash."

He smiled and sipped his coffee. "So, Mr. Van Buren, tell me this . . ." He set his coffee cup down, folded his hands on the table, and leaned in. "Why on earth would I do such a thing as pay off a low-life cretin like Jack Vukovich? Help me here. What would be my motivation?"

He had me. I had slipped and made a rookie mistake, losing my advantage. I couldn't tell him why I believed he would attempt to buy Jack Vukovich's silence without indicting myself. I hoped to skirt the real issue, but there was no reason to bluff or play coy. "Jack Vukovich was in my office the other day. He said you knew he wasn't the real killer of Petey Sanchez and you offered to drop the death penalty specs against him for taking the fall for the killing."

His facial expression never changed. He said, "Of course, you know that is a totally ludicrous allegation from a man with absolutely no credibility. Why on earth would he have pleaded guilty to a crime he didn't commit?"

"Even tough guys don't want to die."

"I have no recollection of the details of the plea agreement—it's been so long—and unfortunately the official records were tragically destroyed in last night's fire. However, if Mr. Vukovich now claims he wasn't the killer and that he was wrongly convicted, that would mean that someone else was up on the hill the day young Mr. Sanchez was killed, wouldn't it?" I didn't respond and he allowed the words to hang in the air. "Given that, perhaps I should ask my son to reopen the case to see who else may have been up on Chestnut Ridge that morning."

"If you did, I wouldn't be the only politician with credibility problems."

"Whatever do you mean?"

"You're the one that sent an innocent man to prison."

Botticelli slowly shook his head. "Mr. Van Buren, I did not get to the point where I am in life by being careless. Not one shred of evidence exists that shows I knew anyone other than the accused—Jack Vukovich—was up on the hill that day. If my son reopens the investigation and determines that someone else killed that young man, I will salute him and proclaim my sincere sorrow that Mr. Vukovich spent so many years in prison for a crime he did not commit. I will call it a tragedy and a terrible, terrible miscarriage of justice. I'll show the proper amount of contrition and the fact that I was the prosecutor will soon be forgotten. What they'll remember, however, is that four boys—a respected preacher, a successful businessman, a former football star, and a candidate for Ohio attorney general—conspired to hide this for all these years." His death-like grin consumed his face. He was a feral cat toying with a field mouse. He leaned in and in a hushed tone said, "Publicly, that's what I'll say. Mr. Vukovich told me all the names of the boys who were up on the hill that morning, but sending a bunch of high school kids to juvenile hall gave me no political advantage. However . . ." He winked and clicked his tongue. ". . . send a pedophile to prison and you're talking about some serious political points, and that's what I did. I sent Vukovich to prison and old man Nash graciously agreed to an arrangement that would keep his kid clean. Funny how things work out, isn't it? The younger Nash brother becomes a successful businessman and I squeeze him like I squeeze his old man. The good reverend periodically supplies me with a pulpit from which I can speak directly to the voters. And now, you're running for attorney general, and I'm sure there will be ample opportunity for you to help me out."

Alfred Botticelli stood and dropped a twenty-dollar bill on the table. "My advice to you, Mr. Van Buren, is to go back to your campaign and make sure the copies of those records never see the light of day, because if they do I will pull the package on you and you won't be able to get elected dogcatcher." Across the room the aide stood and took a few steps toward our booth. Botticelli raised a finger and the man stopped. "Let me give you a little advice, Mr. Van Buren. The people who will be most valuable to you in your political career are those who are weak and those who have much to lose. Sometimes, you can take those who have the most to lose and make them weak, like Carson Nash. He was a strong man, but he was so concerned with protecting the reputation of his precious little boy that he left himself exposed. I simply took advantage of that vulnerability. Remember this—I'm not some penny-ante criminal from Akron. I am a United States congressman and I didn't get there by leaving a trail of breadcrumbs for second-rate investigators like you to follow. It's not the Jack Vukoviches of the world that are the problem. It's people like you. You want the power and prestige of being attorney general, but you allow pipsqueaks like Jack Vukovich to gum up the works. You don't have the stomach to simply take care of the problem. You remember this, son, if those contribution records surface, I'll make sure every voter in the state of Ohio knows you were up on that hill." He picked up his paper off the table and motioned with his head to his aide. "Yes, we do play hardball down here in the valley, Mr. Van Buren, and you are completely out of your league."

"I might just be a little smarter than you're giving me credit for, Congressman."

"I doubt that. You have a good day."

When Alfred Botticelli and his aide had disappeared from the restaurant, I reached into my jacket pocket and turned off my digital recorder.

Chapter Twenty-Seven

I walked out of the restaurant and took a deep breath, cleansing the aroma of bacon and coffee from my nostrils. As I headed toward the far end of the hotel and my room, a familiar black sedan was creeping along the curb toward me. The darkened passenger side window dropped as the car neared, revealing the smarmy face of Alfred Botticelli Junior, who stared up past his thick brows. I leaned down, looked past Botticelli, and said, "Well, well, well, if it isn't the arsonist and his trained chimp."

"Consider yourself lucky that you didn't wake up in the hospital, asshole," the deputy said.

Botticelli held up a hand for silence. "Do we have an understanding, Mr. Van Buren?"

"We?" I laughed out loud. "Let me ask you this: Do you always call Daddy to do your heavy lifting? He comes in to squeeze me, then you do the mop-up work? 'Do we have an understanding?' Give me a break."

He rolled his teeth over his lower lip. "I think it would behoove you to make sure those campaign contribution records get into my hands."

"'Behoove,' that's another good word." I wanted to punch his face. "Go away, junior. If I'm going to be bullied and blackmailed it's going to be by a better man than you." I looked over at the deputy and patted down my jacket. "Sorry, I'm all out of bananas. I'll catch you next time."

Chills ran up my spine as I walked away from the car. I'm sure they were both watching in the rearview mirror until I disappeared around the corner of the building. Once out of sight, I sprinted to my room and locked myself in, quickly stuffing my few belongings into the suitcase. I wanted to get out of the hotel before the goon paid me another visit. I checked out and asked the elderly woman at the front desk to call me a taxi as my Pacifica was—I hoped—still parked in the alley behind Naples Restaurant. I would get the SUV and stop on my way out of town to get some breakfast. I stepped outside the hotel lobby and called Margaret while I waited for my ride. "Enjoying your vacation?" she asked.

"It's been interesting."

"Those aren't the kind of words I usually hear to describe a vacation."

"Well, they're the only ones that fit. I overnighted myself a package yesterday—a thick envelope."

"It just arrived. I recognized your chicken scratch writing on the label. It's on your desk."

"Put it in the safe, please."

"I can do that."

"Anything going on that I need to know about?"

"No, but the day is young. I've been sending calls over to Mr. Lanihan and I haven't heard any explosions from his office, so I assume he's handling things. Your girlfriend hasn't called in the last ten minutes, which makes my life easier."

"Good. I'll be back in the office Monday."

I had not intended to return to the Ohio Valley to create a shit storm, but that's exactly what I had done, and in a ridiculously short period of time. I'm not sure what I had hoped to achieve by visiting my old friends—a recommitment to our silence, guidance, perhaps reassurance that I should stay true to my oath to uphold the law? What I had hoped was to slip in and out the valley unnoticed. Instead, I had set off land mines everywhere I went, the repercussions reaching all the way to the halls of Congress.

I hopped into the back of the taxi and directed the driver to the Pacifica. The tires of the taxi had just bounced onto Dean Martin

Boulevard when my cell phone rang. It was Deak. "What are you up to?"

"Getting ready to blow Dodge. I think I'm pushing my luck staying here any longer."

"You need to stay a while longer. The old man wants to talk to you."

"Which old man?"

"Carson Nash."

"Really? How did he find out?"

"Adrian called him in a panic after your visit. Apparently, he told Carson that everything that happened up on Chestnut Ridge was going to be made public. He also said you had the power to stop it if you wanted to, but you don't want to."

"That isn't what I said."

"I'm just the messenger, Hutch. Carson called Pepper and asked him if he knew anything about it. Pepper said he did and the old man went ballistic—started screaming and cussing into the phone. Pepper called me and said he thought Carson was going to have an aneurysm. He wants to meet us at the bank at six o'clock tonight."

"That works for me. Are you going to be there?"

"I figure we all ought to be there. I can guarantee it'll be ugly. In spite of what Adrian's become, there's nothing more important to Carson Nash than preserving the memory of what his son used to be."

Killing nine hours in Steubenville, Ohio, is no small task. I wandered around the Fort Steuben Mall for a while, stopped by M&M Hardware to look at lawn edgers, ate—sipped, actually—a lunch of chicken noodle soup and lemonade at Bob Evans, then spent a few hours at the library perusing newspapers and magazines. The last two hours I spent cruising the little towns along the Ohio River, recalling days when we did duck-and-cover drills in school, certain the Soviets would target us for nuclear attack because of the mighty steel industry. It would have been a much quicker death.

* * *

At first glance, the conference room at the Glass Works Bank and Trust Company looked like a Crystalton Royals hall of fame, its walls lined with plaques, certificates, and framed newspaper clippings of past athletic achievements. A shelf extending across the back wall was adorned with dustless trophies. Upon closer inspection, however, one realized that the memorabilia did not honor the teams, but a single member—Adrian Nash. In the corner of one wall were a few framed photos of Pepper in his Pitt Panthers uniform and an article about the national championship team, but those were the only mentions of the younger brother.

When I entered with Deak, Adrian was slouched in a chair on one side of the conference table, dressed in the same flannel shirt and jeans he had been wearing the previous night. He nodded when we entered, though it was barely perceptible. Pepper was seated across from his brother, neat in a pressed blue dress shirt and gray slacks. He stood, shook our hands, and said to me, "What the hell happened to your face?"

"Long story," I said.

Carson Nash was talking on the phone in his office. I heard him say, "He's here now." Unless I miss my guess he was talking to one of the Botticellis. Deak sat down next to Adrian. I walked around the table and looked at the clippings, tales of victories of which I had been a part. I wondered what Adrian thought when he looked around a room that was a shrine to his former self. Probably, he didn't think anything. While it seemed like yesterday to Pepper and me, it probably seemed like a lifetime ago to Adrian. He had been so defeated that he no longer considered the depths to which he had dropped.

I sat down and there we were, the Chestnut Ridge four, together for the first time since we sat together at graduation in 1974. The notion of getting all concerned to recommit to silence now seemed like a foolish venture. The realities of June 14, 1971, were known to more people than I could have imagined, all of whom were intricately interconnected. It was inevitable that the truth of that morning would eventually surface. The first domino would fall and nobody would be spared by the fallout.

Carson Nash walked into the room, teeth clenched, his jaw muscles rolling up into his ears. He was in his mid-seventies, but only a grayer version of the man I had known as a boy. The forearms extending beyond his rolled-up sleeves were thick, his belly stretched tight under his dress shirt. I stood and reached to shake his hand, which he regarded as though it was covered with canker sores. Pepper dropped his head. Carson sat at the head of the table, rolling a fist into an open palm, and it seemed to take him a moment to catch his composure. When that occurred, he turned to me and asked, "So, what's this shit all about?"

As I had expected, all eyes turned to me. "We've got a problem. Jack Vukovich was up on Chestnut Ridge the day Petey Sanchez . . ."

"I know that," Carson interrupted. "I've known that for years. What's that got to do with anything?"

The heat of anger was creeping up my neck. "He's now ready to tell the world what really happened up there. If I pursue charges against him on another child molesting rap, he says he'll go public."

"So, who in hell's going to believe him? He a fuckin' child molester."

"He's going to produce a polygraph test that shows he did not kill Petey Sanchez. It's going to be ugly."

"Then don't prosecute him. Let him go."

"Just like that? Ignore the fact that he's molesting a mentally retarded boy?" Carson interlocked his fingers and squeezed his thick hands, staring hard, waiting for me to flinch. "That's not the only problem. There's a state investigative unit, the Main Street Task Force, which works on white-collar crime—banks, governmental agencies, nonprofits. I just found out that its investigators are looking into money being funneled to Vukovich. That's where things are going to get real ugly."

Carson frowned. "What the hell's that mean?"

"It means someone is dipping into the till and sending money to Jack Vukovich. Their investigators don't care that Vukovich is the recipient; they're investigating the source of the money. My guess is it's either coming from the coffers of the Jefferson County Democratic Party, or one of the Botticellis, or from you, Mr. Nash."

"Me! That's preposterous. Where in the hell did you get a crazy idea like that?"

"I saw the campaign contributions you've been making to the Botticellis—contributions in your name and the name of some fictitious political action committee. The contributions began within days after Jack Vukovich was first arrested."

"Don't ever let me hear those words come out of your mouth again," he said, gripping the end of the conference table, his nostrils flaring.

"You can be upset with me if you like, but this is all going to blow up in our faces. I can't tell you how the money is getting to Vukovich, but it's clearly illegal or it wouldn't have the attention of the task force."

He took a few deep breaths. "I'll talk to Botticelli. He can pull some strings and get the dogs called off."

"If there's fraud involved, there's no way he'll get them to back off."

Carson laughed in a mocking tone. "You obviously don't know the influence of Alfred Botticelli."

"Maybe I don't, but I know how hungry reporters act. You think you can make this one go away, but once Vukovich gets his information to the media it will only be the beginning. Reporters will be swarming all over this place like you can't imagine. It'll be like dumping blood in shark-infested waters. They'll do stories about Petey Sanchez. They'll do stories about me, you, Adrian, Pepper, and Deak. None of us will be immune or excluded. They'll talk to Sky Kelso, they'll find out the bank was contributing liberally to the coffers of the Botticellis. It will be an ungodly mess."

"It would seem, then, that you are the only person in the room that can control that. Make it go away."

"I can't make the task force go away," I said.

"I don't give a damn about the task force—I haven't given Vukovich a dime. But you can give Vukovich what he wants."

"There's a kid who's been victimized, Mr. Nash. I don't think I can ignore that."

"You can do anything you goddamn want. The last thirty years of our lives have been predicated on one event." He held up an index finger. "Just one. Everything in our lives has grown from there. I did what I had to do. Yes, I paid off Botticelli. So what? A child molester went to prison and Adrian stayed clean. It isn't anything that any father in my position wouldn't have done. I've paid the Botticellis every year since. I understand how protection money works. It's part of the price of admission. We've all lived around here. We're the ones who have driven past Chestnut Ridge a thousand times and got a sick feeling in our guts every time. You left. Now, all of a sudden it's become an inconvenience to you, so you want to throw us all under the bus."

"I hardly think trying to keep Jack Vukovich from molesting another kid is throwing you under the bus."

Carson Nash slammed his fist on the desk. "Then find a way to shut him up. Do something, but don't ruin our lives."

"I'm waiting for DNA tests to return. If the tests are positive for Jack Vukovich's DNA, I'll prosecute. I'll have no choice. When I indict him, he'll go to the media."

"You're a coward."

My jaw dropped. "Coward? I've got a horse in this race, too, Mr. Nash. My campaign for attorney general goes down the tubes if this comes out."

"In that case, you're not a coward. You're just stupid."

★ ★ ★

Deak and I leaned against the fenders of our vehicles, arms folded across our chests, and watched as Adrian left in his ramshackle pickup truck, dropping over a curb without so much as a glance our way. Carson nodded as he got into his sedan and pulled out of the rear of the parking lot, exiting by the alley and heading toward the old homestead. Pepper came over and hoisted himself up on the fender of Deak's car. The sun was low to the west, balancing atop Chestnut Ridge, preparing to disappear into the Seneca Creek Valley.

"You were awful quiet in there," I offered to Pepper.

He nodded and for a moment looked like he might be fighting back tears. "You know, I run a successful business, several successful businesses, actually, but when I get around that old man I'm like a whipped puppy. I walk into that conference room and I swear I would like to tear it to pieces. I've spent my entire adult life trying to prove my worth to that son of a bitch, and he can't stop polishing Adrian's high school trophies long enough to notice."

"Don't blame your dad, Pepper; he can't help it," I said.

"He can't help it? Are you kidding me?"

"He's a typical parent. He spends time and money on the one that needs the most attention, and that's Adrian. Your dad's fixation on him, though, has moved from admiration to pity. We've all moved on, but Adrian has retreated to a secure place where he can always be Adrian Nash and your dad enables him. Mentally and emotionally, Adrian hasn't progressed much past our senior year in high school. That was the apex of his life and he's content to live there."

"He's just weak," Pepper said. "My dad coddles Adrian and he's content just to be a bum. I don't believe all the psychological mumbo-jumbo. He's a bum, period."

We sat in silence for a moment. We were, I'm sure, in agreement with Pepper's assessment of his brother, but were no less sad for our friend and brother. I asked, "Do you think things would have been different for Adrian if we hadn't run into Petey that day?"

Pepper shrugged. "I don't know. It probably contributed."

"Probably contributed?" Deak asked. "I'd say it was central. Whatever demons Adrian struggles with are a direct result of that day."

"We were all there," I said. "We seem to be doing okay."

"None of us threw the maul," Deak said.

"He uses it as a crutch and to sponge off my dad," Pepper said. "He needs to man up."

We were silent for a long moment. I asked, "So, Botticelli has been squeezing both of you, too?"

They looked at each other. Pepper nodded. "Yeah, for about twenty years. The *Herald-Star* did a feature story on my businesses and that son of a bitch showed up in my office the next morning. It's a cash transaction. He hits me for ten grand a year. I'd have told him to kiss my bare ass, but you saw how my dad feels about this. I just hold my nose, pay it, and try to forget about it."

Deak said, "He has never asked me for money. He said he didn't feel right about taking money from a man of the cloth. Once or twice a year he speaks at the church on Sunday mornings. There are upwards of eight hundred people in the sanctuary. He comes on the pretext of delivering a message, but it's nothing more than a thinly veiled campaign rally. If Adrian had fifteen cents he'd have gone after him, too. You're up next. He'll go after you, especially if you win the election."

"He intimated that this morning."

Deak looked at me. "Remember after Petey died, and you said if we could just get enough time behind his death all would be well?"

Tick-tock, I thought. I nodded. "I missed on that one."

"I think about that a lot. I think about what happened on Chestnut Ridge and the heavy price that's been paid." Deak looked up at the hill where Petey Sanchez had died and the sun was now a half orb. "You went out of your way to protect Adrian, and what's it gotten us? What's it gotten you? Nothing but heartache."

"The fact remains, we were trying to protect a friend."

"But, was that the right call?" Pepper asked. "I mean, in retrospect, if we had gone to the cops that day, what's the worst that would have happened? Most likely, it would have been ruled self-defense and we'd all have gone on with our lives."

"You can't look at decisions we made when we were fifteen years old through adult eyes," I said. "We thought we were doing the right thing at the time."

Chapter Twenty-Eight

My bowels were rattling like castanets, a combination of nerves and too much caffeine. It was not unusual for my intestines to swing like an untethered fire hose when my nerves got the best of me, but at that moment it felt like a mariachi band was playing in my guts. I was working on my second roll of antacids since noon. I burped in staccato bursts and choked down the acid that gurgled into my throat and mouth. My ribs felt like they were constricted by leather straps, restricting each breath. I hadn't been able to fill my lungs in days.

All this because on a hilltop more than three decades before we had decided to surround the pocket and protect our friend and quarterback. Meanwhile, somewhere in a dive bar in eastern Ohio, Adrian Nash was filling his belly with beer and laughing and telling stories of heroics long past. In some perverted way, I felt Adrian wanted the information to come out to inflict pain on Pepper, Deak, and me for having moved on and made more of our lives than throwing perfect spirals on high school gridirons. How ironic, I thought, that Adrian Nash, the erstwhile would-be astronaut and congressman, the pride of the Crystalton High class of seventy-four, now had the least to lose. In fact, with his reputation gone, he had virtually nothing to lose.

It was well after dark when I cruised past Tappan Lake and hopped on Interstate 77 north toward Akron. The radio station I had been listening to had turned to static; the puddle of fast-food coffee in the bottom of a large Styrofoam cup had gone cold. For the tenth time during the trip, I patted my jacket pocket and checked the whereabouts of my digital recorder. I was feeling guilty about recording the conversation with Carson Nash, too, but felt I needed the backup. As Congressman Botticelli had made very clear, they were playing hardball, and I was the outsider. Once upon a time I had been part of the team, but no longer. The recorder would go into the safe with the copies of the campaign contributions as insurance policies. Unfortunately, I had no such policy against Jack Vukovich.

The windshield wipers swatted at the steady rain that I had driven into just east of Cadiz. The rain increased in intensity the further north I drove, the drops sounding like marbles pelting the Pacifica. As I neared Canton, I called Shelly Dennison; the call rolled to voice mail after just one ring. "Hey, it's me. I'm back in town. Give me a call, please." She had hit the "ignore" button, still aggravated at me, no doubt. I was being punished. She would return the call when it was convenient for her. Shelly only played by Shelly's rules.

I pondered my trip to Crystalton. In reality, I could have just picked up the phone and told Deak and Pepper about Vukovich's threats. A psychologist would probably say I was seeking support, hoping one of my childhood friends would tell me to do the right thing. Deak had, but I was still struggling. I had not pursued charges against Elmer Glick because of a lack of evidence, even though I believed him to be guilty of murder. Under law, I believed I was obligated to give Jack Vukovich the same consideration if the DNA tests were negative. But I knew this was different. I didn't like being threatened and pushed around, especially by someone like Jack Vukovich, who was standing directly in front of me, an index finger jabbing me in the chest. If the evidence wasn't there and I didn't pursue charges, he would think I had backed down out of fear. I couldn't win.

I pulled the Pacifica into the garage and walked back out into the rain to collect the newspapers I had forgotten to put a hold on before leaving. The rain had left them swollen and plastered to the sidewalk. I peeled them off the concrete and dropped the wet glob in the trash on my way inside. All I wanted was to crawl into my own bed.

★ ★ ★

"Oh, my God. What happened to your face?" Margaret asked.

"It had an unfortunate collision with a very large, very hard fist."

"Whose?"

"A guy I hope never to cross paths with again."

"No doubt." She arose and followed me into the office, updating me on a host of minor inter-office squabbles and personnel matters that needed attention. As she ticked off the items on the list she kept in her notebook, I rolled through the combination on my office safe and placed the digital recorder on a shelf with the envelope that contained the copies of Botticelli's campaign contributions.

"Order me another digital recorder, please."

Margaret nodded and I saw her catch a glance of the inside of the safe as I closed the door. Her eyebrow raised in that familiar quizzical way, but she didn't ask any questions. "I need some time to catch up on work, Margaret. No calls or visitors unless it's an emergency."

"Understood," she said as she walked out and pulled my office door closed behind her.

The edict didn't last five minutes. I hadn't even gotten my computer booted up before my phone rang. "You have a visitor."

She didn't have to identify the visitor. I knew. "Send her in."

Shelly Dennison was all drama. She walked in and shut the door, slowly, so the latch scraped the strike plate and fell, creating a tiny echo in the room. The look on her face was a contrived combination of disgust and disappointment. She walked across the room with her arms folded over her breasts. "So, you've decided to return. How thoughtful of you."

"Hello, sweetheart, it's good to see you, too."

"You . . . " She stepped closer and squinted. "What happened to your face?"

"Some guy didn't appreciate my sense of humor. I'm fine."

"It looks horrible."

"Thanks for the concern."

She planted her fists on her hips. "Do you know how much ground you've lost while you were out tilting at windmills?"

"No. How much?"

She ignored my flippant response. She didn't know, and if I had lost any ground at all it was infinitesimal.

"Just tell me this, Hutchinson, what were you hoping to accomplish?"

"Who's asking, my campaign manager or my girlfriend?"

"On this point, we are one and the same." I had my doubts. "So, what's going on with your little investigation?" she asked, a mocking tone to her voice.

"I don't know what's going to happen."

She shook her head. "We're supposed to be at a rally this afternoon in Columbus. If it's not too much trouble, do you think you can throw a little makeup on your cheek and nose and work that into your schedule?"

"What time are we leaving?"

"I'll pick you up at two, and change that necktie before we leave, it's hideous." She left without another word.

I worked at my desk undisturbed the rest of the morning. Margaret brought me a cheeseburger from the diner next door for lunch, along with a list of people who had called for me that morning. There were a dozen names on the list, one of whom was Jack Vukovich.

I dialed the number of the man who was the source of my intestinal troubles. "Jack, Hutchinson Van Buren."

"You get to the office at seven forty-five in the morning and don't call me until nearly one fifteen in the afternoon? I still don't think you're taking me very seriously, Mr. Prosecutor."

"What do you want, Jack?"

"I swear to Jesus Christ, if you ask me that question again I'll be in the lobby of the *Beacon Journal* in ten minutes. What the fuck do you think I want?"

"I'm afraid I don't have any news."

His breathing was labored, the sound of a man struggling to control his rage. "That's not what I wanted to hear."

"I'm sure it isn't. Do you think this is an easy process, Jack?"

"I'm not stupid, Van Buren. I know how the system works. If the county's top law enforcement officer kills an investigation, it's dead. Period."

"You said I had a week, Jack. My week doesn't end until Wednesday afternoon. Sit tight. I'll be in touch."

The phone went dead.

It was just before two when Shelly returned. She was carrying a plastic bag from a department store. She handed it to me and said, "Put it on." It was a necktie—navy and gold diagonal stripes. Classy and conservative. There was nothing wrong with the tie I was wearing—red with gold fleurs-de-lis—except that she didn't like it and had been looking for something to pick at that morning. I put on the new tie in the restroom off my office. When I emerged I asked, "Better?"

"Much," she said, with little more than a glance my way. I went back to my desk to put on my jacket and throw a few documents in my briefcase. "We don't have all day."

As I came around the desk I said, "I can see this is going to be a pleasant trip. What about these bruises?"

"We'll touch them up when we get there," she said, leading me out the door to her car. I felt like a scolded second-grader following a teacher to the principal's office.

I was a sideshow at the rally, which was held on the west lawn of the Ohio statehouse and timed for coverage by the evening news. Don Dunfee, the Republican candidate for secretary of state, was the primary beneficiary. He was in a tight race with the incumbent, and the party was hoping for a final surge leading up to election day. My role was to stand up and give a rousing endorsement speech for Dunfee, who I secretly disliked and believed to be a total boob who had no business running for a local sewer board, let alone secretary of state. This is why I hated politics. To be a good team player I was duty bound to stand up and tell a crowd of people that Don Dunfee was not only a great American, but also the only logical candidate for Ohio secretary of state. I gagged my way through the entire speech.

It was a good event for Shelly, who received many kudos for running such a great campaign on my behalf. This put her in a good mood for the ride home, at least until my phone rang just as she drove past the first Mansfield exit. I didn't recognize the number, but whoever it belonged to had tried to call me twice during the rally. This time I answered.

"Jesus Christ, where the hell have you been?

"Who's this?"

"Jerry Adameyer. I've been trying to get a hold of you for two fuckin' hours."

"I've been busy, Jerry. What's up?"

"Want some good news?"

Again, my gut began to constrict. "I always want good news."

"We've got Vukovich. The DNA results came back positive." He sounded like a kid who had just gotten a pony. "We've got him nailed, right to the fuckin' wall. The lab found a pubic hair follicle in the encrusted blood in the kid's underwear. It's Vukovich's."

I thought I'd vomit. "That's awesome, Jerry, just awesome."

"Damn lucky, I'd say. I wanted to touch base with you before we head out to arrest the bastard."

Jerry talked so loud that Shelly was hearing every word. Her jaw flexed and she rolled her hands over the steering wheel.

"Let's hold up on that, Jerry. I want to take this one to the grand jury."

"What? Why wait? He's toast. Let's get the perv off the streets before he does any more damage."

"It's a touchy case, Jerry. Let's make sure we've got all the bases covered. One hair in the kid's underwear is not slam dunk evidence. Let's get together in the morning and talk about it, make sure we're square, and I'll take it to the grand jury."

He exhaled into the phone and was, I sensed, trying to keep his temper in check. "I wish to God I knew what the deal is with you and this case. A few years ago you would have been in my office in ten minutes so you could go with us on the pinch."

"With age comes caution. Can you and Officer Davidson be in my office at eight a.m.?" I asked.

"We'll be there, goddammit."

I snapped my phone shut and looked at Shelly. She held her open right hand toward me and said, "Don't talk."

Chapter Twenty-Nine

Years earlier, just after I was first elected Summit County prosecuting attorney, I attended a leadership and management conference. One of the seminars I attended was put on by a crisis communications and reputation management specialist, who spoke on how to deliver bad news. The one takeaway I recall from his talk was to get the bad news out in the open quickly and honestly. "Sometimes you have to fall on the sword," he said. "Admit to your mistakes, apologize in earnest, show the proper amount of contrition, and state clearly why you will never again repeat the error." It seemed simple enough, though I was reasonably certain that no amount of contrition would elicit any sympathy when the misdeed was allowing someone go to prison for a murder he didn't commit, then remaining silent for many years.

I sat alone at my desk, elbows on its polished mahogany surface, my fingertips touching, my index fingers planted between my brows. The only noticeable noise in the room was the inner workings of the large clock on the far wall. Tick-tock. I felt an odd inner peace. Having come to the decision to beat Jack Vukovich to the punch had oddly unknotted my guts. For the first time in several days, my breaths came without restriction.

It was the morning of Tuesday, September 21, 2004, and I had just met for nearly two hours with Portage Township Police Chief Jerry Adameyer and Officer Clarence Davidson. As I had said earlier, Adameyer was a hell of an investigator and the packet of information they brought to my office was flawless. Under normal circumstances, I would have been thrilled to see such a complete workup. The grand jury was scheduled to meet on Thursday. I would present the case and seek an indictment of rape, assault, and gross sexual imposition with a minor, which was all but assured. "I'll call you as soon as I get the indictment and you can round him up," I told them.

When they had left, I picked up the phone and dialed Margaret. "Would you come in here, please?" She walked in with her notebook and pen. "You won't need those," I said. "Sit down. I want to talk to you for a while."

We sat at the conference table, and I told her of the morning on Chestnut Ridge and how it had spiraled into my current dilemma, omitting nothing. "It's all going to hit the fan in a few days, Margaret; I just wanted you to be prepared."

She had sat through the story, occasionally lifting her hands to cover her mouth, emitting a soft, "Umm-umm-umm-umm-umm," or an equally soft, "Mercy." Holding a hand to her ample bosom, Margaret said, "I appreciate you telling me all this, Mr. Van Buren, but you were only fifteen years old, for goodness sake, a baby. Besides, it sounds like prison was the perfect place for him."

"Bless your heart, Margaret, but I'm not sure my opponent for attorney general or the electorate will share those sentiments. I'm going to get crucified."

I called Pepper and left a message on his cell phone. "I'm taking the Vukovich case to the grand jury on Thursday. I'm certain they will return an indictment and he'll be arrested. What happens after that? Your guess is as good as mine."

★ ★ ★

The Downtown Business Association of Cleveland held a candidates' breakfast on Wednesday, at which my opponent also was in attendance. Shelly said, "You should go over and congratulate her in advance for the miraculous comeback she is going to pull off after your dirty little secret becomes public." I ignored her remarks, gave a five-minute version of my standard get-tough-on-crime speech, and got into Shelly's car for a painful two-hour trip to Toledo for a Chamber of Commerce lunch, followed by a Q&A with the University of Toledo Young Republicans Club. All day Shelly punished me with silence and terse responses to any initiation of conversation. As we cruised along the Ohio Turnpike on the way back to Akron, I began a rambling monologue on the history of the Ohio judicial system in relation to the death penalty. I did this for no reason other than to get under her skin, and it worked magnificently. It took eight minutes before my beloved, her knuckles white on the steering wheel, said, "Hutchinson, shut the fuck up. I don't care."

I knew that.

When we hit the outskirts of Akron she said, "I can't for the life of me figure out why you are so determined to wreck a campaign on which we have worked so hard, and which we are virtually assured of winning."

I looked at her in slack-jawed amazement. "You've given me the silent treatment all day and you start this conversation when we're five minutes from my house?"

"I just don't understand why you are so intent on ruining all we've built."

"I'm not intent on ruining all we've built. I'm intent on keeping a predator, a pedophile, and a reprehensible human being from hurting any more kids. There's a difference. My career is going to be a casualty of doing the job I was elected to do. You don't understand this because it's like a game to you, Shelly. You want to win at all costs. In this situation, I can't do both. I can't do my job and win the election. I don't like it either, but that's a simple fact."

Shelly Dennison shook her head and drove the rest of the way to my house in silence.

I checked my e-mails from my home computer and picked up my voice mails. There was nothing that needed my immediate attention. I ordered a pizza and took two beers into my office to review the Vukovich file, which I would personally present to the grand jury. Half the pizza and one beer were gone, and Dean Martin was singing of a chapel in the moonlight when my cell phone hummed in my pants pocket. I answered without looking at the incoming number. "Hutchinson Van Buren." I could hear labored breathing on the other end of the phone. I leaned forward, pizza crumbs falling off my lap. "Hello?"

"Hey, Hutch. I need a little help here, buddy."

★ ★ ★

I pushed the Pacifica harder than it had ever been driven, flying south on Interstates 77 and 76 before jumping on Interstate 277 east and taking Route 93 south to Portage Township. It was a little less than twenty minutes after I had left the garage when I passed through the entrance to the Thimble Lakes. The black Saab was in the carport. A beige minivan was parked along the opposite side of the house.

The door to the screened-in front porch was open, pressed flat against an inside wall. I feared a trick. There was a lump of fear in my throat and my mouth was parched. I walked slowly to the front door, stepping where the cedar decking was nailed to the joists, trying to avoid creaking boards. The door was unlocked. When I pushed it open, the hinges squeaked and plastic blinds fell away from the door then slapped the window; the silence inside the house magnified the sounds. I pushed the door closed while surveying the layout of the ranch. I moved down a small hallway into the kitchen and eat-in dining area where a faint light glowed over the stove. A plastic bag of groceries sat on the kitchen table. A collection of liquor bottles stood at attention atop the refrigerator. "Back here," came a weak but familiar voice. The linoleum in the hallway creaked under my weight as I made my way toward the voice.

The hallway intersected a living room that extended the width of the house, providing a magnificent view of the lake. I was a half-dozen steps from the metal threshold dividing linoleum and the worn green carpet of the living room when I saw the soles of the shoes, toes down, just inside the room. The shoes extended from a pair of blue slacks that I could see to the crease behind the knees. Another step, two, and the torso revealed itself, clad in a light yellow, short-sleeve shirt that was untucked, exposing a dingy white T-shirt. Blood from the bullet wound in the left ear of Jack Vukovich had created a puddle the size of a dinner plate on the carpet. Gray hair stood erect around the exit wound, supported by congealed blood and hair gel. Brain matter and blood were splattered in a misty pattern seven feet up on the pinewood paneling.

A couch was pressed against the near wall. Propped in the corner was the Reverend Dale Ray Coultas, a Browning .45-caliber semi-automatic handgun in his right hand and resting on his inner thigh, his left hand covering a bullet wound in his abdomen; blood soaked into a white dress shirt and the top of his khaki slacks. He forced a smile and said, "Quite a mess, isn't it?"

"Oh, mother of Christ, Deak, we've got to get you to a hospital." I pulled out my handkerchief to inspect the wound, but when I took my first step toward Deak, he bent his wrist, pointing the pistol at my chest. "Close enough, Hutch." I froze. He pointed across the room to a chair, a battered recliner wrapped in fake leather. "Sit down. We don't need any heroics." He was weak, his words slowed by the loss of blood. His eyelids sagged and his pupils were dilated. The sides of his face were moist with sweat from shock.

I eased myself onto the edge of the seat cushion. He kept the gun trained on my chest. "What'd you do here, Deak?"

"This is the result of gross stupidity on my part. You know, I've fantasized about killing him for years—years, ever since I was a kid. Just daydreams, you know. You dream about things you wish you had the courage to do." He licked at his lips. "I'd been thinking about the harm he had done to Petey, me, and God knows how many other kids. I'd been thinking about how he was trying to blackmail you. Then, I got to thinking about the boy he'd just molested, the one you were telling me about, and I decided Jack needed to die." He held up a bloody left palm for my inspection. "As you can see, it didn't work out quite the way I had intended." His words were soft, strained. "They taught us in seminary school that God protects the weak and innocent. What happened?"

"There's evil out there that even God can't stop."

Deak nodded. "Apparently."

"Where's Vukovich's gun?"

"He used this one."

"How'd that happen?"

"When I pulled up in the yard he looked at me like I was trash. He sneered, 'What the hell do you want?' I said I needed to talk to him for a few minutes. I brought in that bag of groceries, you know, like I was on a mercy mission. I followed him in the house. When he turned his back I pulled the gun on him, but I forgot to take the safety off . . . " He shook his head and forced a light laugh. "I didn't know how to use it. I took it from a guy who was staying in our homeless shelter." He swallowed; his stomach heaved as he struggled to pull in air. "We wrestled over the gun and he twisted it in my hand and it went off into my stomach. I think he panicked." Deak took a few seconds to catch his breath. "He jumped away from me. I said, 'Oh my God, you shot me, Uncle Jack.' And he helped me to my feet. When he did, I raised the gun up and shot him in the ear."

"We've got to get you to the hospital."

He rested the pistol on his thigh, but kept it pointed at my chest. "I don't expect you to understand this, Hutch, but there are worse things than death. When a man loses his honor, he has nothing left."

"That's crazy talk. You've got a lot to live for—a wife and kids, and would you please lower that gun."

He dropped the barrel down along his thigh. "You don't get it, Hutch. It's me they're after."

My brows pinched. "Who's after you?"

"The Main Street Task Force. It's me they want."

"Why would they want you?"

"They know where Vukovich was getting the money. It was from my church's foundation, the nonprofit for at-risk women and children. Uncle Jack there, he showed up at the church a day after he got released from prison. He threatened to expose the whole Petey Sanchez mess unless I helped him get back on his feet. That's how he phrased it. He said he would tell all who would listen that I had sex with him. I was scared and I panicked. I paid him. I shouldn't have. It was like feeding a stray cat. He wouldn't go away. At first, he just wanted a little cash, but then he realized how scared I was. He pushed harder, wanted more, all the time talking about the years he had spent in prison for a crime he didn't commit. First, I drained my personal account. When that was gone, I started siphoning money from the foundation. The board president approached me about it because he thought our church secretary was stealing the money. You know who he called first, don't you?"

"Botticelli Junior?"

"Yep, our corrupt prosecutor questioned me about it. When I told him that Vukovich was the one blackmailing me, he went white. He wanted nothing to do with anything involving Jack Vukovich. He told me to repay the foundation and he'd ignore it. I'd already skimmed about forty thousand out of the account and I was broke, so there was no way to pay it back. When Botticelli didn't do anything, the board president went to the state attorney general. That's when the Main Street Task Force began investigating. Last week when you stopped by the church and the girls told you I was at a conference? I was in Columbus with my board president meeting with investigators." He swallowed and took two breaths. "The board president told them he still thinks it was the church secretary. You know who that is? Darlene DiSabito. Remember her? She was a couple of years behind us in school. Darlene's a wonderful lady. They're investigating her for crimes that I committed, and I didn't have the common decency to step up and tell them that I was the thief."

"You're not a thief, Deak. There were extenuating circumstances."

He tried to sit up, clutched hard at his stomach and winced. Traces of blood appeared at the corners of his mouth.

His voice was growing weaker, like someone struggling against sleep. "The world finds out I'm a thief and a murderer. Everything will come out about Petey. That will make for some juicy headlines—the ignominious fall of the Reverend Dale Ray Coultas. Everything I've worked for, my lifetime reputation, ends in a humiliating prison sentence. No, thanks."

"It's not worth your life."

"Really?" He took several short breaths and swiped at the blood on his mouth, leaving smears of red on his sleeve. "Isn't that why we kept quiet about Petey—to save Adrian's reputation?"

"So, are you just going to let yourself bleed to death? Is that the answer?"

"When I got here I planned to kill myself after I killed him, but I didn't know if I had the courage. Uncle Jack did me a favor by shooting me. It makes it easier."

"Deak, I can't sit here and let you die."

His arm was starting to quiver as he struggled to hold on to the pistol. "If you had just gone to the parole board hearing, maybe this all could have been avoided. You could have kept Jack in prison."

"That wasn't my responsibility. He wasn't in my jurisdiction."

"Then why did you write a letter to Mrs. Sanchez saying you would do everything you could to keep him in prison?"

"How did you know that?"

"Lila belonged to my church. She was a good Christian woman. She wasn't scared of dying; she was just scared that Jack Vukovich would get out of prison and hurt another child. I told her to write to you. She sat in my office at the church and I helped her write the letter." A trickle of blood rolled down the corner of his mouth. His voice was becoming weaker, harder to hear. "I'm the one . . . who told her to write to you . . . because you were a good man and wouldn't let her down. 'I pray that you will be my voice when I am gone.' I remember that line from her letter. It was all hers." He took several short breaths. His eyes seemed to lose their focus. "She showed me the letter you wrote back. She died at peace because of that letter."

"I didn't mean to . . ."

The pistol fell to the floor.

"Deak?"

Chapter Thirty

Ten minutes after the gun hit the floor, I called the 911 operator and told her I needed the Portage Township Police Department and a squad on a non-emergency run to 1288 Little Thimble Lake Drive.

"What's the nature of the emergency?"

"There are two dead men at the residence."

Her tone leaped in volume and pitch. "How do you know they're dead?"

"It's quite evident."

She asked several additional questions, including my name. I hesitated, but said, "Hutchinson Van Buren."

Three Portage Township Police Department cruisers, two Summit County Sheriff's Department cruisers, two township emergency squads, and a pumper truck arrived with lights flashing and sirens blaring. Newsrooms all over the area monitor police radio transmissions. When the 911 operator sent out a call of two dead bodies in a Thimble Lakes house, and the reporting person was Hutchinson Van Buren, not a name that blends among the John and Jane Smiths of the world, reporters, photographers, and videographers were soon crawling over the yard like fire ants.

From my vantage point inside the house I watched as television reporters did live, stern-faced cut-ins announcing two men were dead in the Thimble Lakes home behind them and that Summit County Prosecutor Hutchinson Van Buren was the one who discovered the bodies. Chief Jerry Adameyer had been at a meeting of township trustees when an officer tracked him down forty minutes after the 911 call. He arrived with a red emergency light flashing from the dashboard of the family car, but couldn't get to the driveway because of the congestion caused by the police, emergency, and news vehicles. He jogged across the front yard in street clothes, cursing and waving off questions by reporters with microphones.

"What the hell is going on?" he growled to no one in particular the instant he hit the front door. When he walked into the back room he groaned, "Aw, Jesus H. Christ." Adameyer received an update from Officer Davidson, then walked to the far end of the room and sat down next to me on the fireplace hearth. "Well, at least we don't have to pay to keep the sonofabitch in prison." It was a sentiment I heard from cops nearly every time a bad guy met an untimely demise. "Who's the stiff in the corner?"

"A minister from Steubenville."

Adameyer gave me a quizzical look. "You know him?"

I nodded. "He was a friend of mine for as long as I can remember. He called and asked me to come down, said he was in trouble. I didn't know anyone had been shot until I got here. By the time I arrived he was breathing his last."

Adameyer nodded, but looked confused. "What the hell was he doing here?"

"He was Vukovich's nephew. It's a long story, Jerry."

"Is that what was bugging you about this case?"

I shrugged. "I'll make a statement."

"Give it to Clarence," he said. "You going to be okay?"

"Yeah, thanks."

Officer Clarence Davidson and I sat at the kitchen table while I gave my statement. It was terse. "Call me tomorrow if you have any holes to fill," I said.

"Seems pretty cut-and-dried."

"Agreed."

When I walked out of the house a half-dozen newspaper and television reporters were standing behind the yellow crime scene tape waiting for an interview and looking like a swarm of amusement park carp begging for popcorn. Waving at me thirty feet from the reporters was Shelly Dennison. I got the attention of a uniformed officer and motioned for him to allow Shelly inside the yellow tape. She ran up and embraced me like I was a soldier returning from war. "Oh my God, are you okay?"

"I'm fine. What are you doing here?"

"They cut in on the news and said you were inside the house and had reported that two men were dead. Why are you here?"

"That's Jack Vukovich's place."

In a moment, the realization came over her face. "The guy who was going to go to the press with that story?"

"That's the one."

"He's dead?"

"Quite dead."

"Oh my God. That's wonderful, darling, wonderful. The story died with him, right?"

"One of my oldest and dearest friends also died with him."

"I'm sorry," she managed. "But the important thing is, that man is gone and can't hurt you." She squeezed my arm. "Let's get out of here."

"I need to talk to the reporters before I leave."

"Be careful. Don't say anything that will . . ."

I glared at her. "This may surprise you, Shelly, but I've talked to reporters before."

She patted me on the shoulder. "Sorry."

I answered questions for ten minutes, explaining my role in the drama and being careful not to overstep my bounds, referring other questions to Chief Adameyer.

"Where's your car?" I asked Shelly, walking away from the reporters. It was parked a few hundred yards up the road, past the house that was under construction. When I opened her door she said, "I am so relieved that this horrible nightmare is over."

"The horrible nightmare of losing one of my friends?"

She smiled and rubbed my arm. No, I thought. It was her horrible nightmare she was concerned about—a campaign in free fall and a smudge on her reputation. "How about I come over to your place? You shouldn't be alone tonight."

"On the contrary, Shelly, I think it's a perfect night to be alone."

Chapter Thirty-One

The Reverend Dale Ray Coultas was laid to rest on the slopes of New Alexandria Cemetery on the morning of Wednesday, September 29, 2004. Every seat in the sanctuary of his Cathedral of Peace was filled. Parishioners and friends stood two deep around the rim of the sanctuary, and speakers were set up on the front lawn for those who could not squeeze inside the doors. Pepper stood alone in the back of the church; Adrian was not in attendance.

Deak's wife telephoned me the Sunday after his death and asked me to speak at the memorial service. She said, "Dale thought very highly of you. He treasured the times the two of you spent together when you were young. I think he would be honored if you spoke." Of course, I said yes.

I was up early and on the road by 6 a.m., heading to Steubenville for the 10 a.m. memorial service. I traveled alone. Shelly had declined my offer to accompany me. Oh, she said, I would love to, sweetie. Can't. Meetings. Planning sessions. Crazy times, you know. Got elections to win. You'll do great. I know you'll do great. Okay. Love you. Drive safe. Bye. Mwah! It was now all she could do to maintain some semblance of a personal relationship until after election day, when I would go the way of the state representative from Ashtabula County.

My eulogy took fifteen minutes. I had practiced without emotion. But the words caught in my throat when I looked down from the pulpit at Deak's family—his wife, children, sisters, nieces and nephews, and parents who had grown gray and frail, their eyes transfixed, looking but not seeing, searching for answers to the unanswerable. The memories of our youth flooded back. I cleared my throat and talked of how I would miss Deak. Until his death, I viewed my youth like a completed picture puzzle. But with Deak gone, it was as though someone had stolen a piece of the puzzle and it could never again be complete.

I spoke of Dale Ray's passion for the Lord and how at an early age he had developed the nickname Deacon, which we shorted to Deak. He was destined to walk in the way of the Lord and bring people to follow the teachings of Jesus Christ. When he first became my friend he was a kind and caring boy; he grew up to be a kind and caring man. I told them that I was with their minister when he died. He wasn't afraid. He spoke of his loving wife and children, and of his flock. He wanted you all to know that he loves you still and looks forward to seeing you again in heaven.

Admittedly, I took some liberties in recounting Deak's final moments. Under different circumstances, however, I was certain that is exactly what he would have said.

The funeral procession extended more than a mile, taking a full half hour for the cars to cram into the hillside cemetery and the crowd to gather around the green tent under which the casket was taken. I stayed to the back of the crowd, hoping to make a quick exit when the gravesite service concluded. There was to be a dinner at the cathedral after the interment, but I wanted to avoid further inquisition about his death.

Instead, I drove back up to Robinson Township and had lunch with Pepper at his Double Deuce Steak House. It was the first time that Pepper and I had talked at length since Deak's death. I told him a story that those at the church didn't hear. We ate and hugged and promised to be better about staying in touch.

★ ★ ★

Margaret led Barbara Zeffiro of the *Beacon Journal* into my office at ten o'clock the following morning. I had called her on my way home from the funeral and set up the interview.

I walked over to the mini fridge in my office and grabbed a bottle of water. "What do you want to drink, Barbara?"

"Nothing, thanks."

"You're going to be here for a while. What do you want to drink?"

"Something diet."

I grabbed her a can of diet cola and started back across the room. "You received a phone call last week and the caller told you to ask me about Peter Sanchez, correct?" She nodded. "Do you know who called you?"

"No."

I handed her the can of soda. "I do. It was a man named Jack Vukovich."

"The guy from the hostage situation at the Thimble Lakes?"

"Yes."

"How do you know that?"

"Let me tell you a story, Barbara. It begins on a foggy Monday morning—June 14, 1971. I was fifteen years old and without a care in the world. That morning, my three best friends and I ventured into the hills west of Crystalton, Ohio, a place called Chestnut Ridge, to look for arrowheads."

That's the way it began. I told her everything. I told her that I watched Petey Sanchez die and conspired to keep his death a secret. When Jack Vukovich was accused of murder and went to prison, I remained silent. For years I tried to bury the memory of the event in my consciousness. I couldn't. What I did was wrong. Jack Vukovich tried to blackmail me. He threatened to expose everything if he was indicted on rape charges. He was going to be indicted. He was an animal, and I was glad he was dead.

I told her how Botticelli had gone after Vukovich on murder charges in exchange for kickbacks from Carson Nash. I also gave her photocopies of the campaign contributions and a typed transcript of my conversation with U.S. Representative Alfred Botticelli and allowed her to listen to my recording of the interview to verify the information.

It was just after 1 p.m. when the interview concluded. When she capped her pen and closed the second notebook she had filled, she said, simply, "Wow."

I nodded. "Wow, indeed."

"Let me ask you one more question. Why did you do this? You kept it a secret for more than thirty years, and the only other person who would have brought it to light is dead."

"My silence cost a dear friend his life. The events that occurred on Chestnut Ridge that morning triggered a series of events that ruined lives—Reverend Coultas, Adrian Nash, and his father. They have lived in a continual maelstrom since that summer. Pepper Nash and I escaped, somewhat, but you can never completely distance yourself from such a horrific event. The likes of Alfred Botticelli, and Jack Vukovich, and my own conscience, were always there to remind me of my culpability. Reverend Coultas wanted to tell the truth the day Petey died. If he had, if any of us had, none of this would have happened. But, he remained silent because I wanted him to remain silent. Where has it gotten us? In a way, my life has been no different than that of someone who skips bail and ends up running from the law for years. They live in perpetual fear of being caught. Every time a teacher or a minister would talk about truth and honesty, I felt like they were talking just to me, like they had a portal into my soul and knew I was hiding a deep secret. I've spent my entire adult life worrying about when the secret was going to be exposed. I was tired of it. It's just that simple."

When Barbara Zeffiro left, Margaret walked in. "Did you tell that girl your story?"

"I did."

"Umm-umm-umm-umm-umm. Am I going to have to look for a new job?"

"I don't know, Margaret."

On the way home I called the chairman of the Ohio Republican Party and told him to get ready for a bunch of phone calls because all hell was going to break loose when the *Beacon Journal* hit the streets the next morning.

"What's wrong?"

"I can't tell you," I said. "I always honor a scoop."

"What's that mean?"

He was still pleading for information when I hung up. I can only assume that he then speed-dialed Shelly, because she was calling my phone within minutes. I let her call roll to voice mail and didn't call her back. She could read about it in the morning, too.

★ ★ ★

Inexperienced criminals will hang themselves with their own alibis. Under questioning and in moments of panic, they begin creating elaborate stories of where they were, who they were with, what they were watching on television, adding minute details in an explanation of why it was impossible for them to have robbed the gas station. I have always been astonished at the number of criminals who literally talk their way into jail.

The most experienced criminals, at least the ones that have been through the judicial system a few times, understand the benefits of simplicity. I don't know. I don't remember. I didn't see anything. I wasn't there. I want to talk to my attorney.

When giving my statement to Officer Davidson and during my interview with Barbara Zeffiro, I was mostly truthful. When I wasn't, I kept it simple.

What I didn't tell them was that after Deak died I wiped the .38-caliber handgun clean of his fingerprints, and while cradling it in a handkerchief, pressed it into the lifeless palm and fingers of Jack Vukovich. After I believed it to be properly covered with his prints, I dropped it beside the body, as though that was where it landed after Vukovich committed suicide. Then, I called 911.

Did I know where the pistol came from? How would I know? I assumed it belonged to Vukovich, since he was the ex-con. What would a minister be doing with a pistol? Was I certain that it was a murder-suicide? Absolutely. At least that was what Reverend Dale Ray Coultas had said in the moments before he died. Why did he call me instead of 911? He didn't say. What was he doing there? He brought groceries and was ministering to his uncle. Jack Vukovich was a troubled soul and Reverend Coultas had a soft heart. Did I know why Vukovich used the weapon on the preacher and himself? No idea. Reverend Coultas died before I could ask him.

I justified lying to protect Deak's memory and his reputation. No one was going to shed any tears over Jack Vukovich. Deak was the one who had suffered with the memories of abuse. His family and congregation didn't need to know the truth. What purpose would it serve other than to besmirch the memory of a good man? None that I could see.

The following week I would call the chief investigator of the Main Street Task Force and tell him that Deak said he had given Vukovich the checks from the foundation under threat of death to him and his family. Obviously, the threat wasn't a bluff. Perhaps, I offered, Reverend Coultas had told Vukovich that no more money was forthcoming and that precipitated the shooting and suicide. That seemed the most plausible explanation.

More lies.

Deak would not have approved of my actions. He would have said, "Hutch, didn't you learn anything from the last time you tried to protect someone's reputation?" Apparently not. The difference here was that there were only three people who knew the truth. Two were dead and I'm very good at keeping secrets. When I got home after my interview with Barbara, I called my mom in Florida and relayed my story to her. Except for an occasional, "Oh, my," she listened in silence. When I concluded by telling her I had told the story to a newspaper reporter and that my political career could likely end, she asked, "So, it was Adrian who threw the stone, or the Indian thing. Not you, right?"

"Right. I was there, but I didn't throw it."

"That's good, very good."

With that, she had absolved me of any wrongdoing. I wasn't sure the voters would see it the same way.

The story that began on Chestnut Ridge in 1971 would finally conclude. The last chapter would be set into motion on the front page of the Akron *Beacon Journal* the following morning. That was a certainty. How it would end for me, Congressman Botticelli, Botticelli Junior, or the Nashes, I hadn't a clue.

Strangely, I wasn't overly concerned. There was something incredibly liberating about the future being out of my control. I closed my eyes and once again could breathe in the aroma of the cherry blossoms on Chestnut Ridge.